A Time To Fall

BY JESS VONN

Book 1 of the "Love by the Seasons" Series

Amazon-issued ISBN 13: 978-1975925512

Amazon-issued ISBN 10: 1975925512

First Printing September 2017.

Cover design and author photo by Jess Vonn. Cover photographs used under license from Shutterstock.com.

All characters appearing in this work are fictitious. Any resemblance to real persons, living or dead, is purely coincidental.

For George, the hero I had to nab as quickly as possible, lest he slip away. Thank you for being my corresponding shape.

JESS VONN

Chapter 1

Winnie Briggs gasped in disbelief as she pulled up to her new home and put her 12-year-old car, Fiona the Ford, into park. She did a triple-take at the GPS to make sure she hadn't messed something up and accidentally pulled into someone else's driveway.

221 Lily Lane, Bloomsburo. This had to be it.

She'd seen photos of the place prior to signing a lease via fax, but that hadn't done it justice. She glanced up again, taking in the cozy butter-yellow cottage before her, with its autumn wreath on the red door, white shutters, and hanging plants bursting with red and orange blooms. Fairy lights dotted the roof of the porch, which sheltered two white rocking chairs and a small wicker table.

If it weren't so big, the cottage could have easily passed as a picture-perfect dollhouse.

Not that the cottage was in any way big, but she knew that its tiny size would suit her perfectly. As a single woman in a new town, she didn't need much, and downsizing had made it that much easier for Winnie to pick up her entire life and start a completely new existence in Bloomsburo.

A completely new existence.

The weight of those words felt like lead in Winnie's stomach, ushering in a now familiar wave of anxiety. She closed her eyes and slowly breathed in through her nose, allowing her lungs to fill so full with air that it almost hurt. With a slow exhale, she willed away the anxiety. She breathed in the earthy smells of early autumn foliage and the sound of the first crisp leaves rustling on the branches. She breathed out fear.

There were lessons to be learned from autumn, Winnie mused, about how falling can be transformational. About how growth so often must be preceded with breaking down, with dissolving into something different entirely.

She shook away the melancholy thoughts and looked once more at her new, picture-perfect home. Today was for unbridled possibilities. For forgetting who she was, and for creating who she wanted to be. And all of that started in this adorable little cottage. Tomorrow she'd start her new professional life as the editor of

Bloomsburo's twice-weekly newspaper, but today was for homemaking.

Winnie stepped out onto the gravel driveway, eager to stretch out some of her stiffness from the morning's 343-mile road trip from Chicago. The *Les Misérables* soundtrack and a steady supply of Dr. Pepper had helped to ease a bit of her boredom during the long drive, not that she was lamenting an uneventful trip. She sent up a silent offering of gratitude that Fiona had completed the journey without incident. Given the fact that the car had spent the better part of four years tucked safely away in a downtown parking garage, Winnie knew she was pushing the old gal to her limits with this relocation. Now that her automotive anxiety about arriving in one piece had passed, she could soak in the details of her new home.

Walking up to the porch, Winnie peeked beneath the largest bush in the landscaping and found the tiny cast iron turtle that, as promised by her new landlady, housed a key to the cottage. As she slipped the key into the lock and pushed open the door, delight flooded her heart and the tiniest of squeals slipped from her lips. The inside of the cottage was somehow even more darling than the outside. The online advertisement that led her to the space had specified that it came fully furnished— all the better for Winnie who'd gladly said goodbye to the thrift store furniture she had dragged around since her college days. But she wouldn't have dared to dream of something so cozy. So homey. She felt like she stepped into a Mary Engelbreit drawing.

Honey-hued wooden floors covered the entire space, and abundant windows, including a skylight, flooded the cottage with late-afternoon sunshine. The tiny but tidy kitchen featured a small marble counter top, a round table with two chairs, and a compact stove and fridge that would be more than suitable for cooking for one, especially when you factored in that Winnie didn't know how to cook.

Just past the kitchen was a tiny living room area and in the back corner of the small, loft-style space stood a tall four-poster queen-sized bed covered by an intricate quilt and a half-dozen throw pillows in an array of colors and patterns. In the other corner, beneath one of the windows that looked out onto the flower-studded lawn, a simple wooden desk and chair and a tall white bookshelf stood just next to the entrance of the smallest bathroom Winnie had ever stepped foot in. But with a toilet, a sink and a slim stand-up shower, it would surely cover her basic needs.

Covering her basic needs. That was what she was here for, right? Wasn't that why she had, at twenty-six, decided to flip her entire life on its head? Sure, a fantastically disastrous break up had *technically* prompted the move, but in re-envisioning her new life, Winnie ensured that she wasn't just running away from something, but also moving toward something new. She created two simple goals for herself: to focus on her journalistic skills and to avoid men.

Courtesy of an unfortunate discovery involving her long-time boyfriend Anthony, a blonde intern, and a glass-walled shower, Winnie was the proud owner of a new chastity pledge. No dating. No hand-holding. No whispering of sweet nothings. No kissing. She was going full Duggar.

Winnie could still hear her best friend's voice in her ear from the night she made the decision to pick up her life and restart, and the memory of the way Bree's voice had cracked with emotion when she'd said the words brought Winnie fresh tears.

"You've got to find yourself again," Bree had told her. "And I think you've got to get out of Chicago if you want to do it right. It's time to put Winnie first."

And so, in climbing out of the rubble of what she thought was going to be her happily-ever-after, in her attempts to re-center herself and remember who she was before she had lost herself in an unhealthy relationship, Winnie also had to say goodbye to her very best friend in the world. The friend she'd made the first day of college orientation almost exactly eight years before.

The woman who, Winnie knew at the core of her being, had saved her life during their junior year of college when Winnie's parents and only brother were killed in a car accident. Bree was Winnie's true touchstone, and now hundreds of miles separated them. The women both agreed to go a month without talking, texting, or emailing, just to give Winnie time to settle into her new life in Bloomsburo without getting too hung up on the past.

Winnie scanned the room, contemplating where to begin decorating. Despite the built-in furnishings, Winnie knew that she could put her own impression on the cozy space with the personal effects stuffed into Fiona's trunk. Really, though, there was no question where she would start: the mantle. She'd always wanted one. Instantly she could picture the exact knickknacks she'd adorn it with—a shimmery red scarf, her favorite hour glass filled with sparkly yellow sand, her goddess-shaped candle holders with the honeycomb candlesticks, and the tiny Lego robot that her little brother Johnny made more than a decade before.

Infused with a sweet rush of adrenaline, Winnie's fingers twitched at the thought of unboxing some of her favorite possessions in the world. She skipped to the front of the cottage, swung open the screen door, and, after stepping onto the covered porch, ran directly into the broad, sweaty chest of an unexpected male visitor.

Something between a scream and a yelp flew from Winnie's mouth as she pushed herself off the man, her back slamming against the screen door.

She scanned him over, taking in a dozen details in an attempt to make an assessment of his character in milliseconds. He was a bit older than her, but not by much, and taller than her, by quite a bit. Rounded biceps peaked out from the tight grey T-shirt he wore, which was covered in patches of sweat where it strained across his broad chest.

Confusion and annoyance clouded over his face, which was almost enough to distract from how devastatingly handsome he was.

Almost.

Unethically long lashes fringed his intelligent green eyes. Sweat darkened his slightly shaggy honey blonde hair near his temples, and golden-red afternoon stubble scattered across his strong jaw line.

He was primal. Vital. Muscular. Confident. The kind of man that made a woman's brain simultaneously whisper "get closer" and "stay away."

And he did not look happy to see Winnie.

Well, she was hardly thrilled herself. This porch was only supposed to be for delivering pizza, not eye candy. Seeing how her entire life reinvention hinged on her pledge to avoid men, it was beyond aggravating that just ten minutes after pulling into town, she couldn't even manage to accomplish this task at its most literal. No, she had to go and accidentally chest bump one of mankind's sexiest ambassadors right on her own front porch.

"Who are—?" Winnie started, struggling to compose her thoughts into steady, convincing words. She felt as if she'd been dunked in a pool of icy water, with every inch of her body prickling in awareness of the man before her. "What are you doing here?"

The man's eyes finally locked into hers, and the intensity of his gaze made something in the vicinity of Winnie's stomach unravel.

"Funny, I came over here to ask you the exact same thing," he said, his voice steady and commanding. He held up a sleek smart phone. "And just in case I don't like the answer, I've got my friend, the police chief, on speed dial."

Chapter 2

Now that Cal Spencer could see the woman up close, she clearly posed no threat, but her unexpected presence at the cottage on his mother's property had been enough to spike his adrenaline to unprecedented levels.

And her curvy body slamming into his at twenty-five miles-per-hour sure didn't help to calm him down, either.

He liked to think of himself as a man of routine. A man who cultivated a predictable and consistent life. And since it was the weekend, he stopped by his mom's house, just as he always did on his longest weekly run. The place stood exactly 3.5 miles from his own house, which made it an ideal water break during his weekend runs. He would jog to his childhood home, help himself to a glass of water, and then turn back around and run the same route back for a smooth seven-mile circuit.

At least that's how it typically worked. But today, as he'd caught his breath and grabbed a sip of water at his mother's kitchen sink, he'd glanced out the back window and noticed movement in the souped-up shed his mom kept on the far end of her property.

Knowing that his mom was out of town for the weekend, Cal's protective instincts went into high alert and he made his way out the back door, jogging across the two hundred feet of well-maintained gardens that separated the structure from his mother's main house.

He wanted to just barge right into the shed (the "She Shed," his mother had always— absurdly—called it) but something in his gut told him he should knock. Before he'd had the chance to do so, however, the cottage's screen door swung open and a woman slammed into his chest with all the grace of a Mack truck.

She had pushed herself off him and backed herself up against the screen door, unabashedly surveying his face, his chest, his entire body, surely trying to determine who he was, what he was doing on the porch, and if he posed a threat to her.

Which of course, he didn't. He didn't want to scare her, and the panic washing over her rankled him. Yet he felt more than ready to hear her explanation for what the hell she was doing here.

"So, do I need to call Chief Conrad, or are you prepared to explain your presence on my mother's property?" he asked, his tone uncharacteristically firm as he waved the phone in his hand.

She winced. The woman was clearly unaccustomed to law-enforcement related threats, which he'd now hurled her way twice in twenty seconds. A twinge of guilt tightened his chest, but he shook it off, seeing as how he wasn't the one trespassing. Even if the woman didn't pose an immediate threat, he'd demand an explanation for her presence in the She Shed. Cal looked after his family at any cost. As the oldest and the only son, that had been his role even long before his dad had passed away.

The woman before him was as harmless as she was surprising. His eyes briefly flickered over her, giving her the same superficial assessment she'd just given him, and he might have smiled at the sheer unexpectedness of the woman had he not been trying to ever-so-slightly intimidate her.

She was a quirky thing, at least half a foot shorter than his six foot two inches. A curvy, solid woman with lots of dark hair tied back into a few messy buns on either side of her head. Her fingernails and toenails appeared to be painted about six different colors, perhaps to match her unicorn-print leggings. Her black tank top, featuring what looked like a trail of Cheeto dust where it stretched across her full breasts, declared in flashy silver print: "I'm Sorry For What I Said When I Was Hungry."

Any amusement inspired by her eclectic style, however, quickly evaporated after she explained her presence.

"I'm Rhonda Spencer's new renter. I'm supposed to move in today."

He felt his blood pressure rise at her words. His mother's new renter? What in the hell was the woman talking about? His mother hadn't said anything about renting out her damn She Shed. Surely she wouldn't try to pull off such a stunt without so much as a word to her oldest child about it.

Questions flew through his mind—how could she have coordinated this without his knowledge? Did his little sisters know about this, deciding collectively to leave him in the dark? Where had his mother found this mysterious renter, and had she carefully vetted this woman before handing over a key?

He didn't have any answers, but if he knew his mom as well as he thought he did, she probably just thought up this plan on a whim and hadn't bothered to mention it to anyone. Rhonda Spencer seemed to have a deep, intrinsic need to surprise the people in her life from time to time.

"Her renter?" he repeated, unable to formulate a more intelligent response.

"Yes," the woman said firmly, her brows narrowing as she watched him with suspicion. He ran his hands through his hair. God, he forgot what a sweaty mess he was after running in the unprecedented September heat. This woman probably thought him unhinged, and he couldn't very well blame her.

"She didn't mention anything to me about renting out the She Shed."

At his words, the panic momentarily vanished from the woman's face and he watched it transform into something brighter — something beautiful —which somehow managed to annoy him even more.

"The *She Shed*?" she emphasized, her face softening as she clasped her hands in front of her chest.

He sighed and rubbed his brow. Lord, she and his mom were going to get along swimmingly. His mother's whimsical nature had always mystified him.

"That's *her* ridiculous name for it, not mine."

"That is beyond amazing. I didn't think I could love this place more, but now I do. The She Shed!" the woman repeated, practically swooning, and twirling around in a little circle.

Cal resisted the urge to mirror the happy curve of her lips. He wasn't here to flirt, and he was in no mood to do so anyway.

"But, I have a copy of my signed lease with me, if you need confirmation," she continued once her spinning ceased. "It's totally legitimate."

"Why would she do this?" he muttered to himself, but the woman replied anyway.

"I can't answer that. It sounds like you and your mother have some things to talk about," she said, a touch on the smug side. He tried not to grimace.

His mom didn't need money from a rental. She was hardly rich, but the mortgage on his childhood home had been paid off for years, and she could live comfortably on her modest income, especially in this part of the country. And with four grown children, two grandkids, and dozens of neighbors and clients who adored her, it's not like his mother needed the company.

The She Shed had been her private oasis, one she had tinkered with for years to get how she liked. She never let Cal go in there, and his father had known better than to even ask for admittance back when he was still alive. In fact, no men went into the ladies-only zone.

This meant that his mother would only rent the space to a woman. And it'd have to be a single woman, seeing how the shed barely fit one.

Suddenly Cal's stomach lurched, the same way it did every time he thought about his mother and single young women in the same breath.

Though his mom was semi-retired, he often joked that she continued to work full-time as matchmaker for her only son, whom she believed to be withering on the vine at the ripe old age of 30.

Hell.

He'd seen his mother pull some outrageous stunts over the years to try and put eligible young women in the path of her notoriously noncommittal son, but this would be taking it a step too far even for her.

"Do you happen to have a copy of the rental announcement that you responded to?" he asked.

"I do, but..."

"Could I see it?" he interrupted.

She hesitated. Yeah, she definitely thought he was unhinged.

"I could wait and get it from my mom tomorrow when she's back in town," he relented. No need to spook this woman any further than he already had. As it was, his mother would already be livid about how he'd treated her new renter.

"No, I guess there's no harm in showing it to you. It wasn't private or anything. I found it online. Just wait here."

He couldn't blame her for not inviting him in, but as she began rifling through a bag on the kitchen table, he took the opportunity to peek into the She Shed.

Damn. His mom had certainly been busy. How much money had she sunk into renovations on this place, and could she possible recoup it based on the rent she charged? The last time he'd seen the space, it was little more than a massive tool shed with some pretty paint slathered around. Today the place looked fantastic, he'd give her that.

"You found the ad online? So you're not from around here?" Cal asked, though he already knew the answer. Having grown up in the small town, he knew most everyone within five years of his age around a three-county radius. He would have remembered a woman like the one before him.

"Uh, no, I'm not from around here," she said, avoiding his gaze as she dug through her purse. Since she wasn't watching him, he allowed himself a small smile at the odd collection of items she pulled out of the bag—a pack of Crayola markers, a romance novel, a bag of gummy worms, a sparkly pink notebook, a tiny rubber duck wearing a Hawaiian lei. "I'm relocating from Chicago."

Chicago. That response surprised him even more than the rubber duck in her purse. It was almost unheard of for someone from a major city to relocate to a small town like Bloomsburo, a town that couldn't even claim quite 4,000 residents.

"Wow, so you're pretty far from home, huh?" he asked.

Her rifling stopped briefly. "It wasn't home," she said quietly. Her tone made it clear that follow-up questions were not welcome, and he refused to cater to the part of his brain that hungered for this woman's full story.

She rooted around for a few seconds more, finally locating the desired piece of paper beneath a pair of star-covered socks. She walked over and handed it to him.

"Here you go," she said, her eyes reaching his once more, only bolder this time. The initial fear he saw there had vanished, thankfully, replaced by a spark he couldn't quite identify. "And I'm Winnie, by the way. Thanks for asking."

A surge of shame coursed through his veins. With his adrenaline high now tapering off, he realized what an impolite ass he'd been to this woman. Having grown up with a strong mother figure and three little sisters, Cal always prioritized respect toward women, but today he failed to live up to his own standards.

"I'm Cal Spencer. And I'm sorry for startling you on the porch."

"Are you also sorry for insinuating that I'm a burglar, here to steal the throw pillows and the box of baking soda in the otherwise empty fridge?" she asked, one brow arching.

A hint of a grin pulled at the corner of Cal's mouth despite himself. He took her sass as a small sign of forgiveness.

"Yeah. Sorry for that, too. But in my defense, you've got a dangerous edge about you," he added, his lips spreading involuntarily. "I couldn't be too careful."

She snorted. Why such a graceless sound managed to come across as endearing to him, he couldn't say. All he knew for sure was that his brain was clearly fried, and he needed to finish his run and get his wits back about him.

"Yes, I'm sure that the Chicago PD has already called up your friend, the chief, to warn him about my arrival," she joked. "They probably have my picture on a poster down at the station."

He quirked a brow at her before opening up the piece of paper and reading his mother's rental ad aloud.

> "Single-occupancy studio cottage for rent. Idyllic space for young professional looking for privacy. Austen-esque rural setting. Bountiful flower gardens border on all sides. Cottage is furnished to feminine tastes. Family-oriented is a plus, as grandkids often play in the shared lawn."

Jesus, his mother was about as subtle as a hammer to the head.

"This is going too far, even for her." Cal groaned, suddenly wishing he'd wake up to discover that his whole afternoon had been a dream.

"I loved the description! It caught my attention immediately," Winnie said. It wasn't lost on him that Winnie defended his mother, while her own son griped about her.

"Of course it caught your attention. Because it's basically a single's ad, masquerading as a rental agreement."

Shock swept across Winnie's pretty face.

"A single's ad?" she sputtered, grabbing the paper from his hand and scanning it again. "How do you figure?"

A Time To Fall

"Do you happen to be a single, educated, professional woman with a romantic streak, who happens to love the outdoors, flowers, and dreams of marriage and children down the road?"

Winnie puffed out an indignant sigh.

"Well, I mean, maybe," she stammered, her cheeks flushing the most compelling shade of pink. "I guess that could describe me a little bit. Or maybe me-in-the-future. But that description fits lots of women. That has nothing to do with the ad."

"I would never respond to an ad like this," he said flatly.

"What, you're not a Jane Austen fan?"

"Nah, I've always been more of a Bronte guy," he said, not missing a beat.

She did a double take. He shouldn't have taken so much satisfaction from the quick grin his quip inspired from her, but he did. He felt suddenly grateful for the literary references he learned courtesy of growing up in a house full of little sisters.

"Okay, so your mom put out a single's ad? Is *she*, um, interested in women?"

Cal laughed despite himself.

"Sure, she's interested in women to set me up with."

He'd never seen the blood drain from a woman's face quite that quickly. It was humbling, really.

"She rented me the She Shed because she wants to set me up with *you*?"

The disdain with which she said *you* was a swift kick to his pride, but he felt some relief that at least one other person found his mother's meddling to be as preposterous as he did.

"That's my guess."

"I can assure you, I was just looking for a place to live. You weren't mentioned as part of the package deal. She might have offered me a discount on the rent if that were the case."

He laughed at the jab.

"And my mom was just looking for a potential daughter-in-law. That's what she does."

"I can't say I blame her. You seem like the kind of guy who would need a bit of help in the romance department," Winnie teased.

Had a woman ever simultaneously flirted with him and insulted him? More importantly, Cal wondered why, when Winnie did just this, a small flame seemed to light somewhere deep inside of him, as if she were turning on a pilot light he didn't even know existed.

This uninvited ignition made him want to growl. He didn't do girlfriends. He didn't do "marriage potential." He didn't date cute, quirky, *Pride and Prejudice* loving, girl-next-door types in unicorn tights, and his mother damn well knew it. He had no interest in pursuing something serious with any woman, but especially not one whose romantic sensibilities were even remotely influenced by Mr. Darcy.

"She's barking up the wrong tree, anyway," Winnie conceded. Her gaze dropped to her zebra-print flip flops in a failed attempt to hide the discomfort that flashed across her face.

"So you're interested in women, then?"

"If only," she sighed, a comment he couldn't even begin to interpret. "I'm not interested in women, but I also happen to be temporarily disinterested in men. I'm not dating right now."

He hated the part of himself that interpreted her comment as a challenge.

Damn it, he really needed to go finish his run and burn off this excess adrenaline.

"Well, I'll tell my mom that you already shot me down, and hopefully she won't make you pack your bags and head back to Chicago in order to bring in a new candidate."

Winnie's eyes widened and he saw panic return to them, the same panic that met him when she first slammed into him on the porch. He didn't like it—neither the anxiety he saw there, nor whatever it was back in Chicago that made the prospect of returning so terrifying.

"Hey, I'm just kidding with you," he assured her, his voice gentling. "My mom's going to adore you. She's probably already talked to you on the phone a half dozen times and is completely enamored with you. She's probably already planned to trade me out for you."

She avoided his gaze, but she relented a small smile that confirmed his suspicions.

"Well, I had better get to unpacking, that is if you're going to call off the SWAT team," she said with more than a touch of orneriness.

He glanced down at his sweat-soaked shirt. Satisfaction simmered deep within when she followed suit, her eyes seeming to darken as she scanned the contours of his chest once more.

Winnie Briggs might not be interested in dating, but he'd bet his life that her interest in men was alive and kicking.

"I'll let you get to it, then," he said. "It's time for me to get out of these clothes and into the shower, anyway."

For the three-and-a-half-mile jog home, Cal didn't think about the September heat or the stitch in his side or his irritation with his mother or the work waiting for him at his desk Monday morning. The only thought his mind wanted to mull over was that final image of Winnie Briggs' face—her deep brown eyes wide, her mouth parted, and her cheeks flushed the prettiest pink at the thought of him wet and disrobed.

Chapter 3

It wasn't until Winnie's short drive to the office the next morning that she fully realized how little rest she'd gotten the night before.

Falling asleep had been no simple task. If it had just been her arrival in her new town, sleeping in a new bed, and preparing to start a new job the next day that were working against her, she might have gotten more rest.

But she also had to contend with the aftermath of crashing into the great wall of Cal Spencer.

Sheesh.

Even now, driving across town toward the newspaper office, the memory of that single second of her life filled her with the deepest mortification.

As a rule, she didn't interact with guys like Cal Spencer. Had she seen a man like him on the street, or across a crowded bar, she wouldn't have even dared to look in his direction. He was *that* good looking of a guy.

He was like a magazine cover come to life.

He was like a Hollywood star.

He was so handsome it kind of pissed her off. It was rude, frankly, to flaunt that beauty in everyone else's run-of-the-mill faces.

And she had gone and flown into his broad, muscular chest like a bird kamikaze-ing into a sliding glass door.

Winnie hadn't even bothered putting on blush today. She knew that if she wanted color in her cheeks on her first day at the new job, all she'd have to do was relive that moment in her mind. She found herself really, really wishing she and Bree weren't on a communication break.

Some things you just needed to relay to your best gal who, yes, would laugh her head off at your expense, but then would shift gears and offer up a healthy dose of sympathy.

She also wished she could have talked clothes with Bree. Winnie glanced down at her first-day-of-work outfit. Having never set foot in the newspaper office (securing her job, like securing her lease, had been a long-distance operation), she didn't know quite what the dress code was, but she opted for a dressier version of her quirky style: a soft, mint green V-neck sweater, a grey pleated skirt, some green-and-white striped tights, and her favorite black Mary Janes with the one-inch heels. Her hair was half up and half down, letting her brunette waves follow their natural instincts as they tumbled wildly over her shoulders.

She liked her style. Loved it even, but in a way, it had been crafted in reaction to guys like Cal Spencer. Back in junior high, it had been clear that Winnie, with her round hips, her curvy chest, her unruly brown curls, and her thrift store budget, would never fit the kind of skinny/sleek/trendy/blonde standards required of the most popular girls in school.

The girls who ran with the Cal Spencers of the world.

So Winnie began to craft her own offbeat style, and found that, in time, it empowered her. Among the band geeks and the gamer guys, she was well appreciated, and this suited her just fine. She understood the natural order of things. She'd gladly leave the jocks for the other girls.

And in a way, her unique style also served as armor, because not even all of that pixie dream girl confidence had fully vanquished the intimidation Winnie felt around men like Cal Spencer—well-built, well-dressed, golden, confident, athletic. She'd only seen the man in workout clothes, but she'd bet her life on the fact that he was impeccably well-dressed in his professional life, whatever that was.

And that was what she had to keep reminding herself. Yes, Cal Spencer might have spooked her on her first afternoon in town, but other than the odd chance she'd encounter him in his mom's backyard, she wasn't going to have to deal with him. It seemed highly unlikely, anyway, that a guy like Cal Spencer spent much of his time meandering through his mother's flower gardens. This was just as well, because it meant that Winnie could refocus on her big two goals: professional development and avoiding men.

Winnie first, she reminded herself.

She finally wound her way around to the newspaper office parking lot, and smiled at the sign indicating the spot reserved for her as editor-in-chief. Her salary wasn't impressive, nor would there be a lot of glory in the kind of reporting she'd be doing in the small, rural community of Bloomsburo, so she'd take what perks she could get.

She put Fiona the Ford into park, gathered her purse and her camera, and made her way to the front door, trying not to pay too much attention to the butterflies dancing in her stomach.

Winnie had accepted this job with a full understanding of exactly the nature of the mess she was stepping into. The morning after the previous editor printed a guns-blazing editorial about all his gripes with the town and the paper's parent company, he had hopped in his car and driven straight to Florida, where rumor had it he now worked happily as a fry cook at a seaside shack. The paper, which normally came out twice a week, had only published twice in the past month courtesy of a remote effort by editors from some of the company's other newspapers. The publisher made it clear when hiring Winnie that the subscribers were understandably upset about the state of affairs. Re-earning trust among the readers was among her top tasks as the new editor.

Even with all that added drama aside, the nature of her work at *The Bloom* would be a significant change of pace for Winnie. She'd earned her college degree in journalism, interning at a major metropolitan daily before taking her most recent job, as a beat reporter for the parks and recreation beat of *The Chicago Daily*, where she'd dutifully covered sod expenditures and Porta-Potty lease agreements for the past four years, working with a large staff of editors, stringers and designers.

Here at *The Bloom*, however, she'd be mostly a one-woman show. Given the size of the community, the newspaper was small enough to get by with an editor and a few freelancers for sports, along with a small advertising department. She'd be responsible for writing, editing and designing the small paper twice a week.

The freedom of it was exhilarating but the responsibility of it was daunting. Whatever positive feedback people had about the paper would reflect on Winnie, just like anything negative anyone said about the paper would, too.

The whole thing was on her shoulders, and ultimately, she welcomed it. She was here to bury herself in the job, and doing the work of two or three people would make that all the easier. Walking up the narrow sidewalk in front of the building, she pulled open the glass door to the office, and braced herself for whatever came next.

"You're here!" a friendly woman cried out, holding up a copy of the morning's edition of the paper when Winnie walked toward the front desk, which was adorned with several ceramic pumpkins and a colorful banner of fall leaves. Glancing at the paper in the woman's hand, Winnie's jaw dropped when she noticed what was on it: an excessively large photo of her alongside a brief bio, introducing her as the new editor-in-chief.

"Do you think they could have run the picture any larger?" Winnie asked, grabbing the paper and grimacing. It wasn't a bad picture, just overplayed. It must have been a slow news day if they'd needed to fill up that much space with her portrait.

"Oh, it's a lovely picture," the middle-aged woman behind the desk assured Winnie. With her short, soft blond curls, full face and warm smile, Winnie felt immediately at ease with her new coworker.

"And I'm Gloria, by the way," the woman continued, extending her hand. "I've been the receptionist here at *The Bloom* for twenty-five years, which, I would guess, is just about as long as you've been alive."

Winnie laughed.

"Pretty close," she admitted. "And I'm Winnie, the lady from the front page."

"Well, honey, I'm here to help you get settled into the paper and into town. I'm a Bloomsburo lifer, so feel free to ask me anything. Plus, I've been typing up the police reports for two decades, so it's always a good idea to run any potential beaus by me first. I'll give you the real scoop on 'em."

Winnie's heart skipped a beat because Cal's striking face popped into her mind as soon as Gloria uttered the sentence.

No beaus, Winnie reminded herself.

Gloria escorted Winnie through the narrow corridors of the stuffy office, pointing out the basic amenities of the humble space. It was a far cry from the sophisticated steel and glass of her high-rise building in Chicago.

This office felt more like a country motel in desperate need of redecoration. Dusty fake flowers sat on pine bookshelves and the cheap golden frames hanging on the wall, all slightly crooked, held various newspaper articles and awards.

Taking a quick look, Winnie noticed the paper hadn't earned an award since the late 1980s.

She had her work cut out for her.

JESS VONN

When Gloria led her around the corner to her private office in the back, Winnie surveyed the big, fake wood grain desk that awaited her. The Mac computer sitting on it was older than the version she'd used back in college and one of the phones next to it actually had a rotary dial.

She swallowed back the judgment and superiority that threatened to rise within her, reminding herself that the whole purpose of her relocation to Bloomsburo was to try something new, and she had no illusions that in this specific instance "new" meant "glamorous."

She had prepared herself for quite the opposite, and now, sitting in her dusty office with the fake wood paneling on the walls, she deemed that wise.

Gloria, who had returned to her desk out front, seemed lovely though, and Winnie had worked in enough office settings to know that the relationship you had with the secretary could make or break a job.

Before Winnie could even turn on her computer, she heard the front door bells jingle from around the corner, followed by a woman's shrill voice asking, "Well, is she here?"

Winnie glanced at her watch. It was only 8:32 on her first morning in the office. How could anyone possibly be looking for her already?

"You couldn't have an appointment with her yet," she heard Gloria answer protectively, which warmed Winnie's heart, even from a room away.

"Well you know what they say," Winnie heard the mystery woman reply, "the news never sleeps. And apparently, in Bloomsburo, neither do the idiots. They should be here any minute, by the way."

"The idiots?" she heard Gloria respond, which made Winnie giggle.

"The police chief and the Chamber of Commerce director," the woman curtly clarified, much less amused by Gloria's deadpan humor than Winnie was. "There's another situation."

Then Winnie's brain caught up to her ears. *The police chief and the Chamber of Commerce director were on their way to her office?* Dread filled her stomach. She hadn't even figured out where the office bathroom was located, yet two major town leaders were already on their way to discuss 'a situation' with her? So much for easing her way into her first day on the job.

Realizing that she couldn't hide in her office forever, Winnie reluctantly walked back through the hallway until she could spot the mystery woman standing at Gloria's desk. Short, at least in her seventies, and clad in a bright blue velour tracksuit and a heavily made-up face, the woman looked intense and annoyed but she plastered on a forced smile when she noticed Winnie approaching.

"Winnie Briggs, I presume," she said, offering out a bony hand adorned with perfectly manicured nails and some seriously sizable rings. Winnie shook it, surprised by the tightness of the older woman's grip. "I'm Betty Jean Finnegan, chairwoman of The Blooming Ladies."

She looked at Winnie expectantly, as if Winnie was supposed to know all about the club. Winnie just blinked, her sleep-deprived brain struggling to keep up with this whirlwind of a woman so early in the morning.

"We are Bloomsburo's *premiere* social organization," Betty Jean continued, retracting her hand. "We do talent shows, pancake dinners, holiday parades, sweetheart dances, and of course, we help with our town's signature festival, Bloomsburo Days, which takes place the first weekend of October. No civic organization in town raises even a fraction of what we raise for local charities and causes. Needless to say I will be in touch with you at the paper *quite* frequently."

"Well, uh, it's a pleasure to meet you," said Winnie, trying not to look as startled as she felt by the woman's intensity. She looked to Gloria for moral support, and her co-worker sent her a wink, as if reading her mind. "I'm so excited to get to know the community and help spread the word about important events. Is that why you stopped by this morning?"

Betty Jean let out a dramatic sigh.

"Oh, Winnie, I wish it were that simple," she said, frustration tightening her facial features. "Trust me, I have plenty to tell you about in terms of the coverage our group is going to require in the next few months."

Winnie doubted that Betty Jean intended for that sentence to be a threat, but to her ears, that's how it came across. Not to mention that the idea of a community member *requiring* media coverage didn't sit well with Winnie.

"First of all I –" Betty Jean started before the bells rang on the front door once more. Both women turned their heads to view the newcomer and within seconds, nausea overtook Winnie's body. No, she hadn't slammed into his sweat-covered body this time, but the second coming of Cal Spencer seemed to have an even stronger effect on her than the first incarnation.

That same sexy mouth and mischievous eyes. That grabbable golden hair. If his body had looked delectable in his casual workout clothes, it was beyond fantastic showcased in more professional attire: the dark, perfectly-fitted jeans he wore with tan oxford shoes and an untucked Chambray shirt, sleeves rolled up.

Okay, so the man was out-of-this-world gorgeous. But what on earth was he doing at the newspaper office at this time on a Monday morning?

"Well it's about time you showed up," Betty Jean scolded Cal, as if she had been waiting for him. And that's when Winnie's dazzled brain finally put the pieces together.

No.

Given that Cal wasn't wearing a police uniform, her powers of deduction suggested that he must be the Chamber of Commerce director, which made her want to crawl under Gloria's desk and cry.

That couldn't be his job. Surely she'd misunderstood something. Because after the mayor, the city council members, the school superintendent and the police chief, there was no one she'd have to work with more closely than the Chamber of Commerce director.

And if that person was Cal Spencer, she might as well turn in her resignation today. She couldn't do it. Wouldn't.

"Where's the chief?" Betty Jean interrogated.

"He's tied up down at the station," Cal answered, and Winnie suddenly remembered his comment yesterday, that he and the chief were good friends. "I told him I'd give him a full update about your emergency meeting."

She didn't miss his slightly sarcastic emphasis on the word *emergency.*

Betty Jean sighed dramatically as Winnie and Cal silently sized one another up – Winnie, looking pale and dumfounded, and Cal looking sexy and amused, and Gloria surely wishing she had some popcorn to enjoy while the drama unfolded.

Betty Jean returned her scrutiny to Winnie.

"Winnie, this is a man you will have to deal with quite often," she said almost apologetically, gesturing in Cal's general direction. "Cal Spencer, director of the Bloomsburo Chamber of Commerce."

She watched that lethal grin spread across his lips and cursed her stomach for its overreaction to it.

"It's nice to see you, too, Betty Jean," he said, stretching the truth. When he glanced at Winnie, she couldn't help but mirror his ornery gleam. If nothing else, she'd enjoy having Cal as a co-conspirator against Betty Jean's managing ways.

"Cal, this is Winnie Briggs, the new editor of *The Bloom.*"

Winnie's gaze was still locked into his when he reached out his hand and found hers, squeezing it gently. It was amazing how natural yet electric it felt to be skin to skin with this man who seemed both like a stranger and like someone she'd been waiting for. It felt like a key sliding into its mated lock, the rightness of their bodies connected like that. She held his gaze, momentarily transfixed, until Betty Jean's barking orders snapped her out of it.

"Well, let's get on with it, then," Betty Jean hollered at them from down the hall, where she had already started marching her way toward Winnie's office. That the woman felt at home at the newspaper's headquarters was already more than evident.

"After you," Cal offered, his hand gesturing toward the hall. Winnie sighed, put on her metaphorical big girl panties, and made her way to her office to try and figure out what was going on in this office. In this town. With her life. And to think she was foolish enough to believe that her first Monday on the job might play nice.

Chapter 4

When Cal woke up early Monday, he had exactly two items on his morning agenda: get Winnie Briggs off of his brain and start to finalize some of the planning details around Bloomsburo Days, the town's annual three-day festival that his office organized.

Before 8 a.m., however, one paper delivery and two phone calls suggested that both goals were unlikely to be met.

Of course, he'd already been failing miserably on the not-thinking-about-Winnie front. Cal loved nothing more than being in complete control of his life, and everything about Winnie Briggs screamed "unexpected." Not to mention disruptive. Even his long run home yesterday afternoon hadn't been enough to fade the effects of his strange encounter with her.

Maybe it was the fact that Winnie, with her ample breasts, had crashed into his body out of the blue. Maybe it was the fact that he hadn't been with a woman in longer than he'd ever publicly admit. But he couldn't shake this bodily awareness of Winnie, not last night at his own house, and certainly not this morning when he opened his front door and found her face plastered across the front of his morning newspaper.

During yesterday's interrogation at his mother's shed, he hadn't bothered to ask what work brought Winnie to town. He naïvely assumed that this woman would be a minor hassle in his life. As long as she paid her rent on time and didn't create problems for his mom, he welcomed the opportunity to never think about her again.

But when the newspaper announced that Winnie Briggs would be taking over as editor-in-chief of *The Bloom*, he knew that this would prove impossible. Granted, Winnie's predecessor at the paper had been fairly worthless, but Cal worked intimately with the local media in order to promote the Chamber's initiatives.

And doing *anything* intimately with Winnie filled Cal with dread.

Not because she wasn't attractive. Hell, if he was honest, it was because she was. Sure, she looked cute and mussed in her rainbow-hued loungewear yesterday, but this morning at the newspaper office? All polished and professional?

He didn't want to think about it. About how the soft mint green of her sweater clung to her ample chest. About the way her hips flared beneath her flouncy skirt. About the effect her dark hair had on him, tumbling down over her shoulders like a rowdy invitation to play.

About how she was the first interesting thing to drop into his predictable life in years.

Damn it all, he didn't need this right now, yet here she was.

But it wasn't just the newspaper announcement that had kept Winnie on the forefront of Cal's mind prior to his arrival at *The Bloom Times'* office. He'd started his day with a very early phone call to his mother. He'd woken her up, which pleased him, given that he still felt considerably irritated with the woman.

"Anything you want to tell me about the She Shed, Ma?" he'd asked, his voice tempered just enough to let her know that the question was rhetorical. A brief pause on her end —a rare phenomenon when talking to his chatty mother—indicated that she knew what he knew.

"I've rented it."

"I figured that out."

Another pause lingered as he waited for her to explain herself. He loved his mother endlessly, but no one could press a man's buttons like the woman who created him.

"I don't have to explain myself to you, Charles Calhoun Spencer."

Up, up, up ticked his blood pressure, and not just because she used the full name he despised.

"It is my job to keep you safe, Ma, and how am I supposed to do that when you go off and do something boneheaded like this without so much as warning me?"

"Boneheaded?" she cried in disbelief. "What a thing to say about your only mother. It is *not* your job to keep me safe, Cal. That's a role you gave to yourself without my request."

He chose not to rise to that old, familiar bait. As the oldest and only son of a crummy father, and with three little sisters following in his footsteps, it sure as hell was his job to watch out for his family.

"What do you even know about this woman?" he asked.

"What woman?"

"Winnie Briggs."

"You met Winnie?"

He hated the eagerness he heard in his mother's voice.

"I did." He wouldn't give his mother an extra centimeter as far as the woman was concerned, let alone an inch.

He could practically hear his mother's gears turning in the silence. He knew her better than anyone else on earth, and he felt certain that she was thinking very carefully about how to proceed with this conversation. Surely she'd already crafted an elaborate plan for introducing Cal and Winnie, and now she had to think about how her matchmaking could best proceed given this unexpected start.

"Well, what'd you think of her?" she asked in a tone that might have come off as neutral to an outsider. But Cal knew his mother far too well to fall for it.

"I thought she was breaking and entering, so I threatened to call the police on her," he said. "What did you think was going to happen?"

"I...well..." Rhonda sputtered. "You threatened to call the police on her? Cal, that wasn't very hospitable. You probably scared the poor thing half to death."

That twinge of guilt flickered through his gut for the hundredth time whenever he pictured that panicked look on Winnie's face. He forced it away.

"And what did she say in response?"

"Oh, she made me feel guilty and put me in my place."

"Good girl," his mother said and he could hear the smile in her voice.

"You didn't answer my question," he growled, losing patience. "What do you know about this woman?"

"I trust her," his mom said.

He scoffed.

"Based on what?"

"I talked to her and I sensed that she was a good person. It was a gut instinct."

"Jesus, Mom. Your gut? This is a legally binding relationship. By the look of things, you invested some serious money in that cottage. You can't just let a stranger into a part of your home."

"Actually, I can," she said, her voice getting testy. "People do it all the time. Every day."

"You're not people. You're my mom and I worry about you."

"Cal," she said, her tone softening in that maternal way she had.

"She filled out an application," she continued, the bite dissolving from her voice. "We talked on the phone multiple times. She submitted three references, all of whom raved about her. And I ran a criminal background check. I talked to Jenna at the law firm in town before I started any of this, and followed all the steps she recommended."

Cal sighed. Of course she did. He knew his mother was a smart woman, but it frustrated him when she cut him out of the conversation. How was he supposed to be a resource to her when she refused to keep him in the loop?

"That's good," he managed.

"Now, you answer *my* question," his mother countered. "What did you think of Winnie?"

Mostly that I don't want to think about her.

"I did answer that. I thought she was a trespasser."

"That's not what I meant."

Cal sighed.

"Ma, don't do this."

"Don't do what?" she asked innocently. She wasn't fooling anyone.

"You know exactly what. Don't let your imagination run wild. Don't forget who you're dealing with."

"Who I'm dealing with? You mean my young, professionally accomplished son who's so handsome that he causes fender benders?"

"That happened once, Mom," Cal groaned, annoyed at the memory of the mortifying incident. Getting catcalled in the middle of a busy intersection in the center of town a few years back, and then having that cat caller crash her car into the truck in front of her at a stop sign was not his proudest moment.

Naturally it was one of his mother's favorite stories to bring up.

"Or maybe I'm dealing with the son who is so popular that every unattached woman in town has tried to get a date with him, yet he has politely refused every one of them?"

Oh, how tired he was of going down this road. Why did all of his sisters have to partner up so young? Why did he have to be the only one of the four siblings left to receive the full force of his mother's meddling?

He was barely thirty for Pete's sake. He was hardly an old…well, whatever the male version of an old maid was. He dated a little bit in high school, and a bit more in college. But never women from Bloomsburo. His Friday nights were far more likely to be spent playing pool with Carter and some of the guys at the bar downtown than wining and dining a woman.

"I do go on dates, Ma, just not with people from around here," he said, stretching the truth. Sure he'd done some online dating over the years, hooking up with the occasional woman when the right chemistry presented itself. He was a healthy man after all, amply supplied with physical needs. But none of it had ever grown into anything serious. He never brought anyone home to meet the family.

And he definitely never let these dates or one-night stands happen within the borders of Bloomsburo, because everyone knew everyone in the tightknit town where gossip spread faster than the flu in February.

For as much as he loved the place, the familiarity of his hometown could be suffocating at times.

"Well, you're in luck. Winnie's not from around here."

It wasn't home.

He suddenly remembered Winnie's description of Chicago, the city she'd just left. Just why *had* she shown up at his mother's doorstep?

And why the hell was he so curious about her story?

"Don't meddle," he warned his mother, finally getting to the true purpose of the conversation. "If you care about her, steer her away from me. You of all women should know that Spencer men are best to be avoided."

His mother sighed. Her late husband, Cal's father, was never a topic she enjoyed talking about with the son who despised him.

"I can't do this Cal. Not today."

"Please respect my boundaries, Mom."

"I hope you respect the irony in that statement, given the fact that *you* called *me* at seven o'clock in the morning to tell me you didn't approve of a decision that I made for myself as a fifty-five-year-old woman. You're not exactly the king of respecting boundaries yourself."

He couldn't come up with an argument against that one.

"I've got to get to work, Ma. We'll talk soon."

"I love you, Cal. I do appreciate you watching out for me."

And despite the occasional frustration she caused in his life, he couldn't help but return the sentiment.

But the whole conversation had started his day on a sour note. When his phone rang a short time later, at 7:45 on the nose, he knew it could only be Betty Jean Finnegan. The two had negotiated that time as the *earliest* possible time she could contact him on a weekday for community-related business. Today's call was to inform him of the 'emergency' meeting she was organizing later that morning, which brought him back to his current situation, following Winnie Briggs down the narrow hallway of the newspaper office and trying – and failing – not to notice just how the sway of her curvy hips caused the pleats of her skirt to dance around temptingly. It brought to mind many things, none of which should be spoken in a professional context. Her sheer proximity made him feel like a green boy back in the middle school hallways, lusting after a pretty girl walking by. And this realization also reminded him that it had been unnaturally long since he took comfort with a woman. He suddenly felt like a thirsty man in a desert, and Winnie looked a lot like an oasis.

But, oasis or not, she was a professional associate now, so it was time to convince himself that her temptation was just a mirage. As they rounded the corner into the back office, Betty Jean pulled a seat right next to Winnie's workspace, but he maintained his distance in a chair on the other side of the small room.

"Now, what's going on here? Are you both here for the same reason?" Winnie asked, pulling out a notebook and clearly trying to gather her bearings, all the while avoiding eye contact with him. He took some comfort in the fact that she seemed rattled, too, though it probably had more to do with Betty Jean than him.

"I called everyone here," Betty Jean explained, before her tone frosted over. "Well, everyone who bothered to show up."

Defensiveness rose in Cal's chest, a common reaction when your best friend was the police chief in a small town where petty critiques were common place.

"Chief Conrad has a lot on his plate. I told him I'd inform him if there was anything pressing he needed to know," he offered, trying to keep his tone neutral.

"Well it *is* pressing, and I'll expect you to tell him so," Betty Jean said, desperation cracking her typically polished veneer.

He caught a flicker of a smile on Winnie's face as she observed their exchange. Her gaze met his quickly, sending a spark across the room that seemed to strike him directly in his underutilized parts, but her attention flickered back to Betty Jean just as quickly.

"So, what exactly is pressing, Betty Jean? You'll have to forgive me. It's my first morning on the job and I'm far from up to speed."

Betty Jean cleared her throat, a sound Cal had long ago translated to mean that the woman was attempting to swallow back a sharp comment. He gave her credit for at least attempting civility with a newcomer.

"Well, plain and simple, there's been a pancake dinner sabotage," Betty Jean pronounced.

He hadn't known Winnie long, but he would guess that she was biting her inner cheek in an attempt not to snicker at Betty Jean's silly declaration. Surely this was just the kind of exciting story she had left Chicago to pursue.

Which brought back the question that had been circling in his mind for the last 18 hours: Just why had the woman left such a fantastic city? When he was younger, Cal himself had often dreamed of bolting Bloomsburo, and Chicago was one of his all-time favorite places to visit. Heading to the state university a few hours away for four years had been as close to an escape as he'd managed, though. His deep sense of responsibility toward his mother and sisters and nieces rendered any more ambitious adventures purely imaginary.

"Do you think you could elaborate a bit?" Winnie asked politely, interrupting his rumination.

"Yes, a flapjack fiasco deserves our utmost attention," Cal offered, unable to help himself.

"This is no laughing matter, Cal Spencer," Betty Jean huffed, even as Winnie finally relented the full wattage of her pretty smile, rewarding his orneriness. Such rewards could be addictive.

"Someone altered the sign at Hudson Dentistry," Betty Jean elaborated.

Winnie looked to Cal for clarification.

"Dr. Hudson offers up the big sign outside of his office to community groups for advertising their upcoming events," he elaborated. She nodded and took a few more notes.

"I personally oversaw the creation of the lettering for the pancake dinner sign, after numerous calls to Dr. Hudson's office to discuss the precise wording," Betty Jean continued. Cal could imagine her oversight perfectly, given how often she offered it to him at the Chamber. "It clearly stated that the start time was tonight at 4 p.m. But when I drove by the sign last night, I saw that the start time was listed at 7 p.m."

"It was probably an honest mistake," Cal offered.

"I might be willing to overlook it, too," Betty Jean said, pulling a notebook out of her designer shoulder bag and opening it to a page of scrawled notes, "had it been an isolated incident. But it wasn't."

Cal's eyebrow quirked. "Okay, let's hear your other evidence."

"The 'for sale' sign in Doris Duvall's yard was moved to Hattie Henson's yard. I saw it with my own two eyes on my morning walk."

"What time do you wake up?" he asked, truly astonished. The woman seemed to get more done before breakfast than most people did in a full work day. She didn't dignify the question with a response.

"Was there more?" Winnie asked.

"Yes. The chalkboard sidewalk sign over at Happy Grounds was completely erased."

Cal looked over to Winnie, and whispered "downtown coffee shop."

"And the bulletin board at the senior center has been completely cleared of all of the posters and flyers," Betty Jean continued, "even the Bloomsburo Day signs."

Okay, Cal had to admit that this last part caught his attention, as he'd posted those flyers their himself last week. But still, as far as crime and vandalism went, this seemed far from serious.

"Betty Jean, I'm sure it's just a few kids trying to pull off some harmless prank," he offered.

"Well, you'd know about that, now wouldn't you?"

Lord, the memory of people in this town. You toilet paper a few local businesses during homecoming one time in high school, and it hangs around your neck for the rest of your life.

"So you believe that these incidents are connected?" Winnie asked, maintaining more professionalism than the other two of them combined.

"Yes," Betty Jean replied.

"There's nothing Carter can do about any of this," Cal explained. No laws were broken. He doubted that any of the incidents even merited a formal police report.

"Well, what am I supposed to do in the mean time?" Betty Jean asked desperately. "Our pancake dinner fundraiser is tonight, and now the entire town is being told that the event doesn't even begin until after it's supposed to end! Who knows how many people saw that misinformation."

He sighed. Betty Jean could be a royal pain, but she was deeply devoted to this town and raised a hell of a lot of money for it. He didn't like to think about her event getting ruined due to a petty prank.

"Has the paper been advertising the event?" Winnie asked, and Cal inwardly winced, predicting the reaction that the question would induce from Betty Jean.

"No, the paper has *not* been advertising the event," Betty Jean cried, anger coloring her cheeks even beyond her heavily applied blush. Well, so much for her forced civility, though it was nice for the three full minutes it lasted. "*The Bloom* hasn't been doing anything worth mentioning for more than a month, thanks to that useless former editor and the good-for-nothing, out-of-town publisher who can't even bother to return a phone call."

He watched Winnie's jaw literally drop.

"You make calls to my out-of-state publisher?" Winnie asked in disbelief.

"Only when necessary," Betty Jean said smugly. "Someone has to stop this ship from sinking."

Defensiveness flared in Cal's heart once more, as natural as thirst or hunger.

"Take your claws out, Betty Jean," he said, his cool voice hiding the annoyance simmering beneath his skin. "Winnie isn't to blame for the newspaper's past problems. She's the solution to them."

His eyes made the mistake of meeting Winnie's across the room and the gratitude he saw there simultaneously tied his stomach in a knot and spurred him on.

"It's her first morning on the job. Give her some time to prove herself. She has stronger credentials than any editor that's worked here in my lifetime. She needs our support, not our scorn."

Betty Jean sighed dramatically, but didn't argue back. He took that as a win.

"Now, about the pancake dinner. The fastest way to fix the issue is going to be online," said Cal. "I'll put up a correction on the Chamber homepage this morning, and we can both link to it on our respective e-mail groups."

"I could post a correction on the newspaper's social media feeds," Winnie offered before adding with a laugh, "that is, as soon as I figure out what the passwords are."

He smiled her way, impressed with her calm in the face of Betty Jean's intensity. The woman really was going to be an asset to the newspaper and the community.

"And I guess I could activate the Blooming Lady phone tree," Betty Jean added. "Not everyone in this town uses computers and smart phones the way you kids do."

He and Winnie shared an amused glance.

"So I'll talk to some of the affected establishments and see if there's any larger story here," Winnie offered, before turning to Cal. "Will you have Chief Conrad contact me if anything else comes up on his end?"

Cal nodded, though the thought of his childhood friend calling Winnie shot a strange sensation through his veins, something closer to jealousy than he cared to admit. Not because Carter and Winnie were two single, attractive adults. No, it was just because he hadn't yet fully come to terms with the fact that this woman was now a part of his professional circle.

Right.

"So are we square, Betty Jean?" Cal asked, standing in an attempt to force the meeting to an end. He glanced at his phone and saw that it was already after nine. The pile of work on his desk at the Chamber could only be growing at this point, and he needed some space from the weird things Winnie did to his brain and body.

"I suppose," Betty Jean said. "Winnie, can I get your cell phone number, just in case something comes up?"

Winnie shot Cal an uncertain look. Clearly this was not a line she was accustomed to crossing.

"I've found that resistance is futile," he admitted. "If she doesn't have your phone number, she's more likely to come knocking on your door."

Her brow raised.

"The door of your home, not your office," he clarified. Winnie reluctantly jotted down a number on a Post-it note and passed it to Betty Jean.

"Well, I've got my work cut out for me today, as do both of you," Betty Jean said as she marched out of the office like a velour whirlwind. This left the two of them suddenly alone and facing each other once more. He watched Winnie nervously twist a finger around a curl at her collar bone.

"So, the woman breaking and entering on my mom's property turns out to be the new editor of the newspaper, huh?" he asked.

"Guilty."

"That seals our fate then."

Her eyes widened with concern. "Does it?"

"Oh, yes. There'll be no staying invisible now, Briggs. You've moved into a little fishbowl of a town, one that doesn't get restocked often. As the newest, most sparkly fish, everyone's going to be watching you closely."

He watched her take a deep breath and straighten her shoulders a bit.

"I'm a journalist, which for better or for worse makes me pretty used to being in the public eye."

"Well, good."

Her eyes softened just a bit.

"Are you concerned about any of this?" she asked, glimpsing briefly down at her notes from the 'emergency' meeting.

"No," he answered, and it was mostly true. "It's worth looking into. Even if it's just a few teen pranks, it'd be best to put an end to it. I'll give Carter a heads up, you'll talk to some of the business owners, and Betty Jean will do what she does best."

"Which is…"

"Put the fear of God in people, especially those who try to come between her and her pancake dinners."

Winnie snorted. For the second time in as many days he wondered how the sound managed to be adorable.

"Okay then, I guess that's that," she said. "Now it's time for me to figure out where everything is in my office, who's who in town, and what exactly I'm supposed to be doing as the editor of this paper."

"Should make for a nice, light work day, then."

She laughed again, and damn if he didn't love the sound. His feet suddenly felt rooted to the ground and he fought the urge to continue their banter, just as an excuse to stay in her presence for a few more minutes.

That very awareness proved to be the wake-up call he needed. He had to shake this woman from his system, fast.

"Until next time, then," he said with a smile and made his way to the hallway. And even if he chose to ignore it, the notion that there would be a next time with Winnie Briggs was enough to put a spring in his step as he made his way out the front door.

Chapter 5

By late morning, Winnie's brain had turned to mush. Between the lack of sleep, the bizarre introduction to the town's most relentless busy body, the kick in the gut she felt after learning about the inevitable professional connection she and Cal would share, and the intensity of all the processes, passwords and people she was learning about on her first morning on the job, Winnie didn't know up from down.

Slowly, slowly, the curl of anxiety began to creep its way through her core, and her internal pendulum started to shift toward panic. What was she doing here in Bloomsburo? Had she really picked up her life and stepped into the middle of a community where she didn't know a soul? Who could she vent to? Who could help her process the dozens of conflicting emotions coursing through her veins right now?

And why on earth had she agreed to not contact her best friend Bree for an entire month?

Luckily one familiar sound stopped her from her catastrophizing: her stomach grumbling. She suddenly struggled to remember if she'd actually managed to eat even so much as a granola bar this morning in the all the hubbub. If there was one thing Winnie knew about herself, though, it was that an empty stomach increased her odds of overreacting.

She might be in an unfamiliar city, dealing with a needlessly aggressive community leader and a criminally handsome professional acquaintance, but she could manage a meal. She could do that much for herself.

Winnie first.

She told Gloria she was leaving for a lunch break and walked out of the newspaper office doors, down the block to where the road intersected with the main square downtown. Looking across the street, she noticed a retro green and white sign that read "Dewey's." She glanced at her watch. 10:53 a.m. Too late for breakfast but too early for lunch. Luckily Dewey's looked like the kind of small-town diner that would have her appetite covered either way.

Pushing through the front doors, she heard the attached bells tinkle in welcome, and felt somewhat relieved by the restaurant's vacancy. Her oddly timed meal at least allowed her to beat the lunch rush.

Behind the counter she saw a pretty waitress staring out the window, her face distant. Winnie placed the woman in her early twenties, with a cute retro apron and wild red hair that a low ponytail failed to tame.

"Excuse me," Winnie interrupted. She felt bad, disturbing a woman so lost in her own thoughts, but Winnie had to get some sustenance if she wanted to survive this Monday. A huge plate of fried food may be the only thing strong enough to salvage the day. Not to mention that if she didn't eat soon, she'd be struck by the hangries, and turn really cranky, really fast.

Winnie cleared her throat, trying to gently break whatever spell held the waitress.

"Oh, I'm so sorry," the woman said, shaking her head, as if to bring herself back into the present. "I'm not all here today."

"Trust me, I get it. My mind's wandering all over the place, too. Is it okay if I sit here at the counter?" Winnie asked, dropping her messenger bag down on a shimmery red vintage diner stool next to her.

"Of course. Can I get you a drink?"

"If you could put a Pepsi in my hands right now, you'd be my new best friend."

Surprise colored the woman's face, but she smiled and turned to the soda fountain behind her.

When the drink, filled with the most delicious crushed ice, made its way to Winnie, she gulped it for five seconds straight until her throat began to burn.

"Oh, that's better," she said. "I'm Winnie, by the way. I'm so new to town that I haven't even had a chance to buy groceries yet, hence why I've come to you in such dire, hungry straits."

"Well, I'm Evie Finnegan," the waitress said hesitantly, apparently still somewhat unsure of what to make of Winnie. "And I'm old to town."

"You grew up here?"

"Yep. Born here, raised here. And currently stuck with no real prospects for getting out of here," she said with a forced laugh, though Winnie noted the slight strain in the woman's face as she twisted what appeared to be a wedding ring on her left hand.

The interviewer in Winnie wanted to ask a half-dozen follow-up questions, most of which would be impolitely invasive. She mentally filed them away for later.

"Here's a menu," Evie said, placing a massive laminated sheet in front of Winnie. "Just let me know when you're ready."

"Will do," Winnie said, hungrily scanning the dozens of breakfast, lunch, dinner and dessert choices.

Evie moved back down the counter, likely to give her sole customer a bit of space as she made her decision. But even from where she resumed her post looking expressionlessly out the window, the woman kept sending curious glances back Winnie's way.

As the newest, most sparkly fish, everyone's going to be watching you closely. Cal's prediction had become the theme of the day. She might as well have a flashing sign on her head that blinked New Girl! New Girl! in neon letters.

Then again, the front-page feature story about her in the newspaper had pretty much created the same effect.

Surviving this transition would require a friend, and the pretty, weary redhead seemed as good a candidate as any, not only because of her age, but also because Winnie already knew that Dewey's would quickly become a regular haunt.

A flutter of butterflies whirled through Winnie's belly, acknowledging not for the first time the difficulties of making friends as an adult. Mandatory college ice breakers had thrown her into Bree's path back in college, but everyday life didn't offer such opportunities, so she'd have to be brave. Her survival depended upon it.

"Are the cheeseburger's any good?" Winnie asked, trying to pull the woman back into conversation.

"Amazing. They're best with onion rings."

"That will be perfect. Well-done, please," Winnie said as she slid her massive menu up the counter toward Evie. She watched as the woman jotted a few notes on a tiny pad of paper, and then slipped the order to the kitchen via a window on the far side of the counter.

A fragment of their earlier conversation suddenly sparked in Winnie's brain.

"Wait a minute, did you say you last name is Finnegan?"

Evie looked suddenly worried. "Yes."

"Are you by any chance related to Betty Jean Finnegan?"

If Winnie didn't know better, she'd guess that it was despair flashing in Evie's face in that moment.

"Um, yes. She's my husband's grandmother. And I apologize in advance if she did something to upset you."

Winnie laughed in relief.

"Let's just say it's my first day in town, and she's already made quite the impression. I'm not sure how she feels about me. I didn't get the sense that she was especially pleased with me."

Evie raised one brow, and the effect transformed her serious face into something mischievous.

"Well, if you're on that list, then you're joining me there. After all, I was the no-good hussy who got pregnant in high school, ruining her grandson's prospects."

Winnie's heart swelled. A potential friend who understood the full force of The Velour Whirlwind? She knew fate had guided her to Dewey's this day.

"You have kids?" Winnie asked in disbelief, not only because Evie couldn't be twenty-five, but also because she had the figure of a teenager.

"Three, actually. A five-year-old daughter and two-year-old twin boys."

Winnie told her jaw not to drop but it did anyway. That explained Evie's weary aura, anyway.

"Well, you look incredible for having three kids," Winnie noted.

"And if you come in here once a week and say that to me, you'll be *my* new best friend," Evie said, a genuine smile spreading across her face for the first time during the exchange.

"So if I started venting to you about my day like someone might do to a bartender, would you kick me out?"

Evie grinned, another flash of mischief animating her face. It filled Winnie with joy to see the woman loosening up a bit.

"If you lead a dull life, maybe. If you've got something juicy to share, probably not."

Winnie laughed, and began to tell Evie all about her unusual first day, and to inquire about the ever-growing cast of Bloomsburo characters crossing her path. The warm glow of a new friendship,

JESS VONN

not to mention the cooked-to-perfection cheeseburger, worked like a salve on her anxious heart.

~-~-~-~-~-~-

In her second night in the new cottage, Winnie slept like the dead, and she awoke slowly and with much confusion.

Where was she?

Oh yes, her new cottage. The She Shed. That silly nickname still filled her with unreasonable joy. It probably always would.

What day was it?

Oh yes, Tuesday. She'd officially survived one day on the job.

Why was she feeling disoriented?

Oh, that could be any combination of things. Professional stress. Nutritional deficits. (She really did have to get to the grocery store today. Last night's dinner of Lucky Charms didn't exactly qualify as a meal of champions.) Oh, and perhaps the fact that she couldn't be in her new home without thinking about Cal Spencer.

Just as she slid off the high perch of the new bed that she had already fallen in love with, she heard a knock on the door.

It would have felt like déjà vu had the gentle knocking not so contrasted with Cal's pounding two day before.

Cal's pounding. Now there was a phrase she hoped to never think of again. She'd given up men, but she hadn't yet figured out how to turn off her libido. This combination of conditions presented a problem.

"Winnie, are you up?" a woman's voice sang from the porch, shaking Winnie from her own thoughts. She panicked, remembering that she wore nothing but a taco-printed nightgown. She grabbed the nearest hoodie she could find and threw it on. By the time she made her way to the door, she was glad she had. The early September heat wave had apparently passed and the fall morning air felt crisp and cool.

She opened the door just a crack to see the kind face of a middle-aged woman and in her heart, she knew it had to be the face of her new landlady, Rhonda Spencer, the woman with whom she'd already shared half a dozen enjoyable phone conversations. With her long, strawberry blond hair pulled back into a thick braid that hung over her shoulder, her blue eyes lined with the gentle crinkles of a laugh-filled life, a floor-length sundress covered in swirl of floral patterns, and wrists full of colorful bangle bracelets, Rhonda embodied the picture of a hippie who'd aged magnificently.

Winnie liked Rhonda instantly, even if that required her to ignore the fact that the woman's eyes had the same mischievous glint as her son's. The Spencer DNA clearly trended heavily toward charisma.

"Winnie?" she asked, her face glowing with affection.

"That'd be me," Winnie said. "Rhonda?"

In response, the woman simply pulled her in for a long, deep hug. Winnie willed herself to forget her lack of real clothing, and tried not to imagine the state of her wavy hair after a long, restless night. Luckily, Rhonda's warm presence put her instantly at ease.

"It's so good to finally meet you!" Rhonda cried, releasing Winnie from the embrace and grabbing a basket from where she'd just set it on the ground. "For you!"

Winnie looked down and saw a pretty red wicker basket bursting with a bouquet of tiny purple and yellow asters atop a bowl full of fruit salad and a plate of homemade muffins so fresh that their warmth steamed the plastic wrap that enveloped them.

"What's all this?" Winnie asked, touched. She'd actually have something to eat today!

"An apology."

Winnie glanced up. "An apology? What for? I'm in love with this space. It's more than I could possibly have hoped for."

Rhonda's face softened. "I'm so glad. It pained me to let it go, but as soon as I got your email, I knew you were the perfect woman to hand it over to."

Winnie felt herself blush.

"But the apology is for my son."

Winnie's stomach tightened. Well, she'd made it two minutes, at least, before her mind reluctantly returned to Cal Spencer's visit to this very porch.

"Oh, he felt worried about his mom, that's all. He seems like a very caring son," Winnie said, attempting to tuck a wayward curl back behind her ear.

"That's generous of you to say. He's the best son," Rhonda said, before her tone shifted ever so slightly. "And since he's my only son, I can honestly say that he's also the worst. Either way, he had no right to barge in here and make you feel unwelcome."

Winnie's heart warmed at Rhonda's protectiveness. She didn't harbor any anger over Cal's stony welcome. By now she felt merely resentful about his gorgeous existence more generally, and the way it kept short circuiting her sex-starved brain.

"We resolved the situation well enough."

Rhonda looked unconvinced. "I gave him a piece of my mind when he told me what happened."

"And what, exactly, did he say happened?"

"He told me that he stormed over here and scolded you. And then he said you put him in his place and he went along his merry way."

Winnie couldn't help but laugh. "That sounds about right. And let me guess, Cal gave you a piece of his mind, too?"

Rhonda rolled her eyes, but playfully. "I don't know at what point a child decides he needs to start taking care of his parent, instead of the opposite, but I'll tell you, it's unwarranted. I'm a grown woman who can make her own decisions and take care of herself. I probably should have told him my plans for the She Shed, but you know what? I didn't want him butting in. I wanted one project that existed just for me, not the whole family."

"That seems reasonable," Winnie relented. "But he's a very dedicated son."

Rhonda sighed. "That I can't deny. It just shows itself in unexpected ways. But in any case, I wanted to say that I'm sorry for my absence Sunday, that I couldn't welcome you myself, and to assure you that my overbearing son will not be causing you any more problems around here."

Winnie smiled despite her realization that the man seemed more than capable of causing problems for her regardless of his physical proximity.

"So you've started at the newspaper already?" Rhonda asked.

"I started yesterday. I even ran into Cal at a meeting."

When she saw Rhonda's face light up at this new piece of information, she could practically hear Cal groaning from across town.

Cal groaning. Another phrase to add to the list of things Winnie shouldn't ponder. "But, I had better get ready if I'm going to be on time today," Winnie said.

"Well, I wish you luck. And I can think of at least five people that I truly, truly hope won't find their way to your office today."

"Does Betty Jean Finnegan happen to be one of them?" Winnie asked before she could think better of it.

Rhonda laughed. "Heaven's yes. She's already got her talons in you, huh? It never takes long."

"Well, she's at least attempting to do so."

"Don't worry. She's almost all bark. I wish I could tell you she's the worst you'll face around here, but I've never been a liar."

Winnie laughed as Rhonda gave Winnie one more hug and began the walk across the gardens, back to the main house.

It occurred to Winnie that in the past five minutes with Rhonda, she received more hugs than she had in the past week, a realization that made her feel unexpectedly weepy.

She needed a shower and some caffeine, stat.

~-~-~-~-~-~-

Before Winnie could even set her bag down at the office, Gloria handed her three phone messages. Once again she looked at her watch. *8:36 a.m.* Never what you might call a morning person, Winnie realized it might take a good long while to fully acclimate to the early-morning eagerness of the Bloomsburo community.

"The first call came from the Presbyterian church, requesting coverage of their blood drive later in the week," Gloria said, handing her a quaint, old-fashioned paper message. Come to think of it, with the rotary phone by her desk, Winnie doubted the office featured voice mail capabilities. She'd use her own cell phone if she could figure out how to get decent service anywhere in the center of town – another tangle in her new life waiting to be unraveled.

"The second call was from Diana Knolls, our publisher, who wanted to talk to you about an upcoming special section," she continued, passing Winnie another tiny pink slip of paper.

"And the third one," Gloria said with a sigh, as if she didn't want to have to go into it, "well, the third one is from Esther Hoffman."

"Okay," Winnie said, suddenly wondering if that name made the cut on Rhonda's five-townies-to-watch-out-for list. "Should I be worried?"

"She's eighty-eight years old. She's about four and a half feet tall. She's as sweet as the homemade pies she's famous for. But she calls in at least three times a week with story tips."

"Hmmm."

"And let's just say that her idea of what's newsworthy probably differs from your idea of what's newsworthy."

"So what was it this morning?"

"Well, she's got a summer squash coming up in her garden that, and I quote, 'has some very interesting looking stripes on it.'"

Winnie couldn't help but laugh. No, that didn't feel like much of a news lead to her.

Gloria continued, "She wants to know if you want to drive out and take a picture of it for a small write-up in the next issue of the paper."

"Oh, sheesh."

"And I should mention," Gloria continued, "that she lives at the very far reaches of the county. It's probably a good thirty-minute drive once you get through all the meandering, gravel roads."

"Can't she just take a picture and send it in for our consideration?" Winnie asked.

"Did I mention that she's eighty-eight? She has no camera, and no computer. Hence why she always needs the assistance of *The Bloom Times* staff."

Winnie grabbed the final pink slip from Gloria's hand.

"Well, I think the call from the publisher takes a bit more precedence than the call from Esther for the time being, don't you?"

"I think that's a good assessment."

She turned to walk back to her office, but stopped, remembering one more thing she had to ask Gloria.

"Hey, Gloria, have they sent us an agenda for tomorrow's city council meeting yet?"

Gloria blinked a few times.

"Well, no. They don't tend to send those to us."

"They don't publish the agendas? That's required by law."

"No one's brought it up, I guess," Gloria shrugged. "Are you sure you want to go cover the city council meeting? No one around here has done that for years. Nobody would notice if you missed out this week while you got settled."

Winnie sighed. The fact that *The Bloom* hadn't covered city council meetings since the Reagan administration was one of the first things she planned to change at the paper. Townspeople deserved to know as much as possible about the actions of their leaders, and Winnie took the watchdog function of journalism seriously.

And if they weren't even managing to publish a public agenda for their monthly meetings, the city council needed a watchdog.

"No, I think it's good to let them know what they're dealing with straight out of the gate," she said with a wink.

Gloria gave an almost foolishly big grin. "Like I said, you're going to shake things up around here. I better just put on my seat belt right now."

Winnie laughed softly as she made her way back to her office. She looked at the messages in her hand, and decided to give her publisher, Diana, a call back before she got lost in other tasks. Diana, who hired Winnie, worked out of Minnesota, but managed ten different small-town newspapers like *The Bloom* around the Midwest. Winnie had spoken to her a handful of times in the weeks since her hiring, and Diana had always given the general impression of "slightly stern competence."

Having dragged her finger across the rotary the requisite eleven times, Winnie eventually heard Diana pick up on the other end, informing Winnie that she didn't have too much time to talk, but that she wanted to give her a heads up about an upcoming project.

"At these small, community papers, special sections can be a big money maker, and can generate a lot of community enthusiasm," Diana explained. "You'll put together 8-10 over the course of the year, usually about twenty pages each. Sometimes they focus on holidays, or seasons; other times they have some theme, like home improvement, or gardening. They're usually comprised of a mix of canned and local content."

Well that sounds like a lot of work for me, Winnie thought — silently, of course, because she'd like to keep her job for more than two days.

"I'll get you a copy of the full year's schedule so you can plan ahead," Diana continued, "but the first one you need to know about is coming right up. Bloomsburo Days is the biggest festival of the year in your town, and it's one of our largest and most profitable special sections you'll produce."

"Okay. What's the timeline?"

"The festival is always held the first weekend of October, with events beginning Wednesday and ending Sunday. We need to publish the section the week before. So the special section will be distributed September 30th.

Winnie scanned the calendar on the wall. It was already the 6th. That gave her less than a month to put together the special content. She must have sighed louder than she meant to, based on what Diana said next.

"I know it's daunting, but the good news is that you have lots of help with this one, given who runs the festival."

"And who's that?"

"The Chamber of Commerce."

To Winnie, of course, this revelation felt like the *opposite* of good news.

"And luckily the guy in charge, Cal Spencer, really knows his stuff. He's helped us with this section for the past five years, and as long as you work closely with him, your timeline should be manageable."

"Well, that's great, then," Winnie lied through clenched teeth.

"Sorry to drop all this on you and run, but I have to catch a 9 a.m. flight to Decatur to unravel an HR disaster at our daily down there."

"Okay, well, we'll touch base on this soon," said Winnie.

"Good."

As Winnie hung up the phone, only one tangible thought remained: Was the daily paper in Decatur hiring? Bloomsburo, so it seemed, had it out for her.

Chapter 6

"Want to go easy on those weights, man, or is the Chamber planning on replacing them once you've banged them up beyond repair?"

Cal removed his right earbud, giving his eardrum a much-needed break from the relentless clamor of rock music. He glanced over at Carter Conrad, who seemed displeased with Cal's morning mood. When Cal looked at Carter, he only saw his best childhood friend, who was just a shy, scraggly kid when they met. Everyone else who looked at him saw the town's pleasant-but-respected police chief.

Granted, the man had packed on about thirty pounds of muscle since their high school days, but old memories died hard.

"Sorry," Cal said, glancing down to where the forty-pound dumbbell had just crashed at his feet. Given the fact that no public gym operated in Bloomsburo, Cal appreciated Carter's generosity in letting him work out at the police station weight room. The two friends met up there at least two mornings a week, and Cal typically took better care of the equipment. "I guess I'm in a zone."

And by saying he was "in a zone," Cal meant that he wanted to exert himself to the breaking point in an attempt to work that damn dream out of his system. Every time he closed his eyes, his brain replayed last night's visions with startling clarity.

Winnie, lying on a blanket in the grass on Cosgrove Hill.

All that dark, wavy, hair splayed around her. A soft purple sundress pulled down around her waist.

His hand slipping beneath the dress folds to caress her wet, hot core.

His mouth feasting on her bare breasts as they rose and fell with the moans he coaxed from her.

He bit the inside of his lip until it bled, attempting to tamp the desire that threatened to flood his senses again and bring his focus back to the humid weight room. Sure, he had had his fair share of sexy dreams, mostly as a teenager, but never about a woman from his real life. Never with such staggering specificity. He wasn't going to get caught up in the fantasy again. Not here. Not in front of Carter.

JESS VONN

"You pissed about something?" Carter asked. The brawny cop typically avoided much talk about emotions, but aside from Cal's own mother, no one could read Cal's moods like his childhood friend.

Surprising himself and Carter, Cal took out his other earbud and shut down his music.

"My brain's all scrambled. I can't focus," he confessed with a sigh.

"Work stuff?" Carter asked, pulling up a weight bench to sit on, and grabbing a sip of water.

"Nah, not really. I mean, Bloomsburo Days is coming up soon, so that's always a ton of work, but it's nothing I haven't done lots of times before."

"Your family okay?" Carter asked.

"More or less. Ma's meddling, as usual."

"Better that she's meddling with you than meddling with me."

Cal had to chuckle at that. Carter's name appeared right below his own on his mother's list of single Bloomsburo bachelors she'd like to marry off. Carter carried a hell of a lot of personal baggage though, which served to cool his mother's matchmaking determination.

"You didn't have a date last weekend that you didn't tell me about, did you? Did something go south?"

"Nope. It's been a while now."

"Oh, well that explains it, then," Carter teased. "You're suffering from a drought. That'll mess with a man's brain."

Cal glared at his friend.

"That's not it exactly, but the drought surely doesn't help, as I'm sure you understand."

His friend let out a rueful laugh.

"I'd feel sorry for you, except that I know how every eligible woman in this town, and a third of the married ones, would jump at a chance to be your date this weekend."

Cal shot him an annoyed look. "And the same couldn't be said about you?"

Carter merely shrugged, and Cal let it go. It had only been in the past year that people in the street could look at Carter without growing overwhelmed with pity and grief, but that didn't mean that the man needed to jump back on the market.

A Time To Fall

Given the losses Carter had been through in the last few years, Cal wouldn't be surprised if his friend never dated again. He probably wouldn't if he was in the guy's shoes. Some grief you just don't recover from.

"I don't know though, man," Carter continued. "This feels woman-related. You don't have something brewing that I don't know about, do you?"

"Nothing I *want* to be brewing."

"The plot thickens. It can't be anyone around here. Any decent hometown prospects got themselves married and off the market years ago."

Cal scoffed.

"You don't mean your mom's new renter?"

"How the hell do you know about that?" Cal cried, annoyance morphing into anger. "My mom told *you* that she rented out the She Shed before she told me?"

Carter shot his friend a self-satisfied look grin. "I *am* her favorite son."

Cal sighed. His mother had all but adopted Carter, and he knew she liked him better than her own flesh-and-blood son half the time. If she ever found herself with a dozen extra cookies lying around, they would end up at Carter's house long before they'd end up at Cal's.

Then again, Cal could cook. Carter was hopeless.

"Have you met Winnie?" Cal asked.

"Haven't had the privilege."

Cal stayed silent for a moment, then explained. "I think it's just how I met her that's throwing me off. It rattled me. I just wasn't expecting her to suddenly be a part of my life."

"So she's *unexpected*?" Carter said, his voice hinting at something he should know better than to try.

"Give it a rest. You're as bad as my mother."

"So what's wrong with her?"

Cal jerked his head back. "Nothing's wrong with her," he said too quickly. "I mean, I don't even know her."

"Ask her out this weekend. See if you can find any defects."

"I'm not asking her out."

"Why not?"

"I don't ask women out on dates."

"Oh yeah, that's right. You eventually relent to Tinder matches when the need gets desperate enough. I forgot your masterful strategy."

"You don't date. I don't date. We're in the same boat. You've got no room to judge."

The look Carter shot at him from across the weight room let him know he'd crossed a line. But enough time had passed. Cal didn't need to treat the man with kid gloves any more. He could just as easily decide to move on with his life but, like Cal, he chose not to for personal reasons. It was an unspoken agreement that the men respected this about each other.

"Look, don't get all touchy. It's more than that. We're colleagues. She's the new editor of *The Bloom*."

"Well, shit. That complicates things."

"Yeah. So even if I wanted to, which I don't, it can't go anywhere. But I just have to get her out of my brain. Get a little bit of space between us. I think I'm just worried about my mom."

"Right," Carter said, the word dripping with sarcasm.

"I should finish these reps," Cal said, indicating that the conversation was over. But not before he heard his friend's final comment.

"There are a lot of things you should do, man."

Cal shoved his earbuds back in, blasting his music to drown out his friend's commentary and the devil on his own shoulder.

~-~-~-~-~-~-

When reevaluating her professional goals, Winnie decided she need to add a new item to the list: managing to arrive at a meeting more than twenty-five seconds before it started. She never arrived late, but it occurred to her that she might make a better professional impression if she didn't always arrive right on the buzzer, breathless and with her hair flying everywhere.

However, she hadn't quite figured out how to make that happen yet, and so on Wednesday morning, true to character, Winnie slid through the city hall doors exactly twenty-three seconds before the 10 a.m. city council meeting was scheduled to begin.

She scanned the various corridors of the stuffy historic building, feeling completely lost.

New girl! New girl! New girl! the familiar alert blared in her mind. No one sat out front though; the staff of city hall seemed to be as non-existent as the city council's meeting agenda. She walked down a hallway that she assumed led to the council's chamber, pulling open the heavy wooden doors at the end of the hallway. Her stomach whirled, in part because of all the first impressions about to be made, but also because it seemed at least feasible that the Chamber of Commerce director might be in attendance at a city council meeting.

Really, Cal could be anywhere. That's what freaked her out. As a well-known professional in town who worked closely with area businesses, he had a legitimate reason to attend the majority of the events Winnie would be expected to cover, and not knowing when she'd see him next kept her stomach in knots.

When she walked through the heavy wooden doors, however, she realized she hadn't missed anything at all. Somewhere in the back of the chamber a police officer sat with his arms crossed, looking half bored, half annoyed. She noticed three people sitting up at the front, the city council members presumably, exchange confused glances from behind their respective newspapers. The general seating area was completely empty. No Cal. She felt equal parts relief and disappointment at his absence, a reaction she didn't approve of.

"Can, uh, can we help you?" the older man at the front of the room, who had to have been at least eighty, asked before Winnie could even take a seat.

"I'm Winnie Briggs, the new editor of *The Bloom Times*," she said from the front of the room. Both council members sat up straighter, which she loved. Striking fear in the hearts of public officials was one of the best parts of being a reporter. "I'm here to cover today's meeting."

The men looked at each other again.

"Right, well," the other man said, clearing his throat. "We're just getting a bit of a late start."

He glanced over to the councilwoman sitting to his right, who suddenly grabbed her cell phone, bolted out of her chair and rushed out the door Winnie had just entered through.

"You know how mornings can be," the other man said, laughing nervously.

"Mmmm," Winnie said, not quite agreeing. She was far from a morning person, but a meeting time was a meeting time.

With no agenda to guide her, Winnie tried to figure out what was going on, and who was missing. She knew from the website that the town had three council members plus the mayor, but there were only three people sitting up front today. She recalled the photo of the mayor she'd seen on the town website, realizing he was the one absent from the meeting.

She sighed, unsure what to make of the bizarre situation. At the very least, it looked like she'd have time to gather her bearings after all.

Seeing as how the police officer was the only other person in the room, she decided it was only polite to sit near him. Plus, if she found herself with a few extra minutes, she might as well get to know a community member.

"I'm lucky I got here early enough to grab a seat, huh?" Winnie joked in the man's general direction. On an almost daily basis, she relished the fact that being a reporter required her to talk to strangers, because it forced her out of the shyness that could sometimes paralyze her.

Especially with men like him, who would be intimidating in or out of uniform.

Well not *out* of his uniform. Though surely, that would be intimidating, too. Oh, heaven help her, she was not going to survive this foray into abstinence.

She took in every detail of the man before her: tall, broad and brawny, with thick, close cropped dark hair just starting to show salt and pepper strands around his temples. No wedding ring, she instinctively observed. She resented the part of her brain that always checked for such things. Needless to say, this cop was more Magic Mike than the Barney Fife she might have been expecting in a small, rural town.

What was in the water around here? Bree would never believe her when Winnie told her how much man candy was hidden amongst the cornfields.

Not that it did Winnie any particular good during her sexual hiatus.

The cop smiled at her, a white dazzling smile that seemed to glow amidst his tan skin and the dark stubble already forming on his chin.

He seemed like the kind of guy who'd have to shave at least twice a day to keep his face smooth. Testosterone aplenty with this one.

"No, there's no crowd yet, but something tells me this show is about to get more interesting," he said, gesturing toward the door through which the councilwoman just fled.

"I'm Carter Conrad," he said, extending his hand for a firm shake, "Chief of Police here in Bloomsburo."

The chief? He seemed too young, though he did carry himself with the confidence of a leader.

"And I'm Winnie Briggs, muckraker."

He laughed at that, releasing her hand, and she felt grateful for the ease she already felt with him, another person she'd be working with regularly, though not always under the best of circumstances. Police officers tended not to welcome visits from local reporters.

In a flash, the very first words Cal spoke to her came to mind.

I've got my friend, the police chief, on speed dial.

Naturally, the blond Adonis and the raven Adonis would be best friends. They'd probably been collectively bringing girls, then women, to their knees since junior high.

"I'm assuming you're required to attend these meetings," Winnie said.

"Twice a month," he confirmed, without enthusiasm.

"You'd think the mayor would be required to attend them as well," she said flatly, earning her a snicker from the handsome chief, even if he was too smart to respond to the dig.

"Well, welcome to town anyway. It's not a perfect place, but we're proud of Bloomsburo. It's a great place to raise a family."

She probably looked as dumbstruck as she felt at his words.

"Well, good to know, even if I will not be needing it for those purposes anytime soon," she sputtered, revealing far more than was reasonable or appropriate.

Her cheeks flushed as his eyebrow rose, but in kindness he didn't say a word.

"Do you have kids then?" she asked, and she saw something unreadable flash across his face.

"Nah, I don't use the town for those purposes, either," he said with forced lightness. A story hid behind that delayed response. She made a mental note to ask Evie about his backstory later.

"Well, it's nice to meet you face to face, as I'm certain that I'll be contacting you for some story soon," Winnie said, veering the conversation away from non-existent spouses and children.

"I'd be lying if I said I'll be providing you with much big, breaking crime news," he admitted.

"I guess that's ultimately a good thing. After living in Chicago for four years, I've had my fill of sick, twisted crimes."

He nodded in understanding. She wondered if he'd always been a small-town cop, or if he'd also had a taste of big city life.

"You know, I take that back," Chief Conrad said. "We do see some action sometimes. Just this morning, a squirrel had the audacity to break into Mabel Murphy's four-seasons room."

Winnie laughed. It sounded like the kind of story that Esther Hoffman might call in. Luckily the grandmotherly woman had taken it pretty well yesterday when Winnie called and let her know she would *not* be driving out to her farm to take pictures of her oddly-striped summer squash. Only time would tell what Esther's next news tip would be.

"Well, I'll be sure to hold a spot on the front page for that one. If the squirrel will give me a quote, that is."

Winnie asked him a few more questions about the Bloomsburo community, but before long, the council doors swung open once more. The squat councilwoman returned, her face flushed red and sweaty from exertion, and she brought with her two contrasting guests.

The first, an older man who, by the look of things, had just rolled out of bed.

His sandy white hair stuck up in odd spikes around his sunburned scalp. A printed, wrinkled button-up shirt stretched to fit over his protruding belly. Its buttons were askew, leaving a long tail on the bottom of one half of the shirt. His cargo shorts seemed like an odd option given his tall white athletic socks and his black Adidas sandals. Though the casual attire bore no resemblance to the suit and tie he wore in his official photo online, Winnie quickly identified the man as Mayor Ralph Simpson.

As strange as his frazzled, unprofessional entrance seemed, even stranger was the woman who accompanied him. Winnie couldn't decide what was most striking about the woman, who looked about Winnie's age: the white-blonde hair, the piercing blue eyes, the tall and athletic build, or the ample bust that unnaturally contrasted the firm leanness of the rest of her physique. She wore painted-on white leggings and a soft, silky neon pink halter top that perfectly matched the shade of her three-inch strappy heels.

"That's Greta Johannsen," the chief said, gesturing up to the blonde vision at the mayor's side.

Of course that was her name, seeing how she looked like she emerged from some magical springs in the Alps like a goddess from one of Grimm's fairytales.

"She's the mayor of Broadsville," Chief Conrad continued, referring to the neighboring town.

Winnie did a double take.

"You're messing with me," Winnie said in disbelief. She looked at the woman once more, a woman who wouldn't look out of place on a runway. Winnie felt like a jerk for even having the thought, but the woman was not what you thought of when you thought *small town politician.* Her youth, style and beauty were quite frankly shocking.

"I'm telling the truth," the chief maintained. "She was elected two years ago, when she was only twenty-three. Her dad is a very rich and very well-known figure in agribusiness after he patented some special strand of fertilizer. He made a gazillion bucks, and she pretty much gets what she wants around here."

Cal.

Why would his name pop into her head right now? Why couldn't she keep him off her mind for five solid minutes? But Winnie couldn't help but think that if *she* happened to be a stunning and successful blonde who lived in the area and got whatever she wanted, she'd pick Cal.

Winnie experienced the typical process she went through when an alpha female neared. Nervousness mixed with a desire to be liked, mixed with a splash of inferiority and a touch of nausea. But she'd have to fight through it. This was another professional acquaintance. Granted, not one she'd work with nearly as often as Cal or Chief Conrad, but a colleague nonetheless. Winnie needed to give her the same warm reception she'd give anyone else.

The pair came closer, with the mayor focused up front, not registering Winnie's presence in the room. Greta did, though, a sign of that distinctly female awareness that women seemed to have around one another. Winnie pulled up her big girl panties and offered Greta a warm smile.

In return, Greta offered only cool disapproval, her eyes flickering over Winnie from head to toe, quickly deeming her inconsequential.

Somehow, the dismissal strengthened Winnie's resolve. She might feel social anxiety around a woman with Greta's beauty and confidence, but she didn't feel professional anxiety around her. She jotted down the very first sentence from the meeting in her reporter's notebook: *What is the Broadsville mayor doing at the Bloomsburo city council meeting, and why did she walk in late with Mayor Simpson?*

Winnie knew she wouldn't get the answer today, but she now had an agenda, even if the council didn't.

The mayor finally made his way to the podium he should have been at seventeen minutes earlier.

"Well, uh, hmmm," the man sputtered. "Sorry for the delay, but, well, when the constituency calls, the mayor must answer. Yes, indeed, I had a bit of an... umm... residential emergency this morning, but, uh, rest assured, it was resolved completely, and we have another happy Bloomsburo citizen."

From his bio on the web, Winnie knew that Simpson had served as mayor of Bloomsburo for more than twenty years. If today's weirdness indicated his typical behavior, she struggled to see how that was possible. Nonetheless, he grabbed the gravel and slammed it down.

"Let's get started then." Mayor Simpson looked out into the chamber, still empty except for Winnie, Chief Conrad, and now Greta Johannsen sitting with perfect posture in the very front row. Winnie instinctively sat up straighter.

When the mayor's eyes finally met Winnie's, his expression was hard to read. She merely smiled confidently in his direction, making sure he understood that she was not the type to get scared off.

For the next fifteen minutes, the council did a very poor job of pretending they knew what they were doing, rambling on about new restaurants in town and ideas for a dog park. When the gavel sounded again to end the meeting, they all looked fairly pleased with their performances, but Winnie knew an improvised show when she saw one.

Something was seriously wrong with the Bloomsburo city government, and she had a new mission to figure out exactly what it was.

Chapter 7

Having wrapped up her very first issue of the paper late on Tuesday evening, there was one lingering item on Winnie's to-do list, and it filled her with dread. Winnie reluctantly sent Cal an email at the Chamber on Wednesday evening with some questions about the upcoming Bloomsburo Days special section. She couldn't avoid the man forever.

> Cal,
> I am beginning my work on the Bloomsburo Days special section. Could you let me know how much involvement the Chamber typically has with its production? Do we compile it collaboratively?
> Thanks in advance, Winnie Briggs

By the time she arrived at the office Thursday morning, a response awaited her, but it wasn't from Cal.

> Dear Miss Briggs,
> Mr. Spencer says that the newspaper staff puts the section together, and then the Chamber reviews it when a full draft is available. Please let me know how I may be of assistance in the meantime.
> Sincerely and with kind regards, Danny M. McDonald, Intern

What an odd response, Winnie mused. Not quite sure how to interpret the intern's dispatch on behalf of "Mr. Spencer," Winnie chose to ignore it. Later that afternoon, however, she found herself with some more questions about the section. She wrote Cal once more.

> Cal,

Regarding the upcoming special section, do you sell the advertising, or does that happen through our sales department? Is there a standard ad size, or do they vary?

Thanks, Winnie Briggs

Exactly thirteen minutes later, the reply arrived.

Dear Miss Briggs,

Mr. Spencer says that the Chamber coordinates the advertising. You'll just need to reserve space for 18 advertisements, all three columns by five inches. Please do not hesitate to contact me with follow-up questions.

Sincerely and with kind regards, Danny M. McDonald, intern

What. The heck.

"Mr. Spencer" had a quite a bit to say despite his inability to push the 'reply' button on an email. Winnie set the issue aside for the day, needing to go cover the blood drive at the Presbyterian church, but when the exact same scenario replayed itself Friday morning with a third message to the elusive Chamber director and a third response from her dear friend Danny, she began to take it personally. She stomped up the hallway to Gloria's desk at the front of the newspaper office to investigate the matter further.

"Does Cal Spencer write you emails?" she asked, her voice failing to hide her annoyance.

Gloria seemed surprise by the random inquiry. Either that or she was startled by Winnie's uncharacteristic crankiness.

"Uh, well, yes. We're in touch a few times a week about something. He's really good about responding to emails."

"But does *he* actually write you or does Danny the Intern write you?"

"Who on earth is Danny the Intern?"

"You don't even know about Danny the Intern?"

"I guess I don't."

Winnie sighed.

"What email address are you using to write Cal?" Winnie asked.

"Let's see," Gloria said, clicking around on her computer for a few seconds. "I use director@bloomsburochamber.net."

The same one Winnie had been using.

Winnie scowled, and sulked back to her office, falling to provide Gloria with any more context. She didn't want the woman thinking that town leaders were already actively avoiding her.

Especially since it might be true.

She plunked down in her office chair and crossed her arms over her chest, looking not unlike a pouty toddler. Which felt about right. Clearly Cal still hadn't forgiven her for moving into the She Shed, which was ridiculous. Any frustration on his end should be directed to his mother, not Winnie, who had done nothing wrong.

She breathed out slowly and decided to forget it for the time being. She had an issue to put together before she could go home tonight.

Ugh. Her annoyance with Cal had momentarily distracted her from the fact that her sports stringer contracted strep throat, meaning Winnie would have to cover tonight's Bloomsburo High School football game.

Winnie would cover a hundred stories about summer squashes with weird stripes if it got her out of writing even one sports story.

Her arms collapsed onto the desk in front of her, and her head followed suit, gently pounding into the nook of her arms over and over again, as if the action could change the fate of her day. That was how Gloria found her a few minutes later when she popped her head around the corner.

"Winnie?" she asked, her voice concerned, and with good reason given Winnie's moody behavior this morning. "I hate to bother you, but Esther Hoffman's on the line. Her great niece out in Montana recently won a blue ribbon for her steer at the county fair, and she wondered if you might want to do a story on it."

Winnie silently wished, just for a moment, that *she* had an intern who could field the messages she didn't want to deal with.

~・~・~・~・~・~

Winnie ended up with exactly one hour to spare after she sent the weekend edition of the newspaper to the printer and before she needed to show up at the Friday night football game. Rushing home to change and get some food, she stepped up onto the porch and into the cozy cottage, feeling, as she always felt upon entering it, at peace.

The She Shed had become her oasis. She loved every inch of the space, which felt like a really comfortable combination of Rhonda's cozy style and Winnie's flair. If Cal's every action (or lack of action) filled Winnie with angst and anxiety, his mother had the opposite effect. Her warmth, her humor, the maternal way she checked in on Winnie at odd times, often served as the one comfortable thing Winnie could count on in this new life in Bloomsburo.

She jumped up onto the comfy sea of throw pillows on her four-poster bed, pulled her phone out of her bag and wrote a quick text to Evie, her second saving grace in town.

> Sure you can't come with me to the football game tonight? I don't think I can survive without you!! XO

Evie responded promptly, as usual.

> Wish I could. Have all the kids tonight, husband's out of town. I think that Thomas the Tank Engine on repeat may be worse than a football game. HELP! Working Sunday lunch shift if you need food. Good luck!

Yes, food. Winnie still hadn't quite gotten her act together on that front yet, though she had managed to find Murphy's Grocery for those meals she didn't eat at Dewey's. She hopped up and looked around the kitchen. The oven remained unused, but the microwave had already proven essential. Opening a cupboard, she surveyed the breakfast shelf lined with Pop-Tarts and granola bars, the lunch shelf lined with canned soup and crackers, and the dinner shelf lined with ramen noodle packs and microwaveable cups of mac and cheese.

She sighed. If a toddler could design a dream pantry, it would look like this. Winnie wanted to eat like a grown up, she really did, but she didn't know how to cook. In Chicago, street vendors and Bree kept her alive (her friend possessed serious culinary skills, something that set her apart from Winnie's own parents, who relied mostly on takeout and freezer meals when she was growing up.)

JESS VONN

Here in Bloomsburo she didn't have access to 24-hour food trucks, nor did she find herself with enough free time to begin to learn how to feed herself like an adult.

Oh, and she didn't own any pots or pans, which complicated things further. She did have one spatula, though, and she felt pretty proud of it. The bright orange handle gave way to a flexible rubber top, white with red and yellow stars all over it. She knew it would come in handy one day, doing whatever it is that spatulas do in the kitchen. In the meantime it just looked cute.

Just as she was about to prepare a microwavable cup of noodles, a knock on the door and Rhonda's kind voice floated from the porch.

"You home, Winnie?"

"Come on in!" she yelled, struggling to get the plastic seal off the tiny plastic cup.

Rhonda walked in, a mason jar of wild flowers in her hand. Today her hair fell loose over her shoulders, and Winnie couldn't help but admire the long strawberry-blond curls streaked with silver. So rarely did a woman in her fifties keep her hair that long, but it suited Rhonda perfectly.

"For you!" she said, giving Winnie a kiss on her cheek and setting the bouquet in the middle of her small table.

"These are gorgeous. I still can't get over your gardens," Winnie said. She recently learned that Rhonda had worked most of her life as a tea maker and herbalist, hence the gorgeous landscaping that separated Rhonda's house from the cottage. She hoped to gather up enough courage to ask Rhonda for a tour of her massive, solar powered green house that filled the side yard. "I have a black thumb."

"Oh, there's no such thing as a black thumb. There's only a lack of practice."

Winnie hadn't known Rhonda for long, but she already knew that the woman specialized in helping people take a positive spin on their weaknesses.

Rhonda's eyes flickered over Winnie's sad meal-in-a-cup, and though they didn't linger there long, they expressed the woman's displeasure at Winnie's pathetic meal.

"The flowers were only an excuse to come over here," Rhonda said warmly. "I have an invitation to issue."

Winnie's stomach twirled.

A Time To Fall

"You do?"

"Yes, I do. Every Sunday evening my kids and their families come over and we do a big family-style dinner. I want you to come as my guest and meet everyone."

Emotional reactions flooded Winnie so quickly and so forcefully that she lost track of the order of their arrival. Desire for a cozy family meal. The distant-yet-familiar heartache about her own lack of family. Embarrassment that the sad state of her pantry had led to what could only be a pity invite. Curiosity at what the inside of Rhonda's home looked like and about her daughters' personalities. And then of course, that now familiar fearful/excited combo that she felt any time the prospect of seeing Cal came to mind, which made it obvious what her answer had to be.

"I couldn't," she said, the most truthful answer she could offer without revealing too much. Even if Cal *weren't* a factor, even if the man hadn't been actively avoiding contact with her for the better part of a week, and even if she didn't know in her heart of hearts that he would be livid over her appearance at a family meal, she couldn't ask that of Rhonda. The woman had already been so warm and generous. Winnie couldn't take advantage of it. She had to put up boundaries, even if Rhonda refused to.

"You must. I insist! It would bring me so much happiness," Rhonda said, grabbing Winnie's hand with her own. Oh, she was a hard woman to refuse.

"It's such a kind offer, and I enjoy your company so much, but it just doesn't feel right. That family time is sacred."

"I agree, which is why I want you to be there with us."

It was difficult to wrap her head around, the idea of these big family gatherings, where adult siblings came together in their parents' home. Her brother Johnny would have been 17 by now—a heart-wrenching calculation that she never lost track of. It was unfathomable to her, given that his life was cut short in boyhood. She'd never had the chance to see him grow into a man, but she knew instinctively that she would have adored the grown-up version of her silly and impulsive baby brother.

Winnie just shook her head no.

Rhonda sighed.

"Well, have it your way," she said, looking once more at the sad Styrofoam cup of instant noodles on the counter. "But know that I'll keep asking until I break you down."

Winnie smiled. There was the Spencer stubbornness.

"Anything fun planned tonight?" Rhonda asked.

"Absolutely not. I have to go cover the high school football game. I'd rather pick splinters out of my knees."

"I've never been much of a sports fan myself," Rhonda laughed, "but the people-watching at the stadium should make for some fair entertainment."

"True."

"Well, good luck," she said, giving Winnie's hand one more squeeze before making her way back out of the house.

Chapter 8

Cal took a deep breath of the cool autumn air, braced himself, then walked through the gates of the Bloomsburo High School football stadium.

The place hadn't changed much since Cal himself attended the school more than a decade before, but what the facilities lacked in polish and state-of-the-art equipment, they made up for in enthusiasm. In a small town like Bloomsburo, football played a big role. He never participated in the sport himself, always going out for cross country in the fall, but he usually went to the games to cheer on his friends. By junior year, Carter had packed on enough muscle to survive on the field. As for Wyatt, well, he'd always had what it took to dominate on the field and off.

Wyatt. Now there was a hell of a complicated figure. For as much as Cal wished his high school recollections only included him and Carter, he'd be lying if most of his memories didn't include all three of them. It felt like a damn lifetime ago.

Despite the bitterness that thoughts of Wyatt brought to mind, Cal had to smile, thinking back on his high school days. The best part of not playing football in a football town was the ability to chat up all the girls in the stands while the biggest jocks were otherwise preoccupied. And in a way, though had just hit thirty, his role at the Friday football games each fall really hadn't changed much. As the Chamber of Commerce director, a lot of his job involved getting out in the community, so when most of Bloomsburo gathered at the stadium on a Friday night, that's where he was, making small talk, shaking hands, supporting the sports boosters, and cheering for the home team.

The work suited his personality and strengths, but it could be exhausting. Sometimes he longed for a Friday night at home on the couch, watching something mindless on Netflix.

"There's trouble," a familiar voice called, bringing Cal back to the present. He looked up to see Carter, in full uniform, smiling at the post where he supervised the stadium security check.

Cal took some solace in the fact that if his work required him to show up for every home game, his best friend was in the same boat.

And at least Cal's work never required him to reprimand teenagers after they'd raided the family liquor shelf.

"Go on, pat me down. You know you want to," Cal laughed, reaching out to shake Carter's hand. "Busy night?"

"Not too many problems, but it's early yet."

Cal nodded.

"I get it, by the way," Carter said quietly, and a bit more seriously.

"You get what?" Carter's low voice seemed to be talking in code.

"I met her. And I get it," he said, his brow rising suggestively.

Cal gave his friend a stern look, though he didn't know if it was out of defensiveness or jealousy. Either reaction was ridiculous, of course. His friend could acknowledge Winnie's charms. It's not like Cal held some claim on her. Hell, he'd been actively avoiding the woman all week.

None of these facts helped explain the discomfort that tore at him at the thought of Carter and Winnie.

Carter and Winnie. The pairing felt unnatural and nauseating, like peanut butter and pickles.

"There's nothing to get," Cal said flatly.

"Yeah, you keep telling yourself that."

Cal rolled his eyes and continued his walk toward the stadium.

"One other thing," Carter called.

Cal turned around, annoyed.

"What?"

"I think Greta smelled you on Winnie."

Greta Johannsen. The rich blonde trust-funder from Broadsville who loved mind games and getting her way. She'd had her sights set on Cal for years, and, given that she was a classic narcissist, his rejections had only fortified her resolve to win him.

"What the hell does that mean?"

"Greta didn't give Winnie a very warm welcome at the city council meeting. It's like she could sense your connection to her."

"I don't have a connection to Winnie," he said with more bite than he meant to.

"The hell you don't. Even if you're going to try to maintain like an idiot that you're not interested in the woman, she's living in your mom's backyard. Even that small intimacy is going to have Greta seeing red when she figures it out."

Shit. His friend wasn't wrong, which pissed him off all the more.

"That's just great."

"Hey, don't look so down. A man of your advanced age should be grateful when a cat fight breaks out in his honor. Those opportunities are growing few and far between."

"Go to hell."

"Love you, too, man," Carter said with a laugh, and he turned back to his security duties.

Cal scowled as he walked toward the stadium, but he couldn't indulge the sulk for long, nor did he have time to process the thoughts bouncing around his brain after the brief conversation with Carter.

Before Cal walked even ten steps, he needed to transform back into Cal the Chamber director and hometown boy, shaking hands and making small talk about the September weather, about how the team was doing this year, about the latest addition to his mother's gardens, about how old his nieces were now, about the entertainment lineup for Bloomsburo Days, and about his thoughts on the new stoplight going in at the corner of Maple Street and Twelfth Avenue.

Winding his way through the crowd, Cal ran into family friends, cousins, old high school classmates, business owners, two current neighbors, and a few of his late grandmother's friends, who to this day couldn't resist patting his cheeks with affection. He stopped by the concession stand and grabbed a bite to eat from the sports boosters, bought two homemade friendship bracelets for his nieces from a Girl Scout fundraiser booth, and then eventually succumbed to a seven-minute aside with Betty Jean Finnegan about logistics for the upcoming craft show during Bloomsburo Days.

By now it shouldn't surprise him that the woman could talk about folding chairs for so long, and with such passion, and yet it did.

From a distance he could hear the sounds of the game—the shrill shrieks of the whistles and the crunch of the helmets colliding and the syncopated cheers from girls with pom-poms and the loud murmur rising from the packed bleachers. By the time he actually arrived at the stands, the game was already well into the second quarter, and Broadsville High was kicking Bloomsburo's butt. It looked to be a long, depressing night for the home team.

Cal walked up the bleachers, only making it halfway up before a former coach and his wife stopped him where he stood at the railing.

JESS VONN

They caught up for another minute or two. While talking with them, Cal occasionally scanned the bleachers, trying to determine if there was anyone else he should greet. He saw many more familiar faces, but only one that made his heart pound.

Winnie.

But it wasn't just Winnie who caught his attention, it was the fact that there, in the middle of the bleachers, sandwiched between groups of friends and extended families, she sat alone, surrounded by empty metal bleacher benches on all sides where people had given her room as they turned to talk and laugh with the people they'd come to the game with.

His heart seemed to lurch. It seemed to actually lurch out of his chest when he saw her there, all by herself. Here he was, bemoaning the fact that he had so many people to greet and chat with, and she sat there on her own, rubbing the arms of her too-thin sweater in an attempt to keep warm, and looking down at the notebook in her lap with confusion. No one to talk to. No one to joke with.

Hell. The lust the woman evoked? That he could work out in other ways. But the *lurch.* Well, it complicated things.

Then again, maybe it simplified them.

He tried to imagine if it were one of his younger sisters in Winnie's shoes: relocating to a new town, a new state even, where she didn't know a soul. Sitting alone and shivering, more or less invisible in a sea of people absorbed in their own lives.

Winnie hadn't even been in town a week. She had no family here. She wouldn't have had enough time to make any real friends. If that were his sister, he'd want someone to go say hello.

And even though Cal was probably her closest acquaintance in town, he had spent most of his week blowing the woman off, merely because her presence rattled him, both by day and at night in his dreams.

He sighed. It was time for him to ask a little bit more of himself.

He said goodbye to his old coach, and made his way over to where Winnie sat.

"For what it's worth, our team's not usually this bad," he said, breaking the ice. Her brown eyes were so big and bright, he thought they couldn't grow wider, yet they did as they looked up into his and registered his presence.

It took only a second before they narrowed more cynically, though.

"Is that right? Well, I'm surprised you didn't send Danny the Intern over here to share that dispatch," she said, her right brow rising in that very Winnie way.

Despite the flash of guilt her comment produced in him, he had to grin. He shouldn't attempt to smooth over his bad behavior with humor, but he couldn't help himself. "Well, what good is an intern if you don't have him do all your dirty work for you?"

The firm line of Winnie's smooth lips curled ever so slightly upward. Seriousness didn't come naturally to her.

"May I join you?" he asked, his gaze flickering over her bright floral scarf, her soft navy cardigan, her burnt orange skirt and the polka dot leggings beneath them. Something about the way the woman dressed just made you want to soak in the details. He found himself needing to make a deliberate effort not to stare at her for too long.

After a moment's hesitation, she nodded and he sank to her side. Her eyes lowered to the colorful friendship bracelets twirling between his fingers.

"Doing some jewelry shopping?"

"Have you ever tried to say no to a Girl Scout? It's impossible, the adorable little fiends, especially when my nieces would love these bracelets. It was a difficult choice, but I ultimately parted with the five dollars."

Winnie gave a genuine smile, so different than the distant and lonely look she had just moments before. It occurred to Cal that coaxing those smiles from Winnie's lips could become habit-forming.

"How old are your nieces?"

"Six."

"Both of them?"

"They're twins."

"Twins!" she said her hands clasping near her heart, and his mind flashed back to that first day on the porch when she made the same gesture upon learning the name of the She Shed. "I always wanted twins."

Watching the blush fill her cheeks, he could tell that the intimate revelation embarrassed her. But it surprised him how well he could

JESS VONN

picture it: Winnie, married and content, with a flock of little dirt-smudged, curly-haired kids tugging at her skirt.

"They are amazing, though I'm somewhat biased."

"You must be a good uncle," she said, glancing at the bracelets once more before returning her attention to his face.

"Well, I don't know about that. But I will say that if anyone in this world can bring out something good in me, it's them."

The way she looked at him then softened him. Unsettled him. Her gaze slowly lowered, zeroing in on his lips. She stared at them for a moment, transfixed, completely unaware of the power she held over him when she looked at him like that.

Completely unaware of the many things he wanted to do to her with that mouth. That he'd dreamed of doing.

He pressed his lips together, breaking her gaze on him. She glanced back out at the field, the flush of rose deepening ever so slightly on her cheeks.

"Do you have any nieces or nephews?" he asked, turning the focus back on her.

She cleared her throat.

"No."

And she left it at that, a dozen questions hanging in the air between them. For a woman who made her living asking questions of other people, she sure had a knack for not answering them herself.

They sat there a minute more, Cal very aware of her proximity. She rubbed her hands once more along her upper arms, trying to keep warm in the crisp, cool evening air. It would be so easy to put his arm around her, to pull her into him and let the warmth of his body comfort her as he discovered just how soft she'd feel against him.

Luckily he glanced down just then at the notebook in her lap, and saw her notes on the game, conveniently reminding himself that no matter how good the woman smelled, or how much he might like to offer her bodily comfort, she was a professional acquaintance.

And if he wouldn't pull Mayor Ralph Simpson into his body for warmth and pleasure at a Friday night football game, he damn well better not do it to Winnie.

"So are you covering the game?"

"Allegedly. But it's not going so well."

"Where's Randy?" he asked. *The Bloom*'s sports stringer had been covering the local teams for the paper for at least a decade.

"Out sick."

"That's too bad."

"Bad? It's catastrophic!" Winnie cried. "For him. For me. For our entire readership."

Cal grinned.

"May I?" he asked, gesturing to her notes.

Winnie handed him the notebook and then put her face in her hands as if she wanted to disappear.

He chuckled, reviewing what she'd written so far.

- *Yellow = Bloomsburo*
- *Green = Broadsville*
  First quarter - Green team scores.
- *First quarter - Green team scores again. (But why only +2 pts. instead of +6?!)*
- *Yellow team calls time out. Coach looks like his head might pop off.*
- *Second quarter - beginning to wonder if yellow team actually knows how to score.*

"So you're a real football buff, eh?" he laughed, handing the notebook back to her.

"Don't be cruel. This is serious. What am I going to do? I'm having heart palpitations over here."

Cal thought for a minute.

"Well, I'm sure Randy's listening to the game at home. They live stream the commentary on the local radio station, and then post it online after each game."

"I'm not sure how that helps."

"Well, Randy can listen to that, and add in the play-by-play commentary that he needs for the article. The most important thing you probably need to do tonight is to just get some quotes from a few players and coaches after the game."

Relaxation spread over her face.

"Of course! Why didn't I think of that?"

"Probably because you were planning strategies for surviving a football-induced panic attack?"

She laughed.

"Thanks for the advice."

"It's nothing."

Winnie glanced down at her hands, which now busied themselves by fidgeting nervously with her pen.

"Cal, I'm sorry if my being here has caused you stress."

Cal. His name on her lips for the very first time. So simple, yet not.

He wasn't sure how to respond to her sudden candor. The woman had done nothing wrong, even if her mere presence disoriented him.

"I—" he started, but she cut him off.

"But you really should tell your mom that she doesn't have to be so nice to me."

"I should?" he asked, amused. Clearly Winnie didn't know his mother that well. He'd have better luck convincing Rhonda that the grass was blue than convincing her to ignore her nurturing instincts.

"I know she is just trying to be kind, but I don't want to be an imposition to her. There was no way I could go to your family dinner on Sunday," Winnie said.

He felt the blood drain from his face. "She invited you to Sunday dinner?" he asked, shock tinged with a half dozen other feelings he'd rather not acknowledge. It was his family's most intimate, most important tradition. He'd never invited a woman to a Sunday dinner. Never.

Winnie's hand covered her mouth in regret. "You didn't know? I shouldn't have said anything."

"This is becoming a pattern, isn't it? You knowing more about my mother than I do."

"I'm sorry. But I knew you wouldn't like it, so I said no right away."

Cal sighed. He wanted to be mad at his mother, but Rhonda was an includer by nature. She always had been, and it was one of the things he admired most about her, even if this particular case caused him aggravation.

"You didn't have to say no on my behalf," he said, though he knew full well that his behavior had not supported this claim.

"It wasn't *only* on your behalf. But I didn't want you to feel uncomfortable at your own mother's house."

Fidget, fidget, fidget went her fingers around the blue ink pen. He made an intentional effort not to think of other ways she might preoccupy those hands.

"She does meddle, but she has a huge heart. She likes to take care of people. And like it or not, you're one of her people now."

Winnie's face expressed the strangest mix of happiness and sadness. "Well, regardless, I said no. I'll keep saying no, even though she promised to continue asking until she wears me down."

Cal laughed. "That does sound like her."

"I don't need to interfere with your personal life, or encourage your mom's absurd matchmaking impulses."

Absurd. Right.

"But I do hope that we can be amiable associates," she said, her eyes searching his before they dropped lower, gazing upon his mouth once more, as if something deeper, something stronger, was guiding her.

It wasn't too much for her to ask. The fact that she offered an olive branch in the face of his avoidance this week, rather than scorn or guilt, spoke volumes about the woman. She deserved better from him, and he'd just have to learn to deal with the things she made him feel.

"Do you have your cell phone?" he asked.

"Uh, yeah," she said, clearly confused by the random question.

She reached down and pulled her massive purse into her lap and began digging through it. She pulled out an umbrella, a whistle, a pack of shiny heart stickers, a deck of cards, and a bottle of Elmer's glue before she asked for help.

"Can you hold this stuff for a sec?" she asked, dumping the random items into Cal's lap before he had a chance to answer.

He looked down, chuckling despite himself. She was a regular Mary Poppins.

"Ah ha!" she said before pulling out a smart phone with a case covered in pink sprinkled donuts. "Got it." She held the phone between her neck and her shoulder as Cal passed back the rest of the random contents of her purse.

"Now why do I need it?"

"Let me see it."

She shot him a suspicious look, but she entered her code and passed it to him.

"Your phone background is a photo of John Krasinski?"

"Yes, it is. He's my third favorite pretend boyfriend."

"Out of how many?"

"Roughly seven."

"Dare I ask who number one is?"

"A girl's gotta have her secrets," she teased. "It adds to my general air of mystery."

She was joking, yet spot on. The number of things he wanted to know about Winnie Briggs, and how she landed squarely in the middle of his life here in Bloomsburo, grew daily. Like Dorothy, it was as if a tornado had scooped her up and dropped her right in his lap. Though not literally, unfortunately.

He punched his number, under the name "Cal the Great," into her contacts. "My cell phone is the best way to reach me."

Winnie perked up. "Oh, okay. You mean for work stuff?"

"Yeah."

"Of course, because why would I be reaching you for non-work stuff. That'd just be absurd," she rambled, her cheeks flushing in a way that made Cal want to reach out and stroke them. To see just how much crimson he could fill them with.

"Totally absurd," he said, his eyes locking into hers, probably expressing as many uncertainties as hers did. He passed the phone back to her, and her fingers grazed his, sending tingles up his arm. She pushed a few buttons on the device.

"There, I just texted you. Now you've got my number, too."

His satisfaction with this scenario couldn't be masked.

"And is it safe to say that you'll be sending any texts that come from this number, or does Danny J. McDonald the intern field these for you as well?"

A clever response sat on the tip of his tongue, but before he could reply, a figure appeared in the corner of his vision.

An impossibly blond, svelte, self-possessed figure to be more specific.

Greta Johannsen.

If bantering with Winnie caused Cal to warm into relaxation, Greta's sudden presence blasted him with cold discomfort like a suddenly opened freezer.

He glanced at Winnie, who was less skilled in masking her emotions than Cal. Winnie's face shadowed over. Her hands tensed.

"Well, Cal, if my tempting salary and benefits package hasn't enticed you to come and take over the Broadsville Chamber of Commerce office, maybe the prowess of our football team will," Greta said, her hand stroking his forearm. The woman wasn't capable of speaking to him without also laying her hands on him.

He sighed. When Greta first moved back to the area after going to college on the West Coast, she'd merely wanted him as a man. She was a gorgeous, bored, pampered young woman in a quiet part of the world, and she desperately wanted Cal to add some sizzle to her life.

The feeling wasn't mutual. Sure, Greta may be the most technically attractive woman for hundreds of miles, but she had a cold edge and a hunger for power and control that only bolstered Cal's defenses against her advances. She wasn't looking for a lover or a partner, but a plaything she could sink her hooks into. Cal wanted nothing to do with her.

Dozens of polite rejections had done little to weaken the woman's resolve, so her strategy changed. Now, courtesy of her daddy's money, she was the mayor of neighboring Broadsville, so she had professional reasons to contact Cal on a regular basis. This meant that in addition to hounding him on a personal level, hardly a week could go by without her trying to hire him away from Bloomsburo to serve as her town's chamber director.

He knew, of course, that 'the benefits' of the job went well beyond health insurance.

"Come on now, Greta, you know I'm not a fair-weather fan. I've got to support Bloomsburo, even when they can't manage to get on the board."

Her hot pink lips curved, revealing perfectly white, perfectly straight teeth.

"You're such a good man. It's why I have to have you," she said, her eyes flickering with utterly non-professional intentions.

"Greta, have you met Winnie Briggs?" he asked, deflecting. He didn't want to do this with Greta, and he sure as hell didn't want to do it in front of Winnie.

He watched the woman pry her gaze off him and redirect it toward Winnie. Cool. Assessing. Disapproving. Suddenly Carter's earlier comment made a lot more sense.

"I don't believe we've met," Greta said, offering nothing more by way of introductions.

He watched Winnie straighten her shoulders and extend her hand.

"Nice to meet you. I'm the new editor of *The Bloom*. I noticed you at this week's city council meeting, but I didn't get a chance to introduce myself before you left," she said, polite and composed, if lacking the warmth she'd exuded just minutes before.

"I didn't notice you," Greta said, giving Winnie's hand a brief, light squeeze before recoiling.

Confusion flashed across Winnie's face. Clearly there was more to their first meeting than Greta was indicating.

Protectiveness swelled in Cal's chest. Close behind it was a wave of guilt, knowing that now that Greta had seen Cal and Winnie sitting together, laughing and talking, Winnie would get an even colder shoulder than normal from Greta.

"Greta is the mayor of Broadsville," Cal continued, filling in the holes of the woman's shoddy introduction.

Unsure how to respond, Winnie merely nodded.

"Speaking of, Cal, there's something you simply must help me with," she said, her thin, perfectly manicured hand reaching down and grabbing his own, causing her excessively flashy rings to glitter beneath the stadium lights.

"What is it?" he asked.

"A few of our local business owners are on the away team bleachers, and they were having the loudest debate about sales taxes. They're practically causing a scene. I had to come find you to see if you might help resolve it, given your expertise."

Cal sighed. Only with Greta was flattery served on a knife at his throat.

He looked at Winnie, a silent apology.

"Duty calls," he said dryly, managing about as much as enthusiasm as if he were off to remove wallpaper.

She laughed, a burst of nervous energy released.

"Okay, then. Have a great weekend."

"You, too," he said, surprised at the loss he felt as he left Winnie's side.

Greta linked her arm into his and began to pull him to the stairwell. He looked back at Winnie one more time after making it to the bottom of the bleachers, and he noticed that her right index finger had already made its way into her hair, twirling and twirling those pretty brown curls.

He wondered briefly if she even knew she had the nervous tick.

He wondered for much longer what other little secrets he might learn about her body if given the opportunity.

Chapter 9

Sunday dinners at Rhonda Spencer's house were chaotic, but charmingly so, and Cal, unlike many single men his age who might begrudge mandatory time with their immediate family, looked forward to the occasion each week.

In a way, the Sunday dinners were like a trip back to his childhood, when their cares were fewer. Only now, his father, eight years dead, was out of the picture, which only made the dinners that much better.

Charles Calhoun Spencer! He could hear his mother's voice in his brain, scolding him for indulging such an unkind thought. Ironically, one of the few times she tended to utter his full name was when Cal spoke ill of his namesake.

Without the drama that his father's behavior brought into the mix for so many years, and with Cal and his siblings now past the sometimes tumultuous transition into adulthood, they'd all grown into good friends.

Despite the signature red hair that branded his sisters as Spencer women, the three couldn't be more different.

Haven, twenty-eight, excelled in her role as family know-it-all and, taking after Rhonda, mother hen. Fiercely loyal not only to her mom and siblings, but also to her soft-spoken husband Dan and their twin daughters, Mary and Lulu, Haven was a brash, fiery, passionate force of nature. She was every stereotype about redheads, magnified times ten. As stubborn as Cal and twice as temperamental, he and his oldest little sister butted heads plenty of times growing up, but now as adults, he considered her to be one of his very best friends.

Next in line came twenty-six-year-old Willa, whose coolheaded calmness could only be the result of growing up in the shadow of her larger-than-life older siblings (that, and perhaps a stronger dose of their mother's more peaceful DNA). Athletic and disciplined, Willa participated in lots of fitness competitions, including the Iron Woman, and that was actually how she'd met her long-distance partner of two years, Jane, who lived in New York. Their travel for competitions allowed them far more time together than their long-distance relationship did otherwise, and kept Willa away from more

Sunday dinners than his mother would prefer. Her work as an occupational therapist in town gave her much satisfaction and, at least for now, kept her rooted in Bloomsburo.

Finally came the baby, Rosie, just two years out of college at twenty-four, and working as an assistant in the Disability Resource Center at a small liberal arts college several towns over. Even if she'd *only* been the baby of the family, Rosie, with her sweetness and quick humor, would have likely been doted on. But Rosie was also a fighter. An uncommonly early diagnosis of multiple sclerosis at twelve might have broken the spirit of someone with less resolve than Rosie, who viewed the disease as a challenge she'd never stop fighting. Usually accompanied by her high school sweetheart, Jack, the woman went after everything life had to offer, from music lessons to international travel to the occasional foray into stand-up comedy. Thankfully Rosie's symptoms remained fairly mild and, miraculously, the non-stop checkups and alterations to her medications did little to dampen her bright disposition.

Cal wasn't sure he admired anyone on earth more than Rosie.

Thinking of his sisters, his heart felt full as he walked up the brick steps to his mother's quaint Craftsman bungalow, his arms loaded with his contributions to the evening meal: a crockpot full of minestrone soup and two loaves of still-warm homemade bread.

The house was neither big nor fancy, but like all things associated with his mother, it emitted character and charm. The shingles were a pale teal color, and the windows were framed in cream and navy-blue trim. The house, accented with rambling vines and antique touches, hit that sweet spot between well-maintained and well-loved. Small details that might have otherwise looked tacky or shabby turned whimsical with Rhonda's touch.

By the time he stepped onto the porch, Cal could already hear the familiar voices inside. Balancing the heavy basket he carried in one hand, he swung open the screen door and stepped into the chaos.

"He's here!" two bright voices called, in almost perfect unison, as his nieces, Mary and Lulu, charged him before he'd even had a chance to set down his basket of food and the crock pot. Their little faces shined up at him in love and excitement, missing teeth and all. And damn if that wasn't the best part of his entire weekend.

"Uncle Cal, Mommy said that the woman who moved into Grandma's shed is *very* pretty," Mary said, in that demanding, matter-of-fact way that sounded exactly like her mother Haven. Her big blue eyes, another gift from her mom, peered seriously into his, as if she were daring him to question her mom's opinion.

He shot Haven a look of annoyance as she walked toward him and grabbed the food from his hands, but she merely shrugged innocently.

"What? I saw her from across the lawn the other day. It was just an observation."

When had his sister gotten into cahoots with his mother?

"And don't be worried about me. It's mom you have to watch out for," Haven continued. "You're in trouble about something. Don't ask me what it is. I'm just excited for the entertainment it will add to our evening."

She turned on her heel, delivering his food to the kitchen, and Cal redirected his attention to the sweet nieces before him.

"Well, is she pretty, Uncle Cal?" his other niece, Lulu, asked gently, her face half hidden behind her mess of curly red hair that belied the timidity she inherited from her dad. "Grandma said you're the only other person who's seen her."

Something in Cal's stomach seemed to flip flop. *She's damn beautiful*, he thought, though he knew he'd rather starve than admit such a thing in this piranha's den.

With his hands now free, Cal squatted down and scooped up a niece in each arm, amazed as always at how much they seemed to grow even between one Sunday and the next.

"All I know for sure is that is you two are the smartest, prettiest girls I've ever seen," he said, crushing them in a double bear hug until they squealed in delight. When he finally released them, they were satisfied with the affection and abandoned their inquiry, running back to the heaping pile of toys on the living room floor.

Cal made his way across the family room and into the kitchen, waving at his brother-in-law, Dan, who happily sat at his usual post on the couch. He gladly watched his daughters if it meant he could mostly ignore the sister talk in the kitchen. Cal knew he wouldn't be so lucky tonight. His three sisters were like lions, and they could not be still if there was fresh meat in the room. Needless to say his mother led the pack.

Jack, his youngest sister's long-time boyfriend, had already made his way to the fridge and grabbed a beer for Cal. He was a good man.

"This is all your mom has to drink, though I'm afraid you may need something stronger tonight. They're in rare form," Jack suggested sympathetically to Cal as he handed him the bottle before excusing himself to join Dan in the living room, clearly escaping the line of fire.

Cal popped the cap off his beer and downed a third of it one draw, praying for resolve in the face of the nosy Spencer women.

"Well, is she?" asked his youngest sister, Rosie.

"Is she what?" Cal asked, feigning ignorance.

"As adorable as mom says she is?" Rosie continued with a sweet smile, a smile that usually wrapped everyone in the family around her finger. But not this time.

"She's a work acquaintance. That's irrelevant."

"Notice how he didn't actually answer the question," chimed in Willa, glancing at her sisters with suspicion. "But it felt like a yes."

He heard a pot slam on the counter behind him, making him jump.

"You wouldn't all have to be playing these guessing games about Winnie if Cal hadn't scared her off," his mother said from behind him, uncharacteristically sharp. "She should be here tonight, but she refused my invitation and I believe your brother is to blame."

Haven gave him an I-tried-to-warn-you look before Cal turned around and saw his mom's face, twisted in disapproval.

Shit.

"What did I—" he started, but his mom quickly cut him off.

"Don't you play innocent with me, Charles Spencer," she began, walking over and jabbing a pointed finger into his chest. He could hear his sisters snickering behind him. His mother tended to dote on her only son, so the women enjoyed every glimpse of his occasional fall from grace. "If there is one thing I have tried to instill in you children it's to be kind to other people, and I am getting the strong impression that you have not given this woman a warm reception."

"Shame on you, Cal," Haven said with exaggeration. Channeling the self-discipline he lacked when she used to bait him as a kid, he refused to give her the satisfaction of a response.

Cal opened his mouth to defend himself, but his mother filled the silence first.

"Now, how is it that a man so charming that he could sell wool sweaters at the equator can't direct a little bit of his good-naturedness toward my new friend?"

"Ma, she's not your friend. She's your renter."

Rhonda stepped back, her anger momentarily overshadowed by disbelief.

"You don't get to tell me who I can and cannot be friends with. I handpicked Winnie out of dozens of applicants for that cottage because I liked her, Cal, and my every instinct suggested that she would be a positive addition to my life."

He sighed.

"Can you imagine what it's like to move so far away from the only world you've ever known? Not knowing anyone to call up and invite out to a movie? Not having anyone to share a meal with or have cook for you? No family around to—" she started, but her voice cracked, and along with it, Cal's resolve cracked, too. He could fortify himself against his mother's anger, but not her sadness.

He stepped forward and pulled his mother into his arms.

"No. I can't imagine that. You've built too good of a life for us here. That's why you can't get rid of us. You spoil us." He kissed the top of her hair and she squeezed his ribs.

"I get to decide if I spoil her, too."

"I agree. I'll encourage her to take you up on your next invitation, Ma."

His mom's blue eyes looked up into his, hope returned to them.

"You will?"

"I will," he said, lowering his voice to continue. "But I don't think it's just me. I think she likes some privacy, too. And to set some boundaries. You need to be respectful of that."

Back at the table, his sisters continued their earlier discussion.

"Well, even if Cal won't fill you in on this mystery woman, I will," Haven said. "I saw her, and she's adorable."

Cal groaned.

"Waves of auburn hair piled high," Haven continued. "But she's got that girl-next-door kind of vibe. More Katie Holmes than Mila Kunis. Big brown eyes and a gorgeously curvy figure."

"For God's sake," he muttered, but no one listened. It suddenly dawned on him that he should have begged Winnie to attend the dinner. At least her presence would have forced his sisters to be on their best behavior.

"Is she home now? I wonder if I could sneak a peek," Rosie said, standing and beginning to walk toward the back kitchen window that faced the yard separating his mother's house from Winnie's cottage.

"So that's what it's come to? Treating the woman like a zoo exhibit on display?" he asked incredulously.

"Pretty much," Rosie smiled. He playfully pinched her arm as she walked by.

"Save yourself the trip. Her car's not there, anyway," he said before he could consider the consequences.

"Look at him, noticing that her car wasn't there. It's almost like he has some interest in the zoo exhibit as well," Willa observed.

"That's it. I'm off to play with my little nieces, the only civilized ones among you." He killed his beer and walked to the fridge to grab a second, and his mom stopped him for a private moment, now that his sisters were lost in their own conversation.

"Sorry for pouncing on you the minute you walked into the kitchen," she said regretfully as she gave him one more side hug, resting her head on his shoulder. "You're a good man. I never doubt that."

"I know, Ma," he said. "I love you."

"I love you, too. I just want you to be happy."

"I am happy."

"Well, I want you to be happier, then. I like her a lot."

He sighed, not because he disagreed with his mother, but because he agreed with her. He grabbed the beer, and made his way to the floor where his nieces were engaged in an intricate game of pretend.

Stretching out on the soft rug on his mother's floor, he stacked blocks mindlessly as the girls played out some storyline about a princess who learns to fly. Tonight, though, he couldn't get into their imaginative play.

His mother knew. Somehow she always knew the things he tried to hide. There was something different this time. There was something different about Winnie, and he couldn't remember the last time he'd felt it. Or really, if he'd ever felt it. He liked Winnie. He didn't just want her, though that instinct was plenty strong. He genuinely liked her and it scared the hell out of him, because it would require him to have her best interests at heart.

And that was the crux of it. If her best interests motivated him, then he'd have to be sure that they did not become a couple. His mind flickered back to the night before, to the way Winnie shivered in the stands next to him. To the overwhelming urge to rub his hands up and down her soft, polka dot tights and ignite heat between the two of them. Of the way those random curls escaped the bobby pins that did little to control her dark, unruly hair, sending wispy locks down the side of her cheek. Along her neck. All the places he wanted to explore for himself.

But more than anything, he thought back to the way that two or three times throughout the evening, her eyes lingered absentmindedly on his mouth, as if she wanted to taste him as much as he wanted to taste her.

Though he knew it couldn't move beyond harmless flirting, it suddenly occurred to him that flirting with Winnie was already far from harmless. And what was worse was that he didn't have a damn clue what he was going to do about it.

~-~-~-~-~-~-

Winnie's brain hurt, and she wanted to curl up in bed and read the latest Julia Quinn novel she just picked up from the library, but if she didn't finish this blasted article for the paper tonight, her week would start off on the wrong foot.

It was nearly eleven on Sunday, yet there she sat at the small desk in the back corner of the cottage, working away on a story about the county planning and zoning commission meeting.

If it had been a plucky profile? An education story? A small business feature? No problem. She could have cranked the story out in less than an hour.

But the tedium of the county zoning commission meeting was the same reason the story wasn't done yet. She'd started it that morning, avoided it most of the afternoon, went out on a picnic with Evie and her kids over dinner, and now it was reckoning time.

Her brain was a jumble of unfamiliar zoning jargon—land use tables and right-of-way easements and aquifer protection areas and homeowner covenants.

Gah. Rural legalese was not her forte. But luckily an alert from her phone provided one more distraction from the world's least interesting article.

When the bright, tinkly chat notification sound went off, she'd expected Evie's number to pop up, especially given that she and Bree were on a communication hiatus, and no one else in town used her cell phone. Well, except for Betty Jean.

So when she picked up the phone and saw the alert that read "New text from Cal the Great" she dropped her phone as if it would burn her.

It clunked on the desk and she stood up.

Fear and excitement went rounds in her stomach as she debated whether or not to look at the text. Who knew what it might contain?

Of course it'd be work related. There'd be no other reason for him to contact her. So she should probably just wait and read it tomorrow.

Oh, to hell with it. There was no way she could wait until tomorrow.

She sat down, picked up her phone, swiped through and opened up her text inbox.

Is it past your bedtime, Briggs?

She grinned. And then groaned. Lord, this could be trouble. Her fingers typed a quick reply.

Not even close. Working on a county commissioner story.

Those three little dots popped up instantly, letting her know he was responding this very second. The flickering circles seemed to synchronize with the nervous swirls in her stomach.

A night owl then, huh?

Guilty. You?

Also guilty.

She froze, suddenly unsure what to type. Relief flooded her veins when those 'typing' dots popped up once more. She waited with bated breath to find out his real intention behind the text conversation.

> Wanna meet sometime this week to talk about Bloomsburo Days and the special section?

Winnie couldn't help but smile. His mother must have laid on the guilt at Sunday dinner (an event she'd mostly been able to forget given her outing with Evie's crew.) Why else would he suddenly be playing nice?

> That'd be really helpful. Will your translator Danny M. be joining us? ;)

Oh, sheesh. That was a premature emoji. Too flirty.

> Nope, one on one. But I'm sure he'll miss you. #heartbreaker

Winnie had to snicker.

> Poor guy. Let him down easily for me, will you? When works for you?

She pulled out her planner, excited, but she sighed after opening it, realizing just how booked she already was for the week. She really could use an intern of her own. She might have to talk to the publisher about the possibility of hiring a few more reporters.

> Tomorrow afternoon work? he typed.

> Nope. Tuesday morning?

> Tuesday's no good for me. At an all-day conference. What's Wednesday like?

Meetings at 10, noon and 2. Thursday's just as bad. Friday?

You're a hard woman to pin down.

Focus, Winnie. Focus on this very professional situation, not on that big bed behind you that would be so nice to get pinned down on. He wrote again.

Could do Friday at 3. That's about the only time.

No can do. :(Will be putting the weekend issue together.

Dang.

Dang, she repeated.

Do super journalists take dinner breaks?

I try to. Not always successful though.

Dinner meeting? Wednesday?

BadIdeaBadIdeaBadIdea, her brain warned. Too much like a date. She'd only just recovered from the effect Cal's proximity had on her at Friday night's football game.

And yet, she really needed more information on Bloomsburo Days to get this special section rolling. If it took until next weekend to have a less intimidating daytime meeting, she'd be that much farther behind.

She looked at her calendar. It could work. And it would be one more evening that she didn't have to resort to dinner-in-a-cup by herself in her tiny kitchen.

She started to reply, then deleted it. Started again, then erased it once more. Displaying more clairvoyance than Winnie was comfortable with, Cal wrote once more.

It's just a work meeting, Briggs, not a trick. Haven't forgotten your stance on men.

She laughed, feeling more at ease thanks to his humor.

That sounds great. Thanks for reaching out. Where should we meet? You're the local guy. I only know Dewey's.

Dewey's is good, but you should branch out. Heard of Cafe Gioia? Midway between here and Broadsville.

Nope, but I'm not picky.

A hidden gem—excellent food.

She almost wrote '*It's a date!*' Thankfully she caught herself in time. Because if there was one thing she'd have to remind herself 523 times between now and Wednesday evening, it was that her upcoming dinner with Cal was 100-percent *not* a date.

See you then.

Night, Briggs.

She had a feeling that the anxiety and excitement she felt swirling in her stomach would be with her for much of the next three days, but it wasn't all bad. Already she found herself with an unexpected boost of adrenaline to help wrap up her godforsaken zoning story, and that could only be interpreted as a gift.

Chapter 10

What were you thinking?!

Winnie grumbled to herself for the dozenth time on the drive to the non-date dinner meeting on Wednesday night. When Cal had recommended a café a few towns over for their "business meeting," she had pictured a casual, small town cafe.

Much to her horror, when she Googled the café Cal suggested, she learned that it was all dim lighting and tabletop candles and cozy interiors and Italian food, which was basically the foreplay of the culinary world.

Bad idea. This is a bad idea.

Her hands were shaky and she was uncomfortable in the outfit she'd finally picked (the seventh and final choice). Evie had provided fashion support via text. Winnie would snap a picture of an outfit and send it to her for a thumbs up or a thumbs down. Finally they settled on something that felt pretty but professional: a black flounce skirt paired with a satiny lavender top and a light grey flyaway cardigan. And just for a confidence boost, she wore her highest-heeled black booties.

She felt good in the ensemble when she left the house, but suddenly the top felt tight, as if her boobs had inflated a cup size, and her skirt now felt a bit too short.

She willed herself not to sweat profusely out of anxiety. At least the car's AC could help with that. If she'd done one thing right, it was refusing Cal's offer to give her a ride. Yes, they might have saved some gas, but it would have felt way too intimate.

Sorry, planet. Her unstable libido just wouldn't allow her to go green today. She promised to make it up to Mother Earth by walking somewhere she would normally drive to later in the week.

The most important thing to remember, despite the impending dinner with an aggressively handsome man at a cozy restaurant, was that this was absolutely not a date. Which was good, since she hadn't been on a proper date in about a year, and even that long-ago date would have been with Anthony who was probably glued to his fantasy football updates on his phone the entire time anyway.

She didn't even want to think about how long it'd been since she'd been on a *first* date.

Not that this was a date.

She grabbed her shoulder bag and headed into the packed lobby. The place was surprisingly busy given that it was a weeknight. She didn't see Cal anywhere in the waiting area, so she glanced into the bustling restaurant. Butterflies swam through her stomach as she took in the low, romantic lighting. Then nausea drowned those butterflies when she spotted Cal from across the room. It was a merciful gift of the universe that she spotted him first, because he looked positively gorgeous and had he been watching her as she approached, he surely would have noticed the favorable appraisal.

His cozy booth was lit only by an antique wall sconce, which cast a tempting, soft light onto his wavy golden hair. In his deep blue and perfectly cut suit and vest, Cal looked red carpet ready and far more dressed up than Winnie might have anticipated.

This is only a business meeting. This is only a business meeting.

It was not lost on Winnie, however, that she had never before had a business meeting with someone so sexy.

When she approached the table, Cal did a double take, stood and broke into a smile that increased the wattage in their corner of the restaurant by a few marks.

"Winnie," he said to her in a tone that sounded more like a shocked question than a greeting.

He reached out for her hand. It was a professional enough gesture, but the feel of Cal's skin, his grip firm and warm, unsteadied her.

In the celibacy game, touching a sexy man's hands was playing with fire.

"Hey there," Winnie said, more calmly than she felt. He held on to her hand just a moment longer than she expected before returning to his seat. She slid into the opposite side of the high-backed booth and clasped her hands firmly around the clutch on her lap, so their shakiness wouldn't betray her attempts at composure. The booth, which was covered in a gorgeous canopy of flowers, was at once huge and cozy, and she was aware of just how very close Cal felt across the table. Of just how intimate the setting was.

"Winnie, you look..." he began before pausing ever so briefly. "Lovely." His intense gaze flickered down her body quickly before returning politely to her face.

"Well, low lighting can do wonders for a girl," she joked with an awkward laugh, looking out into the restaurant and wondering just why it was so hard to keep eye contact with Cal.

"That's hardly the case here," Cal said genuinely, leaning in and looking even more intently at Winnie.

"You're awfully dressed up yourself," she observed casually, as if he wasn't devastating her senses.

Cal looked down at his suit.

"Oh, this? Yeah. I came straight from a meeting with some investors in Evansdale," he said, referring to the largest town in the region. "I always try to dress a little nicer when I'm trying to get people to give me money."

"Did it work?"

"Like a charm," he said, and she wondered for a moment if the man had ever been denied anything. Her gaze dared to meet his once more, despite the intensity she felt when they locked into hers. Soon enough, though, her eyes, which simply could not be trusted, skimmed down his handsome face and fixated on his mouth.

He had the perfect mouth, in her opinion. His bottom lip was especially full. Bitable. Inviting.

Why did her mouth suddenly feel so dry?

She quickly grabbed the drink menu, looking for some liquid courage.

"So, when you met with the last newspaper editor to discuss business, did you usually start with drinks?" she asked slyly, glancing at the half-empty beer glass in Cal's hand.

"The old editor usually started with drinks before I started breakfast, so it was somewhat of a moot point."

Winnie laughed a big laugh that somehow seemed to put them both at ease. It felt unfair that Cal could be that pretty *and* genuinely funny.

The waiter came through and she ordered a vodka tonic before turning her attention back to Cal.

"I read your article by the way," he offered.

"Which one?"

"Your best one. The football story."

Winnie snorted.

"If you're going to flatter me, please don't flat out lie while doing it. Plus it was me *and* Randy's story. We shared the byline, which was generous of him, given that he wrote three-quarters of it from his sick bed."

"I was sad that you didn't reference the coach's head almost popping off in anger. It was your best observation."

"Yeah, Randy nixed that line."

"The football story actually wasn't my favorite though. I really enjoyed your piece on the new cultural council."

Pride swelled in Winnie's chest. It hadn't occurred to her that Cal would pay any attention to her writing. It surely had little to do with her and a lot to do with his need to keep up with community goings-on, but it felt more touching than she might have expected.

"You read that? It's a cool initiative and I think it'll be great for the town. I had fun writing it."

"It showed."

"As opposed to the zoning story," Winnie groaned. "I'm pretty sure that the only person who wanted to read that one was the mother of the zoning commissioner."

Cal chuckled.

"It's hard to make some of the stuff that happens around here seem interesting."

"And yet, a fist fight almost broke out at the zoning meeting."

"You chose to bury that detail?"

Winnie laughed. "I hinted at Wyatt Clayton's anger at the commission's decision."

"Yeah, he's the kind of guy who might throw a punch," he said, his face shadowing unexpectedly.

"You know him?" she asked, her curiosity flared. Wyatt had certainly stuck out at the meeting of mostly retirees. He had to be closer to Cal's age. With his muddy boots, torn jeans, deeply tanned skin and his shoulder-length hair tied back in a messy ponytail, the man cut quite a memorable figure. He had an edge about him that made Winnie's skin prickle a bit because she couldn't tell if he was sexy, dangerous, or both.

"I know Wyatt, alright," Cal said, his voice lowering in what sounded like aggravation. "He and Carter and I used to run together when we were kids."

"And throw punches?"

"Yeah, I think the last time I saw him there might have been some of that," Cal said, practically grinding his teeth in not-quite-concealed anger. "Let's just say I don't talk much with Wyatt anymore."

Interesting. Winnie thought about that for a second. Everyone seemed to get along so well with Cal, but it only made sense that someone who had lived in a community for the better part of thirty years would have some bad history with at least one or two community members. It was also clear that he had no interest in elaborating, no matter how piqued Winnie's curiosity was.

"So did you get that tax debacle straightened out?"

He looked momentarily confused.

"The one that was going to cause chaos in the Broadsville bleachers on Friday night?"

He rolled his eyes.

"For better or for worse, it's my job to be civil to leaders in the community, no matter how manufactured their crises may be," he said matter-of-factly, but the ornery gleam never left his eye.

"Well, it was evident that Mayor Johannsen has a very hands-on approach to community partnerships," Winnie said. She'd lost track of how many times the woman found an excuse to touch Cal during their few-minute exchange on Friday night, but she was completely aware of how annoyed it made her.

But the comment got a laugh out of Cal. Winnie's words hung in the charged air between them as he took a long draw from his pint.

"So, how do we do this? How does this go?" Winnie asked, desperate to change the topic away from the awkwardness at Friday's football game. "How do you usually conduct these candlelit business meetings?"

"Well, I tell jokes, you laugh. Then we repeat."

Winnie laughed again, perfectly on cue. Bree had always called her a laugh whore because she gave them away so easily.

"Very good. You catch on quickly," Cal said, seemingly pleased with the reaction he could get so easily from Winnie.

"I feel nervous," Winnie blurted out with a sudden candor that surprised them both.

Cal's shift in demeanor sent butterflies through her stomach. Apparently her insecurity-masking-itself-as-playful-confidence trick had been working. He had no idea how out of place she felt at this table with a man like him.

"You have nothing to be nervous about, Briggs."

JESS VONN

If that was true, why did the mere sound of her name on his perfect lips make her feel as if something inside of her was unraveling?

"This is not my typical work setting, and *you* are not my typical work associate," Winnie said, an early indication that her mouth would be moving more quickly than her brain tonight.

Cal's eyebrow rose.

"And how's that?"

"Well, I interact with cute little kids at school pageants and slightly hostile seniors at the community center and energetic women who run local boutiques. But, not people like..."

Saved by the waiter, Winnie cut off her embarrassing admission mid-thought and took a long, grateful sip of her vodka tonic.

"Not people like me," he finished for her. Mercifully.

"Precisely." Winnie refused to elaborate, though she was certain that her flushing cheeks were dropping some hints.

"I have to say, this is new to me too," Cal admitted. "You make for much more pleasant company than, say, Mayor Simpson."

Winnie grinned, remembering her first, odd introduction to the man. She bet that Cal had some stories he could share about the mayor.

"Seriously though," he continued, "I hoped we might get to know one another first before jumping right into business. We'll be working together regularly, and I think it would be best if we weren't complete strangers."

"That makes sense," Winnie thought, silently continuing... *even if that's also what you do on a date.*

"So tell me about yourself," Cal started.

"Oh that will be quick. I'm terribly boring."

"I highly doubt that. You're all anyone around Bloomsburo can talk about these days."

Winnie blushed a bit, even if she knew he may be right. Fortunately she also knew that this had everything to do with a small town's insatiable hunger for novelty and gossip, and nothing to do with her in particular. It would pass.

"No, really. My life is a model of pathetic-ness. I work. I sleep. But mostly I work."

"Why did you become a journalist?"

Winnie looked taken aback for a second.

"Wow, you don't even ease in with 'what's your favorite color?'"

Cal shook his head.

"It's green, by the way," Winnie offered, unable to ignore the very stunning green eyes smiling back at her from across the table. Had that always been her favorite color, or were recent influences at play? Suddenly she couldn't remember.

"But why did I become a journalist? I always loved to write. At first I wrote fiction, but then I started to dabble in non-fiction, and eventually I came to believe that it's an honor to tell people's stories, and to keep the public informed on the issues that matter to them."

Cal nodded, seemingly pleased with her dutiful career speech.

"Why are you in public relations?" she asked.

"Because I did some research on the average salary for journalists," Cal joked. Winnie rolled her eyes even if the dig was well justified. Nobody went into journalism for the money.

"No, really. Why PR?"

"Because there was a cute girl in the major when I started college," he said, not missing a beat.

"No, *really*," Winnie insisted, her glare firm on Cal, who hesitated, but finally complied. He was an ornery interviewee who did not like to stay on topic.

"Well, there *were* many lovely ladies in the major, that much was true. But I guess I've always loved working with people. I'm good at communicating visually. I get a charge out of the marketing component. I like to take a concept from some messy, scattered idea and polish it into a successful campaign."

"Better."

Cal's eyes narrowed again, alerting Winnie that the questioning was coming back to her.

"What do you do for fun?" he asked.

"What is this 'fun' you speak of? Did you not catch on to my sad work/sleep cycle?"

"You have to do *something* for fun."

Winnie thought for a moment.

"I like to watch junky reality TV because it makes me feel like a better person. I love to see movies in the theater, but my pockets are always full of contraband candy that I've smuggled in from the dollar store because I'm a cheapskate. I still enjoy creative writing."

"What do you write?"

"Nothing for public consumption."

"Just romantic poems in your diary?"

Winnie flushed again, despite herself. "Hey, enough grilling here. I'm the interviewer. What do you do for fun? Or do I even want to know?"

Cal laughed lightly.

"I think you may have the wrong idea about me, Briggs."

"Oh, I'm a pretty good judge of character."

"I'm not so sure, otherwise you might not be sitting here with me now."

The insinuation caused Winnie's heartbeat to quicken. "Touché," she admitted, sipping again at her drink.

This is only a business meeting. This is only a business meeting.

"I cook," Cal finally offered.

"You *cook*?" She knew it didn't make sense, but she just found Cal too handsome to cook. Sure, he seemed like the kind of guy who, like a Matthew McConaughey character in a romantic comedy, would have one impressive meal under his belt that he could use to impress women and get them into bed, but not a whole culinary repertoire.

"Oh, don't look so shocked," Cal defended himself. "What did you think my hobbies were?"

"Jetting off to Vegas for cards and strippers? Conning recently widowed cougars out of their savings? High-contact meetings with the blondest of area mayors?"

Cal laughed in mock outrage. "Well, I hate to ruin your cruel little fantasy of me, but I cook, and then when I'm done cooking, I put on my pajamas and crash on the couch and read *Cook's Illustrated* or *Bon Appétit* and I decide what I'm going to cook next."

Speaking of fantasies, suddenly Winnie couldn't shake the mental image of Cal, lying on the couch in a tight grey T-shirt and plaid pajama pants. But then it begged the questions about what was underneath. Boxers? Briefs? Nothing…

Winnie cleared her throat, her mouth going dry again. She was surprised but not surprised to notice that her vodka tonic was already nearly gone.

"Well, that's a great skill to have. I'm jealous. I can't cook."

"Surely you could learn. You're a smart woman."

Winnie felt disproportionately touched by the comment. Her ex, Anthony, who spent his days with some of the sharpest legal minds in the country, had often treated her like a silly, frivolous thing.

"No, it's a fairly well-established fact that I can't cook. There's at least one Chicago-based fire battalion that can attest to this."

"I could teach you," he offered.

Now Winnie's mental image transformed to Cal (still in his irresistible plaid pajama bottoms, the morning after) standing behind her as she scrambled eggs on the stove, his arms coming around her waist to guide her hand. The feel of his breath warm on her neck...

"I'm not sure I'm comfortable being indebted to you."

"I'm sure we could come up with a creative payment plan."

This is only a business meeting, imagination. Knock it off!

"Have you seen the waiter? My drink disappeared."

Cal smiled, then looked out into the restaurant, signaling to the waiter, who came over and took a second round of drink orders, as well as their meal choices.

"So what do you say, are you up for a lesson?"

Winnie recollected her thoughts. The cooking lesson.

"Oh, that would be a waste of your talent, especially when I've gotten by this long with Pop-Tarts and microwaveable mac and cheese."

Cal clutched at his chest as if he were in pain.

"Oh, you can't tell me these sorts of things. It's inhumane to let you go through life eating those food-like substances."

"So just cooking?" Winnie diverted, trying to change the subject and discourage her wild imagination.

"I also run."

"Clearly," Winnie said under her breath as she took a sip of her replenished drink and tried not to think about the muscular contours of his legs.

"Pardon?" Cal asked, ornerily.

Winnie nervously cleared her throat again.

"Um, clearly, because..." she started, her mind frantically trying to dig her way out of that hole, "because you were running the day we first met. You know, when you tried to arrest me."

He grinned.

"And clearly it's time for me to eat something, since I'm so malnourished by the Kraft company."

He kept his gaze locked on Winnie for a minute, a pleased expression slowly spreading across his face.

Winnie couldn't keep the contact, so she reached to replace the drink menu across the table and with signature grace, managed to smack the edge of it into Cal's water glass, sending it crashing to the table and splashing its contents onto his lap.

"Woah!" he cried, lifting his bottom up off the booth in a natural reflex.

"Oh God, Cal!" Winnie shrieked, bolting up from her side of the booth, cloth napkin in hand. "I'm so, so sorry."

She scooched in next to him in the booth, and began dabbing furiously at his waist and the top of his thighs, which were now sopping wet and three shades darker blue than the rest of the suit material.

"Oh, this is such a good-looking suit. I hope it's not ruined," she said earnestly.

She dabbed fervently several more times before realizing that Cal wasn't dabbing at all. He was simply watching Winnie, his eyes slightly widened at the spectacle unfolding before him.

"So you like the suit, huh?" he asked, his voice low, as Winnie transformed to roughly the color of a beet.

Suddenly so close to Cal, closer than she had ever been and with his arm nearly around her. Suddenly enveloped by his cologne, which happened to be every bit as intoxicating as she imagined. Suddenly so close to that plush, tempting mouth.

Realizing that her hand was still pressing firmly into his very pleasant thigh, she felt the weight of embarrassment crash like a boulder into the pit of her stomach. She desperately wanted to crawl under the table and hide until Cal had finished his meal, paid the bill, and exited the restaurant.

"I'm sorry. I'm making a spectacle. Clearly you're capable of taking care of your own crotch."

The statement flew out of her mouth before she had the chance to capture it and prevent herself serious embarrassment.

She was on a roll now.

Cal didn't say a word, he just maintained his amusement, which made Winnie want to click her heels and disappear, Dorothy style.

"Well, yes, I'm a big boy," Cal said as she moved her way back to her own side of the booth.

"That much was evident during the dabbing," Winnie joked, much to Cal's shock and delight. This time, the big laugh came from him.

Winnie covered her face with her hands.

"I'm kidding. I didn't touch anything. I mean, I was dabbing around...it. I didn't even see anything, not that I would be looking, because what would I even need that kind of information for?" she sputtered.

Cal's grin grew as Winnie took a long drink and grew redder by the second.

"Sorry. Sometimes I forget that I'm not with my girlfriends and I fail to keep my true sense of humor in check," she said, talking into the hands that were failing to cover her bright red face.

"If off-color humor is officially on the table, then you just became my all-time favorite work associate," Cal said.

"Does that mean you're not going to sue me for sexual harassment?" Winnie asked.

Cal almost coughed out his last sip as a laugh took him off guard. "No, no I'm not. Not this time at least."

"Because this is a business meeting," Winnie maintained, repeating the evening mantra that so far had done absolutely no good. "But I promise to keep my hands far from your private parts at all of our future encounters."

"Thank you for the assurance."

Lord, this was only a business meeting, right?

Cal excused himself to the bathroom and Winnie tried to remember how to breathe like a normal human being.

Chapter 11

Cal stepped into the single stalled men's room, locked the door, and raked his hands quickly through his hair in an attempt to regain the self-control that Winnie Briggs seemed especially suited to demolish.

He'd almost kissed the woman, right in the middle of the damn restaurant. She had been there, tucked beneath his arm on his side of the booth, her body giving a merciless amount of attention to his upper thighs. In mere seconds, he could have scooped her closer, devoured her mouth, filled his hands with piles of that unruly hair that always seemed to be springing in a dozen directions. He could have set her atop his lap and let her feel for herself just how much he appreciated her firm touch on his body.

Shit. No. He was in here to cool down, not to get worked up again. Winnie had her charms, but hell, he was hardly an inexperienced teen. He'd been with plenty of gorgeous women with tempting bodies. Yet somehow, none of them had gripped his mind or his balls like the very real woman sitting out at that table fifty feet away.

Tonight's meeting really had been born of good intentions. Winnie needed community information that he possessed, and some professional accommodation toward her would get his mother off his back. Two birds, one stone. So he'd texted her and set the date.

But his first wrong move was suggesting Cafe Gioia. No matter how good the food was, the place felt too intimate. Too flooded with soft, golden light that made the smooth, creamy skin at the top of Winnie's breasts positively glow from where they peaked out above that satiny lavender top.

No, he ordered himself again. No thoughts of her low-cut blouse or her heavy breasts or how nice the latter would be without the former. His dick needed a breather if he was to step back out in public any time soon.

Income taxes. Polar plunges into icy lakes. Nails on a chalkboard. Undercooked meat. His mind filtered through the least pleasant thoughts possible. Jesus, Winnie reduced him to a middle school kid dealing with his first gym class erection.

Somehow, Winnie's absolute lack of awareness about the sensuality she emitted made her all the more potent to him. She didn't understand the effect of her bottomless chocolate eyes. Her infectious laugh. Her pink mouth, so quick to smile. Her full breasts. Her thick, swinging hips atop strong legs.

But none of this was Winnie's fault. Simply put, it had been too long since he'd been with a woman. Six months? Eight? The fact that he couldn't even remember the last time he'd relieved himself in the tight, warm clutches of a woman reinforced the urgency of his current situation. He had set himself up for this.

Last night, feeling rattled about Winnie after the football game and the Sunday dinner altercation with his mother, he'd pulled up Tinder for the first time in months. He flicked through his matches, hoping to identify someone who might be available for some quick, mutual relief, but none of the women's profiles managed to hold his interest. In fact, just looking through the list of random women available one swipe away felt off-putting.

Later that evening, when he'd reached for himself in the shower in a last-ditch effort to quiet the cravings of his body, the only image his mind could form to help him along was of Winnie in there with him—her hair drenched, water catching in her long lashes. Her full lips wet and glistening. A sparkly trail of sudsy soap winding across the full slopes of her breasts and down, down, down to her center where he worked to tempt cries of pleasure from her. Where her sex clenched needily around his fingers as she cried out his name.

Sure, the image had helped him out in the shower, but it wasn't doing him a damn bit of good when it came to keeping his composure around the woman today.

He just plain wanted her. There wasn't any more to it. His body and his psyche clearly agreed on this. It was only his brain that was putting on the breaks. But why?

Winnie didn't date. That much he knew, and he respected it, because he didn't date either. And he sure as hell wasn't in the market for a girlfriend, let alone a happily ever after. That wasn't his birth right. Was it because they were work associates? That excuse wore thin, too, when he realized that it would be no less awkward to be her ex-lover one day down the road than to be her wannabe lover right now.

For every truth he acknowledged about his inability to romance a woman, or to think about long-term monogamy, Cal knew he *could* please a woman and take pleasure from her, and the only person who seemed qualified to meet his body's criteria right now was Winnie Briggs. So why fight such a natural instinct? If there was anyone who needed some mindless physical passion more than him, it was that tightly wound woman sitting out at their booth. If they approached this the right way, both of them would walk away with some satisfaction, and some relief from the churning needs of their bodies, without having to deal with the messiness of a failed romance.

And if they approached it the wrong way? Well, Cal's brain wouldn't quite let him process that possibility. He splashed some water on his face, took a few final deep breaths, and made his way back out to the only woman who could give his body peace, determined to find a solution they could both live with.

~-~-~-~-~-~-

Back at the booth, Winnie's hands returned to the shakiness they experienced at the start of the evening.

What in the holy hell was she doing here? Why did she think she could handle a casual dinner with a man who exuded such bone-deep sexuality? Her traitorous mind flickered back to moments before, when her hand was on Cal's leg. God, the sheer muscularity of it unmoored her. She'd never been with a fit man. Never had the urge to run her palms along the contours of a man's thighs. But Cal's legs had been a revelation. The thought of the novelties that the rest of his body offered made her want to whimper. Until her hands had pressed into Cal Spencer's body, it never occurred to her all the things she hadn't experienced.

She wanted him at a cellular level. Wanted to stretch him across a bed and spend hours examining the shape of him, his intimate patches of hair, his thick cords of muscle and the places on his body that grew sweaty from exertion.

Crikey.

Wanting Cal was no more practical than wanting a forty-room mansion in Los Angeles or a personal chef or a weekly massage. Some things, as nice as they sounded, and for as much bodily pleasure as they offered, simply were not meant for her, and part of being a grown-up was accepting reality.

Ever aware of the man's proximity, Winnie noticed Cal returning from the men's room and, like the mature woman she was, she buried herself behind the dessert menu in an attempt to escape her own mortification.

He resumed his place in the booth, her every cell heightened with awareness of his proximity. She peered over the large menu toward him.

"Seriously, if there is permanent damage to that suit, I will buy you another one," Winnie promised, feeling foolish. "After a few more paychecks, though, because I think your wardrobe reflects a different price point than mine."

"Winnie, forget it. I mean, I won't *ever* let you completely forget it, because it was too funny," he teased. "But really, you can forget it. It's not a big deal at all. It's just water."

He was playful, but sincere and it put Winnie mostly back at ease. Cal was well dressed and criminally sexy, but she was pleasantly surprised to learn how laid back he was, considering. Once Winnie had spilled sweet and sour sauce on one of Anthony's favorite suit jackets and he hadn't talked to her for two days after the incident. She didn't think he ever fully forgave her. She mentally winced, realizing in hindsight just how frequently she chose to overlook those everyday indications of his true nature. It was startling to her just what she had been able to overlook in the name of not rocking the boat.

"So, now that you've completely soaked me, you've got to answer some questions for me. It's only fair."

Winnie's heart beat raced, suddenly feeling like she was back in a middle school game of truth or dare.

"I'll try," she offered, too timid to fully, willingly, submit to Cal's games.

"What brought you here?"

Her heart rate ticked up, up, up.

"A good job opportunity," she bluffed.

He didn't hesitate a moment before saying, "I call bullshit."

Fair enough. The man was sexy, but he wasn't stupid.

She took another long sip of her second vodka and tonic, the alcohol soothing the nerves that might otherwise render her spineless. Perhaps it also helped her forget, ever so briefly, that this was only a business meeting. She met his gaze directly, their deep green depths seeming to reverberate between her legs.

"A man."

He nodded. Senselessly, his lack of response urged her to elaborate.

"A three-year relationship went south. He cheated on me. My world imploded."

"How?"

"Mutual friends, a small professional network—" she began, her mind flooding with all those suddenly distant Chicago memories. Taking the elevator up to Anthony's condo to surprise him with a night out on the town for their anniversary. Following the sound of groans and gasps to his bathroom, where he screwed his blonde intern against the side of his glass-walled shower. Her mixed drink wasn't strong enough to forget all that.

"No, I meant how did he cheat on *you*."

Winnie searched Cal's face for a moment—wondering, hoping, yet knowing that his words couldn't mean what they seemed.

"Lawyer Anthony, in the stand-up shower, with his impossibly slender blonde intern," Winnie said drolly, harkening the phrasing from the classic board game. "A tale as old as time."

"I'm not talking logistics, though that's shitty as hell," Cal relented, his gaze upon her relentless. Hungry.

Winnie's heart beat doubled on itself, and nausea rose through her core at the possible implications of Cal's words.

"You'd have to ask him that."

"I'd like to think I would if given the chance, but to be honest, if I met him, I'd probably just punch him in the face."

And then she found herself grinning. She didn't, as a rule, condone violence, but she might make an exception for her bastard ex.

"And what about you?" she asked, emboldened by vodka and the man's blatant flirtation. "What's your relationship history like?"

He blinked.

"I don't really do relationships," he said simply, as if that settled it.

"No?" she asked, yearning to hear more. She wanted the man's sob stories. His sexy recollections. No man who looked that gorgeous in a royal blue suit could have a simple romantic history.

"There have been women," he allowed. Oh, she could only imagine the parade of women who followed in Cal Spencer's wake.

"Mmm," she offered. Vague. Noncommittal.

"I'm not the slow and steady type. I don't do romance. I don't do long-term. But I take my pleasure where I can get it."

She bet he did. And with another sip of her vodka and tonic, she loosened up enough to imagine what that might look like. His mouth. Those hands.

Mercifully, the waiter arrived just then, delivering the most delectable meal Winnie had seen since arriving in town.

She looked up to Cal in disbelief.

"I told you it'd be good," he offered, before filling his mouth with a forkful of fried ravioli in rich marinara sauce.

Winnie had never before envied a pillow of ravioli, but there was a first time for everything.

And so it went into the evening. Eating. Flirting. Filling her mouth, her body, and her mind with a storm of pleasing sensations—from Cal, from the food, from the charged ambience of the café.

By the time they finished their meal and settled the bill, the restaurant was all but abandoned. They had shut down the place. Transfixed, Winnie walked out the door of the restaurant, only realizing in the very back recesses of her mind that she and Cal had failed to discuss one single pertinent detail of Bloomsburo Days.

Lightly buzzed, not so much from her earlier drinks, but from the food and the sexy company, Winnie arrived at Fiona the Ford in something like a daze. She wanted to linger there. Wanted this night with this beautiful man to somehow, impossibly, last.

The chit chat that had brought them out to the empty parking lot had faded, and there they stood, her body leaning against Fiona, so near to his. Near enough to cause her throat to tighten. For something deep within her to contract with need.

Her eyes grazed upon him, such an uncommonly attractive figure, suddenly thrust into her life, all because of her random response to an online rental ad.

Fate had placed him here, an arm's length away, and she was just content enough not to mind. To not to think that it was a cruel twist of fate. She scanned him once more, not yet able to fathom his beauty, from the honey-gold strands of his wavy hair, to his endless green eyes, to that mouth.

God, that mouth.

"You keep doing that," Cal observed, his deep green eyes alighting with mischief.

"Doing what?"

"Watching my mouth."

Winnie cleared her throat, suddenly feeling cold sober.

"I don't —" she started, but he cut off the lie.

"Yes, you do."

Her eyes widened. In what... annoyance? Guilt? Shock, at the way he seemed to see through her, as if she were made of glass? As if he could see her every accelerated heartbeat. Her throbbing pulse.

But he'd caught her, and the man wasn't wrong. And since she was caught, she relented, her gaze falling once more to his lips. Full. Satiny. Bitable. A plush haven amidst the stubble and hardness of his strong jaw. What was the point of denying the magnetic draw she had to them?

"What are you thinking about when you look at me like that?" he asked, his directness like lightning through her core.

A blush filled her cheeks and her eyes fell to her feet.

"Winnie, look at me," he said gently.

From beneath her lashes, she peered toward him, but she didn't dare open her mouth. His directness gutted her and she knew he caught every signal that her traitorous body sent—the quickened pulse, the shallow breath, the shaky hands. This desire she felt in his presence felt bigger than she could handle.

And surely bigger than she could conceal.

"I'm not asking what would happen if you acted on it, or about the long-term ramifications, or what I might think about your thoughts. Just, what are you thinking? Can you be honest with me?"

His candor made her feel five years old. Why couldn't she just say it? Why was it so hard to acknowledge the overwhelming urge surging through her body? Her every cell knew exactly what she wanted to do to the man, yet she couldn't force herself to be her body's own spokeswoman.

"Tell me," he said, his body inching ever so slightly toward her.

"There's no sense in talking about things that aren't possible," she finally managed, her voice strangled.

"Sensibility and pleasure are hardly easy companions."

It might as well be the man's motto.

"Tell me," he repeated.

Exasperated, she relented.

"I want to feel them," she finally cried. "Your lips look so soft. So tempting. Like they'd know exactly what to do to with a woman beneath them."

Desire burned in his eyes. And confidence. No doubt he agreed with her assessment. He knew full well the expertise he had to offer, and what it could do to her.

"So feel them," he dared her, moving a half step closer to her, the lack of space between them now overwhelming Winnie with wants and needs.

She shook her head no.

"Why not?"

"I made a promise to myself."

"The pledge?"

"Yes. No dating."

"Right. I don't date either."

"Good."

"So, let's not date. That has nothing to do with what's happening between our bodies."

Her heart thudded harder in her chest. She swore he could see it pounding away beneath the thin material of her blouse. His eyes flickered to her breasts and she cursed the attention her own breathlessness drew from his burning gaze.

"I don't know what you mean."

"I think you do. Do you make it a point to deny your body what it wants?"

"What?" she laughed, forced. Panicky. "Of course not."

"You eat the saddest food imaginable. You work all weekend and most evenings. You avoid men. Where do you find your pleasure, Briggs?"

"I find *plenty* of pleasure," she said too quickly, her defensiveness as evident as her arousal.

"Where?"

She thought for a moment, annoyed that an answer didn't come to her more quickly. Damn the man for short-circuiting her brain.

"I take pleasure in my work," she relented, as if career satisfaction held a candle to what his mouth could offer. His fingers.

"Okay," he conceded, however mildly. "So do I. It's a starting place, and important, but not nearly enough. Where else?"

Why was it suddenly so hard to remember what she did just because it felt good? Random thoughts came to her, but they were too outdated to mention—old memories of weekend trips with girlfriends in college, the crafts she used to create but had long since abandoned. She might as well mention "playing with Barbies." She hated how everything she thought of might sound silly. Frivolous.

Mercifully, an idea came to her.

"I take pleasure in my style," she said.

"Your style?"

"My clothes, my fashion sense. How I accessorize. It makes me feel good. Different. I like it."

"I like it, too. I have to force myself to look away from you."

Warmth spread through her body at his approval, followed quickly by a tiny spark of annoyance. She didn't dress how she did for men. In fact, she honed her style in spite of them, as a reclaiming of power.

But damn if she didn't want this particular man to like the look of her.

"What else gives you pleasure?" he persisted.

His body was closer now. Close enough to reach out for, to grab. She could smell him—the expensive woody tones of his cologne that she breathed in despite its potential to destroy her. Need throbbed through her veins.

"Naps," she managed. Though she wouldn't tell him of the self-pleasure that helped her nod off. That was only for her to know.

His sweet lips spread into a grin.

"Hmmm," he said, the low vibration of his mouth unraveling something within her.

"Saturdays and Sundays, I usually take one. They're delicious."

The word set off a spark in his endless green eyes.

"That's closer. But couldn't you do with a little more?"

"More what?"

"Pleasure in your life. I could help with that."

Desire singed every inch of her, each one desperate for this man's touch. It decimated her defenses. Her insecurities. For a brief moment, she felt like a different woman, as if she was somehow floating outside of the self-conscious body that carried her around on a day-to-day basis.

Or maybe she had it all wrong. Maybe this man wasn't here to destroy her. Maybe he was here to embolden her. To teach her to literally reach out and grab what she wanted out of life.

To hell with the pledge. Because at the end of the day, wasn't it just one more way to let men control her life?

Winnie first.

"Yes, I could do with a little more pleasure," she said, surprising them both. She watched his face, searching, as he contemplated his next move. With one more step, he closed the gap between them.

"Name the parameters," he ordered, barely containing the need that coiled his muscular body as tight as a rope.

Her heart thumped in her chest at the thought of the line they were about to cross. She took some solace in the fact the she'd just picked up and moved her entire life hundreds of miles away. If this thing, whatever it was burning between her and Cal, were to go up in flames, if he ignited her entire world and burned it to ashes, she could flee and do it all again.

A small comfort. Her brain whirled, trying to calculate the conditions that might help to minimize the damage this experiment would surely yield.

It didn't help that the man's fingers brushed her cheek, stroking her jawline tenderly. She wanted those fingers to explore every centimeter of her body. She knew they could make her weep with desire.

"Uh, no dates," she managed, closing her eyes in an attempt to focus. "No more sexy business meetings either. We stay professional on the job. Not a whiff of indiscretion."

Had her eyes been open, she might have seen what was coming, but as it was, the soft kiss Cal placed exactly where her ear met her neck shot a wave of sensations through her body, every one of which seemed to ultimately settle in a throbbing pool between her legs.

"Mmm-hmm," he consented, his lips still close enough to her skin that she could feel the sound vibrate off them.

A tiny moan echoed in Winnie's throat, but she forced her mind to focus for just a few minutes more. She would gladly lose herself in this moment with this man, but not before she outlined a few more ground rules.

"It builds slowly," she said as his lips made a trail down her neck to the curve of her collarbone. Already it was so clear the ways he could leverage that mouth to please her. "You cannot incinerate me."

"I'll do my best," he said, his voice husky and warm on her skin.

"Cal," she pleaded, the panicked tone of her voice stopping his mouth's pleasure assault.

He stood to his full height, suddenly so tall, so imposing, so all-consuming pressed there against her body. His green eyes locked into hers, and her stomach dropped.

"I mean it," she said, her quiet voice quivering.

"I do, too. I'll take care of you. One inch at a time."

She looked for a reason to doubt him. For a reason to be cynical. But damn it, she believed him.

"What else?" he asked, his hand slipping behind her neck, his thumb sweetly brushing her sensitive skin.

"No terms of endearment. No sleepovers. And I can call it off at any time."

His eyes flashed at the last line, though she couldn't quite discern the meaning in the darkness of the parking lot.

"I assume that goes for me, too?"

Her stomach sank. Naturally, her thoughts wanted to swirl toward the negative. *Of course he'll want to call it off. You're vastly inexperienced with men. You're beyond complicated.*

But she fortified herself. This hadn't been her idea. He made the offer, and he wouldn't have done it if there wasn't real interest there.

"Of course."

He nodded and she couldn't help but grin. It was amazing how cooperative the man had become now that the topic related to him getting some action.

"I mean, what if I can't handle you? What if you annihilate me, Briggs?"

She laughed lightly, grateful that he could lighten the mood again. She took comfort in her deep sense that Cal would be a playful lover.

Lover. Lord. She'd never had a lover in her entire life. She'd had two long-term relationships, both of which took their sweet time to work up to incredibly basic relationship sex. Now, here she was being mouthed by the sexiest man she'd ever seen.

What a difference a month could make. She couldn't help but smile, astonished at not only this twist of fate, but at how excited she felt about it.

"And most importantly," she continued, "your mother cannot, under any circumstance, know about our pleasure hunting."

He smiled at the phrase.

"As a general rule, I tend *not* to keep her abreast of what I do with my lovers."

She smiled, yet the comment rankled in Winnie's stomach. *Lovers*, plural. How many women had experienced pleasure beneath Cal's hands? His mouth? How would her own sexual history, with only two self-absorbed men, possibly compare?

It wasn't something she wanted to dwell on or talk about. This realization led to another condition.

"No deep digging into each other's backstories or baggage," she said. "Let's focus on the present."

"Gladly," he said, his hands raking up her curls by the handful so he could kiss the side of her neck without obstruction. His fingertips gently massaged her scalp, sending chills all throughout her body.

But thoughts of other lovers brought to mind a final, non-negotiable rule.

"One last condition."

"Anything," he said, his eyes sparked with a lust that empowered her enough to believe him.

"No one else."

His brow quirked, confused.

"We devote some time to getting this thing that's bouncing between us completely out of our system, you teach me a thing or two about manifesting pleasure in my life, but during that time, we have no other partners."

"Deal."

He consented too quickly. He'd shake out of whatever haze he was in soon. He'd remember what caliber of woman he was surely accustomed to, and he'd take his clever hands and hot mouth and sweet ass along his merry way.

Winnie could already imagine the depth of that inevitable loss, of that physical withdrawal she'd experience when his body was no

JESS VONN

longer hers to peruse, but it didn't deter her. Until then, she intended to absorb every ounce of pleasure this man could offer her. Some opportunities came around only once in a lifetime, and Winnie intended to relish this gift, even if it scared her to death.

Surprising herself and Cal, she slipped her arms inside his suit jacket, reaching up his back and rubbing down his broad, muscular shoulders as she burrowed into the comfort of his chest. He felt better than she could have imagined.

He hugged her close to him and the intimacy of it allowed her to speak the final words she needed to say before they started this fiery game.

"I just need you to know that I've never done anything remotely like this," she whispered into the strength of his chest. How something so hard and muscular could provide so much comfort was a mystery. "I'm terrified."

His hands gently ran across her shoulders as he spoke his response softly into Winnie's hair beneath his chin.

"You don't need to worry. You're in good hands."

"Those good hands are exactly what I'm afraid of. And looking forward to."

He laughed.

Having gotten that vulnerable admission of her chest, Winnie felt emboldened to begin her own long-awaited exploration. He filled his hands with her hair as she kissed his chest through his shirt, imagining the hot skin beneath it.

She peeled herself away and slid her hands up to his neck, then his hair. That hair, which had tortured her from the very beginning. She practically pulled herself up with it until her mouth reached his throat. It felt hot and right beneath her lips.

Cal let out a low, satisfied groan, urging Winnie on. She could feel his racing pulse throb beneath her lips near his Adam's apple.

She thought of his mouth, but she couldn't rush. Not after waiting so long. She needed time with every inch of him. He tilted his head as her mouth moved up the side of his neck and under his chin, her breath hot on his skin as she kissed her way up.

"That feels so good," he whispered.

He put her face in his hands and leaned toward her, his mouth landing on her forehead, then brushing her cheek quickly, before finally, mercifully, landing on her lips. Again, then again, he pressed into her before she opened her mouth, inviting him to deepen the kiss with softness and wetness. Their hungry mouths revealed the truth that had been there all along: that these bodies were destined to connect from the inside out.

As his tongue swept between her lips, Winnie moaned, no longer concerned with the ruse of disinterest. The freedom of pursuing pleasure just for pleasure's sake thrilled her. She met him there, in the hot, velvety softness of their connected mouths, and she tasted him.

Perfection.

She could lose herself in this man, but finally she leaned back, desperate for air. She needed a moment to gather herself, but he pushed his lips against hers once more, his hands reaching down across her back, along the sides of her breast, down to the full curve of her backside. As his fingers kneaded her and his tongue caressed her and the thick length of his arousal pressed against her, she knew there was nowhere she'd rather be than here tasting Cal Spencer. Here, holding this magnificent man's full bodily attention.

She'd never known such power.

It was Cal who finally pulled back, pressing his forehead to hers in an unexpectedly intimate gesture. He panted, and it took every iota of self-discipline for Winnie to not stretch onto her tippy toes and press her lips against his once more.

"Slowly," he said, his breath ragged. His desire for her seemed as sharp and as unsettling as what she felt for him. Nothing could have shocked her more.

"Mmm," she managed, the closest semblance of words she could formulate under Cal's hands. His perfect mouth.

He pressed his lips to her forehead, the sweetness of the gesture somehow more devastating than the warm passion that had just surged between their open mouths. It was more tender than she could have imagined. She pictured him rough, aggressive. Not gentle enough to melt her.

"Good night, Briggs," he said, his breath hot on her skin.

She may have whimpered. For her pride's sake, she hoped she didn't, but the quirk of his kiss-swollen lips suggested otherwise.

"Buh...bye," she managed, as the most delicious guy she'd ever met pushed his body away from hers, and began the slow walk across the parking lot.

JESS VONN

Her mouth, her breasts, her sex, her heart, they all ached for the man now too far away from her, and she knew in the pit of her lust-ravaged stomach that no matter what he said, this game they were playing would consume her in flames.

What surprised Winnie was her deep sense that in the end, it would be worth it.

Chapter 12

Lying in bed the next morning, trying to simultaneously remember and forget the feeling of Cal Spencer's hungry hands roaming across her body last night, Winnie's heart and body felt conflicted. There had been so much goodness in Cal's proposition, and in those first tastes of the lessons in pleasure he could offer her with his hands. His lips. His tongue. With that hard length of his body pressed up against hers.

My God, if the man could melt her so thoroughly even through multiple layers of clothing, she'd be putty in his hands once they got naked.

Naked. One word, and her heart sank, all thoughts of pleasure replaced by something less desirable. She had more or less signed up to get naked with Cal Spencer, a man who might very well be sculpted from marble beneath all those sexy clothes.

Winnie's hands involuntarily began to rub across her own body in exploration, over top the thin fabric of her nightgown. They roamed over the full slopes of her breasts. Soft, yes, and beyond a handful, but decidedly more wobbly when she reclined than when she stood. She pressed her hand into her stomach— not round, but far from flat. Pressing her fingers gently down against her midsection, she couldn't think of a single word to describe the area other than squishy.

And she couldn't fathom a world where a man found squishy to be anything akin to sexy.

Traveling farther down her body, she allowed her fingers to trace over the soft silk of her panties, feeling the intimate hair beneath, left mostly natural. She never thought about grooming there much beyond basic bathing suit boundaries.

A man like Cal had probably experienced every kind of woman. He probably preferred some kind of expensive, torturous body hair removal technique named after a tropical country known for its flawless women.

Naked.

Her heart skittered over itself, feeling nervous, anxious, but deep down, if she were honest with herself, she felt damn excited, too.

JESS VONN

And as her fingers traced along the thin underside of her panties, wet evidence of that excitement was more than apparent.

The fact of the matter was that she wanted the man with every fiber of her being, and he'd all but offered himself up on a platter for her to devour. It didn't have to make sense. It didn't have to reflect her assumptions about what men wanted in a partner or her own perceived shortcomings. She didn't have to worry about a month from now, about what would happen "after," not when the days rolling out before her had so much to offer.

From somewhere in the dark and conflicted depths of her brain, her mantra bubbled up to the forefront of her consciousness.

Winnie first.

And for the first time in her entire sexual history, a revolutionary thought occurred to her. A thought that a former version of herself might never have even believed possible.

I want him, and I should have him.

So simple, yet so world-altering.

Cal Spencer, despite his perceived perfection, didn't have to find her perfect, because this wasn't about him. Winnie wanted the man down to the tips of her toenails. She deserved a chance at him. He was willing. She was able.

And she was hungry in a way she didn't even know possible.

Despite this personal epiphany, she had one small caveat for the universe: just give her a day or two away from the man to gather her wits about her. To prepare for the inevitability of needing to tamp down her desire for him in public and professional contexts.

Even if Winnie had come to peace with her desire for Cal, she still had no idea how she was going to subdue it in front of other people. Bree used to tease her relentlessly about her inability to hide one single emotion, even when doing so would benefit her enormously.

Bree. Oh, how she wished she could call up her best friend. How she wished they hadn't placed this stupid communication moratorium. She couldn't even count on indirect peeks into Bree's life on social media because her friend was notoriously anti-technology. The woman didn't even own a smart phone.

And yet, it was working. Winnie was exploring a new friendship with Evie, and a new friends-with-benefits scenario with Cal. Time and distance had dulled her sad memories from Chicago.

But oh, the stories she'd have for her friend when they reconnected. Bree might not believe her. Winnie might have to secure some photographic evidence of Cal's vitality.

But for as much as she wanted to avoid Cal Spencer for the rest of the week, the universe, unfortunately, had denied her request, and when Winnie walked into the Guiding Star community luncheon on Thursday, she zeroed in on Cal immediately, despite the group of more than forty people gathered in the room. If her vagina was a compass, the man appeared to be her true North. Her draw to his body was damn near magnetic.

His eyes met hers instantly, and though he never stopped whatever conversation he was having with the older gentleman at the table where he sat, he shot Winnie a small, pleased nod that seemed to tug at a string attached deep within her womb.

My God, the man was stunning. His thick, golden hair was parted on the side, sweeping over his head in gentle waves tinted with a half dozen shades of blond before it curled around his ears and collar. A soft, chocolate-brown V-neck sweater stretched across his broad shoulders, and she could see a light blue collar and tie peeking out around his tan neck. He looked like the kind of sexy professor all the undergraduates would swoon over.

And Winnie felt ready for a hands-on lesson, right then and there. Her heart raced as she forced her focus somewhere else, anywhere else, after Cal's attention returned to the people at his table. He seemed to be able to act like a normal human being around her, so why was she frozen in her tracks, dumbstruck?

Luckily, Betty Jean Finnegan pulled Winnie out of her lustful reverie.

Now there was a thought she would never have imagined having. But for once, Winnie felt grateful for the woman's meddling. It worked better than a cold shower.

"I'm glad you *finally* arrived," Betty Jean chirped, her voice sweet, but with a bit of accusation, just for good measure. Winnie glanced at her watch and internally groaned. She had a solid ninety seconds before the luncheon was scheduled to begin, which counted as incredibly early for her.

"I knew you'd show up, though," Betty Jean continued. "Why on earth would you miss it? If you want to know the movers and shakers in this town, if you want to be privy to the latest and breaking news in Bloomsburo, then this is the place you need to be every Thursday at noon."

Winnie thought about how to proceed. When she'd flipped through archived copies of *The Bloom*, she was shocked to see how much coverage the weekly Guiding Star Luncheons received in the paper. Nearly every meeting story was run on the front page of the paper with multiple photos despite the fact that it was essentially a social club.

This was a reporting trend she didn't want to perpetuate. On the other hand, Winnie was desperately new in town. Though Gloria and Evie could surely help her find sources for her stories, she would need to create her own network, too, and these weekly meetings weren't a bad place to start.

"Betty Jean, I agreed to attend the luncheons as often as I can," Winnie replied with caution. She didn't want to make any promises she wouldn't be able to keep. "But I will not guarantee any coverage. I will pay dues, just like the other Guiding Star members, and participate as a community member, not as the editor of the paper. If something newsworthy is brought up at a meeting, I will consider it a tip and then pursue it as a separate story, not in any way affiliated with the luncheon."

Betty Jean's brows narrowed ever so slightly, finally betraying her forced pleasantness.

"Well, though I'm glad that we can count on your membership, I must say I'm sad to hear that the citizens of Bloomsburo can no longer read about the good and important work we do in your paper," she said, looking down at her brightly polished finger nails, "a paper that seems so, well, hungry for news."

Winnie took the dig in stride and stood her ground.

"Well, think of it this way," she said. "You'll no longer be giving away the milk for free."

Betty Jean looked up at Winnie, confused.

"If people can just read about the weekly luncheon in the paper," Winnie continued, "why would they spend the money to become official members? If they are as interested as you say in what goes on at the luncheons, they'll surely join once they realize *The Bloom* won't be providing a weekly play-by-play. Your membership numbers will shoot through the roof."

Betty Jean cracked a stiff smile.

"Well, that would be a lovely side effect," she said. "Now, please take a seat before you hold up the entire event."

Winnie huffed as she scanned the room. Granted, she wasn't late, but with only a few seconds left before the luncheon began, she hardly had her choice of seats in the crowded banquet hall. Luckily for her Cal's table was full so she didn't even have to consider that possibility. Her eyes caressed the man once more, watching the casual way he worked his table, the way everyone around him seemed enchanted by him.

Her included.

Making her way to the back of the room, she noticed one seat open and she felt herself relax when she saw who it was next to.

"We meet again," Chief Carter Conrad said with that dazzling smile he had. With his bright white teeth, strong jaw and dark hair, Carter had a serious Superman vibe about him. That sexy uniform stretching over his wide shoulders didn't hurt the situation at all. He had to be close to six-and-a-half feet of bulky muscle.

"May I?" Winnie asked sweetly, gesturing to the open chair next to him. He was up in half a second and pulled out her chair for her. Gentlemanly, too, she mused.

"Sorry you're stuck sitting with me again." Winnie laughed, setting her purse beneath her chair and grabbing a drink of water. The men in this room were leaving her parched.

"I'm grateful for the company. People tend to avoid me at these sorts of things. I think they're afraid that they'll accidentally incriminate themselves during small talk over lunch and I'll have to take them out in cuffs."

Winnie snorted.

"Oh, not on Betty Jean's watch, I'm sure."

Now it was his turn to laugh.

"Yeah, the woman does think she's the law around here."

"Well, I don't think I've broken any laws lately, so I feel pretty safe at your table."

"Is that right?" he asked, unconvinced. "My friend over there sure seems to think you're doing something suspicious."

Winnie followed Chief Conrad's gaze, shocked to find Cal's eyes on her and the chief, flashing with something like annoyance.

Hot damn, could she have made the man jealous? The possibility made her feel giddy and a tiny bit mad with power.

JESS VONN

"Now lean into me and laugh extra loudly," Chief Conrad said, his head lowering closer to Winnie's neck so that she could smell his sexy aftershave.

She did laugh naturally at his wicked suggestion, but she might have amplified it just a bit for the sake of their one-man audience.

"Oh, he's pissed at me, alright," Chief Conrad said with a laugh. "This is the most fun I've had all week."

Winnie laughed and avoided the urge to look back at Cal once more.

"So you two go way back?" she asked, her eyes meeting the chief's once more. They were so blue a woman could get lost in them. That she felt only friendly affection for the man spoke to the power of the spell Cal had cast over her.

"Only to kindergarten."

"Then you probably have some embarrassing stories to tell about the Chamber of Commerce director then. The kind of stories a woman could tuck away until she needed them most."

His eyes twinkled.

"Winnie, I could fill a book with them," he promised with a grin, and she knew in that moment that she had a forever friend in Carter. Unfortunately, before he could share even one incriminating story about Cal, Betty Jean cleared her throat loudly at the microphone in the front of the room and began her introduction to the luncheon speaker.

"I'll take a rain check on those stories," she whispered to Carter, who nodded conspiratorially.

"It's a deal."

Maybe these weekly luncheons wouldn't be such a drag after all, Winnie mused to herself. She looked upon Chief Carter's handsome profile, and she had to laugh. If the only relief she could find from Cal Spencer's sexiness was a flirty friendship with his handsome best friend, well, she'd just have to find a way to deal with it.

Much to her delight, Bloomsburo was growing on her.

~~~~~~~~~~~

Sitting in his office a few hours after the Guiding Star luncheon, where Cal had watched his oldest friend flirt with Winnie Briggs like it was part of his job description, he reflected on just how much he'd wanted to interrupt them. To intercede. To at least text her to put himself back at the forefront of her mind.

Or maybe it was his asshole friend he needed to text, putting an end to Carter's fun. His friend was loyal to a fault, but he'd still enjoy smacking him upside the head all the same.

This train of thought felt wrong. Cal wasn't the possessive type. Hell, he'd never had to be. Most of his energy was spent *avoiding* the possessive types. The clingy women who called too much. Texted too often. Didn't understand the "one" part of a one-night stand. He sure as hell didn't have any claim over Winnie Briggs.

Yet here he was, fingers practically twitching where he sat in his office, just needing to reach out and contact her. To reassure himself that her desire for him was still as strong as it had been the night before.

The night before. He closed his eyes and suddenly he was right back in that restaurant parking lot. Hands full of Winnie's hair. Her soft, full breasts pressed up against his chest as her arms wound into his suit jacket and pulled him closer.

The warmth of her mouth, so soft and inviting.

And those two words that had hitched in his chest. *I'm terrified,* she'd said, so honestly, as her face had buried into his shirt -- all the better to send the words directly into his heart.

As incredible as her body had felt, as hungry as her mouth had made him, those words had the greatest impact on his body last night. Although this experiment they agreed to was about pleasure, pure and simple, he had to remember that Winnie was far outside her comfort zone, and he had a duty to take care with the woman.

Even if she did flirt with his best damn friend right in front of him.

To hell with it. He wanted to connect with her, so that's what he was going to do. Pulling out his cell phone, he typed a quick message, cutting straight to the point.

I'm thinking about you.

He saw three dots appear immediately in response. But then they disappeared. They showed up again, then disappeared. Damn how he wished he knew what she kept deleting.

> Sorry I didn't say hi over lunch. Wasn't ready to face you in public yet.

He grinned.

> Parking lot regrets?

> More like parking lot memories. Not sure how to not pounce you when you're within reach. Working on it.

He had to laugh, as she put words to his exact struggle over lunch. His entire body had risen to attention the minute she'd entered the banquet hall.

> Please don't work on it too hard. I'm a fan of this problem of yours.

> :D

She typed another response.

> Not knowing what's next is killing me.

> So let's plan what's next.

> ??

Hell, why put off what they both wanted?

> My place? Tonight?

The dots appeared and disappeared a few more times. He liked rendering the chatty woman speechless.

> Evening meeting to cover tonight. Tomorrow night?

He glanced at his calendar. Damn it. A guy's night out – poker with some college buddies.

No good. Saturday night?

She responded with a thumbs up emoji.

Good. Well bad, but good.

Bad??? she responded.

Two more days of not touching you = bad.

He sent her a time and his address and took some solace in the fact that at least if he had to suffer through two more days before he could get his hands back on what he wanted, so did she.

Chapter 13

Cal flicked idly through the channels on his flat screen television Saturday night, but in truth he was merely passing the time before Winnie arrived on his doorstep.

He had teased the woman about the pleasureless rut she was in, but the truth was he might as well have been talking about himself.

No one could deny Cal's dutifulness. He was a responsible employee, a good citizen of Bloomsburo, and an attentive and present son, brother and uncle. He kept his house clean, his yard tidy, he paid his bills and taxes on time, and maintained a fit, healthy body with his running and lifting regime.

For all his love of order and control, Cal had begun to realize that he'd created a life for himself that left little-to-no room for surprise or spontaneity. Sure, he spent plenty of nights shooting pool with friends at the bar.

And yes, he sometimes took pleasure in fairly anonymous hook-ups, but he couldn't remember the last time he had so directly invited pleasure into his own life as he did when he made his proposal to Winnie.

And she'd said yes. That was the most amazing part. He took a risk and she more than willingly complied.

He knew he couldn't commit to a relationship. He couldn't date her, get her hopes up for anything long term, no matter how much a woman like Winnie had to offer. But he'd managed to arrange for a situation that was the best of both worlds—the sweet, physical exploration of a gorgeous woman without any concern about what he couldn't, wouldn't offer her in the long term.

He hadn't been able to stop thinking of the woman's hands on him. The way she grasped at his neck, his hair. The feel of her curvaceous ass, finally in his hands where it belonged.

Shit, he was getting hard already and as much as he relished the thought of continuing getting to know Winnie's body, he didn't want to shock the woman the moment she stepped foot in his house. He had to get himself under control, at least for a little while longer.

They'd agreed to take it slow, even if certain parts of him might prefer a different pace. Despite his best efforts to calm his hunger,

A Time To Fall

127

though, when the soft knock finally rapped on his door, his heart and his dick both perked to attention.

Opening the door, he smiled upon seeing Winnie's face before him. Eager. Nervous. Bursting with the same pent-up sexual energy that flowed through his veins.

He widened the door for her to step through, but before he could say a word, she broke the ice.

"I've identified a flaw in your plan," she said, her gaze flickering to his lips, then his pecks, then back to his face. God, he loved it when she sized him up like that. Women tended to be so timid with him, so intimidated by his looks. There was something damn refreshing about a woman who knew that she had full access to any and every part of him she wanted. That was the kind of thing a man could get used to.

"What's the flaw?" he asked, his body inching closer to hers. It was involuntary, this pull he felt toward her.

"The not-kissing," she said, as she took a step closer to him, nuzzling closer toward his neck.

"Huh?" he managed, his brain not fully functioning now that Winnie's heat was within his reach.

"You promised me pleasure, but the not-kissing that we do most of the hours of most of the days?" Winnie said, stretching up on her tippy toes to kiss the hot length of his neck, "That feels much more like pain than pleasure."

"Mmm," he confirmed, content to let this gorgeous woman feast on his throat. His chin. His lips. Any piece of him she desired. She wasn't wrong. The need he'd felt for her the past few days had been all-consuming and bordered on discomfort.

"Anticipating pleasure is nice though, right?" he finally managed between kisses. "It's like the up, up, up of that first hill on a roller coaster. Anticipation heightens the thrill of the pleasure when it finally arrives."

Her mouth met his fully, planting a warm kiss with her soft lips.

God, those lips. Full and plush. He knew they'd feel amazing anywhere, but one body part in particular craved their caress to the point of pain.

She opened wider for him, filling his mouth with her taste, her warmth that hardened him like steel. His hands involuntary landed on her hips, pulling her tightly against the growing need that tormented his body.

"Mmm," she hummed, her lips vibrating to his. "I guess that's true. Maybe, in a torturous kind of way."

He grinned. She pushed herself off him and her genuine smile shone so sweetly from her face that it made his heart squeeze.

Those sorts of observations—about how nice she was? How sweet? About what a good person she was? Those he had to push aside. This had to be a physical thing.

"So is this officially a booty call? I've never had one of those," she asked, her hands trailing down to the bottom of his T-shirt, slipping underneath and gripping the sides of his bare waist.

Jesus, he could take the woman right there on his doorstep. He could have her clothes off in seconds, bend her over the bench near the door and take her so hard she couldn't form a sentence. He shook the thought from his mind.

"No, it's not a booty call," he said, and it was true. He had a different plan for the evening, despite the pleas from his groin. "Though your booty will be involved."

"I wasn't sure what to wear for such an event." Winnie smiled, gesturing toward her ensemble—a tight pair of tie dye leggings showed off the ample curves of her hips and ass, and a flowy, black sleeveless tunic hung from the tempting shelf of her full breasts.

She was damn delectable.

"Well, I think a trench coat and heels with nothing else underneath would be have been ideal, but this will have to do," he said with a wink, which earned him a laugh.

"I'll make a note for next time."

Next time. Now there was a hell of a thought -- that this woman, arriving at his doorstep so hungry for him, could be a regular occurrence.

"You're perfect, as is," he said, and he meant it, even if her rolling eyes suggested she didn't believe him.

"It smells amazing in here, by the way," she offered.

The observation shook Cal momentarily from his lust.

"Oh, that was my dinner. Sausage Choucroute."

"I don't know what that even means, but it sounds French and sexy as hell."

"I thought about inviting you over to join me, but that would feel too much like a date."

"Understandable. I appreciate your adherence to the ground rules. Anyway, I had some SpaghettiOs while I edited a few stories."

He frowned.

"Don't look at me like that," she scolded. "I've kept myself alive this long."

"I'm not sure that 'kept alive' should be the minimum you're striving for in life."

She refused the bait and changed the subject.

"So if not for dinner, and not technically for a booty call, what am I here for?"

"Dessert."

"Oh, I like the sound of that," she said, reaching her hands around his waist and grabbing the contours of his ass.

Cal couldn't help but laugh at the feisty little manhandler. He grasped her wrists with his hands, pulling them up over her head and pinning her against the back of his front door.

She writhed a bit, resenting her sudden inability to feel him up.

"Not that kind of dessert, Briggs," he said, both hating and loving his role as the disciplinarian. He relished the woman's enthusiasm for his body. He craved it. But he also knew they had to pace themselves, at least at first. "We're talking about a different kind of pleasure. Dessert, with a lesson."

Contented that she wouldn't maul him, he released his hold on her and held her hand, pulling her into the kitchen. It surprised him how intimate it felt to have her small hand tucked in his as he guided her through his home. He couldn't even remember the last time he'd held a woman's hand. Those were the smaller, more intimate connections you went without when you opted for casual hook ups over monogamous dating.

Perhaps more significantly, he *knew* he'd never had a woman over to his house to cook with him.

They turned into the kitchen. The space wasn't overly large, but it was modern, with steel appliances, marble countertops, and top-of-the-line cookware hanging from a mount in the ceiling above a kitchen island with stools on one side. The counters were filled with late-fall produce in every color of the rainbow—eggplants and onions and squash and a half-dozen different types of apples. He

JESS VONN

watched as Winnie ran her fingers over their shiny curves. The woman could even make that look seductive.

"You could host a cooking show in here," she marveled. "It's picture perfect."

"It's functional. That's what matters."

"And freakishly clean. Like all the rest of your house seems to be."

He shrugged.

"Which only confirms the fact that we can never date."

He didn't know why the comment made him internally wince.

"Oh, I'm sure I could straighten you up in no time," he said, involuntarily leaning in to nuzzle Winnie's neck. Her ear. Those warm, intimate spots that he wanted to know so much better.

"No, I don't think you could," she said, leaning back. "And the very first time you came home to find my toothpaste in with the silverware or my underwear in with the DVDs, I think you'd head for the hills."

"I don't know," he said, grabbing at the woman's full bottom, which was quickly growing to be his very favorite part of her body. "I kind of like the idea of finding your panties stashed around my house."

She laughed beneath his touch.

"I have to admit I've put some thought into imagining what kind of panties you wear. Lace? Polka dot? Hello Kitty?"

Her cheeks flushed a deep crimson as she laughed.

"All of the above. That part of my wardrobe is as eclectic as the rest."

He could only imagine. And literally, he was doing just that before her next comment refocused his attention.

"I'll have you know that I've put some thought into what's in your pants as well."

He felt his cock twitch, reminding him just how hard he had to focus to keep his body in control around this woman. And when she let comments like that slip from her full lips, it was damn near impossible.

"I think you're going to have to do some research to find out that answer."

She surprised him by reaching around him and squeezing the sides of his ass, first just to get a feel for the shape of him, but then more gently, feeling for the outline of his underwear.

"Mmm, so you're a brief man," she murmured, nipping at his bicep while her hands squeezed and explored. "Very nice."

"Except when I sleep," he clarified. "Then I'm a nothing man."

Winnie swallowed.

"Well, it's a shame I'll never get to see that in action."

He tilted his head in confusion.

"No sleepovers. We agreed."

"Mmm," he said, his mind lingering for a moment on the thought of his body sleeping next to hers, his mouth breathing deeply as it rested near the warm cushion of her breasts. Both of them content and barely conscious from screwing the hell out of each other.

"That's true. But you never said no naps. Maybe I'll have to crash one of your weekend rituals."

"Now that doesn't sound very restful."

"Not at first, anyway. But once I was through with you, I bet we would sleep like babies."

She pulled his strong frame fully against her while she backed up against the refrigerator.

"You're making it very hard for me to prepare for your cooking lesson, Briggs."

"I can feel that," she said, rubbing her core against the evidence.

"Patience," he said, nominally to her, but damn if he didn't need the reminder just as much. He hadn't anticipated Winnie coming on to him this strong. Now that the floodgates were open, the woman seemed surprisingly eager to explore what was zinging between them.

She pouted, but finally removed her hands from his pants in an attempt to behave.

"I think you'll like this lesson."

"I told you I can't cook. This is futile. I don't want to burn down your gorgeous kitchen."

"If you can read, you can cook. I'll be supervising you every step of the way."

Winnie sighed, looking adorable in her helplessness. "So what's the lesson?"

"Chocolate layer cake with buttercream frosting. Sound good?"

He watched her face light up.

"Sounds heavenly. Chocolate is probably my biggest non-Cal Spencer pleasure."

"Well, it should be a nice evening then, huh?"

"Mmm," she confirmed, pressing a kiss to the side of his neck, and then fully onto his lips. He returned the gesture, deepening the kiss. Feeling the warm connection of their caressing tongues. Feeling his cock harden against the cradle of her sex where it pressed.

"Patience," he repeated, prying himself from her tempting lips. How strange that the gesture could feel so natural and yet so unexpected. Cooking with Winnie could become habit forming.

"So where do we start?"

"Here."

He held up a large index card with the recipe and instructions, which he knew by heart, written in dark ink with his own masculine scrawl. He watched Winnie smile as she brushed her fingers ever so gently over his handwriting on the page with a smile. The gesture felt unnervingly tender, causing another uncomfortable ache in the vicinity of his heart.

Over the next half hour, Cal explained every step of the cake making process. Ever the investigator, Winnie asked question after question, and Cal enjoyed answering each one with confidence, from the purpose of a flour sifter, to the reasoning behind letting the eggs warm to room temperature, to the advantage of greasing *and* flouring the layer cake pans.

Eventually, with only a few spills and a few egg shell extractions, the two-layer cake pans full of shiny chocolate batter made their way into Cal's oven to bake. In the meantime, they started the learning process over again, this time with all of Winnie's questions related to frosting. Along the way, Cal learned something too: watching Winnie Briggs lick chocolate buttercream off her fingers was now officially one of his favorite pastimes.

The time with Winnie in his kitchen flew by. Cooking, drinking the red wine he opened, chatting idly about their days, about the town, their favorite movies.

Sheer pleasure.

And the night was still young.

Before he knew it, the timer beeped, the cakes were out and cool, and Winnie held the icing spatula in her hand, gingerly spreading the soft buttercream around the cake. He guided her hand at times, showing her how to flick her wrist ever so gently in order to create waves and peaks in the frosting, and by the time she had finished, the cake, sitting on a simple glass cake stand in the middle of Cal's kitchen table, looked stunning and delicious.

"You did it," Cal said, drying his hands. He'd washed the last of the dishes while Winnie finished decorating the cake.

Her mouth hung open, seemingly stunned at what her hands had created.

"I've never made anything so beautiful," she whispered in awe.

"I told you that you could cook," he said.

"I cannot believe I just did that. Thank you so much!" She bounced over and threw her arms around him in a tight squeeze. The affection in the gesture unsteadied him.

"And now's the best part," he said.

"What do you mean?"

He looked at her to see if she was messing with him, given how obvious the answer was.

"We eat it."

Her face fell.

"Oh, no," she said, putting her body protectively between Cal and the cake. "We can't eat it. It's too perfect. I'll never make anything so perfect again."

"We can make another one. This doesn't have to be the end. Maybe the next one will be even better than this one."

"Impossible. The first is always the best."

He grinned. There wasn't a first with Winnie yet that had left him filled with anything but pure satisfaction.

"What if we—" he started, but she interrupted.

"Wait, just let me get my phone. I have to take some pictures of it." Winnie scurried out of the kitchen, back to the bench by his door where she'd left her purse.

It only occurred to him then just how in-the-moment he'd been, cooking with Winnie. For almost two hours, they talked, laughed, tasted, worked side by side, and not once did he think of a single care outside of his kitchen. Not even one of his knee-jerk, workaholic impulses to check his email or texts. He chose not to dwell on the significance of the way the woman could hold his full, undivided attention.

She slid back onto the wood floor of his kitchen in her polka dot socks, her donut-printed phone in hand.

"Can I adjust the lighting?" she asked. "I want to capture our cake at its most magnificent."

Cal laughed then nodded, pointing to the switch on the back side of the room. He tried not to overthink how much he liked the sound of Winnie describing something as *theirs*.

She slowly turned the knob that controlled the lighting over the dining area until it was just right, then proceeded to take photos of her first cake from a half-dozen angles.

He stood back and enjoyed the bond between Winnie and her creation, while also savoring the image of Winnie, bent over his kitchen table in her attempt to capture the perfect angle for a photo.

Now that was an image that could stick with a man.

"Think you got its best side?"

"They're all its best side. That's the problem!" she said, coming back over by his side and flipping through the series of photos she just took.

"I'm sure photographers have the same problem with you."

"Oh, please," she scoffed. "I don't hold a candle to this cake. Though we probably should get one shot of me with it, don't you think?

"Absolutely." He watched as she went over to the table and crouched toward her cake, gesturing with her hands toward the chocolatey creation like a game show beauty might showcase a big prize.

Taking a few shots and passing the phone back to Winnie, Cal couldn't help but observe that the woman outshined the cake by miles, but he didn't dare tell her that. She might storm right out, and he wasn't anywhere near done with his lessons in pleasure for the night. In fact, he was damn tired of not tasting her. In two steps, his hands were back home where they belonged—on Winnie Briggs' luscious body.

Chapter 14

One minute Winnie had been snapping photos of the most stunning baked good she'd ever laid claim to, and the next she felt Cal's hot and hungry hands all over her. She'd long thought that nothing could come between her and chocolate, but Cal shot that theory straight to hell.

In an impossibly smooth motion his hands grasped the backs of Winnie's thighs and hoisted her onto the kitchen table, planting his body firmly between her spread legs.

Cal caught her tiny yelp of surprise in his mouth as he devoured her. The sudden nearness of him, the hardness of his body pressed against hers, made Winnie feel as if a flood gate had lifted in her body. Desire and need and hunger rushed through her veins, drowning out any propriety or insecurity or doubt.

Her mind scrambled to process the sensations overwhelming her—not only what she wanted to do to Cal, but also what he was doing to her—his lips on her mouth. Her neck. His hands in her hair. The heat and hunger that radiated from every inch of him.

An overwhelming sense of urgency fueled her as fear and desire comingled into desperation. They commanded every part of her body to experience as much of him as possible. Her hands squeezed at his waist. Grabbed his shirt. Her legs wrapped around his ass and pulled his hardness even tighter against her sex. She needed all of him at once, right now, on her, in her.

"Christ," she heard him groan at her hungry gasps. His own loss of composure only stoked her desire.

"Cal, please," she cried out between frantic kisses. "Please. I'm sorry. I lied."

His head cocked up in concern and his busy hands paused.

"You lied about what?"

Shoot. She was accidentally cock blocking herself.

"I can't take it slow," she panted, wondering why there never seemed to be enough oxygen when Cal touched her body. Her voice shook but the words flew out all the same. "I don't want to take it slow. I want everything you could possibly offer right now, on this kitchen table. Tonight."

Relief washed over his face and a wicked grin twisted his lips. "That wasn't the deal, Briggs."

"I want a new deal."

He shook his head no, his face serious. "You set the ground rules for a reason."

Winnie growled. "I was younger then. Stupider."

He laughed. "Sometimes waiting makes the pleasure that much better."

"I don't have time for more roller coaster analogies, Cal. Just fuck me."

His eyes flashed with shock and hunger as his mind processed her uncharacteristic vulgarity, but as always, his stubbornness trumped all.

"No."

She whimpered.

"You're a woman to be savored," he explained.

Damn the man for trying to flatter her into not having sex. But surely his dick would be on her side, if only she could directly communicate with it. Her shaky hands reached down and fumbled with the button of his jeans.

"Cal, I can't wait. It'll destroy me. I want all of you. Now."

His hands grasped at her wrists and easily pushed them behind her, firmly onto the table so that she reclined before him.

"We made a deal, and we're sticking with it," he said through gritted teeth. "You're not getting in these pants tonight, Briggs."

She sighed in resignation, suddenly wondering if self-control was Cal's greatest superpower.

His gaze grew darker. "Now keep your hands on the table unless I tell you otherwise," Cal ordered.

Pleasure pulsed between her legs at his sudden display of dominance.

"If you think I don't want to rip your clothes off and take you this second, Briggs, you're dead wrong. If I let my body have its way, I'd have been inside you before you even stepped foot past my entryway." His eyes met hers with devastating intensity. "But I said I'd bring you pleasure one inch at a time, and that's what I'll do, even if it literally pains me."

To prove his point, he inched closer, pressing the erection straining his jeans against the cradle of her legs. Her hips bucked instinctively, wanting to increase the pressure and heat between them. She groaned at the sweet, tormenting contact and the singing pleasure it foretold.

"Are we clear?" he asked, that sexy firmness holding steady in his voice.

She nodded reluctantly.

His hands returned to her body, filling her with relief and desire. His strong fingers rubbed along the tops of her thighs, then up over her hips, which squirmed with need. His hands swept under her shirt and she gasped at their warmth on the delicate skin of her stomach.

"You feel so good, Briggs," he said as he feasted on the new parts of her being exposed. She couldn't form words as his hands rose higher and higher until her top bunched up over her cleavage and her lace-covered breasts were in full view. She might have felt self-conscious if his hungry green eyes weren't so worshipful.

"Jesus, Briggs," he whispered as he scanned over her. He slid his hands onto the small of her back and lifted her to a seated position so that he could pull her shirt off over her head.

His hands moved down to her hips and he grabbed them greedily.

"Take off the bra," he demanded. With shaky fingertips, she complied, and she watched his eyes grow wider. She felt wanton, spread open to him like that, topless on his kitchen table and straddling him while he remained fully clothed. He was issuing the orders but she was unraveling him and it felt unbelievable. The power of it brought out a side of her she'd never known.

Winnie leaned back on her hands once more, presenting her bare, reclined body for his consideration. He bent over her and his mouth met hers in a deep kiss. Every inch of Winnie's body hummed as his mouth moved slowly, torturously, down to her neck. Over to her ear. His lips brushed the line of her collarbone and no matter how sensual each connection was, she feared that he'd never arrive at where she needed him most.

"Cal, please," she begged, arching her back, offering her breasts up closer to his face. His hands rubbed up her waist until they cupped her breasts, and a groan ripped from his throat.

"You're even more beautiful than I imagined," he offered before his mouth kissed the taut tip of her rosy nipple. "And trust me, I imagined it."

That she could capture the sexual imagination of a man like Cal Spencer was too much to consider now, especially with his mouth opening wider, sucking her nipple into the hot, silky warmth of his mouth.

Right now she couldn't dwell on anything except the sensations this man created in her body. She moaned as bolts of pleasure shot through her body and set her sex throbbing.

His mouth moved to her other breast and her hands involuntarily clutched at his shirt, desperate for it to get out of her way. She wanted his skin. She wanted to feel the warm expanse of his body pressed up against hers and despite his cruel restrictions regarding his lower half, he hadn't said a damn thing about her having to keep out of his shirt.

He leaned back and, in that distinctly male way, whipped off his cotton tee in a fraction of a second. She wished she had the composure to play it cool and not gasp, but gasp she did when his lean, toned body was suddenly revealed to her.

"My goodness," she muttered. Never before had she imagined a man of this sheer physical flawlessness, beneath her fingers. But he was here and she'd enjoy every inch of him while she could. For the first time in her life, Winnie swore she wouldn't overthink it. She'd just appreciate the opportunity literally at her fingertips.

She caressed her hands across the strength of his chest, through the sparse patch of soft hair that covered his pounding heart, the narrowing plain of his torso, across the abs slightly scored into his golden skin and the faint trail of hair that inched down, down, down toward a land of forbidden pleasure.

"Cal, you're too perfect," she whispered, her mouth kissing his chest. The hot skin. The soft patches of hair. The hard tautness of his nipple. She breathed him in, those woody undertones of his cologne mixed with something distinctly male. His skin felt warm and salty beneath her lips, a taste that could quickly grow addictive.

"How are you real?" she whispered into his ribs as her hands stroked the strong contours of his back. He groaned as her lips pressed into his solar plexus, tasting him for her own satisfaction. Her mouth moved hungrily, up, up, toward his collarbone, his neck. She pulled down on his shoulders, needing to bring every inch of him within tasting distance. He leaned into her until their bare chests pressed together, melding in a symphony of sharp desire and fiery heat. The warmth of their bodies, the sweat and the pheromones, overtook her. She'd never before pressed her bare flesh against this man, yet somehow it felt like a reconnection. Like a coming home.

He kissed her like that, long and slow, syphoning off from her mouth the pleasure that percolated up from between her legs. The weight of him pressing into her made her sex throb. It seemed impossible how she could be at once flooded with pleasure and desire from this man, yet still starved for him. She wanted him everywhere at once. There could never be too much of him. Enough of him.

He pressed harder against her, gently grinding his hips so that the hardness of his erection tormented the cradle of her legs. When his mouth took in her breast once more, she cried out his name, the only word her mind could conjure.

Without moving from his sexy perch between her legs, Cal's torso twisted as he reached toward the table, revealing the outline of side muscles Winnie never even knew existed. Luckily she didn't need to name them, she only had to run her fingers along them. His hand reached out toward their tempting cake, which patiently waited a foot away. He dipped his thumb into a wave of buttercream frosting.

Turning back toward Winnie, his hand slowly reached toward her face and she parted her lips as his thumb, covered in sweet softness, entered her mouth. She moaned around it, sucked it, entranced by the hotness of the gesture and the sweet, indulgent satisfaction of the thick cream on her tongue. It was her first taste of being filled by him and she didn't want it to end. He groaned as her tongue and lips stroked him long after the frosting was gone.

Eventually he pulled his thumb away, but before she could process the loss, his lips replaced it, opening her, tasting her, hungry for the warmth and lingering sweetness her mouth could offer.

"More," was all she could say. More of his body. His heat. More of his mouth. More of the sinful chocolate confection the two of them had whipped up with their own hands.

He leaned back, grinning, as if there were no other word he'd rather hear fall from her lips. He reached again for the cake stand, pulling it closer to them. Smiling at the sticky, wicked game he started, she stretched out a finger, shaking slightly from the pleasure flooding her veins, and scooped it through the velvety cream. She began reaching it up to his perfect lips, but he surprised her by shaking his head no.

Her eyes narrowed in confusion, but she watched, transfixed, as he grabbed her hand and guided the finger to her own bare breast, swiping a sweet, chocolate peak onto her tightened nipple.

And then his mouth lowered, a groan escaping his lips as he tasted her cream-covered bud, as his tongue pressed firm and hot up the inner slope of her breast, and the sensations bombarded her—skin and heat and pressure and sweat and chocolate and all that was right in the world. She lost track of time, of place and of any lingering doubts that she wasn't exactly where she was supposed to be.

She returned the favor, feeding him cream from her fingers, sucking it from the hard plain of his stomach. She'd never look at frosting the same way. Or chocolate. Or kitchen tables. Or sex. Or anything. She never thought she'd be led so consensually to her demise. This man would obliterate her, but she'd volunteered for it and would do it again in a heartbeat.

The center of her sex throbbed harder, making her feel like she would burst.

Cal leaned back, and she shivered from the sudden lack of connection to his strong warmth.

"Are you wet for me, Briggs?" he asked, his green eyes ablaze with intensity.

"God, yes."

"Are you thinking of what you wish I'd do about it?"

"Mmm-hmm," she purred in agreement, her hands grasping around him to cup his impossibly muscular ass. That ass would be her downfall.

He rubbed his hands along her neck and breasts.

"Are you thinking of what you want to do to me?"

She nodded.

"Good. Then I'm going to send you home."

"What?" she cried desperately as her stomach sank. She had too much hard evidence between her legs to suggest that he wasn't just as ready to keep going as she was. "Why are you such a mean person?"

Once more, he met her pout with a grin. He reached down and grabbed her lacy bra from where it sat on the floor and handed it to her. She laced her arms through and after a bit of anatomical jostling that appeared to captivate Cal, she managed to attach the hook in the back and get everything back in place.

"I do have a homework assignment for you, though," he said.

Now that peaked her curiosity. He placed her shirt back over her head. His hands brushed across her shoulders, along her breasts, smoothing everything back into place.

Well, everything but her tortured libido, the bastard.

"Homework?"

He walked to the other side of the kitchen and Winnie couldn't help but admire the sheer sex appeal of the man, walking around his gorgeous kitchen in a perfectly fitted pair of jeans and nothing else. Muscles all through his arms and back flexed as he reached up to grab a Pyrex dish and lid from a high shelf and a cake cutter from the drawer below.

He walked back to Winnie, who'd scooted herself off the table and was slowly regaining her land legs. He rotated the cake plate to the side of the confection that hadn't been destroyed in their seduction and he cut off a massive slab, sliding it into the glass container and sealing it up with the round red rubber lid. He grabbed the handwritten recipe card, and placed it on top of the container for her to keep, pushing it toward her.

"For you."

"My homework is eating cake? You may be my favorite teacher ever." And wasn't that more of a truth than she wanted to consider... One night of fairly chaste foreplay with Cal Spencer had already rocked her sexual world.

"That's part of it. The other part though..." he started, cupping her face with his hands and pulling her in for one last deep kiss—one final sweep of warmth and sweetness that plucked her deepest sensual strings. Her free hand clutched at the strong heat of his back while it was still in reach. His voice grew low and raspy. "I want you to go home, crawl into bed, and touch yourself thinking of me. I want my name on your lips when you come. Can you do that for me?"

Winnie's heart thumped in her chest and her swollen sex ached with need but she nodded with a small smile. She'd never been the best student, but something told her she could ace the hell out of this assignment. She might even secure the title of teacher's pet.

Chapter 15

On Sunday afternoon, Cal found himself exactly where he had been two weeks earlier: trying to run Winnie Briggs out of his system.

His feet pounded the pavement in an especially strenuous pace, crushing the crisp leaves that the afternoon winds had blown from the trees. But he wasn't heading toward his mom's house like usual, because that would mean running toward Winnie, too.

After last night, he needed some space. Not because she presented a problem. Hell, to be honest, it was because she didn't. Instead, she presented the kind of temptation that filled Cal with anxiety. He felt the urge to physically escape whatever powerful hold the woman seemed to have over him.

Geographic distance didn't seem to be helping much, though. Despite his labored breathing and screaming muscles, his double-crossing mind happily floated back to the night before, to memories of cake and cream and the soft heat of Winnie's divine breasts under his tongue. Memories of the warm suction of her mouth that foreshadowed the deep pleasures her body could offer.

Jesus, he hadn't restricted himself to such heavy petting since high school, yet somehow, with that woman, it had turned him on beyond measure. He wasn't accustomed to waiting for what he wanted, and doing so heightened the hell out of every minute.

After Winnie left last night, Cal had done a little homework of his own, needing to take his pleasure from his own hand. As he'd stroked himself, it was only Winnie his mind could imagine. Her plush lips moaning. The feel of her tongue on his fingers. Her eyes flashing with pleasure. Her hungry hands. The taste of chocolate on her skin.

The orgasm that ripped violently through him had left him shaking with its intensity. Frankly the power of what they were conjuring scared the hell out of him.

He needed space from her energy—from that damned pull she seemed to have on him, and punishing his body for its fixation on her on this run seemed like the best solution. So cloudy was his own mind, however, that he didn't notice the actual clouds gathering above him. A few fat sprinkles of rain on his face and arms shook him from his daydreams and he realized a downpour was imminent.

Shit.

He'd run at least four miles from home by now, so he braced himself for complete saturation. Except that he suddenly realized where he actually was—less than two blocks from Carter's place.

He sprinted the remaining distance in the quickening rain, taking shelter on Carter's porch before the worst of the downpour began. Carter must have heard him sprint up the steps, because the front door swung wide open.

"Well, look what the storm washed up," Carter said with a laugh, opening the door to let his soggy friend step in and get relief from the downpour.

"Happen to have a spare towel?" Cal asked as rain dripped off his hair and lashes onto his cheeks. Carter dashed to the hallway closet and grabbed a hand towel to toss to his friend.

"Looks like it should blow over soon enough, anyway," Carter offered while Cal dried off, glancing out the front door before closing it behind them. Having grown up in the Midwest, both men were accustomed to the sweeping thunderstorms that could start and stop in less time than it took to pop up a bowl of popcorn. "Come in. I'll get you something to drink."

"Thanks, man," Cal said, scanning the home that his friend had lived in since moving back to town and joining the Bloomsburo police force seven years earlier. "I hope I'm not interrupting anything."

Cal noticed the model car kit in progress on the kitchen table, and he had to smile. Carter had been tinkering with those kits for as long as Cal could remember, though he could attest that Carter's skills had improved greatly from those early attempts back in elementary school. Today he was damn near professional at it. Cal had always lacked the patience, not to mention the fine motor skills, to join in his friend's hobby.

He glanced around Carter's house, taking in the familiar-yet-unfamiliar space. There had been a time when Cal wiled away hours here, but that was before. Before Carter had lost everything. Before fucking Wyatt had twisted all of their worlds into something ugly and broken.

He tried not to notice the feminine touches that still lingered in every room of the house. He tried not to think of the room upstairs that was supposed to be the nursery.

Cal wasn't proud, and he knew it didn't make him a great friend, but only a freak rainstorm four miles into a run could get him back inside Carter's house. There were too many ghosts here, even if those ghosts were probably why Carter himself chose to stay.

But here he was. And for better or for worse, the shit-eating look on his friend's face shook Cal from his depressing train of thought.

"So," Carter started vaguely, and Cal's brain caught up. The last time he'd seen Carter had been at the Guiding Star meeting, sitting next to Winnie and flirting openly with her just to piss him off.

"So," Cal countered, refusing to give an inch.

"How's Winnie?"

"What the hell kind of question is that?" Cal asked, his temper flaring much faster than usual. Other than his mother, there was no one who could see through Cal's bullshit quite as quickly or as thoroughly as his oldest friend. It never failed to piss Cal off, given his preference for opacity.

"It's an honest question. I saw the glares you were shooting me at the meeting on Thursday. I'm not an idiot."

Cal scoffed.

"If you want to pretend there's nothing between you and Winnie, then fine, I'll pretend, too."

Cal ruffled his hand through his wet hair. "Jesus, Carter. I don't know."

Carter stood quietly, waiting for his friend to elaborate.

"There's a thing," Cal begrudgingly relented.

"A thing?"

"Yes. We...well, we're feeling things out."

"Literally?"

Cal glared at Carter, but his non-answer was as good as a confirmation and only made his friend's grin grow that much wider.

"No shit," Carter said, his tone coming off as partly shocked, partly impressed.

"It's nothing I planned. It's the opposite of what I planned," Cal confessed. "I just... well, I couldn't help myself. And she's happy to participate."

"So, what's the problem?"

"The problem? Only that we're professional associates. That my meddling mother is her landlady. That..." He trailed off, lost in his thoughts.

"What?"

Cal sighed deeply. "It's just... it's stronger than usual, my attraction to her. Not just physically, either. It's not good. I shouldn't have started this."

Carter assessed him in that haughty way he had. Granted, the man had survived an unfathomable personal loss, but Cal didn't appreciate the sense of moral authority he came out the other side with. It was as if Carter's own experience with loss and grief gave him the right to issue out carpe-diem style life advice to everyone in his midst.

"Have you ever wondered, just once in your life, what would happen if you could get your head out of your own ass?" Carter asked.

Cal stood up from his stool, testosterone surging defensively through his veins.

"Carter—" he started before his friend cut him off. If anyone understood Cal's legacy, understood just what a selfish bastard Cal's father had been, it should be Carter.

"No, man, I'm serious," his typically cool-headed friend shouted. "You're so used to playing the victim, I'm not sure you'd recognize happiness if it walked up and slapped you across the face. Winnie's a hell of a catch. She's adorable. Funny. Smart. Professional. And I'm just sitting here wondering why you're wracking your brain to find every possible reason not to give her a chance."

"It's not like that—"

"It is, Cal," his friend countered, "and don't tell me it isn't, because I know you better than you know yourself."

Cal scowled.

"You ever consider actually giving someone a chance? If anyone ever deserved a fair shake, it's Winnie."

"I know she does, damn it. She has nothing to do with it. It's me."

You couldn't grow up with a father like Cal's, with the memories of his spectacularly selfish failures as a husband and a dad, and not decide then and there to keep your distance from sweet and lovely women like Winnie Briggs. He would stay single forever before he'd accept that fate.

Carter shook his head.

"You just keep telling yourself that, man."

Cal began his way to the door, feeling recuperated, resentful, full of testosterone and more than ready to get out of this space.

"Looks like the storm has passed."

"Cal—" Carter called out after him, but he was already out the door. He ignored his friend. He ignored his pleading eyes, and his damned frustrating rationality. He ignored his heightened perspective on what it was to have loved and lost.

"Thanks for the water, man," he yelled behind him on the way out the door.

And just like that, Carter joined Winnie on the list of people Cal was trying to run out of his brain.

~-~-~-~-~-~-

"So, where is Corey again?" Winnie asked about Evie's husband, pulling a warm slice of pizza out of one of the two boxes she brought to her friend's house for dinner Sunday evening.

Before Evie could answer, a tiny set of footsteps pattering through the dining room toward where the women sat at the kitchen counter.

"I want to be with Winnie!" Ella, Evie's five-year-old daughter, cried, her special blankie trailing behind her as she ran straight into Winnie's embrace. They'd only met a few times, but Ella was already deeply enchanted with Winnie, and the feeling was mutual. Winnie knew that the little girl's fieriness made Evie's life hard now, but she also knew it would serve her well down the road.

Winnie gave her a squeeze, taking in her wild, curly blonde hair and her Strawberry Shortcake dress. She was like a little Princess Merida in the flesh.

"Ella, you're supposed to be having a picnic with the boys," Evie sighed, glancing across the house to the family room where a blanket was spread on the floor and her two-year-old twins were destroying their respective slices of pizza in front of the TV. Evie had already confessed to Winnie that the boys skipped their nap today, meaning they were even touchier, and she even more exhausted, than normal. (Hence why Winnie offered to show up with pizza in hand.)

"Are you two having a girl's night?" Ella asked, her lips turning into a well-rehearsed pout as she spied the chocolate on the coffee table. Winnie couldn't engage with Ella without remembering her own little brother. Born into the family as a complete surprise when she was 9, Johnny had been like her very own baby doll.

"Maybe," Winnie offered.

"Well, I'm a girl!" she offered, her hands shooting dramatically onto her hips.

"You're a little girl. This girl's night is only for big girls."

"That's not fair!"

"I'm sorry, sweetie. How about if I come and watch ten minutes of your show, only if you promise that after that you'll stay put and help watch your little brothers?" Winnie asked.

"Okay!" she cried, delightedly sprinting back to the family room.

When Winnie returned ten minutes later, she was glad to see Evie halfway through her first glass of wine and enjoying the dinner she didn't have to cook.

"You're amazing. Thanks for handling that," Evie said gratefully.

"Um, no. You're amazing because you handle that every other night of the year."

Evie just rolled her eyes.

"What will truly be amazing is if I survive these years, that's for sure."

"So, where is Corey?" Winnie asked again. She tried to keep her tone neutral, she really did, even if the man seemed like bad news. Evie didn't like to talk much about her husband or her marriage, but the clues Winnie had picked up during their various conversations did not paint the guy in a very positive light.

"Every fall he has these home shows he goes to all over the Midwest," she explained about her husband, who helped run the family business, Finnegan Building Company, in town. "He's usually gone Friday through Monday, at least a few weekends a month."

So, he's gone the only time of the week he actually has to spend with his family, Winnie silently observed. But she wouldn't trash talk him. Not yet. At least not out loud.

"That's got to be hard."

"It helps when friends come over and deliver pizza and wine."

"Well, I am always available for such support services," Winnie laughed.

"Plus, I usually try to book some extra shifts at Dewey's. For everything else you could say about Betty Jean, she's happy to watch the kids for me any time I ask. I know she really enjoys it."

"That really is great."

"Enough about my pathetic existence. Why did you call an emergency girls' night? What happened?"

"I did a very good thing that is likely to end up being a very bad thing," Winnie said, her cheeks flushing as she thought back to the night before. God, had it only been last night that Cal's hands and mouth had explored her so body so thoroughly?

Well, her upper body at least. Thoughts of him lowering his explorations to her bottom half made her fingers tremble. She'd probably be rendered speechless by the time they rounded third base.

"Spill it now and if you leave out a single torrid detail this friendship is officially over," Evie demanded, refilling her glass of wine and settling in for a sexy, voyeuristic story, which lasted almost as long in the re-telling as it did in the actual moment.

Winnie was a storyteller by trade, after all, but rarely did she have such extraordinary source material.

"You are officially my new hero," Evie concluded after Winnie finished the play-by-play, a dopey, pleased look on her face. "That man has never opened up the gates for someone around here. If word gets out about this, some women are going to be very displeased with you—women who've been trying to wear that man down for a decade. Then you waltz into town and seal the deal in two weeks, you saucy minx!"

Winnie snorted.

"One, I did not seal the deal. Though I hope to," she said with a wink. "And two, word cannot get out. That's part of the deal. So this conversation between us tonight never happened, alright?"

Evie nodded eagerly.

"I can't remember the last time I had a juicy secret to keep," Evie said. "This is so much fun. I'm loving being able to live vicariously through you."

Winnie smiled, but before she could respond, she heard a cry of despair from the family room. Evie sighed as they both realized that the kids had likely entered the time-to-go-to-bed-before-someone-gets-hurt phase of the evening.

"That's probably my cue to get out of your hair so you can wrangle your beasts into their beds," Winnie said, standing and picking up their dirty plates. Evie shoulders slumped, but she looked much more relaxed and content than she had when Winnie arrived. "I'd offer to stay and help, but something tells me that it would only make it harder for you."

"Yeah," Evie sighed, "it's probably time to stop pretending that I have no human lives I'm responsible for." She met Winnie at the sink and gave her a huge hug.

"Thank you for dinner. And grown-up conversation. I can't begin to tell you how much I appreciate it."

Winnie was surprised at the tears filling the woman's eyes, but grateful for the bond that had already formed between them. As much as she missed Bree with every fiber of her being, it was so comforting to be growing a new friendship with someone right in town.

After giving each of the pizza-covered kiddos a hug and a kiss, Winnie made her way to her car and drove the short route home to the She Shed. Getting out of the car, she felt full of contentment after her conversation with Evie. Humming quietly to herself, she didn't pay much attention to her surroundings as she walked up to the porch. That is until she heard some giggling in the flower bushes in front of the cottage.

She stopped in her tracks, momentarily convinced that she'd lost her mind. She took one more step toward the door before she heard another bout of laughter, this time louder. She turned on her heel and walked quietly over to the noisy bush, where she discovered two tiny fairies peaking from beneath the blooms.

Twin fairies, with matching pairs of sparkling wings on their backs and identical manes of curly, strawberry blond hair, a clear gift from their grandmother's DNA.

Cal's nieces.

She glanced quickly over to Rhonda's house, suddenly remembering that it was Sunday and thus all of the Spencers would be gathered for their weekly family dinner. While she could see figures moving inside through Rhonda's windows now glowing in the twilight sky, luckily no one seemed to notice her out in the yard yet.

Well, except the fairies. She turned her gaze back to her visitors and her heart skipped a beat when she noticed the matching friendship bracelets both girls wore—the same bracelets Cal had been twirling between his fingers at that first football game.

"I didn't know this was a fairy garden," Winnie said, her eyes widening in wonder as she glanced at the girls.

More giggles.

"We're not real fairies," said the one on the left.

"We just like to pretend," her sister elaborated.

"I like to pretend, too," Winnie confided. "I'm Winnie, by the way. I live in the cottage now. Do you visit here often?"

"That's our nana's cottage," the sister on the left said once more. She clearly seemed to do most of the speaking for the pair. "No one would tell us about you so we wanted to catch you for ourselves."

"Ahh," Winnie said. "Now you know I'm real. If you're not fairies, who are you?"

"I'm Mary," the talkative one said, before answering for her sister, too. "That's my sister Lulu. We love to play in our nana's gardens."

"I don't blame you. They're so beautiful. And they feel a little magic."

"Yes!" the quieter girl agreed excitedly, before dropping her gaze shyly to the ground.

"Nana is about to serve up cake," Mary explained, looking back to the house. "You should come over and have some. She makes the best cake in the world."

"No, that's not true," Lulu countered. "Uncle Cal's chocolate cake is probably the best in the world."

A crimson blush rushed to Winnie's cheeks as her brain made the erotic connection between Cal and chocolate cake—memories that felt too naughty to even *think* about in the presence of innocent children. She needed to hide herself away in the She Shed before she was forced to face the man in front of his family.

"Oh, I hate to miss out on dessert, but I have some work I need to do," Winnie offered as the girls stood up, preparing to make their way back to the house. "Thank you for the offer, though. I'll have to take a rain check."

The girls nodded, prancing their way back through the gardens, the sunset sending soft rays of light bouncing off their sparkly wings. She laughed as she heard one ask the other, "What's a rain check?"

Winnie wasn't convinced that the girls weren't at least part fairy, but there wasn't time to dwell on that now. She rushed up the stairs, into the cottage, and shut the door behind her, her heart beating wildly, as if she were fleeing from a crime scene.

She turned around and peeked through a tiny crack in her kitchen blinds, watching the girls bound their way up the deck steps toward a sliding glass door leading into Rhonda's house. The door opened and Cal's unmistakable frame filled the space. Though she was too far away to see their expressions in the darkening night, she could see the girls tugging on his arms excitedly and pointing back toward Winnie's cottage.

Winnie could feel his gaze directed at her, even if she couldn't read his expression from the distance. How would he react to learning that his nieces were just as meddling as his mother?

She'd have to wait to find out. He affectionately tousled both girls' hair, and then closed the door behind him, separating them once more neatly into their two separate worlds. His night would be spent with his warm, loving family—sharing food and laughter. And she'd be here in the cottage on her own.

Her heart squeezed in a way that it had almost every single day since her parents' accident. That squeeze that reminded her of the irreplaceable things her life was missing.

Tears threatened. That familiar wave of self-pity and melancholy wanted to wash over her, but she took a deep breath, poured a big glass of wine, and pushed the urge aside. She didn't have time to feel sorry for herself. She had a story to edit before going into the office tomorrow. And for the millionth quiet, lonely night, work once more served as the dam that held back a tidal wave of grief.

Chapter 16

"I understand, Mrs. Hoffman," Winnie sighed into the phone, trying to conjure up a bit of patience for the woman and her endless story tips. It seemed as though no amount of refusals was enough to dissuade her. She was currently trying to persuade Winnie to pursue a story about cat-carrying backpacks. She'd seen a feature story about the trend on a morning talk show and wondered if anyone in the Bloomsburo area was using them.

"It is a very unique product. I'll tell you what," Winnie relented. "I'll keep a look out for anyone using one around town, and if I find someone, I promise to pursue a follow-up story."

This contented the woman for the time being, though it would be another five minutes before Winnie could get her off the phone due to a meandering story about the origins of the apple slab pie recipe that she used this morning when baking some treats for the fire station.

Winnie huffed as she finally set down the phone receiver that had grown heavy in her hand. For an octogenarian, Esther Hoffman demonstrated a heck of a lot of tenacity.

And even better, her ramblings kept Winnie's mind of off Cal, which was no small task. Almost daily, the man seemed to occupy a larger and larger part of her mental space, and given the smallest opportunity, her thoughts drifted happily toward memories of chocolate cake and satiny lips and muscles she didn't know the anatomical names for, but she could now recognize by touch.

Alas, this afternoon was not about any of those things, so when the call ended, Winnie returned her attention to her cluttered desk, sifting through various Post-it notes and a hastily scribbled to-do list. She needed to lay out a two-page photo spread for the next issue. She needed to follow-up on a phone call with a state representative running for re-election. She needed to edit her story on the tax levy proposal by the school board. She needed to review the city council meeting agenda for Tuesday (since they actually bothered to send her one this time) and follow-up with the city clerk on some information requests that could help her begin to untangle some of the mayoral nonsense.

And she needed to make some progress on that special section about Bloomsburo. God, she'd totally forgotten about her lack of progress on that front. She and Cal's dinner "meeting" had so quickly dissolved into blatant flirtation that they hadn't so much uttered the words "Bloomsburo Days."

Despite Cal's wicked proposition and his delicious follow through on it over the weekend, Winnie knew she'd soon have to face him in a more professional context. They had work to do together that had nothing to do with their bodies. That is unless he passed her off to Danny the Intern again, but she imagined that they'd worked past that particular situation by now.

But something told her that calling up Cal to talk shop wouldn't necessarily end in professional productivity either. That was a problem she was going to need to solve, because the special section needed to get put together in the next week despite her interest in interrogating the Chamber director in other ways.

She pulled out her phone and began a text message to Cal.

We need to talk about Bloomsburo Days!!

His response arrived in seconds.

We need to do lots of things, Briggs. Did you do your homework?

The smile that spread across her face was involuntary. This was why she shouldn't have started with the to-do list item related to him. Though if she were honest with herself, this was exactly why she started with him.

A couple of times.

A+

Lord, this man was trouble.

Cal, I have stuff to get done. I need your help.

I have stuff to do too. Stuff = you.

She rolled her eyes, loving every second of his absurdity. He wrote her more.

> Promise to meet me tonight and I'll answer any questions you email me.

> Tonight!?

> Yes.

One arrogant word. As if she couldn't deny his beckoning. And dang it, he was right. She told herself she'd have to wait much longer to reconnect with the man. She'd toyed with the idea of avoiding him until the weekend, which seemed torturously far away from where she sat on Monday.

> You'll send me answers to my questions by the end of the day?

> I swear.

> If you don't, I'll stand you up.

> OKAY, now I actually mean it.

> You're bad.

> True. But isn't that why you're writing me?

Touché. The man understood his appeal. She texted again.

> Where? When?

He stayed silent for a moment and she wished she could read his thoughts. The She Shed would be off limits for the foreseeable future, given that one of the most important clauses of their agreement was that Rhonda couldn't catch wind of what they were doing. That would prove tricky if she found her son's car parked outside of Winnie's cottage late at night. She also didn't want to overextend her welcome at his house, no matter how nice of a time they'd had there over the weekend.

Cosgrove Hill. Moonlight hike. I'll bring the blanket.

Winnie's heart thrilled at the possibility. An outdoor tryst? That'd be a first for her. She had a feeling that Cal possessed an endless string of tantalizing firsts for her to experience. She had a stronger feeling that she'd like to knock them off her to-do list with as much haste as possible, starting tonight.

It's a plan. Unless I have to stand you up for bad behavior.

Send the questions already, woman.

And she did just that. With the detailed answers returning a mere twelve minutes after she sent them, his response time was record-breaking.

~-~-~-~-~-~-

Winnie didn't have much time at home between wrapping up her workday and grabbing a burger and some quick conversation with Evie at Dewey's, but in the twenty minutes she was there, Rhonda Spencer managed to catch her.

The soft knock on the door made Winnie jump, and her nerves didn't calm even slightly when she saw her landlady's sweet face at the door. It was less than comfortable to face the mother of a man whose sex appeal was short-circuiting her brain.

Winnie focused on the woman before her who, once again, held a red wicker basket of food—brownies and banana bread and some homemade jam, by the look of it.

The Spencers were a family of feeders, and Winnie wasn't mad about it.

"For you!" Rhonda said warmly. Today her strawberry-white curls were twisted in braids that hung down her chest. They fit well with the distressed overalls she wore over a striped boat neck shirt. Her feet, like usual, were bare.

Winnie reached out for the basket and lifted it closer so she could smell the goodies inside. "You're too kind. This looks amazing!"

"I love to bake, and always end up with more than I could possibly use."

"Do you want to come in?" Winnie asked, moving aside to make room for Rhonda to enter.

"Just for a minute. I don't want to bother you if you have plans."

Must. Not. Think. About. The plans.

"I have a bit of time."

Rhonda took a seat at the round table she'd furnished in the kitchen, and Winnie joined her.

"The place looks wonderful," Rhonda said as she quickly surveyed the space.

"Oh, it's a mess."

"That's what's wonderful about it! It looks lived-in. The mantle looks fantastic. I left that clear on purpose. I figured that whoever came here next would appreciate a few blank canvases around the space."

"Did you have lots of interest in the rental ad when you first put it up?"

"Heavens, yes," Rhonda laughed. "Far more than I expected. I didn't know what I was getting myself into."

Winnie couldn't bring herself to ask the next obvious question, but Rhonda answered it anyway.

"You were an easy choice. I probably read twenty responses to the ad before I read yours, and the second it arrived in my inbox, I knew you'd be the one."

"How?" Winnie asked, unable to help herself. She'd never been "the one" in *any* context.

"You could spell, you had a lovely voice to your writing, and you said that you were looking for a place to both find yourself and to get lost in. That was it, because that's what this space had always been to me. Then after we talked on the phone, I knew it was fated."

Winnie couldn't help but smile. "So did you just stop by to drop off sweets and lavish me with compliments?" Winnie joked.

"No, I'm afraid I didn't. Though if they softened you to me a bit, that would only help my cause."

Winnie's stomach sank. She had a feeling she was about to be issued another Sunday dinner invitation. Accepting would be more impossible now than ever, given the sudden shift in her relationship with Cal. A sizeable part of her heart ached at the realization that she could have the man, but not his family.

"I have a favor to ask you," Rhonda said, her brows narrowing slightly in determination.

"What is it?"

"I'm having a special celebration this Friday."

Butterflies swarmed her stomach. She hated nothing more than saying no to this generous woman, but some things had to be done.

"Before you say no—and you can say no," Rhonda continued, "let me say that it's a once-a-year event, so you won't have to worry about signing up for a weekly commitment for the foreseeable future. Plus, other neighbors and friends will be there."

That made it a little more palatable, even if Cal wouldn't like it at all.

"What's the celebration?" she asked, her curiosity getting the better of her.

"It's my annual equinox feast and bonfire."

Winnie's eyes widened.

"Mabon is what the Pagans call it. A time to give thanks for bounty and harvest. And this year, you are part of my bounty. You have to be there."

Winnie sighed. The woman was as flattering and persuasive as her son, despite their very different aims.

"I just don't know..." she lied. She'd love nothing more than to go. To meet Cal's sisters and see those cute little fairies once more. To eat as much of Rhonda and Cal's food as she could possibly manage in one sitting. To revel in the pleasure of joining a big family for a special annual event. Even if she would be an interloper, she wanted to soak up those feelings of togetherness and warmth and affection so that they could sustain her during on the months ahead. Her least favorite time of the year was upon them, with its endless string of family holidays that she'd spend alone, given just how spread out her distant cousins were. Cost made the travel difficult, and if she were honest, she always loathed being the add-on orphan, even if she knew that's not how her extended family felt about her.

Her heart sank at the realization that this year she wouldn't even have Bree by her side during the holidays.

"Plus, it'll take over the whole yard." Rhonda continued her pitch with the dedication of a car salesman. "You really can't avoid it. The cottage is an intimate part of my outdoor space, and it would just feel wrong to cut you out of it."

Yes. Yes. Yes. Winnie's mind whirled. But what would Cal think about her presence there? It was a special family event, and she wouldn't want to ruin it by her awkward presence. She concluded that her only option was to ask the man himself.

"For now can I say that I'll think about it?" Winnie asked.

Rhonda reached over and pulled Winnie into a deep hug, squealing in delight. Winnie knew that Rhonda interpreted Winnie's maybe as a yes. Only time would tell if she'd have to disappoint the woman again.

"Okay. I'll take that for now."

"I'll try to let you know by tomorrow. I do appreciate the invitation. You've made me feel so welcome."

"It's impossible not to love you, Winnie. I do hope you realize that."

She gave Winnie's hand a squeeze and made her way back out the door before she could notice Winnie's tears welling.

Chapter 17

Cal wasn't sure how Winnie would respond to his suggested meet-up spot, but he felt more than pleased with the possibilities that Cosgrove Hill held, and not just because it was the town's infamous make-out spot.

Ever since that first fantasy he'd had about Winnie, he'd been desperate to see the woman spread out on a soft blanket in the grass. Tonight seemed like an ideal opportunity, and what better way to help her acclimate to her new community than with a little bit of heavy petting on The Hill? The sky was already dark, the fall air was cool and the light breeze rustled the crisping leaves in the trees.

He was so grateful she'd texted him today. He told himself he'd let her make the next move. He arranged everything about their last meet up. Part of him wanted to see how long it would take her to reach out. Part of it felt like an act of self-preservation. Now that he equated Winnie's breasts with the taste of chocolate, the woman—and her many compelling assets—became that much more difficult to stop thinking about.

His stomach dropped when her headlights pulled into the otherwise empty parking lot. He figured the place wouldn't be too busy on a weeknight, and he was right. Their solitude and the opportunities it presented thrilled him.

Winnie stepped out of her car, practically bouncing her way over to him. Her jubilance was infectious. She threw her arms around his neck and pressed a soft kiss to his lips, sending all the important parts of his body into alert. As he wound his arms around her lower back and pulled her softness tightly against him, he couldn't help but notice how good it felt to be connected to her in the crisp, cool fall air. Without the complications of a relationship, without the weight of expectations, they could just plain enjoy one another. It was damn refreshing.

"You showed up," he teased, his hand pushing back a curl from where it fell on her face.

"You did what you were told."

"Well, you were extorting me. I really had no choice."

She grinned, her eyes shining with humor in the final minutes of twilight.

"And you were bribing me with promises of sexy time. I had no choice, either."

"I guess we're well matched."

He offered her the hand that wasn't holding a folded-up blanket and when her fingers curved into his, when he felt the warmth and softness of her skin on hers, his heart tightened.

"Hey, can I ask you something quick," Winnie said, stopping in her tracks and turning her suddenly serious eyes up to his.

"Of course."

"Your mom stopped by tonight," she said with reluctance. "She brought me some really delicious treats."

That sounded like his mom.

"She was trying to butter me up," Winnie continued.

And that sounded even more like his mom. "What for?" he asked.

He watched nervousness wash over her face.

"She wants me to come to her equinox celebration."

Cal controlled his expression carefully. One wrong quirk of his brow, and Winnie might read far too much into it.

The bonfire. He'd nearly forgotten about it himself. It was one of his favorite annual events at his mom's. Of course she'd think to include Winnie, if for no other reason than that the She Shed's windows would be shining with the fire all evening. It'd be rude not to invite her over. Plus his mom was an inviter. Hospitality was her forte.

"Do you want to go?"

Winnie blinked up at him.

"Of course I *want* to go. It's your mom. If she invited me over to help her clean out her chimney flue, I'd be there in a heartbeat."

Cal chuckled. His mother did have that effect on people. He didn't like that he was preventing Winnie from making another friend in town, especially a friend as loving and thoughtful as his mom. And despite his better senses, his mind and body were now motivated by one firm principle: the more Winnie, the better.

"So, what's the problem?"

"You. Like usual."

He snickered. "I'm okay with you being there."

Her face lit up like a Christmas tree just plugged in. Damn it, it was easy to please the woman, and doing so made him feel like he'd won the prize.

"You mean it?" she asked, her hands clasping in front of her chest in delight, that signature Winnie reaction. "Because I'll be on my best behavior. I'll stay quiet. I'll just eat the entire time. That'll keep me happy and out of trouble."

"Well, I don't like all this talk of you being on your best behavior, but I suppose it makes sense for Friday evening."

She threw her arms around his waist and gave him a tight squeeze. The depth of her affection, and how good it felt, threw him slightly off kilter.

"And only as long as you promise *not* to be on your best behavior tonight," he said, moving his hands down to cup that ass that'd been torturing his mind for the past two days. It was just as round and soft as he remembered.

She giggled that infectious giggle she had and whispered, "Oh, that's a guarantee."

She laced her fingers in his once more and they began their slow ascent up the hill, making idle talk about their days. The ease of it, of every step of this connection with Winnie, floored him. He didn't want to dwell on it too much out of fear that it might disappear.

By the time they made their way up to the clearing on the top of the hill, the moon had risen well up into the sky, its nearly full circle glowing white with faint swirls of grey. Its light flooded the clearing with a white-yellow aura, and shadowy trees framed the edges of the field.

Cal let go of Winnie's hand to spread out the quilted blanket he'd carried from the car. He lay down first, looking up to Winnie and admiring the way the nearly-full moon framed her head like a halo. He could make out the spring of each curl in the moon's silhouette. He wanted to run his fingers over every one, but that would require her to be closer. He extended an arm toward her and she closed the distance between them, crawling slowly toward him on the soft blanket. Instinctively, as if she needed it like he did, she pressed the length of her body against his, like two magnets attracted to one another on an atomic level. Her knee slid between his thighs and he tried not to think about just how good it felt to have her leg brushing up against his groin.

Her face nuzzled into his neck, the exact same spot her mouth had gravitated toward at his house. And earlier in the parking lot. A spot, Winnie helped him realize, that he'd never given enough credit to with regard to its erotic potential. When her lips, her breath, were on his neck, hot and damp and hungry, he knew he could deny the woman nothing.

"So, this is make-out hill, huh?" she asked, her lips pressing into him. Her tongue gently swiped across his collarbone.

"Mmmm," he responded. Sure, he'd fumbled around up here with girls a few times in his youth, but he found himself suddenly unable to remember another moment here before Winnie. Another woman before her.

"So how much time do you suppose you've spent up here with your conquests over the years?" she asked, the puff of breath from her laugh tickling his neck.

He rolled onto her to better command their entwining. To take, rather than to receive. His mouth pressed into her temple. Her cheek bone. Her jawline. Her lips.

"In minutes? Hours? Days?" he asked, his lips spreading into a wolfish smile against hers before moving along to her jaw line and the side of her neck. "Couldn't say. Though I'd estimate that I've sired at least four offspring on this very field."

Winnie snorted, that ridiculously adorable sound, and longing throbbed in his chest. He hated the way he needed her laughter. It wasn't enough that she desired his body, or found pleasure beneath it. That was physical. That was the biochemistry of the human species. But when she curled up in laughter next to him? Well, it didn't get better than that.

"Well, I'm sure they're all beautiful," she joked about his fictitious children.

"You're beautiful," he said, that word, in its earnestness, shifting the mood to something more reverent. Her mouth opened to him, and the warm, sensual connection of their exploration sent lightning through his chest. The woman was electric.

His mouth traveled down to the soft crevice between her breasts where they peaked out from the hem of her shirt, that spot he could settle into for hours.

"You drive me mad, Briggs." He heard her whimper. He could feel the erratic beat of her heart beneath the spot where his lips pressed into her soft flesh.

"Let me see you," he pleaded.

Her breath caught. "Here?"

"Here. Now."

"Cal, I don't know…" She trailed off.

"Briggs, we're alone in the woods. The sky and the trees won't report us. I want to see you here, bathing in the moonlight."

He wanted to see Winnie's bare, voluptuous breasts in every possible context. Glowing beneath the night sky, sweating in the midday sun, shimmering in the rain, cooling in the shade, drowning beneath a shower's hot torrent of water.

Before he had to beg, she began to unbutton the tiny pearl buttons of her blouse, one at a time in a brutally slow pace. Each flick of her fingers revealed another two inches of the treasure beneath—her satiny skin and the lacy texture of her bra in a shade he couldn't quite determine in the moonlight. Maybe a soft grey or a baby blue. When her shirt fell open to both sides, her fingers clasped between her breasts and snapped open the bra's front clasp, and then suddenly she was bared to him. Bared to the night.

He sighed at the beauty of this woman and the unprecedented strength of this physical connection with her.

Her breath still seemed shallow, nervous. But his hands on her seemed to create a calming effect, soothing her as he cupped her. She lay fully back, closing her eyes as his thumbs brushed across her nipples, followed quickly by his mouth, because it always wanted to further investigate what his hands discovered first.

"I need more of you," he said. She groaned with desire, but it didn't suffice. He couldn't proceed without her permission.

"Please. Tell me to keep going." His eyes looked up to see hers, darkened with pleasure and desire so deep that words failed them both. But she nodded. His heart and his dick thrilled at the permission.

He offered up a small prayer of thanks for the soft, stretchy skirt she wore, for the way his hand could slide beneath it so easily, for the way he could push it up and out of the way around her midsection, revealing the satiny silver panties that shimmered beneath. He marveled at the curve between her waist and the width of her full hips.

He kissed one hip bone, then the other, feeling Winnie's hips buck ever so slightly. His name, soft as a feather, floated from her lips. He could smell that subtle scent of her arousal, and the knowledge of how wet she already was for him shot a bolt of desire straight to his dick. His need to taste her in the most intimate way nearly overwhelmed him. But it wasn't time yet.

Moving his body between her legs, he gently spread them until her knees fell apart. He took her in like that, body open to him, breasts bared to him and his breathing became labored. Her eyes met his briefly, opening sleepily with pleasure, before quickly turning to her side with modesty. She probably prayed for a sheet to cover up with, but he'd campaign ardently against such a move. Her body was one to be feasted upon in any and all ways possible.

"Watch me, Briggs," he said, his voice soft. Her gaze slowly returned to his, and he knew from memory the exact shade of pleasured pink that tinged her cheeks even if the subtle moon light made it impossible to detect. "Watch how I want you."

He saw her swallow nervously, the hollow of her neck jumping up and down, but she pushed herself onto her elbows to improve her vantage point. The shift in weight changed the shape of her breasts, and they sat fuller, heavier against her ribs. Jesus, he could while away the night with those breasts again. It felt like torture, his need to have his mouth and hands everywhere on the woman all at once.

His dark jeans did little to conceal the magnitude of his desire for her, and he leaned closer to rub his hardness against that soft patch of silver satin between her legs, the delicate fabric that separated him from the only thing he truly wanted in the world. He heard her breath catch in her throat. A groan ripped from his own throat. He felt amazed at how the heat of her, the rightness of the connection of their bodies, could penetrate him so thoroughly even between their layers of clothing.

He grabbed her hips, tightening their connection and shifting his angle so that the hard length of his bound erection could grind against the sweetest bud of her sex. However good it felt to him, and he was quite certain that nothing in his entire life had ever felt so good as stroking the cradle of this woman's legs with his cock, nothing could compare to the privilege of watching Winnie Briggs's face slowly unravel with pleasure. Her widened eyes expressing some mix of desire and disbelief. Her full ruby lips parted into the sweetest gape. Her chin titled ever so slightly to the sky, accentuating her sexy neck. Her breathlessness causing her breasts to bounce ever so slightly.

"Cal, please," she whispered, not sure exactly what she requested, but knowing he'd gladly give it to her a dozen times over.

He thrust across her clit again and again, slowly and methodically, ensuring that the high, sensuous note he played on her with the bow of his body sang on and on without pause. Watching the slow buildup of her desire, watching the frantic need build in her eyes and on her lips and in the involuntary thrusts of her own hips and in the thoughts she couldn't formulate so that they just fell out of her mouth in erotic moans and gasps, Cal knew he was playing with fire. He knew that his own release wanted to barrel down the door of his restraint. He could picture it so perfectly, unbuttoning his jeans, grabbing the length of his erection with one hand and pulling aside the wet satin of her panties with the other. Plunging himself into her hot, slick depths. Watching her lush mouth drop open and her eyes close in pleasure as the thick length of his desire stretched them both to the brink.

He forced his breathing to slow down. Forced his mind to return to Winnie's pleasure and to the other ways he needed to experience her before they both came right through their damn clothes.

"Cal, yes," she said, her voice so quiet. Her pleasure nearly muted her and somehow, with this woman, it was sexier than if she screamed with desire. Her eyes suddenly turned to his, pleading, desperate, and the look alone was nearly enough to finish him off. "I need... Please," she started, but couldn't articulate the request.

In a matter of seconds he pushed her thighs together, grabbed the elastic of her panties and pulled them off her ankles before spreading her open again. A soft triangle of those most intimate curls framed her sex, and goddamn, he could see how wet she was without even touching her.

He wanted to taste her. To explore the innermost treasures of her body with his mouth. But he didn't want it as much as he wanted to watch her shatter beneath his touch. There would only be one first chance to watch Winnie climax, and he intended to soak in every detail.

JESS VONN

He steadied himself on his knees between the softness of her pale thighs in the moonlight.

"Like this, Briggs?" he asked, his fingers stroking in circles up and down her inner thighs.

She shook her head frantically, her face wild with need for him. For his touch.

"N-no. That's..." she stammered, her curls cascading down her bare, moonlit chest. "It's not enough."

He grinned. He shouldn't enjoy this sweet torture so much, but he did.

The fingers of one hand raked through the small, sweet patch of hair that framed her sex while another reached up to caress her heaving breast.

"Cal," she cried in desperation, her voice getting tighter. "Please."

"Please what?" He knew it, damn it, but he wanted to hear her desperate and dirty words. *Just fuck me,* she'd begged at his house, on his kitchen table. For the past two days his brain couldn't stop replaying those three uncharacteristically naughty words that had fallen from Winnie's tempting mouth.

"Please touch me. I—" She gasped, her head arching back. "Your fingers."

"What about them, Briggs."

"I need them," she said. "On me. In me. Please, Cal. Please make me come."

And with that final request, the game was over. He couldn't deny the woman any longer or he might be the one who burst. He'd never known anything as singularly erotic as Winnie Briggs, nearly naked in the night air, begging him to get her off.

And a gentleman didn't keep a begging woman waiting.

From his position on his knees between her thighs, his thumb ever so gently brushed against her aroused clit.

She cried out, her voice finally rising above a whisper. He stroked her again, amazed at what the back of his broad thumb could coax from one square inch of this woman's glorious body.

The fingers of his other hand slid near her opening, the warm evidence of her desire slick to his touch. One knuckle brushed into her sex, his other thumb still devoted to its work above, and then he gently pressed one finger inside her folds. Up higher, deeper, to where her hot wetness surrounded him.

She cried out in pleasure and he nearly joined her. Jesus, the hotness of it. The rightness. He slipped in a second finger and pushed deeper, wanting more of her surrounding him. Wanting to get lost in that most erotic embrace. His dick and his mouth protested, not understanding why they weren't invited to the erotic exploration.

"Yes, Cal, yes," she muttered mindlessly, frantically, beneath the work of his hands.

His fingers fucked her slowly, unhurriedly gliding across the hot syrup of her desire. Her clit pulsed beneath the steady, rhythmic stroke of his thumb. It might have gone on like that for a while. He'd have gladly stayed there, busying himself with the work of satisfying this woman. But he looked up at her, and everything heightened. Still propped up on her elbows, her head fell back, her mouth hung open and her breasts heaved in rhythm with her moans. Wanton for him. Her hips squirmed beneath his touch, wanting more than his hands could offer.

"Look at me, Briggs," he ordered. It wasn't enough to feel her orgasm burst around his fingers. He'd denied himself the pleasure of mouthing her for the very purpose of maintaining an ideal vantage point for her climax. He needed to watch it in her eyes as well.

She shook her head softly, as if awaking herself from a daze. When those huge brown eyes, frantic with the discomfort of not-quite-met desire, locked into his, and her mouth begged him *please* once more, his hands intensified their focus, stroking her, rubbing her. Her gaze held his right up until the moment the sensations overtook her and she closed them in a broken cry of pleasure. He tried to process it all at once, tried to burn the dozen elements of Winnie Briggs's rapture into his memory to preserve indefinitely. How her lips cried his name in gratitude. How the slick cushion of her sex clenched his fingers inside of her. How trembling overtook her body as she struggled to regain her breath.

Moments later, as her shuddering eased, he pulled back his fingers and put them instinctively to his lips, tasting her desire for him. Foretasting future pleasures.

Winnie didn't move for a good long while, and he smiled, cuddling down next to her, proud of the pleasure coma she'd slipped into. Her gaze stayed steady on the stars above and a small smile spread across her lips as she reveled in the aftershocks of her climax.

Slowly her head fell to the side, and her eyes met his. They looked softer now, relaxed, not dark and wild and needy like they'd been just minutes before. She surprised him by throwing her arms around his neck and pulling him in for a tight hug that pressed her bare breasts up against his shirted chest.

"Thank you," she whispered near his ear as her hands softly raked through his hair. The sweetness of those words, her earnest gratitude, grasped his heart in a surprisingly powerful way. It was almost as if she had no clue that he'd gotten as much out of it as she had.

"You're very welcome. The pleasure was all mine."

"Now that is not even remotely true, but addressing your pleasure just happens to be the next item on my to-do list." Her eyes glinted deliciously and suddenly her mouth was on his, hot and desperate to return that most glorious of favors.

"Have I ever mentioned how much I adore your to-do lists?" he managed breathlessly before his hands slipped into her hair, grabbing handfuls of curls and pushing her deeper into the kiss. Tasting, exploring. He wanted his hands on her breasts. Her ass. God, he wanted to make her come again already. Wanted to make her body sing until his name was the only word her brain could formulate.

But before he had a chance to complete even a fraction of what he intended to do with the woman, a sudden rustling in the trees behind them caused her to sit up in shock. She hastily pulled together the sides of her unbuttoned shirt.

"What was that?" she asked, her face suddenly filled with a mix of worry and modesty.

"That was a very inconsiderate squirrel, interrupting us like that," he teased, his hands reaching up and trying to sneak their way back into Winnie's shirt and onto her fantastic breasts. "You must have woken him up in your throes of pleasure."

She punched his arm lightly and ease began to replace her fear-- that is until the sound came a little closer and a little louder, as if two animals were having some sort of territorial squabble in the rustling leaves. Cal wasn't the least bit concerned with anything other than getting his hands on the woman in front of him, but she gasped again when a particularly aggravated animal yelp sprung from the dark trees behind them.

He sat up, pulling her into an embrace.

"You okay?"

"Umm," she hedged. He had to smile. The truth was that he didn't have a lot of experience with city girls. He wasn't afraid of woodland animals in the night, but Winnie clearly was. At least her fear helped bring his desire slightly into check.

"We can get out of here," he said, the back of his fingers gently stroking her cheek.

She sighed, her eyes scanning over his body hungrily.

"We've got nothing but time, Briggs," he said, before reluctantly reaching down to either side of Winnie to grasp the two ends of her front-opening bra. He stretched them to her center, and twisted the tiny clasp in place until the contraption covered her bounty. It felt like a crime.

He kissed the top of one full breast where it crested above the lace, then did the same on the other side before beginning the work of slowly buttoning up Winnie's blouse. For as much as he didn't want to tuck her back away behind her clothing, the act of dressing the woman was surprisingly sexy.

Then again, he was beginning to believe that Winnie could make damn near anything sexy.

Neither of them said much on their slow walk back down the hill, but Winnie had begun her nervous hair twirl with the hand that wasn't holding his. What was going through her mind?

Damn it, this wasn't how he wanted the night to end, and he didn't like not knowing how long it might be before they'd get to resume their investigations of one another. But Winnie was startled, and his body wouldn't allow him to beg for her touch if her mind wasn't at ease. For better or for worse, he was slowly learning to live with the low hum of need he felt constantly now that Winnie was in his life. Blue balls had become the norm.

Damn squirrels.

They passed by a storage shed tucked into the shadows at the base of the hill when Winnie suddenly stopped.

"You okay?" he asked, turning back and scanning her face. Maybe the rustling in the woods had scared her more than she let on.

"No," she said, her voice shaky and her face unreadable.

"It was just—" he started, but he didn't get the chance to offer his words of comfort.

"It's not okay."

"What isn't?" he asked, starting to get genuinely concerned. Perhaps he'd done something wrong and hadn't even realized it. Coaxing a climax out of Winnie had been an unspeakable pleasure for him, but maybe the moonlight tryst had gone one step too far for her. She pulled him to her side, then back farther still, until they stood in the shadow behind the concrete structure.

"We can't leave it off there, Cal," she said, her voice hinting at the desperation he heard in it earlier. Her hands pushed on his chest until his back pressed up against the scratchy concrete of the structure. His dick responded in full at the feel of her hands on him again. At the implications of her words. "It's not fair."

In seconds, her mouth met his. Hungry. Demanding. Her fingers grasped at his chest. His hair. At his hips. They slipped below the back of his shirt until they found the hot skin of his lower back and she scraped her nails along his flesh, coaxing a growl from his throat.

So disoriented by the sudden change in the trajectory of their evening, the sensations overwhelmed him and he hardly knew what to do with his hands. They fumbled in Winnie's hair. Reached down and scooped up her ass until she pressed hard against his erection. He could take her right here. Turn her around. Hitch her up on the side of the building and thrust into her until she shattered again.

Her hands tore him from the fantasy, though, as they squeezed between them and grasped his hard length through his jeans.

"Jesus," he groaned at this woman. Her touch. The hungry way she grabbed at him. Making quick work of his button and fly, she pulled down his briefs until the full hardness of his erection strained out into the evening air.

She gasped at the sight of him before dropping to her knees, and he promptly lost all semblance of control.

"I couldn't go home without feeling you," she panted, her fingers encircling his cock and rubbing the length of him.

He should say something. Respond. Encourage this divine act. Thank her for being the goddess she was. But he couldn't form a thought beyond *please don't stop.* It was only sheer force of will that had kept him from coming at her very first touch.

"Cal." Her voice was soft and her breath hot. "I have to taste you," she said, kissing the tip of him before her tongue stroked his length. She tasted her way down to his balls, and when they sank into her mouth, profanity was the only sound he could manage.

Mercifully, her plush lips encircled his cock, tenderly at first, getting a feel for his size and shape. Then faster. With more force. The tight, soft wetness of her mouth foretold of other sensual pleasures her body held for him and he knew he couldn't avoid his climax for long.

One of her hands grabbed the base of his cock and the other curled beneath him to cup his balls, making sure not an inch of him went without her glorious attention. She stroked him into the warm depths of her mouth. Even with her mouthful of him, she groaned hungrily. He'd never known a woman to take such pleasure in this act. Winnie's enthusiasm for satiating him unmoored him. His hands grabbed hastily at her hair as her head worked over him.

"It's too good," he sputtered, wanting this moment to last forever, but knowing, as her grip quickened and tightened, that he was seconds away from coming. He wanted to give her fair warning, not sure where she wanted him to spill himself. But as his climax became more imminent, she doubled down and showed no sign of switching gears. His hips pushed forward to meet her mouth more fully, knowing that he could never be deep enough in this woman. Heightened by the unexpected location and Winnie's unbridled enthusiasm, Cal's orgasm shuddered through him, and he pumped into her hot mouth with one final groan of pleasure. He thrust a few more times for good measure, not wanting to disconnect from this woman's body, but eventually his hips crashed back against the wall behind him as she swallowed, catching her breath. Her hands stayed on him, gently stroking the hardness that still lingered. She tenderly kissed the tip of his shaft, then nuzzled into the patch of hair at the base of his cock.

She clutched his hips and pulled herself back up to standing, swaying ever so slightly, as if her body was as unsteady as his own from the intensity of what just passed between them. He pulled her tightly into his chest, knowing exactly what he needed to say but lacking the mental capacity to form the words. The only word he could conjure in his mind was *good.* She was good. It was good. Life was good. She kissed his chest. She kissed the crook of his neck that she loved so much, and simply said, "That's better." Her eyes met his once more, mischievous and satisfied.

"Good night, Cal," she said, dropping one soft kiss on his lips before making her way out to her car in the lot. He stood there, still hanging half hard out the front of his jeans as his mind desperately tried to catch up with what his body just experienced. At the sheer unexpectedness of Winnie Briggs.

He'd proposed this arrangement with the intent to teach her about pleasure, but with each passing day, it became apparent that the woman had as much to teach as she had to learn.

Chapter 18

As Winnie walked into city hall Tuesday morning, she wondered, briefly, if she'd become transparent. Could everyone see what she'd done the night before on Cosgrove Hill? Did everyone know just how transformed she was courtesy of the sexual favors of one Mr. Cal Spencer?

When she awoke that morning, she had shot straight up in bed, awash in a variety of emotions inspired by the outdoor tryst. Pride. Pleasure. Embarrassment. But more than anything else? Astonishment.

What Cal had done to her body... The way he worked over her and in her with those clever fingers. The way he perched above her in the moonlight and watched her intently as she burst into a thousand shards of light. That had been rapturous. Transforming. Divine.

But what she did to him at the back of that concrete shed?

Her lips curled just at the memory of it. The Winnie of the past would have never taken what she wanted. Hell, former Winnie would have never wanted a man in that way with even half the enthusiasm. That, combined with the sheer shock on Cal's face... that she'd rendered a magnificent man into a speechless, desperate, groaning animal. That was a power she'd never known, and now that she had experienced it, she only wanted more of it.

Yet here she was, reporter Winnie, back on the beat, going on about her professional business as if last night hadn't been life-altering. She had trouble making eye contact with people on the street, lest her new insatiable wantonness show. How could it not?

Making her way into the city council chambers felt like déjà vu. The chairs in the audience sat empty, save for Chief Conrad flipping through a notebook near the back. The only difference was that this time, the mayor was in place before the meeting began. He didn't look any more composed—his sandy-white hair still stuck out in tufts around his head, and his crumpled Polo shirt looked as though it had been picked up off the floor only a few minutes prior, but at least he was here.

Winnie's stomach flipped when she considered Carter in a new light. He was no longer just the friendly and sexy-as-hell police chief. Now she also knew him as Cal's best friend. Did he know anything about what Winnie and Cal were up to? Would he judge her if he did? Maybe she should just sit up near the front today, and avoid that particular situation.

Just when she was about to do so, Chief Conrad's mesmerizing blue eyes flickered up to her and a grin unleashed its dazzling brightness. He gave her a small wave, and she knew that she'd go to him.

"Hey, Chief," she offered as she plunked herself down on the folding chair next to his.

"Hey, Winnie. Please, call me Carter."

"Are you sure?"

"Yeah. As long as I'm not arresting you, Carter suits me just fine."

"Okay, I'll keep that distinction in mind."

She grinned, grateful for his teasing. Even if he did know anything about what she and Cal were up to, Winnie suspected he wouldn't hold it against her. Relief flooded her, given that next to Cal and Evie, Carter was the closest thing Winnie had to a friend in Bloomsburo.

"So how are you settling into town?" he asked.

"Oh, pretty well. Each day seems to introduce some new challenge or challenging personality, but it's all part of the job."

"Yeah, we have our fair share of challenging personalities around here. But most in our town have pretty good hearts."

She nodded. His gaze met hers, as if he wanted to ask a question he couldn't quite allow him to utter.

"Did you ever make any headway on the pancake sabotage?" she asked, fully aware of how ridiculous the phrase sounded. Before he had a chance to answer, though, the gavel struck and Mayor Simpson called the meeting to order. He still seemed suspiciously rusty at running a city council meeting, but he went through the approval of the last meeting's minutes (a step he completely skipped over last time, though Winnie doubted that previous minutes were even taken.)

"Our first order of the day is to discuss the issue of temporary special permits," Mayor Simpson began. "It's come to our attention that the city is not managing its costs adequately on these special events, and that we may need to raise this fee."

Winnie raised her hand, and the mayor looked at her in annoyance.

"Yes?"

"What types of events require these special permits, and what is the current fee?" The mayor looked over to Councilwoman McDonald, who cleared her throat loudly.

Winnie wasn't shocked that the mayor didn't have the answer himself.

"These permits are used for special one-time, annual or semi-annual events, such as seasonal sales of holiday merchandise, farmers markets, festivals, fairs, carnivals, special sheds or structures needed on construction sites, et cetera."

Winnie nodded as she took down notes furiously. So basically, they were talking about the kind of events that were the bread and butter of Betty Jean's Blooming Ladies.

"The current application fee is $150. Some events require a deposit as well. The length of the license varies based on the nature of the activity."

"Thank you," Winnie said, rounding out her notes.

The mayor continued. "These sorts of special events can put extreme pressure on city resources, including law enforcement, facilities and clean up teams," the mayor explained, somewhat dramatically.

Winnie knew from her time working in Chicago that these types of special events were more likely to affect *where* government employees needed to be more than the hours they worked. These were often roles that were being filled regardless of what events were happening on a given day.

"Thus," Mayor Simpson said, "I'd like to propose raising the application fee from $150 to $1,500."

Winnie gasped, and she heard Carter whisper the quietest burst of profanity she'd never heard, but the other bodies in the room— the city council members—merely nodded in agreement, clearly having discussed this figure ahead of time.

That kind of fee inflation was not only unprecedented and unethical, but it would be absolutely devastating for small business owners and non-profit organizers like The Blooming Ladies. Some of their events wouldn't even bring in $1,500 in profit. They surely couldn't be expected to pay that kind of money to apply for a special event license just to hold a fundraiser.

"Given our current fiscal realities, I feel like this is a move in the right direction," said James Dolittle, the youngest councilperson by at least a decade (which was saying something, since he appeared to be in his sixties).

"I agree," the third councilman said quietly. Joe O'Loughlin was by far the eldest council member. Winnie wouldn't be surprised if had been in office during the JFK administration.

"It is a time for financial prudence," Councilwoman McDonald said.

"I'm sorry, but are you suggesting that this fee money could be used to balance out deficits within the city budget?" Winnie butted in, incredulous. "And aren't you concerned about how this high fee scale will deter community organizers from hosting local events?"

"Young lady, this is an official government meeting, and you may not burst out with questions whenever one pops into that pretty head of yours," Mayor Simpson roared, now standing from his position of power up front. His face reddened with an anger that dissolved the harmless, nutty-professor vibe he gave off up until then. She thought he was mostly daft; her heart sank at the knowledge that he was also a misogynistic jerk.

Young lady. Her blood boiled.

"If you have questions about the particulars of our budget, Miss Briggs," said Councilwoman McDonald, "you can access that information via the city clerk."

"That doesn't answer my question," Winnie pressed, but the mayor continued on.

"If we're all in agreement, let's set an action item for the next meeting regarding this proposal."

"But—" Winnie interjected, but her plea fell on deaf ears. Whether she liked it or not, she didn't have a vote at the meeting. The council voted unanimously to put a vote on the next agenda.

She looked incredulously at Carter, who merely closed his eyes, shook his head, and rubbed his fingers across his brow. Winnie knew he couldn't speak his concern about his boss in this forum, but she took some small comfort in the fact that someone in the room found this new proposal as preposterous as she did.

"Our final agenda item: as may arise," the mayor said.

"Nothing from me," said Councilman O'Loughlin, followed by identical statements from the other two council members.

What mindless sheep, Winnie thought grouchily to herself. She couldn't help but shake the feeling that this entire meeting had been orchestrated carefully before hand, in clear violation of open meetings law.

"If there is no other topic to discuss, I'd ask for a motion to adjourn."

Before Winnie even had a chance to ask another question, the motion had been made and seconded. Like cockroaches when the lights turn on, the mayor and the council members scattered out of the chamber the second that gavel hit to adjourn the meeting. There would be no time for follow-up questions today.

Her shoulders slumped dejectedly.

"Cal is going to be so pissed," Carter quietly observed, pulling out his phone and beginning the text message to his friend.

"I doubt he'll be the only one." Winnie sighed. As helpless as Winnie felt at the lack of transparency and the poorly reasoned decision, she took some comfort in knowing that a story about the fee spike in *The Bloom* would force the issue. Neither Cal nor Betty Jean would let something like that stand without contention, and Winnie had a feeling that in a small town like Bloomsburo, there were dozens more where they came from.

~-~-~-~-~-~-

It was almost two p.m. before Winnie rushed into Dewey's Diner, hungry and burnt out from the city council nonsense she'd dealt with that morning, among other things.

"I knew you were working today, and I had to see you!" Winnie said breathlessly to Evie, plunking down her messenger bag on the stool next to hers at the counter. "And I knew I had to catch you before the dinner rush, so that we might actually have a chance to talk."

Evie smiled and Winnie glanced down the counter where she saw a man about her age in a white T-shirt, jeans, and a black apron, flipping through a binder. He was husky and handsome in a 1950s kind of way, with short dirty blond hair, sideburns and strong, wide shoulders.

"Is that Dewey?" Winnie whispered to Evie, pointing in the man's direction. Evie's face flushed ever so slightly as she nodded.

Interesting.

"Will I be in trouble for talking to you while you're working?" she whispered again, but not as discretely as she thought. Dewey looked their way and his full lips slipped into the subtlest of smiles, first at Winnie then at Evie, before returning his attention to the clipboard.

Evie looked down at Dewey again to see if Winnie's personal visit was going to be a problem. He said nothing, but waved his hand as if to gesture "go on," much to both women's delight.

"You're the best, Dewey!" Winnie hollered down the counter, forcing familiarity on him. He said nothing, but shook his head as he continued to look through his paperwork, and she saw his lips quirk ever so slightly at the corner. It was quickly apparent to Winnie that Dewey was not a man of many words.

She looked back to Evie. "Not to make you wait on me, but can I get a soda, a burger and some fries?"

Evie laughed. "It's kind of my job to wait on you."

"Right."

They talked about their days, about the bizarre city council meeting, and about Evie's children. Winnie hinted at some juicier stories about the night before that she wanted to share once Evie was off the clock. In the meantime, eventually Winnie mustered up the courage to ask the question that had been eating away at her.

"Can I ask you to divulge some of your townie knowledge?" Winnie asked, grabbing her soda for a long sip.

"Sure."

"What's the deal with Cal's dad? Was he ever in the picture?" The question had been burning in Winnie's mind since she first met Rhonda. Though her landlady had mentioned in their very first phone call that she was single, she'd never offered up any backstory on the subject of her marriage and Winnie had yet to find an appropriate time to ask.

She saw Evie's face fall and Winnie's heart sank.

"That's a sad story," Evie offered, looking down to her fingers. "Maybe you should talk to Cal or Rhonda about it."

A bolt of guilt flashed through Winnie, but she pressed on anyway. She just needed the general outline of the situation, and then she could follow up with Cal or Rhonda about the details. The journalist in her hated little more than unanswered questions.

"Just the basics?" she pleaded.

Evie sighed. She didn't seem to want to tell the story, but she did anyway. "You know how his little sister, Rosie, has MS?"

Winnie nodded. Rhonda had brought it up more than once talking about her family.

"Cal was probably a junior in high school when Rosie was diagnosed," Evie continued. "When they started doing tests and seeking treatment, they found out that his dad, Charlie, was the one who carried the genetic predisposition for the disease. He received his own diagnosis a short time later."

Winnie's heart tumbled in her chest as she tried to imagine what it would be like for a parent to process that kind of information.

"His dad spiraled right when they needed him the most," Evie said with a sigh, her voice getting quieter. "First it was drinking too much. Then it was drugs. Then affairs. There were arrests."

Winnie's heart sank. Poor Rhonda. Poor Cal.

"It ramped up and up until finally he was killed in a drunk driving accident, along with a woman he was sleeping with."

Winnie felt tears welling. "Gosh, that's horrible."

"It really was. Thank God no one else was hurt. They just crashed into an underpass. It was a tragedy and a huge town scandal. Cal was several years ahead of me in school, but everyone knew how it affected him. He was mortified, but he stepped up. He took care of his little sisters like it was his job. Which, for better or for worse, it was."

She'd already loved the man's body, but damn it if her heart didn't crack open for him now, too.

"Jeeze."

"Yeah. He had to grow up really fast."

Winnie nodded, poking around at the fries on her plate and no longer finding herself hungry.

"I was going to ask about Chief Conway's story, too, but something tells me that one sad story is enough for today."

Evie's shoulders slumped, confirming Winnie's suspicions.

JESS VONN

"Yeah, if Cal's backstory is sad, Carter's story is straight-up tragic," Evie said with a sigh. "That one requires whiskey as a minimum."

Winnie glanced down at the Coke in front of her. "Alright, I'll take a rain check on that one. But only for now."

Evie nodded, taking Winnie's plate and walking back toward the kitchen. In the meantime, Winnie tried her best to will away the feelings of heartbreak and injustice that bubbled up in her heart for Cal, as well as how to navigate them alongside her physical attraction to him.

She failed.

Chapter 19

It was a good thing she had such a late lunch, Winnie thought to herself, because she'd worked through dinner and the end of her workday wasn't in sight. She looked at her phone and groaned when she saw it was already after nine. She still had two more pages to finish up before she could let herself quit for the day.

Just how the publisher expected her to produce these special sections in addition to all the work of creating an entire newspaper twice a week, she didn't know. But this was the price she paid for taking last night off and playing out in the woods with Cal, and in that way, it was worth it.

But still, a lady could use some sustenance.

Just then, as if destined, her phone alerted her to a new text from Cal the Great.

Tonight is officially not as fun as last night.

She laughed.

Agreed. Haven't even left work yet.

You're still at work?

:(

Let me guess, Pop-tarts for dinner?

Not even. Ran out and haven't had time to go shopping. Did find some animal crackers in my purse though.

I'll be there with rations in 15.

Excitement blossomed in Winnie's chest, which she tried to appropriately convey in a string of emojis. The adrenaline rush motivated her to fly through the final edits on the page design she was working on. With Cal on the way and only one more page to complete, the night was looking up indeed.

She heard the bells on the front door of the office ring a short time later before Cal appeared in the doorway of her office, looking handsome in dressy sneakers, camel colored slacks, a red and white flannel shirt, and a navy down vest. She grinned like an idiot at the site of him there, holding a bag of something delicious, but his eyes were serious.

"It's nine thirty and you're working in here alone. Why is that front door unlocked?" he asked, leaning his strong shoulder against the doorframe.

"So that handsome men can stop by and deliver me food, of course."

"Briggs," he scolded.

"Sorry," she said, and she was. Until she heard the bells ring she hadn't even realized that she failed to lock up behind Gloria like she normally did in these instances. "I usually do. I'm just swamped."

He glanced at the piles of edited stories and printed pages covering her desk.

"You have to take care of yourself," he said, finally walking toward her and placing his bag on the only clear corner of her desk. Ugh, the man smelled so good it should be illegal. "You have to feed yourself. Even if Winnie food is all you can manage, it's better than nothing."

He reached into the bag and pulled out a thermos of warm chili, a huge hunk of homemade cornbread and a little baggie of chocolate chip cookies.

"Are you kidding me?" she squealed, walking around the desk to where he set everything out. "You just had all this sitting around the house?"

"Well, yeah. I had to reheat the chili. I'd already put it away after I finished eating dinner at a reasonable hour. You know, like a normal person," he teased. "The bread is what I didn't manage to eat tonight, and I had the cookies in the freezer. When you cook for one, you end up with lots of leftovers."

Her need to eat was at the forefront of her mind, but another kind of hunger began to take precedence in her body. With Cal so close now her mind filled with memories of the night before. Of the glorious exploration of hands and mouths and fingers.

"Do you charge a delivery fee?" she asked, aiming for coyness as she looked up at him sweetly from beneath her lashes.

"I'm open to negotiating a creative payment," he said, placing his hand on the small of her back and pressing her tightly against his body. His lips met hers, hot and hungry. As her fingers wound into his hair she felt his hands lower, grasping both sides of her hips and rubbing her harder against his obviously growing need.

And just like that, it was as if no time had passed between evenings. As if they'd never stopped touching, tasting, taking and giving. She reached around beneath his vest and felt the strong muscles of his back flexing as his hands explored her body. He groaned as she nuzzled into his neck, breathing in his scent and his warmth. Tasting him there.

Everything felt so good, yet desperation made her fingers twitch. She needed to feel more of his skin. Her hands worked their way around to the front of his shirt and her shaky fingers began the work of undoing the top button of his soft flannel shirt.

She would have gotten away with it, too, if her stomach hadn't betrayed her, but the hungry growl it unleashed was enough to snap her scrumptious delivery boy out of his lustful haze and remind him of the whole purpose of his trip.

"Food first," he insisted, gently removing her hands from his chest and refastening the button she'd managed to set free. She saw how heavily he was breathing. Had felt the quickened beating of his heart beneath her touch and his growing hardness pressed against her core. She could convince him.

"Food second," she insisted, her hands making another attempt at the buttons, but he easily caught her by the wrists before she made any headway.

"Briggs, I'd like nothing more than to make you my late night snack right here in this office," he said, his eyes darkened with desire, "but I'm a feeder. I come from a long line of them. You're going to get something to eat before we continue to negotiate my delivery fee."

She sighed, but complied. He pulled the corner chair closer to the desk, which she sat on, not wanting the width of it to separate her from Cal. Her very being just somehow felt more right when he was within an arm's reach.

Sitting on the desk proved to be a good choice. As she grabbed the thermos and dug into the amazing chili, he reached out to her calf where it hung near his knee, gently stroking her with his strong fingers through the soft cotton of her ribbed lavender tights.

"You're the sweetest person in the world for bringing me this food," she said, closing her eyes and reveling in the sensations that the man's food, and touch, ignited in her.

"I'm far from sweet, Briggs. It'd be best to remember that," he said, his fingers following the grooves of her tights up, up, up until they slid under her corduroy skirt. He squeezed her upper thigh, then stroked her with his clever thumb, causing her core to throb in jealousy.

It was hard to remember anything when he touched her that way. She took another few bites, knowing he wouldn't let her play until she'd eaten enough.

He could deny being sweet all day, and rub her in those wicked ways he so excelled at, but deep down she couldn't shake the feeling that he just might *care* about her. She chose not to dwell on how much the idea warmed her. She told herself that his thoughtful gestures weren't really about her. He was just Rhonda Spencer's son. He was raised to be considerate like that.

This train of thought brought forward the memory of the story Evie told this afternoon, about Cal's father, and the circumstances that shaped the man sitting beside her now. Her heart ached. She wanted to know as much as she could about him. She wanted to open him up like a book and read every word of his life story.

Her gut told her to let it be. He was feeding her. Expertly massaging her very upper thigh. But dang it, she wanted him to know she cared about him, too.

"So, you're a feeder, and I know your mom is," she said tentatively. "Did your dad cook, too?"

The stroking on her leg stopped and she could sense Cal's shoulders tense.

Shoot. Why couldn't she just leave well enough alone?

He sat back in his chair, disconnecting their bodies, and met her eyes.

"No."

Okay, then. She took another bite of chili with the hopes of smothering the comment that wanted to escape. The *one* statement she knew she should just keep to herself. The plan failed, because her mouth tended to disregard her brain's advice in moments like this. Not to mention that awkward silences had always been her nemesis.

"It must have been so hard, losing him at such a young age," she blurted out. As someone who'd lost not one but two parents, she felt a deep need to offer empathy to others with a similar story, even if it was a decade too late.

She watched his facial expression harden as he slowly clenched then unclenched his hands.

"Was my mom talking to you about him?" he asked with an unnatural, forced calmness.

Winnie set down the thermos, her appetite suddenly gone. *Stupid, nosy brain.*

"Uh, no," she said, because she couldn't lie. It'd get back to Rhonda, which would create a whole new set of problems.

"Did someone bring him up to you?" he asked, his gaze penetrating. With every second it became more apparent that his father might be the topic he least wanted to talk about. She wanted to rewind, to go back to two minutes earlier when his delicious food was filling her body and his hand was invading her skirt.

"No, not exactly," she said, squirming where she sat on the desk.

He stayed quiet, waiting for her to spill it. He'd figured out her tendencies by now.

"I asked Evie if she knew what the story was with your dad."

She watched him swallow hard and cross his arms, but he didn't speak. Fueled by mounting guilt, she rattled on.

"She didn't want to tell me at first. She thought I should ask you about him."

He let out a small, humorless laugh.

"I kept on her though, until she told me…" She cleared her throat nervously. "…the basics."

"The basics?" he repeated. "At Dewey's, I'm sure."

Winnie's cheeks warmed. She hadn't even thought about the public nature of her and Evie's conversation until that very second. But how could she have known what a scandalous story she was requesting? For all she knew, Cal's dad had remarried and lived a boring life as an accountant in New England.

"Yes."

"I'm sure the rest of the diner enjoyed getting a refresher on the sad story. It was the primary grist of the gossip mills for years. How thoughtful of you to remind them all of the skeletons in the Spencer family closet."

"Cal, I'm sorry, I had no idea – "

"You set the ground rules, Briggs," he interrupted, standing up now. He wasn't angry. He hadn't even raised his voice. But his warmth and humor were long gone, which was somehow worse.

She stood too, so he didn't seem quite so imposing. Something about his irritation made him seem half a foot taller.

"What do you mean?"

"No digging through each other's baggage. That was your rule."

"I—" she started, but he interrupted again. And she didn't have a good response anyway. He was absolutely right.

"I don't know if it makes me feel better or worse that you didn't even bother to ask me about it."

She shook her head, knowing that she was within seconds of tears.

"I figured you would have brought it up if you wanted to talk about it," she said, her voice shaky.

He let out another small, sad laugh.

"Exactly."

Ugh. She was officially a prying jerk.

"I didn't mean to overstep, Cal. I just wanted to know a little bit more about you. I'm sorry."

"Some of us have chapters in our lives we'd just as soon keep shut. I doubt that's the case for someone like you. I'm sure you've had a charmed, uneventful life with two perfect parents who always did and said the right thing. Who were always there for you, no exceptions."

That's when the tears finally fell, as he jabbed his finger right into the center of her pain without even intending to. In that way, they were even, and she silently accepted it as penance. When he noticed she was crying, his face softened.

"Hey," he said gently, which only worked to increase the tear output. He sighed as he brushed the wetness away with the back of his thumbs. "Look. You've got work to do, so I'll leave you to it. We'll talk tomorrow, okay?"

She nodded, unsure what to say. Unwilling to acknowledge the fear and insecurity fluttering in her heart. This couldn't be the end. Not when it had just started to get so magical. He put his finger beneath her chin and tipped her face up so that she was forced to meet his gaze.

"Eat something," he said sternly, though the care behind his words made her heart squeeze. Calmed her down a little. "And lock up behind me."

With no goodbye hug or embrace, he made his way out of the office. Winnie sat at her desk, dazed, not quite able to process the quick turn of events. She couldn't overthink what had happened, or what her and Cal's status was. She had work to finish tonight.

All she'd now knew for sure was that it was impossible to avoid relationship baggage. Even if you tried to, you'd just end up tripping over it eventually – and falling flat on your face in the process.

~-~-~-~-~-~-

An extra-large coffee and an enormous pumpkin spice muffin from Dewey's bakery window the next morning made Wednesday a bit easier to manage despite Winnie's lack of sleep the night before. She was more than exhausted when she finally made it home at eleven, but anxiety about her kerfuffle with Cal made falling asleep next to impossible. The only benefit of her insomnia was a bit of time to finally start combing through the copies of annual Bloomsburo budget reports that the city clerk had begrudgingly handed over.

She was no accountant, but even at first glance, some oddities and troubling patterns jumped out of the numbers. Winnie needed to get to the bottom of it. For as little as she wanted to go into the office this morning, she'd much rather be there than at city hall this morning as the community woke up to find news of the exorbitant fee hike on the front page of the paper. She winced a bit, worrying about the shadow the news would cast over Cal's day. But then she took a moment to appreciate the fact that Betty Jean would have someone else to harass for once.

So she was dragging this morning, but she felt determined to tackle her to-do list with gusto. She would have done just that if it weren't for that blasted office phone.

Winnie slowly began to realize that being the editor-in-chief of a small town paper was basically like one continuous game of Whack-a-Mole. No matter what else she had to do, huge chunks of her days were spent dealing with unexpected things at unideal times: pancake dinner sabotage and missing-in-action mayors and the passing of policies that were far from the best interest of the community, just to name a few.

And before she'd even managed to clear out her inbox, the first task Winnie tackled each morning at the office, Gloria appeared around the corner, with the newest 'mole' to whack.

"Winnie, there's a call for you. It's Poppy Hughes."

"From the Teal Tea Hutch?" It was one of Bloomsburo's most charming Main Street attractions, a cozy tearoom with authentic sweets and fancies. Winnie had yet to meet Poppy, or to visit the spot.

"Yes, that's the one. But the thing is, Poppy's quite hysterical."

"Is she upset with the paper? Did we screw up an ad?"

Winnie sure hoped not. The Teal Tea Hutch was one of the paper's largest local advertising accounts. They had taken out a full-color, full-page ad in the upcoming special section and her publisher would kill her if she did something to compromise that relationship.

"No, she's not upset with you. But she wants your help."

Winnie could hardly get a word in edgewise when Poppy came on the line. Her voice was a barrage of panicked shrieks and only a few dramatic words came through: sabotage, ruined reputation, vengeance.

"How quickly can you be here to help me sort this all out?" Poppy finally asked, breathlessly and desperately.

"I'll be right over."

Winnie grabbed her notebook and camera and flew out the door, speed-walking her way down the side street that met up with Main Street. Luckily The Teal Tea Hutch was just a few blocks away. So determined was Winnie to get over to the shop and figure out what the fuss was all about that she didn't even notice the figure approaching the business from the opposite end of the sidewalk.

As she walked up to the door, however, she saw a man's arm block the entrance.

"Briggs," a familiar voice said.

Her stomach flip flopped when she looked up to see Cal no more than a foot away from her, looking smart in a pair of grey jeans and a lightweight black V-neck sweater with a white T-shirt underneath.

"Oh, hey, Cal," she said, tucking her hair nervously behind her ear and looking at the ground, avoiding his green eyes in case she didn't like what they communicated. She felt nauseous, not knowing where they stood.

"I'm sorry. Again," she muttered into the pavement.

"I know. I am, too." His voice was somber, uncharacteristically so. But not angry. She couldn't tell if his resignation stemmed from her inquiries last night, or the hassle with the city council vote, or both.

She looked up.

"I overreacted. I apologize."

"No, I didn't mean to pry, Cal, I just —"

"It's okay."

"We're okay?"

He nodded, a small smile playing on his lips.

"Let's just stick to the ground rules," he said.

She nodded, too eagerly. But her need for things to be *right* between them was all consuming. Being at ease with Cal Spencer had quickly become one of the most energizing aspects of her life, and she needed it to resume ASAP.

"I'll be on my best behavior."

"Briggs. That's enough. Please don't promise away all your naughtiness."

Her eyes looked up once more and saw mischief there. Relief washed over her.

"I—" she began, but she never had the chance to finish the promise. Just then the tea shop door flew open to reveal a sixty-something woman.

"Thank goodness you're both here," she said. With well-coiffed salt-and-pepper hair and designer heels, Poppy Hughes was impeccably dressed with a sophisticated Helen Mirren-esque air, despite the panic in her eyes. "You two must help me get to the bottom of this."

Stepping inside, it became instantly apparent why The Teal Tea Hutch was such a local favorite. The décor could be best described as vintage eclectic. The walls were painted different shades of teal, and the shelves and built-in hutches were brimming with retro embellishments. Victorian-esque art hung on the wall next to the occasional antique stitching sampler. Quirky, one-of-a-kind chandeliers hung over each table, several of which were filled with happy customers, and upbeat classical guitar music piped gently through a sound system.

"This place is just wonderful," Winnie commented as Poppy finally took a seat at a table in the back with a laptop set up on top, looking out of place in the quaint shop.

"Thank you, dear. I'm so sorry. I haven't even introduced myself yet. I'm Poppy Hughes."

"And I'm Winnie Briggs."

"It's nice to finally meet you. We all think you're doing such nice work at the paper."

"Oh, that's kind of you to say." Winnie's cheeks flushed.

"And do you know Cal Spencer?" Poppy asked hurriedly, her anxiety obvious as she forced her way through formalities. Winnie looked up into his face, which now featured a toned down version of his familiar ornery grin. She was relieved to see its return, even if it was somewhat subdued.

"Yes, uh…" Winnie said awkwardly. "We've met."

Surely his mind was also in that moment showcasing a highlights reel of just how intimately they'd gotten to know one another.

"Well sit, sit. I don't know where to begin." Poppy cried, running her hand through her short silver hair.

"Just take a breath, Poppy. I'm sure whatever it is, we can work it out," Cal offered gently, putting his hand affectionately on her forearm. Winnie could see Poppy relax. It had never occurred to Winnie before that Cal could actually be a soothing presence. Perhaps if Winnie's libido were as "seasoned" as Poppy's, it'd be a different story.

Poppy took a deep breath before continuing. "Well, as Cal knows, but you may not, Winnie, my tea room has a fairly positive reputation in the area."

"Not just in the area," Cal interjected. "This is a tourist destination. People drive well off the beaten path to experience Poppy's hospitality."

Poppy beamed at Cal, and suddenly it occurred to Winnie that there may be no libido too seasoned to be completely immune to his handsome charm.

"That's definitely the impression I've been given," Winnie added.

"Well, as Cal could tell you much more eloquently then me, we've really been working to increase the shop's online presence. It's one of his initiatives at the Chamber, and it's been a definite success."

Winnie looked at Cal, who smiled humbly.

"He's hosted all these wonderful trainings to get our local businesses online. I'm active on social media sites, I post on tea room forums. I even network with B&B listservs, since we share a similar audience."

Winnie was impressed. It made her feel like a jerk, but she'd been so consumed by Cal's handsomeness and charm that she hadn't given much thought to his professional capabilities. Suddenly it dawned on her what someone young and technologically savvy could offer a small town in the middle of nowhere in terms of publicity and marketing. Cal was clearly good for Bloomsburo.

"But perhaps most importantly, Cal has encouraged the food and entertainment people to get on Howl," Poppy continued.

"That's the website with the restaurant reviews?" Winnie asked. She'd heard of it, but never visited.

"The user reviews can really drive business," Cal explained, turning technical. "People trust reviews written by what they perceive to be *real* people. It feels more authentic than an establishment bragging about itself. Word of mouth marketing is really making a big difference for many small town attractions."

Poppy nodded. "I've run some promotions that encourage customers to get online and write a Howl review for The Hutch."

"They've been through the roof," Cal explained with obvious pride, "by far the highest of all the Bloomsburo establishments."

Poppy suddenly groaned in frustration, her hands running through her hair again.

"That seems like a good thing," Winnie offered. "I don't understand what the distress is about."

"I can't even say it out loud," said Poppy. "You just have to look."

She slid her laptop in front of Winnie. Cal scooted his chair closer, putting his arm across the back of Winnie's chair so he could lean in and see the screen. The gesture was so simple, yet so suddenly intimate, and she feared she might get taken away with the subtle scents of his delicious cologne. Her every cell charged at his proximity. She didn't dare look his way.

On the screen was the Howl page for The Hutch, but the average customer rating was listed as only half a star out of five.

"You were just averaging four and three-quarters stars last month," Cal said in disbelief. His arm pulled away from Winnie's chair and reached across her body to grab the mouse, which she had been operating.

"May I?" he asked, his perfect face so close, but so uncharacteristically serious. Winnie nodded quietly. He began reading some of the anonymous reviews.

The pastries were stale and the service was lacking. Don't waste your time going off your route for this place. Big letdown.

Poppy let out another groan as Cal finished reading the quote. It was clear how much of her own sense of self was wrapped up in the teashop's reputation.

Highly overrated. Tea was bitter, and had an unpleasant aroma. The snooty owner acts like you're inconveniencing her by ordering, then she'll mess up your bill to try to make some extra money.

"You of all people, Cal, know that I only serve the very best tea available!" Poppy cried.

Winnie looked at Cal, who was nodding in agreement with Poppy. "My mom's own blends," he explained. Winnie failed to see how anything produced by Rhonda Spencer could be anything less than fantastic.

Bathrooms were filthy. Waited 20 minutes just to get a menu, then they were out of our first three choices. Disappointed, and won't be back.

Poppy pushed her chair away from the table and pointed a stern finger at Winnie.

"Will you do me a favor, Winnie?" she asked, though it was phrased much more like a demand than a request. "Go and look in that bathroom."

Winnie looked at Cal for help. *Was she serious?*

Cal shrugged.

"I mean it," Poppy ordered like a stern schoolmarm. "Stand up. Walk over there." Then her voice softened. "Please. For my sanity's sake."

Winnie pushed off her chair and walked over to the pale teal door marked "Ladies' Room." She opened the door and actually gasped. She'd never in her life considered a public bathroom to be beautiful, but that was the only word to describe the private room. The walls, a serene eggshell blue, were as well decorated as the rest of the shop, and there was even a sitting area near the sink, complete with a wicker love seat covered in big throw pillows in coordinating patterns. Recessed lights on the ceiling and a small rock fountain in the corner created a soft, inviting effect, and the entire room smelled delicately of oranges.

Winnie came back out.

"Well?" Poppy asked desperately.

"I noticed one major problem," Winnie started.

"What?" Poppy gasped, eyes bulging.

"It's far too pretty to pee in," Winnie said. "But if you are willing to rent it out as a tranquil day spa, I'd sign up immediately. I could bring some books in there. You could deliver some fresh scones. It'd be paradise."

Poppy couldn't help but laugh with relief.

"I'm sorry I shouted at you," Poppy apologized. "I'm just so upset."

"Clearly these reviews are inaccurate," Winnie said as she resumed her seat next to Cal. She could sense the frustration coiling in his body and it tied her own stomach into knots. Surely he felt responsible for how this well-intentioned PR initiative had turned sour. Her desire to reach out and stroke his back, to give him some sort of physical comfort, was staggering.

"I could keep reading, but I probably don't have to," he said. "The reviews go on like this for about seven pages until you get back to the honest reviews."

"Please don't read any more," Poppy pleaded. "My heart can't take it. Plus I've read them all about a dozen times already anyway."

"Did you have any unpleasant incidents with customers in the last few weeks?" Winnie asked, wondering if a new enemy might be taking his or her revenge in cyber space.

"Not that I recall. This is a peaceful place. People come here to unwind and escape the chaos of the rest of their lives."

"To curl up in the bathroom with their bunny slippers, some pastries and a good book for a little 'me' time," Cal teased mildly, his face finally cracking in to a small grin aimed Winnie's way.

Winnie couldn't help but lean her shoulder into his as a reaction against his teasing. It felt good to be joking with Cal again, even if the circumstances weren't the best.

"It's not a place of confrontation," Poppy said. "I've been racking my brain, trying to think if I've created any new enemies lately."

"Are there any other business owners in the surrounding community that you've had a disagreement with?" Cal asked.

Poppy thought for a moment, but eventually lifted her arms in defeat. "Not that I can think of. You know how it is. There's not really any competition for this sort of venue. Not in a fairly wide radius."

Cal nodded. "Well, I guess we knew this was always a risk when we went online," he relented.

"Yes. You did brace us for this possibility."

"But I don't think this is a fluke. Someone is trolling your site," he said. "They're trying to send a message. And it wouldn't be someone local. Either all of our businesses survive or none of them do. No one can afford to screw someone else over, or they go down with the ship, too."

"Where do we go from here?" Poppy asked.

"Well, I'll go back to the office and call Howl. Surely this is not the first time someone has tried to sabotage someone else's business with bad reviews. There has to be some precedent for dealing with these situations."

Poppy nodded.

"Have you talked to Chief Conrad?" Winnie asked.

"No. You two were the first I thought of."

"Winnie's right though," Cal said. "Carter would want a heads-up about the situation. If someone is angry at you, or wants to hurt your business, they may try to make a move in the real world, not just online."

"Oh my," Poppy said quietly, her elegant hand grasping at throat. "I'll call him next."

"And how can I help?" Winnie asked.

"I'm not sure," Poppy admitted. "It just felt right to bring local media into the loop."

The reviews seemed suspicious, and if Winnie thought there was a story here, she'd run it. But she didn't think they were quite there yet.

"It may be best if we don't go public with this right now," Cal suggested. "That might only drive people to the review site, and we can't delete negative reviews ourselves. That defeats the site's mission of honest reviewing. But if I do some digging with Howl, figure out where these negative reviews are coming from, they may be willing to remove them, and the whole thing could blow over before anyone's noticed."

"That's true," Winnie agreed. "Local customers know your true reputation, and they wouldn't be going on Howl to check you out. At worst, this could cost you a few new out-of-town customers. But I'm sure Cal will get it all straightened out before anything serious happens."

Poppy nodded, resigned.

"Well, I've got some calls to make," Cal said, standing. "Will you be okay, Poppy?"

Her face was grim, but she nodded again.

"Call me if anything else comes up," he offered, leaning in and giving her a hug.

"Thank you, sweetie," she said. Her genuine affection for Cal was evident.

"Same here," said Winnie. "Once we have enough to make a story out of it, I'll run it on the front page."

"Thanks, dear," Poppy said, reaching to shake Winnie's hand once more. "And it was great to meet you, despite the circumstances."

Winnie and Cal wound their way back to the front of the shop, where smiling, relaxed customers proved just how off-base those online reviews were. As they made their way out onto the sidewalk, it was time for them to go their separate ways.

"So do you think this is connected to the other stuff happening around town?" Winnie asked.

He sighed in response.

"I think we need to start taking everything more seriously," he said. Winnie nodded, even as a nervous wave fluttered through her stomach.

"Well, good luck unraveling the Howl stuff," Winnie said, looking into Cal's face, which was now full of defeat.

"Thanks." He turned to start his walk up Main Street. Winnie surprised herself by reaching for his hand.

"Cal?" she called. He stopped, and let his hand be held by Winnie. His skin felt so warm, so right, against her own. Her urge to comfort him was as irrepressible as her urge to pleasure him had been days before.

He turned and looked at her once more.

"This isn't your fault," she said firmly.

His eyes dropped down to the ground in disagreement.

"It's not," she said, giving his hand a squeeze, not giving a damn who might drive by and see. "You're doing wonderful things for these businesses. You can't let some online trolls get you down."

He nodded in compliance, not agreement, and then let go of her hand, treading back up the street to his office. Winnie watched him walk away for a while, his hands shoved dejectedly in his pockets, before turning and making her way back down the hill to her own office.

She thought it was a flirty, charming Cal that would torture her the most, but it turned out that a forlorn Cal was even worse. She was determined to help get to the bottom of the case. Sure, she wanted to ease his mind and help Poppy's business, but she had her own motivations, too: bringing Cal back to all his lovely, flirtatious glory.

By the time she'd walked back to her office, she'd hatched a plan to investigate the situation. She called in a favor to one of the data analysts who worked at her previous newspaper, a woman who was an absolute whiz when it came to aggregating and investigating online information, even when it seemed difficult to trace. With any luck, Winnie would have some useful information in a matter of days.

Chapter 20

"Just set everything there on the buffet, sweetie," his mother called out when Cal walked into her kitchen with bags full of food for the equinox party. One by one he added his contributions— butternut squash soup, cider-braised chicken, and apple scones with maple butter—to the spread before tucking his extra bags away in the mudroom.

Yeah, he'd probably made too much, but carving out a few hours in his kitchen at the end of this hectic week had been an act of self-preservation. Between Bloomsburo Days looming, the absurd fee-hike approved by the city council, the dust-up with Winnie, and the Howl review crisis, it had been a hell of a week, so he welcomed the opportunity Friday afternoon to go into his kitchen, blast his favorite music, and cook away the stress. His mom never asked him to bring anything to her Equinox party, but knowing his sisters' complete disinterest in cooking, it always felt important to him to contribute something.

Plus, he just enjoyed it. Other than running, cooking was his go-to stress reliever. In fact, he enjoyed it even more than usual because now, as he moved between the sink and the stove and the island, as he scanned over his own kitchen table, he could picture Winnie Briggs there, whisking satiny batter and licking sweet cream from her fingers.

Winnie.

For all the professional stresses the universe flung at him this week, perhaps the biggest annoyance was how they'd sidetracked his progress with the woman. Had it really been just Monday when they'd taken that moonlight hike?

And had he really, completely, overreacted to her innocent inquiry about his dad?

He mentally kicked himself for the hundredth time since that night in Winnie's office. She'd shown compassion, and he'd made her feel like a jerk for it.

He thought of the way she'd looked at him outside of The Teal Tea Hutch midweek. The rightness of the way she gently grasped his hand and offered him encouragement. Feeling 'off' with her, even for a few days, made him feel like a limb was missing, and he was ready to feel complete again. Reflecting back on his week, the only bright spots involved Winnie.

He didn't know what to make of it all.

His mind focused back on the party, where his mother was now bustling to and fro in the kitchen. He appeared to be the first to arrive.

"What else can I do to help?" he called to his mom, who was whirring quickly between rooms.

"Hug me," she said, stopping in her tracks, and he gladly complied. He'd surpassed six feet a decade before, but somehow he still couldn't quite believe how small his mother was compared to him. But he'd always stop what he was doing to get a squeeze from the woman.

"It looks great in here," he said, and it did. His mom's house was always artsy and whimsical, but her fall decor really took the place to an enchanted level. Even though much of the evening would be spent out in the lawn, there wasn't a corner of her house that wasn't decked out.

"Thank you. And thank you for whatever you said to Winnie to get her to join us."

"Ma," he warned.

"Deny it if you want, but I know you must have encouraged her. She wouldn't have said yes otherwise." And he couldn't deny it. He inwardly winced, remembering how Winnie had texted him just that morning asking if it was still okay that she came, given their mid-week tension. He hated that she had to ask, yet he felt grateful for the realization that yes, he did still truly want her to be here, with his family. That was a hell of a thing to process.

"I just told her that resisting you is pointless. You'd wear her down eventually. I merely expedited the process to spare her some hassle."

His mom pinched at his sides, tickling him in response.

"Are the girls on their way?" he asked as his mom moved back toward the kitchen where she lifted a few Crock-Pot lids and stirred the contents, filling the room with delicious scents of cumin and tomato and onion and beef.

"Haven and Dan and the girls should be here any minute. Rosie had to work until six, so she and Spencer should arrive sometime after that," his mother explained. "And Willa? Well, we never do know with Willa, do we?"

Punctuality was not his middle sister's forte and they'd long ago given up on trying to fix it. Whenever she said she'd arrive, you had to factor in "Willa time" and add at least thirty minutes to her estimate. His sisters wouldn't be the only guests, though. Some neighbors and friends would join them, too, and soon the house would be bustling.

A knock on the back door made Cal's heart skitter. Winnie could be the only guest coming from the back yard. She was here, on his mom's doorstep, and a line was about to be irrevocably crossed.

It seemed irrationally monumental. Save for the odd prom date arriving for pictures, Cal had never once brought a woman to his mother's house. Sure, that wasn't exactly what was happening here. He hadn't invited Winnie, his mother had. And she wasn't his girlfriend. No, she was merely the smart, sexy, kind and competent woman he couldn't manage to stop thinking about for five minutes. Despite his attempts at resisting sentimentality and keeping it physical, he had to acknowledge that he felt more in his heart for Winnie Briggs than he'd felt for any woman before. And now she was about to enter his most sacred, inner circle.

Hell. This was about to get complicated, but if he was honest, it was excitement, not anxiety, that the milestone evoked in him. He wanted to show his family off to Winnie, and vice versa.

His mom had already rushed through the mudroom to usher her in.

"Winnie, I'm so glad you're here. Really, I could just cry," he heard her say, and he could tell that she was squeezing the life out of her guest as she said it.

They rounded the corner and came into view from where Cal leaned casually against the kitchen island. His heart revved at the sight of her. The woman was damn adorable. She wore a navy, button-up corduroy dress on top of a printed long-sleeved shirt and blue-and-green striped tights. Grey booties with a heel gave her a bit more height than usual. Something about the contrast between her sweet and upstanding behavior in public and her aggressive and passionate actions in private unraveled him.

What an honor it was to experience both sides of this woman.

His mind wanted to wander back to their adventures at the top (and bottom) of Cosgrove Hill, but tonight demanded more self-control than that.

His eyes made their way to her big brown ones, and he saw nervousness there. He saw that finger twirl in a curl, a dead giveaway that the woman was not at ease. He couldn't blame her, given his overreaction to her questions about his father just days before, and his moodiness after the Teal Tea Hutch meeting. She was so worried about screwing this up. About upsetting him. And that didn't sit right in Cal's stomach.

"Hey, Briggs," he said with a small wave and a smile. He forced himself not to imagine the greeting he'd prefer, which would involve more hands. Their mouths. He tried not to think of how she had bounded over to him at the bottom of that hill earlier in the week, throwing her arms around him. About how her hands excitedly worked to unbutton the front of his shirt just days before, like she had free rein over his body.

Which, frankly, at this point she did. He wondered briefly if she realized this power she held before her voice shook him out of his own thoughts.

"Hi, Cal," she said formally, before turning her attention back to his mother. "I brought some pumpkin bread. Don't worry. I didn't make it. I picked it up from Dewey's."

His mother took the loaf with a laugh and added it to the quickly growing spread of food on the buffet.

"Rhonda, your home is stunning."

"Thank you, hon. I love nesting. Want a tour?"

Cal was happy to see Winnie's eyes widen in delight, diluting some of the anxiousness in them.

Rhonda linked her arm in Winnie's.

"Sweetie," she said to Cal on their way out of the kitchen, "Could you make up some whipped cream? We'll want it for the pies."

He nodded, grateful for a task to distract him. Even above the whir of the hand mixer that was frothing the heavy cream and sugar into something sweet and fluffy, he heard the women's voices bouncing around the small house. He had to smile, imagining the stories his mother surely shared about her children's younger days. She was so good at remembering the positive, not the hard times. Not the dark mark of his father's contributions to those later years.

He shook his head, derailing that train of thought instantly. He never liked to think about that bastard, let alone tonight of all nights. But those memories had a way of creeping into his consciousness at the most inopportune times.

The fact that his bitterness over his father could sour what was happening between him and Winnie, even for a conversation, was enough to give Cal pause. That was a hell of a lot of power he was giving to a ghost. But tonight wasn't the night for unraveling all that old tension.

He shook the old, sad memories out of his mind just as Winnie and his mom returned to the kitchen. As he was covering up the bowl of cream and putting it in the fridge to cool, he heard the front door of the house open and the unmistakable clamor of the family's tiniest members. The sound of it caused a lightness to rise up in his chest. He didn't know much for sure, but he did know that being an uncle was the best damn gig in the universe.

Two sets of feet ran into the kitchen. "Hi, nana," his nieces said in unison, stopping to embrace Rhonda. He smiled just looking at the girls, a collective explosion of color and glitter and sequins and ruffles and bows from their head to their toes. Cal braced himself for their inevitable launch toward him, but the preparation was premature.

Uncle Cal, it turned out, was not the main attraction.

"Winnie's here?" Mary gasped, looking to her twin sister in disbelief. Lulu just started jumping up and down excitedly. Without haste, the girls ran toward Winnie and enveloped her in that collective little hug he knew so well. Winnie laughed in surprise. When she bent down to return the gesture, affection shining from her pretty face, Cal's heart grew three sizes.

"My fairies!" Winnie said, and his nieces giggled in delight.

"I'm Mary, remember?" Mary said. "I'm the one who always talks first, and I'm the one who's missing a tooth." She bared her teeth to show her jack-o-lantern smile.

"And how can I remember you, little fairy?" Winnie asked, turning her attention to Lulu.

"I'm the quiet one, and I have the freckle on my hand," she said softly, holding it up to prove her point. That tiny beauty mark had been the only way Cal had been able to tell the girls apart the first few months of their life. By six months old, however, their drastically different personalities made it impossible to mistake one for the other.

"Got it," Winnie assured her.

Cal clear this throat dramatically until the attention in the room turned to him.

"So what am I, chopped liver?"

The girls giggled and ran over to him, and he hoisted one up in each arm. It wouldn't be long before they were too big for the familiar gesture, but he'd do it for as long as he could.

Their little arms flew around his neck and each one kissed a cheek while he gave them a squeeze.

"Hi, Uncle Cal," Lulu whispered.

"Hey, Lulu Belle," he whispered back.

"Aren't you so glad Winnie's here?" Mary cried.

His eyes met Winnie's across the room, and unspoken words and heated memories flickered between them.

"I am," he said. And damn it, despite those old truths he knew about himself, about what he could and couldn't offer the woman, he was. It was as simple as that. Life was just better with Winnie Briggs near.

He put the girls down after one more squeeze and they went bounding toward the yard. Haven and her husband Dan made their way into the kitchen and the introductions continued.

"You must be Winnie," Haven said with friendliness, extending a hand to shake. She shot her brother a sly look. "And I have to say, any woman who can ruffle my brother's feathers is a friend of mine. So welcome."

Cal sighed and crossed his arms over his chest, resigning himself to the reality that this was how it would be for the remainder of the evening as one by one his sisters arrived, armed with a lifetime worth of stories they'd been dying to share about their only brother.

~-~-~-~-~-~-

Despite his sisters' endless ribbing, the night had turned out to be damn near perfect. Hours later, the neighborhood guests had all returned home and only Winnie and Cal's immediate family remained, gathered in wooden Adirondack chairs around the low, glowing bonfire. Cal felt a contentment that he couldn't have expected, having Winnie here with his family. Sharing in their special, ordinary moments. After his sisters got the teasing out of their system—which took a good long while—they'd all chatted comfortably throughout the evening, discussing favorite movies, favorite recipes, and plenty of Spencer childhood stories that all seemed to end with something embarrassing happening to him.

But he didn't mind. His siblings had always bonded through teasing. There was no need to act differently just because Winnie was here. He'd just have to make her promise to never utter a word of those incriminating stories outside of this yard, lest he be forced to torture her into compliance with his favorite tactics. The ease of it—how right it felt to have Winnie here with his favorite people on earth—that was something he'd have to think long and hard about.

He was stuck in his chair now, with a sleeping niece curled into his chest. Mary was always the first of the twins to nod off. It probably had to do with all the extra energy she burned with her never-ending chit chat. Lulu was snuggling with her mom, her eyes heavy, but still awake and quietly absorbing all that was happening around her in that way she had.

He glanced over at Winnie in the chair next to him. She was curled up in a blanket now for warmth, smiling peacefully into the fire. She looked so cozy there, the warm golden light from the fire flickering over her curls and her sweet countenance. The feel of her there, with them, filled him with the deepest satisfaction.

He wished he could feel anything other than fear when those sensations came over him—sensations that suggested that Winnie wasn't merely a fun physical distraction. Sensations that reminded him that she was kind and smart and funny and lovable as hell. Sensations that confirmed his hunch that everything was better when the woman was near. He watched her face twist into one of her big, charming laughs, responding to some story Rosie was telling. He hadn't caught the joke, though no doubt it had been at his expense.

"How about you, Winnie, do you have any plans for the holidays?" he heard his mother ask, snapping him back into the conversation.

He looked at Winnie then, just in time to see the discomfort flicker in her eyes. For all their time together, and all their conversations, he still hadn't learned much more about her story. *Chicago wasn't home.* He'd never forgotten those words from their very first interaction, but that's about all he knew. Even though it was part of the deal they'd made to not pry into one another's backstories, the gaps in what he knew of her history suddenly bothered him. In the beginning, it was her body that he'd obsessed over, eager to get to know each intimate inch. But now, forcefully and without warning, he wanted to know how she came to be the woman she was today. There wasn't a piece of her past that he wasn't fascinated to learn more about.

"No, I have nothing much planned for the holidays. Work will keep me busy." Her finger found its way to her hair where it began its nervous twirl. Cal didn't like the way he could feel the shift in Winnie's energy.

"Surely your family can come to you for Thanksgiving or Christmas though, right?" Rhonda asked, pressing ever so gently. He knew that the thought of a family not being together for a major holiday was unfathomable to her. Cal looked at his mother, hoping to signal her to back off a bit. She didn't spare him a glance.

Winnie cleared her throat nervously, her eyes gazing down toward the ground.

"No, they can't," she said softly.

The group turned quiet, with Cal's sisters shooting silent glances of concern between one another.

"Why, dear?" Rhonda asked, leaning to the edge of her chair so that the flames reflected that much brighter in her concerned eyes.

"Ma," Cal cautioned. He didn't want Winnie to feel uncomfortable. Not here. Not with them.

Winnie cleared her throat again and took a big breath, as if steeling herself for what she'd say next.

"It's really just me. There's no family to be had."

A heavy silence fell upon the group, broken only by Rhonda's soft whisper of heartbreak: "Oh, honey."

No family? Processing that revelation felt like lead sinking deep into Cal's gut. How could that be possible? A warm and fun-loving woman like Winnie didn't just rise out of nothingness.

"My parents and my younger brother were killed in a car accident when I was finishing college," she elaborated, her voice shaky despite her best efforts to control her emotions. Clearly this was a topic that the woman preferred to avoid, and understandably. Still Cal felt sick that he hadn't known. Sick, irrationally, that he couldn't

JESS VONN

travel back in time and somehow spare her the pain that now darkened her sweet brown eyes. Horrified at how he'd spoken to her earlier in the week, with his assumptions about her pain free past and her picture-perfect family, and the tears that had filled her eyes at his words.

What an ass he'd been.

"I have a few distant relatives, but they're far flung. We don't keep in touch much."

"Oh, my dear Winnie," Rhonda sighed. Cal could hear his mother's voice crack with emotion. "How truly awful. I'm so sorry. I had no idea."

"You couldn't have," Winnie said. "It's been five years now. It's been awhile now. You figure out how to move on. The only silver lining is that you don't mind working through the holidays quite so much."

Cal wanted to reach out to Winnie, wanted to hold her. To kiss her. To whisper in her ear how strong and lovely she was and how, if he had anything to say about it, she'd never again know that kind of loneliness. The thought scared the hell out of him, but for once, he put his own baggage on the back burner.

The sleeping niece on his lap made all of this impossible, though, not to mention the complication of the many people watching them right now. That didn't do anything to lessen the need, though—that bone-deep urge to comfort the woman. To pledge himself to her.

When had this changed? When had this physical game turned into something emotional? When had Winnie Briggs wrapped his heart and his soul in a velvet bow and claimed complete ownership?

He looked at her, wanting her eyes to meet his. Wanting that silent connection they had, without any words being shared. Her gaze stayed fixed on the fire.

The mood of the night had shifted irrevocably now, and Cal hated it. Hated it for Winnie. Hated the tears he saw her fighting back. Though a few of his sisters had made some gracious attempts at small talk, the conversation never really recovered and the end of the evening loomed over them all.

"Well," Winnie finally said with a forced laugh, sitting up in her chair. "This has been such an amazing party, Rhonda. I can't thank you enough for your invitation."

Cal's focus shifted to his mother, whose heart and mind were still trying to process the revelation Winnie had shared. But she was nothing if not gracious, and she forced herself to smile in return.

"You made it that much more special, Winnie. The fall equinox is about gratitude for abundance. You, all of you," Rhonda said, her gaze landing on every single person sitting around the fire, "you are my abundance. And I'm grateful."

"I second that emotion," Haven quipped, trying to lighten the mood. He was grateful for that.

"We love you, Mom," Rosie offered, and the rest of the group slipped into quiet conversation and the subtle shift toward departure.

"I hate to leave, but I'm afraid I'll turn into a pumpkin soon if I don't get home," Winnie said, standing and folding her blanket neatly and placing it on the chair where she'd just sat. He wanted to stand. To walk her home. To hold her. But the sweet, sleeping six-year-old affixed to his chest made that an impossibility.

"Will you take some extra food, Winnie? We've got so much leftover," Rhonda insisted, walking over and finally giving Winnie the hug that he knew she'd been desperate to give her for minutes.

"Maybe I can pick some up in the morning?" she asked, a compromise.

"It'll be waiting for you," Rhonda said, giving Winnie's arms a warm squeeze. He saw his mom whisper something in Winnie's ear. Saw Winnie close her eyes and hug his mother that much tighter for it.

Winnie gave Cal quick look. An apologetic, tearful look. But she didn't say a word. She merely turned back and began the short, dark walk to her cottage in the back of the yard.

He watched her walk away, shocked at the loss he felt from her departure. He wasn't sure he'd ever felt a stronger need to be by someone's side than he felt in this exact moment. Practicalities snapped him back to the moment, though, as he watched his sisters begin to gather up their items, put out the fire, and prepare to say their goodbyes. He gathered Mary up in his arms and carried her out to Haven's van where he bundled her into her booster seat so smoothly that she didn't stir once from her sleep.

He said goodnight to his sisters in the driveway, and made his way back to the kitchen to see if his mom needed help cleaning up. She shooed him out quickly, with one, unmistakable order. "Go," she said her head gesturing toward the She Shed. There was no pretending any more. No more hiding. Not from his mother. Not from himself. Cal nodded and headed toward the only place he could possibly imagine being in this moment—Winnie's side.

Chapter 21

By the time Winnie slipped back into the She Shed, her hands were shaking uncontrollably and the tears that she'd worked so hard to hold back had unleashed into a torrent of warmth and wetness on her cheeks.

A sob unfolded from her throat, one that had built up over the weeks of this transition to a new life in Bloomsburo. So much of these last weeks had been a denial of her loneliness, her lack of familiarity with anyone or anything in this new community.

Tonight had been among the first moments she actually felt at home here, and she'd ruined it. The night had been magical—talking and laughing and eating with the Spencers. Rhonda was so hospitable, the little fairies were so sparkly and affectionate, Cal's sisters were delightfully merciless in their teasing of the man who seemed beyond reproach, and Cal had been a swoon-worthy uncle and a gentleman, casting only the occasional discreetly hungry glance toward Winnie to hint at their after-hours activities.

But the question about her family came up, as it always eventually did, and changed everything, like it always did. Winnie hated dropping that bomb about her tragic backstory, but it couldn't be avoided forever. Once that sad truth was out in the open, though, everything changed. It stilted conversation. It made people uncomfortable. It resulted in friends disconnecting from her, so certain were they that their own stories about weekend trips to their parents or attending their siblings' graduations would unravel her. So certain that keeping distance from her was the best way to protect her. Bree had been the only one to truly look past it. To accept this unfortunate part of Winnie's life story, to witness and sit with her in her grief, and to love her unconditionally anyway.

It would always hurt. The loss Winnie experienced had been incalculable, and she suspected it would haunt her at the most inopportune parts of the rest of her life—every holiday, every birthday, her wedding day, the births of her children. She had no home base on which to land, seeking comfort or care. But she didn't deserve the awkward, pained silence that so often resulted from sharing her story, that emotional disconnection, just because people weren't sure how to talk about it or how to handle her. She may have a crack deep in her soul, but she wouldn't break. She was stronger for what she had been forced to survive.

A soft knock on her front door jarred her from her sad reverie, and dread joined forces with the hurt and embarrassment flooding her. This conflicted need – to be at once connected to others and yet wanting to be alone, embraced yet safe from the pitiful stares of outsiders and the torment of being handled with kid gloves due to her losses—it never got easier to navigate.

But she couldn't very well pretend she wasn't home. Everyone had just watched her walk into this cottage. There was no hiding now.

She expected to find Rhonda on her step with a basket of food as an offering of comfort, so her mouth fell open in surprise when Cal's inimitable frame filled the doorway, emitting that same virility and strength it had the first day she'd found him there. He said nothing, just looked seriously into her eyes. Looked at the tears streaking her cheeks. At the tiny tremble in her lower lip.

Winnie stepped back instinctively, ushering him in without a word and closing the door behind him. Before she had to bother coming up with the right words to convey her sorrow at how she'd screwed up, for interfering on his sacred family time and souring it with her sad story, his hands cupped her face and his mouth met hers in a kiss so deep, so sensual, that she momentarily forgot that there was anything to possibly be upset about. She grabbed his waist to steady herself with his solidness.

That kiss was a messenger, with its sweetness and passion and depth. Every sweep of his tongue communicated a level of care and affection that her brain couldn't process. She wanted nothing more than to anchor herself to this man, to let her connection to his body, just for a fleeting moment, serve as her sole tether to this world.

His lips made their way to her cheek, covering the trail of her tears with the sweetest series of kisses. The gesture comforted her in a way that a thousand words couldn't.

He pulled her head into his chest and filled his hands with her hair, massaging her scalp gently with his strong fingers.

"Winnie," he sighed into her hair, and her heart seemed to stop for a full second.

Winnie.

He'd never called her by her first name before. Never referred to her as anything but Briggs, that roguish, unemotional term of address that always reminded her of the limitations of their connection. No endearments. No emotional intimacies.

Tonight, though, her name on his lips was a declaration of walls tumbling down.

The intimacy of it transformed their sweet affection into something hotter. More urgent. Her hands ran across his back, across the muscular ridges of his shoulders as she pulled herself tightly against his strength. She'd never been more grateful for anything in her life than this man's offering of his body in this particular moment.

"Winnie," he said again, more of a groan, and she felt him harden where his hips pressed against her. His eyes, their green flashing with untempered desire, met hers. Asking without words how to proceed. A gentleman would see if Winnie wanted to talk about what happened, what was shared. He would offer words of comfort and support. Cal Spencer knew differently, though. He knew the exact type of release Winnie needed to push away the pain.

She confirmed her consent with her body, her hands, her lips. Devouring him desperately, fitfully. What little sensual grace she might normally muster dissolved away into something messier. Rougher. She wanted to be taken hard and fast and mindlessly.

Cal had other ideas, and he met her frantic need with torturously slow consideration. No matter how she grasped and pulled and scratched, he continued with heart-searing tenderness. In between his kisses and caresses, in between the work of his mouth on her heated skin, words of affection sprung softly from his lips, falling light as a feather on her skin.

Sweet Winnie...

Beautiful...

My lovely...

Each phrase clearly violated the terms of their agreement, yet one by one, as the words floated into the space between them, they seemed to stretch a taut string between his heart and hers, creating a web of soft spokes that would bind her to this man forever.

She wanted to respond in kind. Wanted to tell him how thoughtful he was. Tell him what a generous lover he was. To thank him for helping her awaken to the pleasures available to her. Thank him for offering the cradle of his body to her on this night. But she couldn't form the words, and instead tried to communicate them with fingers, her mouth, on his body.

She began to unbutton his plaid shirt, her fingers refusing to work fast enough for her satisfaction. Eventually she finished and he shrugged it off before yanking off the T-shirt he wore beneath it. Her breath hitched at the sudden feast before her—warm skin stretched over hard muscles, and that intimate smell of his skin and spice and something distinctly Cal. She rubbed her hands over him as he returned the favor, unbuttoning the front of her jumper, pushing down her tights. Tearing off the shirt that kept her breasts hidden from him.

Bared down to her magenta bra and panties, Winnie reveled in the touch of their stomachs skin-to-skin. She gasped in shock as he lifted her up onto his hips, forcing her legs to wrap around him in support. He pressed her back up against the kitchen wall, allowing her to feel the force of his erection where his straining jeans connected with the thin cotton of her panties.

Her memory sparked back to Cosgrove Hill. To all the ways he could make her body sing. To the thickness and taste of him in her mouth. She had to have all of him, right now. There could be no more waiting. She needed the man to fill her in every conceivable way.

"Take me to bed, Cal," she pleaded, and he wasted no time carrying her over to the tall four poster bed in the back corner of the cottage. He set her down gently on the edge, keeping himself firmly between her legs. He cleared the bed of its abundance of throw pillows in mere seconds. But he didn't move her, and he didn't sit next to her. He stayed right there in between her thighs.

Reaching behind her, he unhooked her bra, freeing her breasts from their torturous capture. He gently reclined her down onto the bed, her legs still dangling on either side of him. Her nipples peaked just anticipating his touch and when his fingers, then his lips, found their way to them, she gasped in pleasure. The suction of his mouth sent shards of sensation to Winnie's deepest core where desire pooled and pulsed. He nuzzled against her, rubbing the stubble of his jaw against the soft swells of her breasts and groaning with pleasure.

"You feel so good, Winnie. All I do these days is want you."

She wanted relief. She wanted him to crawl on top of her, to thrust into her until the fullness cleared her head of all other thoughts and needs.

His mouth pulled back and Winnie whimpered at the disconnection. In one quick move, he had her panties off and flung onto the floor behind him. Completely naked now, and completely vulnerable, Winnie should have felt self-conscious, but her wants left no space for insecurity. Her need for this man's sensual talents superseded all other possible thoughts.

"Winnie, Winnie, Winnie," he whispered reverently, looking upon her and taking in her fully exposed body softly lit from the light of a lamp across the room. Any lingering shreds of intimidation dissolved as she watched his face process her with unfiltered hunger. "How did you fall into my life? How did I get so lucky?"

Her heart and sex clenched simultaneously as his hands fondled her breasts.

"So sexy," he murmured. His fingers traced down the length of her stomach until they reached her thighs, doubling her need. Tripling it. She'd never needed release so badly. She was close to begging him when his hand slipped down between her legs, gliding through her moisture and rubbing delicately over that most sensitive notch.

A sob of pleasure tore from her lips, even if his touch only deepened her panicked desire. She was aroused to the point of near pain, so desperate for Cal to drive her over the edge with the full force of his hardness.

His lips spread into a small smile as he observed the agony she felt beneath his hands. There could be no sexier version of Cal Spencer than the one before her, reveling in the pleasure he could coax out of a woman.

"Please," she groveled, needing a climax more than oxygen.

"Do you need more, Winnie?" he asked, his eyes serious with a spark of mischief.

"God, yes," she managed, closing her eyes as she bore out the relentless stroking of his fingers on her clit. Her wanting knew no limits. "There can never be enough of you, of what you do to me."

"I'm going to kiss you," he said, her brain barely processing the warning. He could do whatever he wanted to her as long as his fingers didn't lift off her quivering body.

Unless…he wasn't referring to kissing her mouth.

"Cal, I…" she started. Her heart skittered all over the place. Wanting him. Fearing that divine intimacy she'd never experienced even as her clit pulsed at the promise of it.

"You're going to come," he promised, his head leaning forward as he kissed her mouth, "and it's going to be on my lips." His wicked eyes met hers, daring her to challenge his vision for her rapture.

She couldn't.

He sank to his knees between her legs. She waited with heightened pleasure. Waited for his lips to make contact, and when they finally did, they brushed her inner thigh.

Damn the man.

"Please," she choked out. The vulnerability that came with what he promised to do scared her to death, but she needed it, now. Her sex throbbed with pent-up desire just waiting to be unleashed and, importantly, she trusted Cal intrinsically. She gasped as his lips moved a fraction of an inch at a time, up the sensitive skin of her inner thigh. Gasped again when he kissed the soft hair that surrounded her sex. And when the plush heat of his lips finally landed at the core of her desire, she moaned. The feel of his lips, full and warm and wet, cast a ray of golden light up into her throbbing body.

His mouth opened her up to a pleasure she couldn't have fathomed. She'd read about it in books. Seen it portrayed in films, but nothing could have prepared her for the raw sensuality of Cal Spencer turning the full power of his mouth to her sex. Nothing had ever felt so generous. So intimate.

Just like with so many of his other kisses, his mouth was gentle at first, exploring her softly and stroking her with his tongue.

"Jesus, Winnie, this is making me so hard," he groaned between kisses before sliding his tongue harder against her, adding pressure and suction and rhythm and depth. She grasped the sheets, certain she'd float up off the bed if she weren't anchored.

"Cal, it's too good," she whispered, wondering if a woman could pass out from pleasure this intense. How had she made it to the age of twenty-six unaware that it could feel this good? The sensations grew so high and so strong that it became almost uncomfortable. She grabbed at his thick golden hair, and the feel of him working over her, working for her pleasure, took her that much closer. The pleasure seemed to fly through her body in wild, intangible sparks. She wanted to rein it in. Contain it. Magnify it.

He hooked his hands under her thighs, grabbing her ass and pushing her harder into the pleasures his mouth offered. No longer exploring, his mouth and tongue fell into a rhythm, working their way over that most sensitive spot, steady and firm. Helpless, her body surrendered to him, shattering in ecstasy, in wave after powerful wave of glittery release. She trembled, stunned by the intimacy and the beauty of what Cal had just offered her. What he still offered her as his mouth and fingers gently stroked and caressed her overwrought body while it came down from the stars.

It was so good. So bright. Winnie couldn't help the tears that fell from her eyes, no matter if they embarrassed her. The physical and emotional release she felt in that moment couldn't be contained. Cal kissed his way back up her body, caressing the softness of her stomach and the hills of her breasts until his fingers reached her neck, caressed her face.

"Winnie, I need you."

His words set her sex throbbing. For as perfect as her climax had been, for all of the mind-numbing goodness he'd evoked from her body, it still hungered to be filled with the man.

For Cal, this was sex. This was about pure, physical connection. But Winnie knew deep in her heart that it had extended to more than that for her. There was a place deep inside of her that only Cal could fill. She'd stupidly gone and fallen in love with a man she could never have. A man who touched her only on the condition that it wouldn't mean anything. Couldn't lead anywhere. The acknowledgment of it sent a new torrent of tears down her cheeks, which he rubbed gently with the back of his hand.

She couldn't play this game anymore after tonight. She knew from the beginning that Cal would open up doors to unbelievable offerings, but that the time would come when she'd have to walk away again. It would kill her to end it, but it would hurt even more to go one like this, having his body but not his heart.

She'd let herself have this night, though. One gorgeous parting gift.

"I want you inside of me," she whispered, pressing her mouth onto his. The warm connection stoked the embers of desire that still pulsed deep within her. The faint taste of her own climax lingered on his lips, and it only made her hungrier for the man. He pulled a condom out of his pocket as her hands fumbled at the button and zipper of his jeans, shoving them down to reveal tight green boxer briefs that barely contained his desire for her.

Sexy as hell. Her hands gripped at the waistband, and he groaned as he sprung free from the fabric. She hadn't gotten a good look at him in the shadowy haste of their fun on The Hill, but the man was magnificently hung. Hard and thick and satiny. Her mouth watered remembering her first introduction to his dick. Remembering the salt and the warmth of his climax in her mouth. She grabbed at him, needing to feel the weight and heat of him in her hand, on her lips, against her cheek, before he protected himself.

He didn't let her play that way for long, though. She could hear his breath quickening, could see his own pent up need tightening his torso as he handed her the condom. She unwrapped it, and rolled it slowly down the hard length of his cock. She backed her way up onto the bed and when he followed her, his naked body crawling up between her legs, she moaned in anticipation.

The weight of his body pressed down onto her, and he kissed her mouth. Her neck. Her breasts. She could feel his dick twitch against her core at each connection. She could tell how much desire coursed through his strong body. She could sense how desperate he was to spend himself inside of her. Slowly, his cock slid into her slick depths, and inch by inch he deepened his penetration. They both cried out at the rightness of the joining.

"Christ, Winnie," he said, giving voice to her very thoughts as he pushed deeper and deeper. His hardness stretched her and filled her in the most satisfying way. He looked so beautiful like that, planted between her legs, his strong, hands holding on to her hips, his eyes closed, his face twisted in pleasure, inaudible moans of satisfaction falling from his tempting lips. She could see how he willed himself to take it slow, how he resisted his own release from the moment he penetrated her. It felt so right, to have their bodies connected so intimately, to know that his body could take such pleasure from being inside of her own.

"I can't take much more of this, Winnie," he said, looking down at her, making eye contact with her for the first time since he'd entered her. Her sex tightened at the intensity of it, and somehow, impossibly, he grew harder inside of her. She couldn't fathom the pleasure this gorgeous man brought her but she didn't have to understand it. She only had to feel it.

"Winnie," he pleaded, his eyes locked into hers as he quickened the pace of his thrusts. His breathing quickened with exertion. She wanted to break the intimate hold his eyes had on her. It felt too powerful. Made her feel too vulnerable. But she couldn't. She was transfixed by this man. By his body. By his heart. She needed to memorize every second of what was happening so it could nourish her in the lonely days ahead. She needed to remember what it felt like when love transformed sex into something truly, inexplicably, sublime in case she never felt it again.

"I need you to come, Cal," she whispered. "Please." She rocked from the way he pounded into her now, no more signs of the tenderness or care he exhibited earlier. Now it was animal need, raw and unfiltered. His athleticism took over, ushering in those final, powerful plunges. With each thrust into her core in those final moments, he called her name, until that sweetest agony washed over his face, cried out from his lips, and he shuddered on top of her.

As his body collapsed onto hers, sweaty and breathless and deliciously heavy, Winnie clung to him like only a woman about to say goodbye to something glorious could.

Chapter 22

Cal woke up slowly, and in phases.

First, his body. Unrecognizable contentment weighed down on his relaxed muscles. He felt rested in a way he hardly recognized, so long had it been. It felt as if he'd let go of something that had long been troubling him.

Then, his mind awoke. His eyes opened sleepily, seeing an unfamiliar bookcase. He noticed the soft play of morning light on someone else's lace curtains.

He wasn't at home. Finally, his mind caught up to where he was, and how he'd arrived in this particular cottage on this particular morning.

Winnie.

Memories flooded over him. Kissing tears off her cheeks. Stroking her breasts against his jaw. The taste of her climax on his lips. The unspeakable pleasure of making love to her.

His heart caught at that last thought, because it dawned on him now last night had been a first for him. Yeah, he'd had sex before. Good sex. He'd screwed women. Fucked them, quick and hard and to the satisfaction of everyone involved. But nothing like what he experienced last night with Winnie.

The acts of last night hadn't involved any elaborate techniques; rather, the magic of what happened between Cal and Winnie originated solely from the chemistry of their two bodies.

He suddenly, and forcefully, craved more magic. It felt as if a pin had been pulled from him, activating something new. Something desperate and insatiable. Physical desire anchored to something sweeter, more caring. His fingers twitched from their emptiness. His mouth watered and his cock hardened.

Rolling over with a smile, he prepared to see Winnie's soft, sleeping body next to him. She'd be so warm. So sweet in her morning state. He might not take it slow this morning. He might devour her rough and fast like she'd wanted it last night before he'd worked so deliberately to slow down the process and savor every minute of it.

But instead of seeing a mass of mussed brown curls on her pillow, all he saw was a folded piece of paper on the otherwise empty side of the bed. His eyes flickered up to the rest of the cottage. Its quiet emptiness made him scowl. Damn his deep, contented sleep. Winnie had slipped out.

He sighed as he grabbed the paper. Maybe she'd run out for coffee and donuts and would return in a few minutes. Maybe she'd walk back through that door, ready to ease his aching morning hardness with her curvy offerings. There could be no better start to a Saturday morning than kissing trails of powdered sugar off of Winnie's soft skin.

Unfortunately, her note quickly shot that fantasy straight to hell.

"Shit," he growled as he scanned the message a second, and then third time.

Had to take off early for a work thing. Will text you later. Lock up please? -W

Winnie's message was curt and dismissive and he easily read everything it communicated between the lines. She didn't want to talk about last night and now she wanted him out of here. Her morning, unlike his, had been marked by neither an overwhelming sense of satisfaction from the night before, nor an unshakeable need to reenact its highlights.

That was a hell of a thing to contemplate.

When he'd followed Winnie home last night and knocked on her door, he had no idea how the evening might unfold. All he knew was that her eyes at the bonfire had expressed such sadness and vulnerability that he had no choice but to find his way to her side. He would have gladly stayed up all night talking to her, holding her, letting her cry into his arms.

But one look at her at the door of the She Shed, and he'd known what she needed. Her body craved his touch and his strength, and he more than gladly complied.

It had been a consensual and mutual, he knew that then and he knew it now. But in the harsher clarity of morning light, he realized he had broken several tenets of Winnie's relationship agreement. The love words he whispered into her neck, her breasts...technically forbidden, yes, but they were involuntary. The woman was sweet and lovely and gorgeous and to ask him to deny those truths as he explored her body wasn't reasonable.

He'd also slept over, another broken rule. Another honest, happy accident. It had happened so naturally. After the sheer tidal wave of pleasure he experienced with Winnie's luscious body, not a word was shared between them. He had nestled in behind her, one arm draped over her so his hand could rest gently against her soft stomach. His pelvis hitched up against the sweetest fullness of her bottom. The front of his knees tucked into the back of hers. His face burrowed into the warm and fragrant nest of her hair.

He might not remember falling asleep, but he sure as hell remembered the last thought that flickered through his pleasure-drowsy mind, because it was a thought he'd never had before.

This is it.

It freaked the hell out of him at first. If his genetics revealed one truth it was that he was not the settling kind.

He should run. He should protect Winnie from the heartbreak he would unleash upon her.

And yet... a deep, abiding since of *rightness* filled his body and his heart. The challenge of it, of being enough for a woman like her, overrode every insecure, doubtful instinct that bubbled up in his consciousness.

There had been a moment in his father's life where the man decided he wasn't enough for his wife, for his kids. Instead of fighting to become a better person for them, instead of turning to them for comfort and connection, he fled. He did everything possible to resist the love and the foundation right in front of his face.

All of Cal's life he'd wanted to prove that he was a different kind of man than his father. It looked like he'd finally found his chance.

No trumpets blaring, no cupid's arrows or dizzying love-at-first sight spells. Just the unfaltering realization that his body and his mind and his heart had all somehow arrived at the unanimous conclusion that life was immeasurably better with Winnie at his side. More importantly, he knew deep in his bones that he wanted her to feel the same way about him.

It wasn't just the sex. That had been amazing, but it was just one piece of why he'd fallen for her. It was her heart, how it worked to unravel his complex past. It was the humor with which she approached her work, and the challenging characters she encountered there. It was her warmth and ease with his mother, his nieces, with him. Her tenderness and humor.

He didn't know if he could be a better man than his father. Couldn't know that. But damn it, for the first time in his life, he felt ready to try. To be more than he ever thought he could be. He loved nothing more than a challenge.

Yet here he was, waking up alone. For all that Winnie had made him feel in his body and his heart, clearly things had not been properly reciprocated.

"Shit," he growled, getting up and finding his clothes in a pile on the floor. Putting them back on, he could still smell the bonfire on them. He sighed loudly. As if the morning couldn't get worse, he now had to do the walk of shame through his own mother's back yard.

Glancing at a clock on the wall, it was later than he thought. His mother would be up by now. She'd have already noticed his car still in her driveway. Then again, she'd probably known pretty well what was going to happen when Cal had made his way to the cottage the night before. The jig was up.

And damn it, it wasn't a walk of shame. Frustration at Winnie swelled in his chest for having made him feel that way. What they'd shared had been sweet and powerful and pleasurable and mutual, and she owed him more than a hasty note on the bed afterward. But then again, hadn't he set the precedent earlier in the week for running out when things got tense?

He stomped his way out of her cottage and through the shared yard, making sure to avoid looking up into his mother's back kitchen window lest he find her concerned face there. With each step, an unrecognizable ache deep in his core twisted and grew. He hopped into his car, slammed the door shut, and began the short drive back home.

All these years, Cal had told himself that there could be no fate worse than settling down. He'd convinced himself that feeling deep affection for a woman would bring out the worst in him. That he'd only bring her the type of misery that he'd seen his mother experience at the hands of his father.

For so many years, he couldn't fathom a fate worse than that. What a blow to the heart to figure out what trumped it: the realization that his deep affection might not be mutual.

~-~-~-~-~-~-~-

Winnie didn't have a plan when she crept out of her own cottage at dawn. She hadn't even realized she'd fallen asleep until she woke up to find Cal's gorgeous, sleeping face just inches from hers. In the peace of sleep, he looked so sweet, so non-threatening. He appeared almost childlike, the way his criminally long lashes fringed his contented eyes while he slept.

The sight of him there, the memory of what they shared, had filled her with such an overwhelming mesh of anxiety and pleasure that she simply had to flee. She pulled on a mismatched outfit, slipped into her flip-flops, and drove Fiona the Ford out into the yellow-and-blue streaked dawn of the early September morning with no destination in mind.

Ninety minutes later, after countless rambling twists and turns, she finally pulled into a mall parking lot in a town she'd never heard of, though her GPS told her she was more than an hour away from Bloomsburo. It had been her first big trip out with Fiona the Ford since she'd arrived in town.

How was it possible that so much could change in a month?

She put the car into park and took her hands from the wheel, marveling at how they still slightly shook.

This. This was the moment she had known would be inevitable since the very first minute she saw Cal Spencer. From that day she'd made the choice to let his sexiness and charm ease their way into her life and onto her body. It was always going to be a deal with the devil. For however good it felt in the short run, and by God had it all felt better than her wildest imagination could have conjured, she knew that it would come at a price.

She'd hardly slept the night before. She'd noticed the second Cal had fallen asleep, his arms and his legs growing heavier where their weight cradled her body affectionately. She'd noticed his breathing growing deeper, with the occasional deep, contented rumble in his chest. That heavy-bodied ease with which men slept.

That was the moment, spooned up against the most sensual, most stunning man she'd ever known, that she'd let herself imagine, just for a minute, what it could be like. Her want for him, her lust for all that a life with him could offer, surrounded her until she nearly drowned in it—that vision of what her world might be like if Cal was her home.

Certainly there'd be nights of pleasure like she'd just experienced. Endless hours of his hands and mouth upon her, his hardness inside of her. His body collapsed in satisfaction next to her as they drifted off to sleep. But it wasn't merely the promise of physical pleasure she envisioned. She could picture long weekend trips to wineries and B&Bs and wooden cabins surrounded by the crisp rustling of brilliant fall foliage. She could picture them snowed in at his cozy house, curled up for days at a time on his comfy sectional couch, binge watching entire seasons of their favorite TV shows while they ate the cookies he'd baked for her. The happy chaos of holidays with his big family. She could picture them walking down Main Street, holding hands in public like a real couple, stopping to greet the familiar community characters that colored both of their professional lives.

Her traitorous, masochistic brain could even picture him in a perfectly cut suit at the front of a quaint, rural church. In a hospital room, gazing adoringly at a newborn bundled in soft blankets.

Her eyes blurred again, correcting her earlier assumption that she'd already wrenched every final tear from her body.

Hope. The emotion that helped her realize that things had to end with Cal immediately. Hoping was the one thing she couldn't allow herself to do given what she'd already lost in her lifetime. In hindsight, it was now clear to Winnie that an aversion to hope had been the only explanation for why she'd stayed with Anthony for as long as she had. She stayed with him not because she *could* see their picture perfect life together, but because she couldn't. She couldn't get lost in the possibilities of a long and happy life with him. She couldn't force her brain to consider the kind of husband or father he'd be. That's why she took comfort in the mediocrity of their relationship. Why she put up with his digs and his controlling ways and the suspicions of infidelity that ultimately proved to be true. If she didn't even bother to dream of where it could go, she couldn't be crushed by that dream's failure to manifest.

JESS VONN

Cal was a lot of things—sexy, confident, kind, professional—but he wasn't a living Ken doll, ready and willing to help the new girl in town construct her happily ever after. He was the kind of man who took what he wanted from life. Though it was clear that their casual ground rules pleased him, it was now evident that Winnie couldn't possibly keep up the charade that a physical, no-strings-attached tryst could be enough for her. Not given the white picket scenarios that her heart and mind had traitorously conjured.

No matter what fun they'd had these past weeks, the truth was that eventually, a man like Cal Spencer would be on the lookout for another adventure, and even the thought of him making another woman feel how he made her feel, physically and emotionally, left her distraught. Heartbroken. She took small comfort in the familiarity of those feelings, a dull silver lining along the edges of her monstrous pain.

She was being selfish. A coward. She knew it this morning when she fled her and Cal's shared bed, and she knew it now, but this was likely her last chance to control how this ended, and to end it before she grew even more attached. He had so much to offer her, and he was such a good man, but she couldn't lose herself in him. Already it felt so easy to hitch her star to his, to hinge her happiness on his contributions to her day-to-day life. But it made her feel too vulnerable. Too exposed. So even though it took every ounce of courage to walk away from that delicious, naked body sprawled across her bed, it was ultimately an act of self-preservation.

Winnie first.

And now it was time to close the deal. He deserved a phone call or a face-to-face conversation, but her voice would reveal too many truths that she prayed he'd never learn.

With trembling fingers, she typed the words that would seal her fate, sending a mortal blow to the hope that had so audaciously bloomed.

Our deal was that I could call it off at any time. I've got to do that now. I'm sorry. :(

She pushed 'send' and contemplated throwing up. The nausea only amplified when those dots indicating his response appeared instantly. For better or for worse, there would be no waiting on his reply.

Was it something I did? Are you okay?

The guilt and concern in his response gutted her. *Was it something you did?* she thought to herself with a bitter laugh. *Yeah, you made the mistake of doing everything right, you bastard.*

No, just need some space. Will be fine.

In a year or two, she silently amended. One minute later, her phone registered the arrival of what would likely be the last text message she'd ever receive from Cal Spencer. It consisted of only three little words. Not *those* three words, but they somehow managed to be just as devastating.

I'll miss you.

Winnie took little comfort in the fact that the feeling was mutual.

~-~-~-~-~-~-

On one level Cal was aware of the Sunday dinner conversation swirling around his mother's kitchen island, but he was so lost in his thoughts that he may as well have been alone in his house across town. He heard snippets of his sisters' talking points: PTA meetings and new movie releases and the latest news about the royal baby, but he hadn't said three words all night.

Grateful to be on lead cooking duty tonight, he busied his hands mashing potatoes and steaming vegetables and checking on the roast in the crockpot, but his mind was still trying to process where he'd gone wrong with Winnie.

On Friday evening she had seemed so grateful for his presence. She seemed as enchanted as he was by the powerful connection of their bodies. Yet somehow, between falling asleep with the woman in his arms and waking up the next morning, she'd rejected him. Rejected the connection that damn near vibrated between them and had him contemplating the one word that he never even knew existed in his vocabulary: *forever.*

Her text hadn't made any sense. If he could just talk to her—just sit with her and stroke her face and tell her what he was feeling—things would be different. But clearly she didn't want that. She didn't even have the courage to call him to break it off with him over the phone. He didn't know how to interpret that, because if there was one thing he knew for certain, it was that Winnie Briggs possessed courage in spades.

It just didn't add up, and he felt sick about the way that his disconnection from her corresponded exactly to the moment he'd finally figured out what she'd meant to him.

He didn't have a damn clue how to proceed. How did you give a woman space when what you really wanted to do was give her everything you had and more?

"I think those are good and mashed, sweetie," his mom said as she walked up behind Cal and put her hand gently on his. He looked down and realized that, lost in his own thoughts, he had pulverized the potatoes.

"This will all keep warm," she said, handing him a glass of red wine. "You come with me for a few."

Rhonda led Cal out to the rockers on her front porch. The twilight sky was a lovely shade of purple, and the calmness of the space stood in contrast to the chaos of Cal's mind.

He and his mom sat side by side on wooden rocking chairs.

"Please talk to me, honey," his mom said quietly. "I'm worried about you."

Cal sighed. He didn't want to have the conversation, even though he knew he needed it. If he couldn't talk to his mom about what was troubling him, who could he talk to? He didn't want to betray Winnie's confidence, yet somehow he knew that his mother had been onto their connection from the very beginning. He'd never understand it, but mothers had that sort of sixth sense.

"It's Winnie," he managed. His palms felt sweaty and his pulse raced. Why was it so damn hard to talk about his feelings?

"I figured," she said. "Is she okay?"

"I don't know. That's the problem."

He felt his mother's concerned gaze on his. She stayed quiet, though. She knew from years of experience that the best way to get her son to talk was to keep her own mouth shut and give him time.

"We'd been getting to know each other," he said, staring down at the glass in his hand.

"That's wonderful, honey."

"It was," he said, sure his eyes were filled with angst he didn't even bother to conceal.

"When I went over there after the bonfire…" He trailed off.

"I figured," she said, squeezing his hand affectionately, not requiring him to finish that sentence. He had the most sex-positive mother on earth. There was no need to be ashamed of his adult behavior, but that didn't mean he necessarily wanted to go into details.

"I thought it was a really amazing night. I thought she felt the same way, too, but yesterday she texted me and told me she needed some space."

He heard his mom sigh next to him.

"And how does that make you feel?" she asked quietly.

"Angry. Sad. Confused. Mostly sad."

"Oh, honey," she said, running her back across his shoulder, a gesture of comfort she'd done thousands of times before.

"I don't understand it," he said, "but it's probably in her best interest." He sensed his mother tense next to him, knowing this was not a path she liked to go down.

"Cal, you have to let go of those old stories you believe about yourself."

It was his turn to stay silent.

"Do you think I'm a stupid woman?" she asked, the emotion in her voice forcing his eyes to meet hers.

"Of course not," he said, taken aback. His respect for his mother was boundless, and she knew it.

"Well, let me tell you something, son. If I had this whole life to do over, I would choose your father again. In a damn heartbeat."

Cal's jaw clenched. How his mother could speak fondly of his father after all he'd put them through, he'd never understand.

"And you know what, you *do* remind me of him."

"Huh," he said bitterly. "So then you understand why it's best if Winnie keeps her distance."

"The biggest problem with your dad in the early days was his looks. Maybe it's just my nostalgic recollection, but he may have even been more handsome than you are now, which is saying something."

She laughed lightly and Cal silently cursed his handsome face. Every time he looked in the mirror he saw the spitting image of his dad. Even his first name, Charles, was another hand-me-down from the man he'd rather not think about.

"I worried, at first, about dating him, because he was so good looking," his mother continued nostalgically. "Girls were always throwing themselves at him. He could have had his pick of anyone. That can be really intimidating to a woman."

Cal stayed quiet, letting his mother speak her peace, and trying not to think about his dad's later decision to take those other women up on their offers, even when he was still married to Cal's mom.

"But he was so kind. And I found that combination to be so attractive. He could have been a jerk. He could have been a cad. But he was a good man. And he proved it over and over again as each of you precious children joined our family."

He heard his mother's voice crack at the fond memories. He squeezed her hand. Even if he didn't understand it, he knew his mom still missed his father every single day.

"He was a loving dad. I know you try to block out everything that happened before Rosie's diagnosis, but surely you still have some memories of those happy moments tucked away in that stubborn mind somewhere."

He did, even if he generally refused to let them out. Even if he vowed never to admit it.

"There was nothing that made him happier than being with me, with you kids. Providing for us. It's what he lived for. I see so much of him in you when you watch out for your sisters, and wrestle with your nieces, and humor your doddering old mother."

An involuntary laugh slipped from Cal's lips.

"Life got hard, Cal, and no, he didn't make the best decisions that last year," she said, her voice full of emotion as she remembered the events leading up to his death. "But that doesn't erase everything that came before it. That doesn't change who he was, or the love and commitment he was capable of."

Cal let out a long sigh.

"Whenever you decide to give away your heart, you need to know that it's not going to be a perfectly smooth road for the two of you," she continued. "You'll make mistakes. So will she. But hopefully you'll grow together, learn from one another, and be all the stronger for it."

Cal considered that for a moment.

"She won't hurt us, Cal," his mom said quietly, finally putting her finger on the heart of the issue for Cal. "You don't have to keep up that boundary anymore, between our family and the rest of your life. We're on solid ground now. And what we have is worth sharing with those who are special to us."

On a rational level, he knew his mother was right. It had just been a really, really long time since he'd allowed himself to be rational about his personal life.

"Winnie adores you, and if she tells you otherwise, she's lying," she said plainly. He took comfort in her assessment, even if it made his heart constrict. "She's terrified of what you could mean to her. And I'd guess that feeling is at least in part mutual."

He sighed in agreement.

"So what are you going to do about it?" she asked.

He shot his mom an annoyed glance. "What do you mean?"

"I mean, what are you going to do to earn her trust?"

Resentment flared in his chest. "I didn't do anything to lose her trust. Why should I—?" he started, but she cut him off midsentence.

"Cal Spencer, I love you more than life itself, but you've not had to work for much in this life."

He shook his head in disbelief. Only his mother would pick this particular moment to lecture him about his work ethic, which, for the record, was outstanding.

"You're tall, athletic, intelligent, handsome as sin, and twice as charming."

He rolled his eyes.

"The world tends to unfold for you. Women beat down your door. Friends seek you out. You've landed every job you've ever applied for. The good life's been handed to you, kid. You haven't been asked to work for much."

Okay, now she was going too far. The woman pushed his buttons just to get a rise out of him. And damn it, it worked.

"Haven't been asked to work for much?" he repeated incredulously. "What about stepping up at seventeen to become the man of the family when my asshole father lost all ability to function as an adult?"

His mother's eyes flashed, and he suddenly remembered exactly from whom he got his obstinate streak.

"Yes, Cal. You grew up faster than I would have liked. But you didn't have to earn our love. You always had us—me and your sisters. We would have loved you no matter what you did or didn't do. You stepped in, you took such care with the girls, you—" Her voice cracked, which made his heart do the same. "You probably saved my life those years. You were the reason I got through."

He squeezed her hand, hating to see that old pain reliving itself across his mother's face.

"But you weren't scared of us, and we weren't scared of you," she continued. "In her young life, Winnie has lost more than most people can fathom. And her last boyfriend cheated on her and humiliated her, dissolving whatever sense of confidence and security she had built up."

Cal's heart stopped, remembering the story Winnie had told him weeks ago about how she ended up in Bloomsburo. He'd been so caught up in enjoying her that he'd forgotten how mistreated she'd been in the recent past. Defensiveness swelled through his chest. A defensiveness he hadn't known since caring for his younger sisters all those years ago. Not to mention a flood of shame as he realized just how close he was to becoming one more asshole who took Winnie Briggs for granted.

He raked his hands through his hair, his mind whirring with new possibilities.

"You do not come across as the safe and steady rebound, Cal," Rhonda continued, "especially the way you were carrying on in private as if you were ashamed of her."

He shot her daggers. "That's not how it was, Ma."

"Well how was it then?"

And damn it, he wished he had a better answer.

"The rest of the world knows that you're handsome and charming and persuasive," she said. "That's surface stuff that you couldn't hide if you tried. You've got to show her what only your family truly knows. That you're protective. Proud. Loyal. That when you choose to love, it's for life."

He blinked away some moisture in his eyes.

"She's worth it, Cal," his mother said. "Worth the fear and the vulnerability."

He sighed deeply, the anger dissipating, replaced with astonishment at how his mom managed to hit the nail on the head every single time.

"What's the worst thing that could happen?" she asked.

He thought for a minute.

She might not choose me.

I'd be without her after learning what life could be like with her.

Put another way, he'd be in the exact same spot he was in right now. Which meant he had nothing to lose and everything to gain.

Ideas whizzed through his mind faster than he could process them. How could he begin the work of giving away a heart he'd kept under lock for more than a decade?

It would take time and thought, which meant it would have to wait until after Bloomsburo Days. Starting Tuesday he'd be working fourteen-hour days through the weekend. But before he could give any more thought to his strategy for winning Winnie, his sister Haven stuck her head out of the sliding glass door, her playful attitude dissolving the intense mood on the front porch.

"Hey, chef boy, are we ever going to eat? The girls are starving."

"So what you're saying is that *you* are starving," he said lightly.

"Well, yeah, but I thought I could inspire you into action more quickly if it was for your sweet nieces instead of your pesky sister."

"You know me well. I'll be right in."

Haven tucked back inside and Cal leaned over and gave his mom a kiss on the cheek.

"You're a wise woman."

"So you'll work for it?" she said, her voice full of a hope she didn't even bother to temper.

"I'll take it under consideration."

"Because I take it personally, you know, when you sell yourself short. I raised a good person. I want someone to appreciate him. I want someone to come home with you for Sunday dinner and tell me what a fine job I did raising this handsome man, thanking me and praising me profusely. Especially after I went to the hard work of hand-delivering the perfect woman to you."

He grabbed her cheek affectionately.

"You're a meddler *and* a narcissist," he said with a grin, before helping his mom up and walking arm-in-arm back into the boisterous kitchen.

He might not know yet how he was going to try to win Winnie's trust, but even the knowledge that he was going to fight for her made him feel lighter and the long days ahead seem more bearable.

Chapter 23

The new message Winnie found in her inbox on Tuesday morning felt like a slap in the face. Even worse, it felt like a slap in the face that she had all but begged for.

The message was from Danny M. McDonald the Intern, and Cal's return to his use of a go-between only served to remind her of the distance she put between them—a distance that still felt like a knife in her gut.

She'd asked for space and Cal had complied. What she couldn't figure out was why his cooperation hurt so much. Probably just because it was one more reminder of what a fine damn man he was. A fine man who would never be hers again.

She scanned the message and groaned inwardly. "Mr. Spencer" thought the special section draft looked fine, but the Chamber needed an extra full-page, full-color ad. The twenty-four-page section was set to go to print the next day. Although Winnie wouldn't need to design the ad—that was all handled in the print shop—she did have to find room for it. This change of plan would only make more work for Winnie. You couldn't merely add one page—the section had to be printed in groups of four pages, which meant she now had to add or cut a whole lot of content to make it work.

Of course she had to comply, because the section was mostly just a money maker for the publisher. It was hard to make that money if the editor rejected paying ads because it created more work for her.

Luckily she'd already finished tomorrow's issue of the paper. Increased productivity had so far proven to be the only upside to insomnia and heartbreak. So it was that most of the rest of Winnie's day was spent shifting content, reducing photo sizes, and editing her writing in order to accommodate the new full-page ad, which she stuck on the back of the section. It would be sent to the printer tomorrow, and be published Friday morning, just in time to let the good people of Bloomsburo know all about the events that their favorite weekend held.

It seemed impossible that Bloomsburo Days was now nearly upon them. It was still a far-off concern when Winnie had arrived in town a month ago, and now the events began tomorrow.

Winnie looked forward to the event, she really did. Through her work on the section, and through her conversations with people around town, she now fully understood how the festival was the cornerstone of the community.

Her only wish was that every mention of Bloomsburo Days didn't make her think of a sexy, golden-haired Chamber director. It would be a long, awkward week of trying her best to avoid the man around town.

Gloria's voice around the corner prevented her from sinking too far into the woe-is-me hole that she kept finding herself in these days. Once again, she felt gratitude that her job seemed to never end. All the better for burying herself in her work rather than wallowing in her heartbreak.

"Winnie, can you take a call?" Gloria asked. "It's Chief Conrad."

Winnie's brow rose in concern. She'd talked to Carter plenty of times around town, but he'd never directly called her. Her stomach sank. What were the odds he was calling with good news?

She picked up the phone and greeted Carter, who cut straight to the chase.

"Could you meet a group of us after work tonight? Seven, at the station?" he asked, his voice serious. "There's another development related to the suspicious activities around town."

He said little, but communicated so much. Winnie tried not to think too hard about who "us" might include, but she prepared herself for the worst. If something else was happening in the town, and Carter was concerned about it, then certainly Cal was part of the conversation.

"Umm, yeah. I should be able to make it," she said, glancing at the time on her computer. It was already 6:15 p.m., but she'd just wrapped up the adjustments to the special section.

"Great. See you then," Carter said before hanging up the phone.

Over the course of the next forty-five minutes, Winnie did her best to avoid the mounting dread that filled her stomach—for the town, of course, but if she was honest, mostly for herself at the thought of facing Cal again after what she had done.

She would have reeled in that anxiety if it weren't for an email that popped into her inbox ten minutes before she was to depart for her meeting with Chief Conrad.

A message from her friend, the data analyst at her old paper who was helping do some digging on the Howl reviews popped into her inbox. The woman had a lead, and when Winnie read through the message, the blood drained from her face. Shock flooded her system so thoroughly that for the first time in recent memory, the pain of her broken heart faded from her consciousness. She printed the email and sped her way through town to the police station.

~-~-~-~-~-~-

Winnie had expected to find Chief Conrad at this meeting, and she had expected to see Cal, despite her deepest wishes, but the person she could not have predicted to be in attendance at this clandestine gathering meeting at the Bloomsburo Police Station was Betty Jean Finnegan.

Yet by the time Winnie was ten feet from the conference room, she could hear the woman's unmistakable harping. Walking in, the sounds of distress became more defined.

"I need you to tell me exactly what you plan to do about this," Betty Jean cried as Winnie entered the room. She met Betty Jean's frantic gaze, before scanning the room to find Carter, looking stressed. Finally her eyes moved to Cal, who wore a soft, long-sleeved green Henley shirt the exact color of his eyes. He nodded, a silent greeting, but he looked somber and tired. Cal just wasn't Cal without that distinct spark of life emanating from him.

Winnie willed herself not to think about the last time she'd seen that spark. Tried not to think about the last time she'd seen the man, period—ass up in her own bed, stretched out in satisfaction.

Her brain simply couldn't reconcile the two versions of Cal—one sexy and satiated, the other exhausted and frustrated. Despite her current awkwardness, how small and petty and unworthy she felt in the moment, she knew it was for the best that their reunion had been forced. The only thing worse than seeing Cal again after the way she'd cut things off so abruptly was her panic at wondering when a reunion might happen. At least it was now behind her.

JESS VONN

"Good evening, Winnie," Carter interjected, the only person to fully acknowledge her arrival. "It's time to bring you up to speed."

Winnie's heart raced, and seeing Cal wasn't the only thing to blame for it. She also worried about whatever had happened in town to call the meeting in the first place.

"There was a suspicious act at tonight's spaghetti dinner fundraiser," Carter explained.

"Winnie would have known this had she bothered to show up and cover the event," Betty Jean spit out, sending a make-up laden glare Winnie's way.

"Betty Jean, let's stay focused on the real issue at hand," Carter gently chided the woman, earning Winnie's eternal gratitude. Betty Jean huffed and crossed her arms in displeasure, but miraculously she let it drop. Winnie had opted out of the event in exchange for finishing up the special section.

"Someone called in a bomb threat at the Veteran's hall."

"A bomb threat?" Winnie gasped. Her gaze instinctively went to Cal, who nodded quietly in confirmation. "Was anyone hurt?"

Her mind quickly flickered through all the people she knew and cared about in Bloomsburo. The two men in the room, of course, though clearly they were unharmed. But her mind whirled to Evie and her kids, to Dewey, to Rhonda, to Cal's sisters. *Her fairies.* Her throat constricted, both at the realization that she already had so many people she cared about in her new town, but also from the knowledge that someone would have put them at risk.

"No, no one got hurt. We evacuated the building, giving people the vague explanation of safety concerns. We searched the entire facility and found nothing," Carter said before Betty Jean interjected.

"We didn't get a chance to serve a single meal," she cried. "It took them more than an hour to secure the building, and by that time, no one was still waiting around for a spaghetti dinner. So not only did we not make any money, but we actually lost several hundred dollars in food costs."

Winnie's heart sank for the woman. Betty Jean might drive her nuts, but she did a lot of good work in this town to raise money for important causes. It wasn't right that someone's prank -- or worse -- got in the way of that.

"Were you able to trace the number?" she asked Carter, who shook his head no.

A bomb threat. Winnie's heart thumped wildly in her chest. She felt suddenly, acutely, aware of the folded paper she carried in her bag—the lead her friend had identified related to the negative online reviews. Should Winnie bring it up right now? Could the two incidents possibly be related? Her hands began to shake in uncertainty, which did not go unnoticed by Cal, whose serious eyes watched her with concern, as if he was as tuned into her as she felt to him.

What did this mean for the rest of Bloomsburo Days? What was going through Cal's mind right now? And why did she have to want, more than anything else, to walk across the table and throw her arms around him? She'd gotten too addicted to the physical strength and comfort the man could offer. Without it, she now felt completely unmoored.

"So what happens next?" she asked to no one in particular.

"We've enhanced our security plan for the rest of Bloomsburo Days," Cal explained, his voice landing on Winnie's ears for the first time in days. It lacked its typical playfulness, yet the sound of it still tugged at something between her legs.

"I've called in back-up officers to work the event for overtime," Carter added. "We're installing some extra security cameras in high-traffic places around town. When time allows, we'll conduct some interviews, and see if anyone has any leads."

"What do you need from me?" Winnie asked. "Unfortunately tomorrow's paper is already at the printer, so I can't add in a story about this to the next issue. I can write a news brief for the website, though." The newspaper's web presence was about a decade behind where it should be, but something was better than nothing.

Carter nodded. "Cal mentioned that you were privy to some of the other situations going on in town. I'm just asking you to keep your ears open. You'll be talking to more people in the coming days than the typical townsperson. Let me know if you see or hear anything suspicious."

Winnie nodded, but she couldn't force herself to bring up the information she'd learned about the Howl reviews. She knew she had to talk about it with Cal first, even if it would be more comfortable to go on avoiding him.

"Now can we discuss security plans for the next few Blooming Ladies events?" Betty Jean demanded. Carter sighed but agreed, ushering the woman into his office and waving his goodbye to Winnie and Cal. Being alone in a room with him made Winnie feel paralyzed—with fear, with desire, with guilt.

He stood, pulled his messenger bag across his body, and began to walk quietly out of the room before Winnie finally worked up the courage to open her mouth.

"Um, Cal," she squeaked out, her voice shaking. He stopped in his tracks and turned to face her. He was so close now. She could reach out and touch him. Stroke his chest through that criminally soft shirt. Rise up on her toes and meet his lips.

She *could* do those things, but wouldn't. It had been her decision to give up those privileges and she had to stick with it, even if it hurt like hell. Even if her body craved his.

"Yeah?" he asked, his green eyes searching hers. Not with anger, but with confusion and hurt and exhaustion. She could only imagine how the Howl situation and now the bomb threat had added to his stress of what was already going to be his busiest work week all year.

"Can we talk outside for a second?" she asked. His brow narrowed in concern as he nodded, leading the way until they were out in the parking lot behind the station.

~-~-~-~-~-~-

He had almost lost himself there, so close to Winnie after too much time apart. She'd looked small and worried, with her huge eyes looking up into his in the middle of that conference room. He could have so easily swept her up into his arms. Pulled her up onto the table and hugged her and kissed her and stroked her until that damned shaking in her fingers stopped.

What was she so anxious about? Was it just the bomb threat, or something more?

It took every fiber of patience in his body to resist the urge to win her over right now. It wasn't the right time, not with Bloomsburo Days right around the corner and more of this bullshit going down around town, no matter how wrong his world felt without Winnie to orbit around. He'd put a few plans into motion, but he had to get this right. He had to make her know exactly what she meant to him. Just not today.

But she'd wanted to talk to him. Could it be about them? Because if she went there, he'd follow along happily. He tried not to get his hopes up, but his heart thumped like a damn bass drum.

They made their way to her car and Cal leaned against its side.

"What is it?"

She glanced down at her bag, from which she pulled out a folded sheet of paper.

"I called in a favor to a tech analyst at my old newspaper," she explained. "I asked her to see what she could find out about the Howl reviews. Not just for the Teal Tea Hutch, but for five other Bloomsburo establishments that had seen an influx of negative reviews."

Cal's eyes widened. He'd gotten nowhere with the company in the hours he'd spent on the phone with its representatives. He couldn't believe that Winnie had gone out of her way to help the cause.

"And?"

Winnie fidgeted with the paper in her hands.

"I wasn't sure if I should talk to you or Carter first. But she traced the reviews to the computer they were posted on. They all originated from the same IP address."

She passed him the paper and he scanned it quickly.

Holy hell. Thirty-seven Howl reviews posted on the same day, and each one sent from Broadsville City Hall.

Greta Johansen.

"Do you think it's related to the bomb threat?" she asked.

"I think we need some more information before we jump to any conclusions." He knew Greta was determined, but he didn't think the woman capable of criminal acts.

"Should we let Carter know?"

Cal thought for a moment. If he had more information to suggest that Greta was behind any of this, that'd be one thing. But all they had was an IP address. Given that Carter was already overtaxed with Bloomsburo Days, especially now that he had to bring in and quickly train a bunch of outside officers to provide back up, he decided a conversation with Greta would be a reasonable first step.

"Not just yet. He's always a phone call away."

Winnie nodded as his brain continued to imagine possible strategies. Greta would deny her involvement, especially if the

JESS VONN

police were involved. He was certain of it. They had to find a more subtle way to get her to talk.

Winnie's mind was clearly on the same page.

"I had an idea, but I'm not sure you'll like it," she said, concern etched across her face.

"I'm all ears."

For the next ten minutes, he listened to Winnie lay out her plan. And it was a good one. He wasn't looking forward to his role in it, but she was absolutely right that it would get the job done.

Having agreed upon the time and location of their meeting the next day, he watched Winnie climb into her car. He saw the conflict in her eyes as she looked at him one final time. He saw pain and regret and beneath it all, he was damn certain that he saw longing. What he didn't see was an explanation for why things had to be like this between them when their relationship had been nothing but goodness and satisfaction.

He didn't want her to go home without him, damn it. He didn't want her to leave without his mouth meeting hers, or without feeling the press of her softness against the length of his body. But if everything went according to plan tomorrow, and when the events of the weekend went off without a hitch, they could put this town drama behind them once and for all, and he could get back to the most important task on his to-do list: winning Winnie Briggs's heart.

Chapter 24

By twilight the next evening, Conroy Farm was packed. The local spot, known for its fresh produce and delicious ice cream, served as the site for the annual Bloomsburo Days bonfire, the unofficial kick-off of the festival. The sun was gradually setting in the clear night sky, and the fire burned brightly, flickering specks of amber before the enchanted faces of little kids covered in sticky marshmallow residue.

Winnie enjoyed distraction in the form of coverage. She shot photos of kids making s'mores and feeding hay to the horses. She interviewed the farm staff dishing up huge bowls of fresh-baked apple crisp topped with their homemade vanilla bean ice cream.

Most of all, she tried not to think about what she was about to do, which was so far outside of her comfort zone it wasn't even funny. She had very little experience with investigative journalism, and she certainly didn't have any experience using gorgeous Chamber of Commerce directors as bait to get crooked politicians to confess their crimes.

Yet here she was, about to do both.

She'd seen Cal around town all day as she'd scurried from event to event. The man was everywhere and in constant motion, which suited Winnie just fine. She could watch him work, watch his confidence and his charm and his competence keep this elaborate festival running like clockwork. Watch the way he wore those grey corduroys like they were invented for the sole purpose of highlighting his exquisite build. Paired with a navy button-up shirt and a vest, he looked picture perfect.

Her heart cracked a bit deeper with every sighting of him. Her longing for him would have to cease eventually, she told herself. It couldn't just go on deepening and deepening, could it?

As the sky grew darker and the bonfire burned brighter, she'd lost track of Cal, but she knew where he was headed and when. He'd texted Greta earlier that afternoon, asking if she could meet him for a talk near the corn crib tucked in the back of Conroy Farm where other visitors were unlikely to wander. It had only taken seconds for

Greta to respond that she'd be there, and Cal had let Winnie know that the plan was a go.

Winnie tried to stay casual, milling about the hayride line. She checked her notebook and flipped through the photos on her camera in an attempt to look busy. But when the clock struck quarter 'til eight, she made her way to the small firewood shed just adjacent to the corn crib, where she planted herself in hearing distance from where Cal and Greta would meet. It might not be legal to record the conversation without Greta's consent, but both Winnie and Cal agreed that having a witness to a potential confession was an integral part of their plan.

Her heart beat wildly in her chest when she saw Cal approach. In the nearly full moon she could just barely see him glance to where she said she'd be, wordlessly acknowledging her. He wandered over to the side of the corn crib, and when Winnie saw the unmistakable outline of Greta Johansen's slim figure sauntering toward the barn in the highest of heels, Winnie thought she might actually get sick. Only the knowledge that her retching would give away her presence allowed her to keep control over her body.

For better or for worse, Winnie was close enough to take in every word, every facial expression, that passed between Greta and Cal as they stepped into the soft light of a lantern near the corn crib. His face lit up when she walked toward him. If Winnie didn't know any better, she'd have thought the man was in love with Greta. Somehow the knowledge that he was acting didn't make her feel any less heartsick about him looking at another woman that way.

"Greta," he said, his voice smooth and sexy.

"Hey there, Cal," she cooed back, her voice as sultry as his. A tight lace top hugged her massive breasts and highlighted her narrow waist. A spandex skirt did the same for her legs, which stretched on endlessly courtesy of Greta's high heels.

Damn, Winnie observed, as much with awe as with envy. The two were certainly a well matched pair when it came to sheer sex appeal.

"I'm glad you could meet me."

"I've been waiting for you to reach out to me for some time now," she said, her hand reaching up and stroking Cal's shoulder. Winnie had never known such possessiveness as she felt coursing through her blood in that moment.

Mine. That was the only thought she could manage, and it was a lie. Cal was no more hers than he was Greta's, and it was her own stupid fault.

"You heard about the bomb threat, I'm sure?" he asked, his hand reaching out and stroking the perfectly straight length of Greta's white-blond hair. "If it was just that, I could maybe overlook it. But more and more, this town seems to be a mess. It's got me rethinking whether Bloomsburo is the right place for me to be establishing my career."

"Is that right?" she said, placing her other hand up on Cal's chest. The contact made Winnie's heart race furiously.

"Is that all you're rethinking?" she asked, and Winnie watched Cal's eyes smolder in Greta's general direction.

"I'm not sure," he said. "I want to know exactly what I'd be getting myself into."

"Oh, I think you're getting yourself into trouble," she said, practically salivating.

"Is that right? Are you going to be trouble for me, Greta Johannsen? I've had bad girls before. They can be a lot of fun."

Winnie's stomach turned. He was so good. Too good. He might be faking it with Greta now, but even the thought of him turning that genuine charm onto another woman made her feel sick. Not to mention the hypothetical bad girls of his past.

"You don't know how bad I can be," Greta cooed, playing right into his hand.

"Is that right?"

"Mmm," she purred. Her body was up against his now.

"Bad enough to try and scare me away from my own hometown?"

A coy smile spread across her red painted lips.

"Maybe."

"You wanted me that much, huh?" he asked, his fingers brushing down the impossibly thin-yet-muscular contours of her upper arm. "You'd break the law for it?"

"You have no idea how much I want you, Cal Spencer. And I always get what I want. Even if that includes calling in a bomb threat."

Winnie's heart thumped at the admission. Jesus, this was really happening.

"You did that for me?"

"Yes. Only for you."

"Is that all you'd do to get me? I expected more…" he said, his hand, now resting on her narrow waist. "It turns me on just to think about it."

"Oh really?" she said with a sharp laugh. "Then you might like to know that I did my very best to run a bunch of low-brow businesses into the ground with some nasty online reviews."

"That was you?"

"That was me, baby."

"What else…?" Cal rubbed his thumb back down her arm, bringing it within a few inches of the curve of Greta's breast. An interrogation had never sounded or looked so much like a seduction.

Winnie didn't know of any other incidents around town. Maybe Carter had told Cal something more? Or maybe he was just trying to figure out if there was anything more to learn?

"I've suffered for you." Greta turned her body into Cal's hand and pressed more fully against him, and Winnie ground her teeth together until her jaw ached.

"I'm sorry to hear that. How so?"

"Your idiot mayor," she sighed.

Surprise flashed across his face now, the first crack in his otherwise flawless performance. Winnie couldn't breathe, her mind flashing back to her odd initial introduction to the mayor. To Greta there at his side when he finally bothered to show up to the city council meeting.

"What about him?" Cal asked.

"Well, I may have convinced him to pursue a policy or two that wasn't in the town's best interest."

The fee hike.

"Now how did you get him to do that?"

"How do you think Cal?"

Winnie gasped, but the sound never left her lips. By that time a hand had found its way to her mouth and clasped her face violently.

"You better not make a sound, young lady," a familiar voice whispered into her ear. Even amidst her fear and her shock, Winnie recognized the voice of Mayor Ralph Simpson, not to mention his obnoxious word choice. *Young lady.* She'd been so caught up in Greta's confession that she hadn't even heard him approach from behind. The man smelled like a bar at closing time and she could

A Time To Fall

sense his drunken unsteadiness from how his large body pressed against the back of hers.

"She's a hell of a little minx, now isn't she?" he whispered into Winnie's ear as they both watched Greta running her hands across Cal's shoulders. "Used those same tricks on me. Got me to do her bidding even if it meant I threw my career, my marriage, down the shitter just for a chance to take her tight little ass to bed."

Winnie tried to wrench free, but he only clasped his hand that much tighter in response.

"She said she was mine. She said if I did what she asked, we could be together, and now I find out it was about the golden boy the entire time."

From her peripheral vision, Winnie could see the mayor slowly raise his free arm, and despite the deepening darkness of the night sky around them, she saw the unmistakable outline of a black pistol. She tried to scream but couldn't find the breath. She felt faint. As much as she wanted Greta to face punishment for her disturbances around town, Winnie surely didn't want to see her hurt.

"If I can't have her, that slick-talking bastard sure as hell can't either," he said, his words slurred by drunkenness and jealousy.

Winnie's heart stopped. He didn't point the gun toward Greta. He aimed it at Cal.

Miraculously, she mustered up the lung power to scream, and though the sound was muffled by the mayor's sweaty hand over her mouth, it was enough to draw Cal's attention to the small outbuilding where they hid.

"Winnie!" he cried, the blood draining from his face, and his eyes widened in fear. Instinctively, he pushed Greta behind the protection of his body. Her heart tightened watching how even in the midst of all this drama, even with this woman who had caused so many problems for the town he loved, he was still just an astonishingly good man.

"Don't make a move, pretty boy," Mayor Simpson yelled across the space, turning the gun toward Winnie's chest in front of him. She yelped in fear, yet she'd rather have it facing her than Cal again. Anything but that. "You get whatever the hell you want around here and I'm sick of it."

"Ralph, it doesn't have to be like this. Greta used you, just like she's trying to use me now. I'm not going to fall for it."

JESS VONN

"What?" Greta called out incredulously from behind his strong frame.

"The only thing I could possibly want from you was a confession. So thanks for that."

Even with the fear surging through her body, Winnie took the smallest bit of satisfaction from the sheer rage that contorted Greta's picture-perfect face.

The mayor appeared to enjoy it, too, as he laughed loudly.

"Well, looks like Mayor Johannsen's not the only one who can use her good looks to get what she wants."

"Ralph, put the gun down," Cal said, slowly inching closer to her and the mayor.

"I said stay where you are," Mayor Simpson roared, pushing the gun that much more tightly into Winnie's chest.

She could hardly process the man's words. She scanned all around her, looking for a possible escape. She strained to look down at the pistol pointing at her when one key detail jumped out her.

The mayor's finger wasn't on the trigger. It simply held the grip. Relief flooded Winnie's body and she took a moment to mentally review what she'd learned long ago in the self-defense classes Bree had forced her to take with her when they'd first moved to Chicago. Winnie hadn't wanted to bother with it. Didn't want to spend the money. But as with most things, Bree ended up being right.

She'd kiss her friend the next time she saw her.

"Let her go and we can talk, Ralph," Cal said, fear gripping his voice. "This has nothing to do with Winnie."

"Oh, what do you care about her? Any trained monkey can come on board and write for that rag of a newspaper."

What do you care about her? Winnie couldn't bear to hear the answer. The time to act was now, while Mayor Simpson was distracted in this back and forth with Cal. A second later, the back of her head smashed into the mayor's jaw, disorienting him enough to allow her to twist herself out of his hold and wrap herself around his arm to take control of the weapon. The attack and his drunken state left him so disoriented that he put up no fight. He merely fell to his knees and grabbed at his aching jaw. Cal was at her side in a fraction of a second, first unloading the gun's ammunition, then grasping Winnie tightly against his chest.

My God, how she'd missed the fortress of his body. It wasn't until the danger had fully passed that shock seized her, causing every limb to shake and a cold clamminess to overtake her entire body. Cal's strong embrace was the only thing keeping her upright. She saw Greta flee the scene, but couldn't let herself worry about that now. Greta had confessed in front of two witnesses. Her time was up.

"Winnie, it's okay," Cal murmured into her ear as he stroked her hair. "Everyone's going to be okay, sweetie."

"I'm not okay!" the mayor moaned from where he writhed on the ground. "She broke my tooth!"

"If I could fathom letting go of this woman for one second, I'd personally ensure that your tooth was the least of the injuries you had to worry about," Cal growled, but his touch on Winnie stayed firm and comforting. Winnie closed her eyes, overwhelmed by the fear she'd felt and by the intoxicating comfort of returning to Cal's embrace. Overwrought with how it would break her to separate from this man again when this awful night was over.

She heard heavy footsteps coming up behind her and she grasped for Cal in fear before opening her eyes and seeing the steady strength of Carter Conrad appear next to them in full uniform.

"What the hell happened here?" he asked, scanning the scene, particularly the gun on the ground surrounded by unloaded bullets.

"This man threatened me!" the mayor called out from the ground as he pointed to Cal.

"Did you do this to him?" Carter asked Cal, looking at the major's jaw that grew puffier and more purple with each passing minute.

"No, Winnie did. He had her at gunpoint."

"Are you okay, Winnie?" Carter asked, with such genuine concern that Winnie's heart ached. She nodded silently from where her head still rested on Cal's broad chest, and Carter smiled. "You always struck me as a woman not to be messed with."

He scanned the area once more.

"Cal told me to meet him here right after eight," Carter explained, "This is not the scene I was expecting." He reached to his waistband and pulled out his radio, calling for extra help.

"Me neither," Cal said. She could feel his low voice vibrating where her cheek pressed into his chest. "All we wanted was a confession from Greta."

"Greta?"

"She was behind the bomb threat. The Howl reviews, too."

"No shit?"

"Winnie got the lead on the story, and she came up with plan," Cal explained, looking at Winnie with pride.

"I'm beginning to think I should offer you a position on the force, Winnie."

She smiled faintly.

"He was the unexpected piece of the puzzle," Cal said, jerking his head toward the mayor. "Jilted lover of Greta's."

"No shit," Carter repeated.

Mayor Simpson groaned louder from where he still sat on the ground, more out of pride than pain.

"Well, he can tell me his whole sad story down at the station," Carter said, reaching for his handcuffs just as two more uniformed police officers arrived on the scene.

"Can I take Winnie to the medics?" Cal asked. An ambulance and a few EMTs stood ready all through the weekend just in case any first aid needs arose at a Bloomsburo Days event.

"Yeah. I'll need to get official statements from you both, but that can wait a few."

Cal nodded and finally let go of Winnie.

"I'm fine," she lied. Her head hurt from the impact of the head butt, and dizziness and chills still coursed through her body.

"I don't care," Cal said, lacing his fingers through hers and slowly leading her back out into the crowded area of the farm.

"People will see us," Winnie said, glancing down at their clasped hands.

"I don't care," Cal repeated, tightening his grip to make his point.

Her heart fluttered. She told it to knock it off.

"You've got work to get to, I'm sure of it, Cal. I'll find the first-aid station. It's fine." Her heart ached. She couldn't do this again. She couldn't fall back into his arms only to have to wrench herself from them when the intensity of the moment subsided and she remembered the limits of their connection. She'd barely survived it once.

"You and I have a lot to talk about, Winnie Briggs," he said, his green gaze staring into hers with an intensity that shook her. "But the only thing you need to know for tonight is that I will not leave your side. Is that understood?"

Fear and hope and relief collided through her shocked system at the thought of the very scenario she had not allowed herself to imagine: another night by Cal's side.

Chapter 25

It was after eleven by the time Cal pulled into his driveway with Winnie in the passenger seat of his car. The medic had checked her over thoroughly. A concussion was unlikely, but he'd said she'd likely experience head pain for a few days. Carter had met them there, taking their statements in the back of the ambulance, and by the time he'd finished, Winnie claimed that the symptoms of shock were mostly gone. Now she just felt dazed and exhausted.

"Cal...your house?" Winnie said hesitantly.

"I said I wasn't leaving your side tonight. I'll sleep in the guest room."

He helped her out of the car, up his front steps and into the peaceful darkness of his living room.

"Are you hungry?" he asked, wanting more than anything to make her comfortable.

She shook her head.

"Just tired. The only thing I really want is the one thing I can't have. A bath."

"Why can't you have a bath?"

"Have you seen the bathroom in my cottage?" He suddenly remembered the harsh plastic lining of the narrowest stand-up shower he'd ever seen.

"Take one here."

She blinked at him, not following.

"I've got a whirlpool tub in the master bathroom."

And just like that, he watched her anxious face soften with longing. He wished he had inspired it, but if his luxury tub excited the woman, brought her some sort of peace, he'd take it. Visions of Winnie's buoyant breasts covered in water and soapy bubbles floated through his mind but he quickly regained control. Tonight wasn't about that.

"I couldn't possibly..." Winnie whispered unconvincingly.

"Winnie, I brought you here to make sure you were comfortable tonight."

"It's just..." she hesitated. He gently pulled her hand and led her upstairs to a part of his house she'd never seen. They made their way to his master bedroom and she paused at the threshold, her eyes widened with an unreadable emotion. They passed the tufted frame of his king-sized bed on their way to the door leading into the bathroom. When she took in the size of the Jacuzzi tub, the gorgeous stone work that surrounded it, and the ambient lighting that Cal had turned on to showcase it, she gasped.

"Oh, my." For the second time in as many minutes he was envious of his damn bathroom.

"Let me draw it for you, and then I'll give you some privacy, okay?"

She nodded her consent, leaning against the door frame while he turned on the water.

"My gel soap works pretty well as bubble bath, if you're into that kind of thing," he offered. She nodded with a small smile and he added a few squeezes of it into the faucet's strong stream.

When the tub was full of hot water and fragrant bubbles, he turned off the faucet and showed Winnie the controls on the side—one slider for the front jets, another for the back jets, and a third for the lights.

He set out a fluffy towel and washcloth, some shampoo, and an unopened travel toothbrush and toothpaste.

"Take your time," he said, walking through the door. "I'm going to go grab a robe you can put on when you're done."

She nodded and he closed the door behind him. He tried to keep his thoughts gentlemanly. Tried not to think about her undressing. Tried not to think about the water slipping temptingly over every inch of her body.

He found the robe he was looking for in the guest room closet, made his way back to the door and knocked gently. When he cracked open the door, he saw that her eyes were closed and her face looked peaceful as she rested beneath the bubbles, which was a marked improvement.

"I'll just set this here," he said, looking at the hamper where he placed the soft, white terrycloth robe. He closed the door quickly behind himself and willed himself to get a grip. Winnie had a lot of needs tonight, and his body needed to remember that right now, they had little to do with him. As for tomorrow, or next week, or next month? Only time would tell.

He paced the house, emptying the dishwasher, changing into a soft T-shirt and flannel pants, checking his emails on his phone to make sure there were no Bloomsburo Days-related emergencies to address, though anything that came up at this point would be pittance compared to what the day had already brought.

He could hear through the ceiling that Winnie was draining the tub, and he slowly made his way back to the bedroom where he found her standing near the edge of his bed wrapped up in the robe he'd provided. Her cheeks were flushed a healthy pink, and her hair fell down her chest, heavier and longer and darker from its wetness.

"Better?" he asked, shoving his hands in the pockets of his flannel pants.

"Much."

"Is there anything else you need?"

She shook her head no, the sadness—her quietness—nearly killing him.

"Okay, well you can just crash in here," he said, turning down the duvet for her and clicking on the lamp on the bedside table.

"I'll be in the guest room just down the hall if you need me," he continued, forcing himself to walk away from this woman in his bed. The woman he wanted to hold more than anything in the world.

"You sure you aren't hungry?" he asked, turning back to her once more in a last-ditch effort to delay the inevitable. Not to mention that his need to feed the woman was damn near pathological.

She shook her head once more and he slowly walked out of the room, turning out the overhead light and half closing the door behind him. He stood in the hall for minutes, unsure what to do with himself. He couldn't go to sleep. Not like this. Not with his mind reeling from the events of the day. Not with the woman he needed like oxygen just a few feet away, tucked into the bed he'd never shared with another.

The memory of the evening's events suddenly hit him like a bullet train. He'd been so busy making sure Winnie was okay that he hadn't even fully processed what had happened. Suddenly the image of that gun pointed at Winnie's throat burned into his mind, and panic gripped his chest once more.

He'd never known such fear. Any lingering doubts about what he felt for Winnie had disappeared in an instant. That minute, the longest of his life, when his mind considered the possibility of a world without Winnie, had been devastating. He didn't want to know a tomorrow without her light in his life.

With her courage and quick thinking, she may have saved his life. Had he even thanked her?

He walked quietly back toward his bedroom door, debating whether or not to knock, when the sound of her soft sobs floated from his bed.

"Winnie," he called, opening the door and seeing her crumpled in her robe in a pile on top of the sheets. He crawled up onto his bed in record time, pulling her into his arms.

"Shhh," he comforted her, hating the feel of her body shaking with distress in his arms. "Winnie, what is it?"

"You're not even mine to lose," she cried, hugging him tighter as her warm tears wetted his T-shirt.

"What are you talking about?"

She sniffled and her face looked up at his, looking splotchy and vulnerable in the soft light from the night stand.

"Everyone's okay now, Winn," he whispered, rubbing his hands in circles on her back and instinctively rocking her in his arms.

"He was going to shoot you, Cal. He pointed his gun at you, and he threatened you, and I've never been more terrified in my life," she said between sobs. "I couldn't survive it if something happened to you..."

She grasped at his shoulders.

"The most ridiculous part is that you're not even mine to lose."

Desire and defensiveness shot through his chest with startling force.

"Like hell I'm not."

Her sobbing stopped in an instant, replaced by a look of shock in her deep brown eyes.

"What?"

He wiped her tears away with the back of his hand before putting his fingers to her lips. Tracing them down the smooth line of her neck. Pressing them under her robe to where he could feel her heart pulse.

"I'm absolutely yours."

She shook her head no. He dared her to challenge him on this front. She might reject him, but she wouldn't deny what he felt and neither would he. Not for another minute.

"This was just supposed to be physical," he continued. "And my God, what a start that was. The pleasures you can draw from my body have haunted me from the beginning." He leaned in and kissed her lightly on the lips, coaxing a soft whimper from deep in her throat.

"You're so gorgeous, Winnie. But you turned out to be so much more," he said, brushing his hand against her cheek. "You are so determined. Considerate. Talented. So damn goofy that I can't help but laugh every time I'm with you. Each time you leave my side, I feel like you take half of me with you. It's only when you're right next to me that I feel whole again."

His lips met hers in a deep, sensual connection. The earth suddenly felt as if it was back on its axis as their tongues glided together. As if every wrong had been righted and things were back to the natural, beautiful order that this woman had revealed to him.

He felt her breath hitch in her gorgeous neck.

"I can't..." she whispered.

"What, love?"

"I can't lose myself to you. I'm not in your league, Cal. I know it."

"Don't," he said in warning. He wouldn't accept this from her. Not now. His entire life had been spent listening to this kind of nonsense. Women suggesting that his handsomeness rendered him incapable of commitment. Of mutual attraction. Of basic decency. Hell, he'd told himself the same stories at times. But he wouldn't stand for it now, though. Not with Winnie.

"Cal, don't you think you might get bored with me before long?" she offered, vulnerability radiating through her. "You could have any woman you want."

He grabbed her chin, and oriented her face to focus her directly into his eyes, lest there be any doubt. He wouldn't stand for it.

"Winnie, I'm not going to lie. A fair number of women have had access to my body, and no, I didn't have to twist any arms in the process. But they only had my body. None of them had my heart. I didn't know I was capable of giving it to someone until you literally crashed into my life."

She snorted, a sobby sort of snort. Still adorable.

"When I thought I'd lost you after our first night together, that was gutting," he said, his lips pressing against her temple. Her cheek. Her neck, where her pulse throbbed. "But at least you weren't in danger then. Not like tonight. That prospect, of any harm coming to you, even for a second? That's when I knew I was ready to stop pretending like you don't mean the world to me."

She hugged him close.

"I'm sorry I ran out on you," she confessed into his shoulder, her voice shaky. "The time with your family, followed by a night with you. It overwhelmed me. It let me start to imagine it."

"Imagine what?" he asked, gently massaging her scalp with his clever fingers.

"Our life together. Being a part of your family."

"It was that horrifying of a prospect, huh? Being stuck with me and my family? I know my mom is meddling, but…"

She laughed, sending a fresh set of tears down her cheeks and onto his t-shirt.

"I didn't run because I was scared of it. I was scared by how much I wanted it. How good it could be. How easily I could get lost in it. How awful it would be to have it taken away from me," she said, a sob catching in her throat at all of those deep memories of loss. "Losing you would be one thing. But losing your family, after I'd fallen even more in love with them, that was just too much to imagine."

He rocked her gently in his embrace as the tears worked their way out.

"You make me a better man, Winnie," he said into her hair. "The aftermath of what my dad did messed with my mind for a long time. I couldn't ever let myself be like him, and the surest way to do that was to keep women away. To never even toy with a serious relationship."

"Hence, our deal."

"Hence, our deal," he repeated. "I chalk that deal up as one of the biggest failures of my life."

Her head snapped up in surprise.

"I had one job, and that was to give you physical pleasure while keeping my heart out of it. But the truth was, you'd stolen it before we'd even negotiated the terms of our agreement. Your hand's been on it since that first afternoon on your porch, in those damned adorable unicorn leggings."

She laughed, a beautiful sound.

"Winnie, I will never be perfect, but I want to be your lover," he said, his soft words electric. He kissed her forehead. "I want to be your best friend."

Cal's gaze locked into hers with a newfound intensity.

"I want you to be your home, Winnie. And I want you to be mine. So the only question left is—will you have me?"

Her body answered swiftly. She climbed up on top of him, straddling him while she hugged his head into her chest where her robe gaped open.

"Yes," she said, his new favorite word. The only word he wanted to hear from Winnie Briggs's lips from this day forward. "God, Cal, how is this real?"

"I don't know, but I'll fight for us as hard as I've fought for anything in my life. For your happiness."

"Deal," she said with a small laugh, but her wet eyes showed the depth of her joy at their reconnection.

He kissed her slower then, sensuously. He tried to convey the depth of his convictions through his mouth.

Her hands busied themselves around her waist and then suddenly, mercifully, her robe fell in a heap around her knees where she straddled him.

"My happiness starts like this," she ordered, grabbing his hands and pressing them against her breasts—soft and fragrant from her bath.

"Yes, ma'am," he said, feasting on the full slopes before him. His tongue found her nipple and the pressure he yielded there made her moan breathlessly.

"Cal," she said breathlessly.

"Mmm," he said, moving his attention to the other breast. Another suckle. Another moan.

"Do we need new ground rules?" she managed between her gasps of pleasure.

His eyes made their way up to hers.

"I suppose we do," he said, his hands rubbing down her ribs and around her back until her perfect ass filled them. He squeezed her hungrily. A naked, writhing Winnie on top of him made it very difficult to think, but he tried his best.

"I get to wine and dine you whenever the hell I want," he said. "I'm tired of not dating you."

She smiled in agreement, running her hands tentatively across the tops her own bare breasts. He watched her hands hungrily, with complete approval.

Jesus.

"Terms of endearment are back on the table," she insisted, plucking at her own nipples. His cock rose that much harder, which didn't go unnoticed by her. She rocked her hips in slow circles, beckoning his throbbing arousal through the thin material of his pajama bottoms. "Is that okay with you, babe?" she asked, her eyes like fire.

"That's more than okay," he said. Jesus, no one could combine affectionate and sexy like Winnie Briggs. No one. He'd be her baby. Her honey. Her sweetie. She could call him whatever the hell she wanted as long as he got to keep touching her and watching her touch herself.

"Anything else?" she asked, her hips working more intentionally now as she continued to cup her own breasts in her hands. It was evident on her face that his hardness tormented her sweet spot.

"Sleepovers?" he asked. He knew where he stood on the matter, but he wanted to hear her thoughts first. His thumb made its way to her clit and his heart thrilled, watching her face absorb the pleasure of his stroke.

"Umm," she said, leaning forward and grabbing the headboard behind Cal so she had more leverage. She rubbed harder against him, her breasts now jostling dangerously close to his face. "I..." She couldn't form a thought beneath his touch, and he fucking loved it.

"I think the answer you're looking for is that we should have sleepovers as often as possible," he finished for her.

"God, yes," she cried, answering his question and reacting to his body all at once. Her hips moved with desperation now and he was more than ready to get his pants off.

"Cal, can we stop talking now? Please?" she panted. "Your mouth is needed elsewhere."

He grinned as she took her weight off him for just enough time for him to slip off his pants and shirt. She straddled him once more, her aroused sex hovering centimeters above his aching dick. The distance might damn well kill him.

"Shit, I don't have a condom up here," he growled. He never brought women home, so his own bedroom wasn't well-stocked for sexual adventures. He wanted nothing less than to wrench himself from Winnie's naked body to go on a scavenger hunt through his house while he was rock hard.

Winnie's eyes softened with shyness.

"I'm on the pill and clean as a whistle," she offered shyly. "I trust you are, too." *Shit.* Just when he thought he couldn't grow harder, she had to go and say something like that. He got himself tested on a regular basis, yet he'd never taken a woman without a condom. That was just the deal a man made with himself when he avoided the monogamy of committed relationships. He'd fantasized about it plenty, though. And the thought of experiencing such a first with Winnie, well that was too good to be true.

"Winnie, are you sure?" he asked, his mind frenzied at the thought of the act he'd imagined so many times.

"I want to feel all of you," she begged, her sex writhing above him. "Now."

He sat up straighter against the headboard, grabbed Winnie's hips and slowly, slowly pulled her down until inch by inch the unfathomable warmth and wetness of her sex drew him in. Christ, he didn't think he could feel more for her. More connection. More intimacy. More desire. Yet here it was, this unsheathed melding of their bodies unraveling him beyond what he could have ever imagined.

"God, Winnie," he cried out at the connection, right as a moan tore from Winnie's throat. She threw her head back in pleasure and her hand slipped down to stroke her own clit as he thrust into her again with more force.

"Yes," she purred, gazing down at him with affection and heat and need. "Cal… please," she muttered incoherently.

Quickly they found their rhythm with Winnie on top, slow and steady at first then faster, with more need, with more desperation. Winnie's breasts quaked each time their hips crashed together and she put her hands behind her neck, riding him like she'd trained for it. She came first, her cries of pleasure serving as the final straw for him. His own release barreled quickly behind hers and with one final thrust his orgasm surged within her, leaving Cal dizzy with the singular satisfaction of coming deep into her warm depths. Nothing had ever felt so right.

Seconds later, she collapsed next to him on the bed, panting and breathless with a silly grin animating her face. He scooped her into the cradle of his body, feeling her warmth, her softness, feeling just how perfectly they fit together. And just like that, those three words popped into his head once more. *This is it.*

Physical and emotional satisfaction, mixed with the lingering exhaustion from the eventful day and a staggering orgasm, resulted in a deep drowsiness overcoming him. He was nearly asleep when her voice roused him again.

"One more new ground rule?" she whispered into his chest.

"Mmmm?" he replied sleepily.

"I get unlimited access to that bathtub."

He chuckled softly. "Deal. As long as you're open to company in there from time to time." He kissed her forehead.

"You drive a hard bargain," she said sleepily into his chest. "But I accept your terms."

Content that all major guidelines had been addressed, the pair fell into the deepest of sleep.

~-~-~-~-~-~-

Winnie woke up face down in the soft depths of Cal's king sized bed and she briefly wondered how she could ever force herself to leave it.

The bed, like everything about the man, was pure sensual pleasure. Now that she had been given the green light with his body, Winnie tried to imagine a future that didn't involve the two of them naked, but it was next to impossible. They'd never leave this bed again. They'd lose their jobs. They'd starve to death. But oh, what a way to go.

She sleepily reached over to his side of the bed, wanting to feel his skin. His warmth. She wanted to reenact the naughty dreams of the man that had flooded her mind all night.

All month, to be more accurate.

But she felt only empty sheets next to her.

She sat up and her heart leapt to her throat when she saw the folded up piece of paper on Cal's pillow.

He wouldn't possibly…

She opened the note anxiously and laughed in relief when she read the message written in his sexy scrawl.

I promise I haven't fled -- I'm just making you breakfast downstairs. I put the special section from the newspaper on the night stand if you want to take a peek. Looks awesome!

Right. It was Friday. Winnie had officially lost all sense of time and place. She picked up her robe off the floor where it had been hastily abandoned the night before, wrapped it around herself, and grabbed the Bloomsburo Days special section off the stand.

Unfolding it, her heart sang. It looked fantastic, she had to admit. Well designed. Nice photos. And the color printing looked vibrant and sharp. She noticed no glaring typos in the headlines she skimmed, which was a comfort.

She leafed casually through the pages, taking special interest in the advertisements—the only part of the section she hadn't seen yet. She merely left space for them—the production staff at the printers actually plugged them into the pages.

They looked pretty good. She didn't notice any obvious errors or distorted photos. All in all, she had a lot to feel proud of. Hopefully her publisher would be pleased. She closed the section and tossed it on the bed, when suddenly an image on the back page caught her attention.

She grabbed it for a closer look and her jaw dropped open.

The back full-page ad had been the last-minute request that Danny J. McDonald the Intern had sent over from the Chamber of Commerce. Four huge sprinkle-covered donuts that looked just like the ones on Winnie's phone case covered the top of the page. Below them a message was written in a huge, quirky purple typeface.

Donuts are sweet
And so are you,
But there is one little thing
I 'donut' want to do—
Pretend that I'm not in love with you.
Wanting, more than anything, to be yours, Winnie.
-Cal Spencer

She read it again and again, her head shaking in disbelief. Her hands trembling. She couldn't decide whether to laugh or cry, so she did both. She was still crying when she reached the bottom of the stairs, where the tantalizing smell of bacon greeted her. Making her way to the kitchen, she headed straight for Cal, putting her arms around his waist where he stood and worked at the stove in those sexy plaid pajama pants and a soft grey T-shirt. His hair, rumpled from sex and sleep, stuck out in irresistible swirls.

"Morning, beautiful," he said, wiping his hands on a towel before turning around and facing her. "Winnie, what is it?" he asked spotting her tears.

She held up the back page of the special section and a nervous excitement washed over his handsome face.

"Do you mean it?" she asked, her voice trembling.

The grin that transformed his expression was the most glorious thing she'd ever seen.

"Hell yes, I meant every word. And I'm ready for the world to know what I feel about you."

Winnie looked at the ad again, then hugged it to her chest in disbelief.

"You prepared this ad days ago."

"I did. Right after you dumped me."

Winnie rolled her eyes. "I thought it was just pity sex that first time."

He shook his head.

"And then this morning I worried that maybe it was just near-death-experience sex."

He laughed. "Is that a thing?"

"I don't know. You're the sex-pert."

"Now that's a term of endearment I could get behind," he said, pulling Winnie in for an embrace. But his eyes turned uncharacteristically serious.

"The truth of it, Winnie, is that I've fallen in love with you. The sex is just a bonus. I don't know if I'll be the perfect man. I don't know if I can overcome whatever shortcomings defined my father…"

Winnie, wondering if her heart could actually burst, leaned up and kissed him.

"But just in case you were on the fence about your feelings for me," Cal said, "I ran out and picked these up this morning."

He reached behind himself to grab a bakery box from the counter. Opening it, Winnie saw a half dozen pretty pink-frosted donuts covered in the most dazzling rainbow sprinkles.

"You fight dirty, Cal Spencer," she teased, running her hands over his chest. "If I tried my hardest, I might be able to resist you. But when you're wielding bacon *and* donuts? Well, game over. I'm yours."

"Lucky me," he said, pulling her in for a deep kiss.

"Mmmm, lucky us," she said, looking up into his eyes as she clutched at his mussed hair. She finally concluded that morning-after Cal was the sexiest Cal of all. "I'm not going to be the perfect woman," she admitted.

"And I know I'll never be the perfect man..." he offered with a kiss to Winnie's jaw line. A nip at her ear.

"But I love you," she whispered. The deepest truth she'd ever known. He answered with his mouth. His hands. His body. Even bacon and donuts could wait when Cal Spencer was on the menu. And that was saying something.

Epilogue

December

As Winnie walked back through the crowded banquet hall, she caught Cal smiling at her from across the room.

Despite the months they'd now been together, Winnie still hadn't quite come to terms with the fact that he was hers, especially in very public settings like this. He was kind of like your nicest necklace or your most expensive pair of shoes. Part of you was dying to wear them out and show them off, but the other part of you worried that it would be too flashy, that it would create too much envy.

But in the months since Winnie and Cal had finally accepted the fact that they were in love, Winnie had gradually grown comfortable with the way other women looked at Cal. It made her proud. It turned her on, because those looks were never returned. He was hungry only for her, and that was something she would simply never tire of.

Just as satisfying as the statewide newspaper contest award she'd just received—first place in breaking news writing for *The Bloom Times'* coverage of the Bloomsburo/Broadsville mayoral scandal—was the feeling when she returned to the banquet table, and Cal pulled her into a congratulatory embrace. Despite the fact that all eyes were still on her, having just accepted the award, he gave her a long and passionate kiss that left her light headed.

"Congratulations, Winn," he murmured in her ear, his hand moving down to give her a playful tap on her backside. "You deserve all of it and more."

He looked perfect there, wearing the same sexy, blue suit he'd worn that first night at Café Gioia. He called it his lucky suit, because it was what he wore when this pleasure-filled journey began. She made him wear it whenever possible – once even while he made her waffles, just for the heck of it. He was a good sport like that.

She could feel herself beaming as she resumed her seat and looked at the plaque, her first first-place award for writing. She hoped it wouldn't be her last, but if it ended up being her only, it would go down as one of her favorite professional accomplishments.

JESS VONN

She'd come to Bloomsburo with two goals in mind: to become a better journalist and to avoid men. She'd met one goal, and now thanked God she failed at the other.

Her only regret was that she could only bring one guest to tonight's awards ceremony. How she would have loved to share this with Gloria, Rhonda, and even with Betty Jean, who had actually become an incredibly important source when Winnie began to investigate the political history of the town.

She was on cloud nine for the rest of evening, eating the delicious food, sharing sweet glances with Cal, and laughing with the other journalists who filled out her table. She practically floated out to his car when the ceremony ended.

"We have to swing by my mom's," Cal explained as he took an unexpected turn on the drive back to his place, where Winnie now spent most evenings. "I promised her we'd stop by to show off the award."

"You didn't know that I was going to win the award," Winnie said suspiciously.

"I absolutely knew you would take home that award, hon. You deserved it. It wasn't even a contest."

She had to grin. She didn't go into the evening with nearly as much confidence, but she never tired of Cal's support. Frankly, she was just honored to be a nominee amongst journalists from fancier papers with much more impressive budgets. Winnie was happy about the award, but she was really looking forward to the final stop of the night: Cal's bed, and all of the magical things that happened therein. They stayed at her place sometimes, too, but his bathtub, and the delicious rituals they'd developed within it, made his place their favorite.

They pulled up to Rhonda's and Cal grabbed the plaque, more eager to show it off than even Winnie.

"Well, come on!" he urged her, like a kid ready to charge downstairs on Christmas morning.

"Ladies first," Cal insisted when they reached the porch. He pushed the door open and Winnie's jaw dropped when she took in the scene inside Rhonda's house.

A huge banner hung across the wide entryway, spelling out 'Congrats, Winnie!" Beneath it stood all of Winnie's favorite people: Rhonda, Cal's sisters, his nieces, Evie and her little ones,

Dewey, Carter, and even Betty Jean. She turned to Cal in disbelief, but he just stood back, pleased with the surprise he was able to pull over on her.

One by one they rushed up to Winnie, smothering her in hugs and kisses and congratulations. Once everyone had a chance to celebrate with the award winner, the party moved into the kitchen, where Rhonda's island was covered with a gorgeous pink layer cake, pies and other assorted desserts, alongside ice buckets of champagne and sparkling cider. Cal promptly poured them two glasses of champagne.

"To the award-winning journalist," he toasted her, and their glasses clinked. They kissed, and the room cheered before breaking into side conversations.

"Don't forget her present, Uncle Cal!" Mary called out, sneaking up beside them and slipping her hand into Winnie's.

"Present? Cal, this is too much," Winnie protested, though it did little to mask her delight. He spoiled her and she loved every second of it.

He handed her a long, thin velvet box with a pink ribbon on top.

"I picked that out the ribbon," Lulu said quietly, pointing to the ribbon.

"It's lovely."

"Wait 'til you see what's inside!" Mary said, jumping up and down as if she were the one getting the gift.

With slightly shaky hands, Winnie removed the bow, placing it on the top of Lulu's head, earning Winnie a giggle. She gingerly opened the hinged box and gasped when she saw the drop necklace inside—a long, gorgeous white gold chain that featured one sizable teardrop shaped diamond at the center and two tiny diamonds a few inches above it on either side. It was breathtaking.

"Cal, it's gorgeous."

"Hmm, just like you, what a coincidence."

He took the necklace and slipped it over her hair until it sparkled and shone against the black satin of her formal dress.

Winnie clasped it in disbelief. She'd never had a diamond. Never had a piece of jewelry so beautiful.

She threw her arms around Cal and kissed his neck profusely.

"I can't thank you enough, Cal."

"We can find some creative ways for you to try, though," he said with a wink.

She grinned and then he leaned in to whisper in her ear. "These won't be the last jewels you get from me, Briggs." His words were hot on her ear. "I'm having trouble waiting a respectable amount of time to give you one diamond in particular."

Her heart skipped a beat at his implication. At the thought that all of this could actually be forever. She leaned in, eyes wide and her lips found his immediately.

"I love you so much."

"I'm a lucky man."

She grinned and turned her attention to the little girls now flanking her. "Can we see?" Lulu asked. Cal's cell phone started to ring and Winnie nodded, encouraging him to take the call while she showed off her new sparkles.

A few seconds later she heard Cal clear his throat.

"Uh, Winn?" he said, his hand gently touching her arm. "It's Bree."

Bree?

Her first instinct was excitement—her sweet boyfriend had even tried to include her long-distance best friend in her celebration. But something in Cal's eyes told her that the call was under less ideal circumstances. The two women had been in touch since their month of non-communication passed. They talked on the phone every week or so. They'd even taught Bree how to use Skype so her friend could see Cal with her own eyes. (Bree now referred to him as The Masterpiece, and often called Cal in order to reach Winnie, given that Winnie's cellphone tended to go missing or uncharged so often.)

"Winn, congrats on the award," she heard her best friend's voice offer shakily. Uncharacteristically edgy. "I'm so sorry to interrupt. I just... Winnie, something's happened."

Winnie's eyes grew wide, looking silently at Cal, and he guided her to the quieter privacy of the mudroom with a comforting hand on her hip.

"Bree, what is it? Are you okay? Are you hurt?"

She heard the sigh across the line. Across the miles.

"No, I'm not physically hurt. I will be okay, but I have to get out of here."

"Out of Chicago?"

"Yes."

If there was one urge Winnie understood completely, it was the need to flee Chicago. She'd never forget the support Bree gave her to do what she needed to do in her time of need, and she welcomed any opportunity to return it.

"What can I do, Bree? How can I help?"

There was a pause, and then an unexpected answer from the most independent, globe-trotting woman Winnie had ever known.

"Can I come bide some time in Bloomsburo?"

Winnie's eyes widened as they met Cal's, whose face showed only concern. Lord, he could even make concern look unreasonably sexy.

"Absolutely. When?"

After Bree answered, Winnie said goodbye, ended the call and oriented herself toward Cal, who was already pulling her into the comfort of his strong embrace.

Home.

"Is she okay?" he asked, pressing a kiss to Winnie's forehead as he rubbed her back. "She sounded shaken up."

"I'm not sure. But she's going to be here tomorrow, so I guess we'll find out."

"Tomorrow?" Cal repeated back, surprised, but not upset.

"Is that okay?"

"Whatever you ladies need is fine with me. You two can catch up, and I'll keep you well fed."

She squeezed him close, taking comfort in the fact that whatever was coming down the pipeline, Cal would be there to help her navigate it. She also secretly reveled in the realization that all her favorite people in the world would soon be in one zip code.

If Bloomsburo could help Bree sort out her life even half as much as it had helped Winnie, she'd be just fine.

"But in the meantime, how about some of that cake I saw? A Cal creation, I presume?"

Cal nodded, pulled her in for a warm, soft kiss, and then ushered her back into the night. To a celebration of her. Of them.

Of Bloomsburo magic.

Acknowledgements

I never, *never,* never would have had the courage to publish this book without my incomparable support system.

To the guys on the ground who make my creative work possible day in and day out: George and our four rowdy boys who let me slip away when the muse beckons and accept frozen pizza as a legitimate dinner option way more than might be reasonable.

Thank you to my parents for everything, but particularly your unwavering support and the genetic blessing of your humor. You are always among the very first people I want to tell about anything in my life, and I do realize what a gift that is.

A huge bouquet of thanks to Katie as well as the unparalleled and esteemed members of the Stars Hollow Intellectual Roundtable: for your humor, encouragement, cheerleading, and perfectly-timed gifs. You are my sisters by choice and make every day better.

A word of gratitude for the sage advice of my super talented peers in the New England Chapter of the Romance Writers of America. I promise to pay it forward.

Many thanks to Melissa for your helpful and humorous feedback during the developmental edits for this manuscript, and Rebecca for the recommendation and the very earliest nudge to move this project forward. And thanks to May Kelly's in North Conway, NH, for showing me how beautiful a restaurant bathroom can be.

And finally, this book is in memory of my two grandmas, the namesakes of the Spencer nieces/fairies: Lu, who, like Rhonda Spencer, always arrived with a basketful of something delicious in hand and a kind word to brighten someone's day, and (Mary) Rita, the Irish matriarch who always had a paper bag full of romances to share with the rest of us.